THE RED HILL

by

Jeff Williams

This book is dedicated to my mother, Joyce Williams and to my wife, Ann Williams.
My mother for bringing me into this world and being my MUM and Ann for being the best wife one could wish to have. She has put up with me over the years, especially whilst writing this book and then helping to edit and pushing me on to publish it.

Cover artwork is by Angie Baxter Ayr Qld

Published with assistance by InHouse Publishing
www.inhousepublishing.com.au

PREFACE

The idea for this book started when I heard a radio news report about a UHF radio call from a person lost in the outback. He was injured and didn't know where he was. The message turned out to be a hoax call, but the seed was sown. In 2003 I began writing and from a small idea the tale seemed to take on a life of its own. It just kept getting bigger and bigger.

After humble beginnings in Adelaide, brought up by my mother and two sisters after my father died too young, I left school early, aged 15 years and 3 days after failing Year 10 and being told not to come back by the Principal. By the age of 20 I was living alone in Brisbane where after a series of different jobs I found myself in Darwin in the summer of 74 delivering bread. Fate took a turn and after Cyclone Tracy I ended up back in Brisbane where I married and had four children with my beautiful wife Ann. Somehow I ended up in entertainment and for the next 30 years performed full time as a puppeteer, then a clown, a balloon artist, a magician then back into puppets again. Today I work part time as an entertainer and as an escort for oversized wide loads around Brisbane. I am still married to my lovely Ann.

The Red Hill

CHAPTER ONE

Burton Downs
Maranoa District. Central Queensland.
Early 1884

The Barlow's woke to another dry morning with not a cloud in the sky. A slight breeze blew from the south-west, tossing a little dust into the air, enough to sting one's eyes, enough to make ones teeth feel dirty with a slight coating of red outback dust. Enough also to roll tumble weeds across their selection. The ground around the Barlow's humble little farmhouse was barren and the few shrubs or weeds that had survived the ravages of the long dry spell looked brown, thin and weak. There was not a bit of green to be seen on the ground anywhere. Even the trees had taken on a slightly grey look, instead of that rich green that goes hand in hand with healthy productive seasonal rainfall. What was once green grass now crackled under foot as you walked on it. This country usually looked lush after good summer rains, but it had been so long since they'd had any useful rainfall that it was hard remembering what it was like. It would have been an understatement to say they needed rain.

A bad drought meant animal carcasses could be seen, and smelt, rotting near water troughs and dried up dams. Introduced species such as cattle and sheep lay rotting in the sun

1

along with native animals such as kangaroos, wallabies, emus, possums and wombats. The big, the small, the old, the young, they all fell as one, caught in the grip of a horridly slow and extremely sad death. The water troughs sat empty and rusting, a faded dry coloured rust, not the dark coloured rust that occurs when the troughs were full. The dams exposed dry and cracking bottoms on which nothing lived or moved, except for the odd lizard scurrying across leaving nothing but a small puff of dust. The animals had suffered agonising deaths from malnutrition caused by the lack of grass and water. It was a constant reminder to the Barlow's that a serious life and death struggle was going on, and if rain didn't arrive soon they would be making the harrowing decision of packing up their meager belongings and moving on before the drought took a serious toll on their lives as well. Years of hard toil and sweat hung precariously on the fickle winds of the outback. They needed rain-bearing storms, and soon.

A few of the district's farms, those blessed with an abundance of healthy capital, sank bores which provided life giving water, but most farmers around the Burton Downs area where just battlers living close to the poverty line at best. No money in their coffers to spend on expensive drilling ventures. They were the ones who felt the drought hardest and longest. They relied wholly and solely on the gods in heaven and the fickle whims of Mother Nature, but they endured in silence. The spirit of these hardened people came to the fore in times such as these. They tightened their belts, waited and prayed.

The drought was particularly hard on the young children. They didn't fully understand why they all had to bath, one after the other, in a mere few inches of dirty soapy water, when during better times, they splashed around merrily, each with a full tub to themselves. They didn't understand why there was never enough food on their plates to satisfy their hungry bellies. They didn't understand why their Mother and Father yelled at each other more and more each day as they never used to do that. They didn't understand why the beloved pets, their 3 dogs, looked skinny and underfed and why the air was often filled with dust and the smell of death. One of the new chores for the older members of the family was to move dead carcasses away from the homestead area. Each carcass as it was dragged away and burned probably lessened the chance of the Barlow's selection surviving.

The drought swept its way into every corner of their lives, and made it hard, so hard, to try and live normal, happy lives. If rain didn't blow in soon, desperate decisions would have to be made to try and keep Burton Downs afloat. Walking off their property and moving back to Brisbane was looming as a reality.

The cattle and sheep breeders of the Maranoa, not only struggled against the harsh elements, they also had to contend with a new and ever growing scourge, bushrangers. They were known to raid isolated farmhouses in the outer reaches of Central Queensland, stealing and plundering anything of value. These pirates of the land were brutal and fearless, most were escaped convicts fighting to stay alive themselves and keeping away from the clutches of the law. To them it was do-or-die and to hell with whoever got in their way.

Then there were the cattle duffers, men who quietly stole stock to sell in some far off cattle auction for self-profit. These were also hard men, not the type to challenge if caught. Sheep or cattle, it didn't matter to them, both tasted good and both fetched a fair price at the right markets. Most properties in Queensland in the 1880's were unfenced and that allowed duffers to roam at will to rustle stock, sometimes moving and selling the stolen stock before the owners had even noticed them gone.

Life in any region of Outback Australia was never easy and it took a very tough breed of human being to not only survive out there, but to raise a family in such extreme conditions.

In 1884 in an area just north-east of what is today the township of Injune in the Maranoa district of Queensland, John Barlow and his family bred cattle on a property they called Burton Downs. John had named it after the village in Scotland where he had grown up. Along with his wife Mary and their family of six children they struggled under the iron grip of a serious drought. Over 5 years now they had struggled on with precious little rainfall. Mother Nature was at her most unyielding.

The two eldest sons, 24 year old Matthew and 18 year old Charles, had been restless for some time, as young people often are. They had discussed on many occasions where they would go when the time came to strike out on their own. They were reluctant to leave when times were tough, but they also thought it would mean two less mouths to feed at Burton. Three girls aged between 16 and 11 helped around the farmhouse along with the youngest in the Barlow family, 8 year-old Will.

'Father, I've just been down to the river,' said young Will, 'the waters all gone!'

Young Will had never attended school. All that he had learnt was what his family had taught him.

'Yes I know Will,' replied his father, without any real thought given to his answer.

'Where does it go Father? There was enough water near

the bottom paddock to swim in before, and you said years ago, that it would sometimes get way up over the banks. Where does all that water go?'

John Barlow realised it was one of those moments that needed more than just a simple response, a throw-away line. He was aware that the education of his young children was all about moments like these, so he took young Will by the hand and led him to the nearest gum tree. There they sat in its cooling shade. John reached over, picked up a small broken branch from the ground and scratched a long line in the dusty dry earth.

'A river is like a long winding track through the bush. When we want to go somewhere, like when we go to town for provisions, we travel down that track to where we need to go.'

It was a hot day so John took off his hat, wiped the sweat from his brow and continued.

'The river has a destination too and nature takes the water to other places.'

'But why can't we keep some of it?' asked young Will trying to grasp what his father was saying.

'Well son, that's the way nature works and we can't change that. We can only use it to our best advantage while it's here.'

'Where does it go then?' asked the inquisitive boy.

'Well it eventually runs down into a bigger river called the Maranoa, from there…', he paused a moment to think, 'Well to be honest I don't really know where it goes to from there.'

Will nodded, but John sensed that his young son looked a little confused and was probably only nodding to be polite.

'I'll tell you what,' added John, 'we'll write to the Survey Office in Brisbane. I'll ask them to mail us the latest surveyor's maps of the rivers in this part of Australia and we'll both find out together just exactly where that water ends up going. As for the water in the dams and troughs, well what the animals don't drink gets evaporated by the big old sun up there.'

'What's evap….. evaputated.'

'Evaporated, well that's a fairly difficult one to explain.'

They sat in the shade and talked about a number of things that day, including John's version of just what evaporation was. After about an hour John decided it was time to get back to work. He was happy with his discussion with young Will and set about finishing what he had been doing earlier. Will also seemed satisfied with their discussion and headed off to play with his brothers and sisters.

That night, following the constant insistence of young Will and by the light of a old kerosene lamp, John wrote to the Chief Surveyors Office in Brisbane requesting any information they could get on the inland rivers of Eastern Australia, especially the ones that either start or run through the Maranoa. A few days later a neighbour called in on his way to Injune to see if the Barlows needed anything while he was in there. The letter went with him.

The trek to Injune was always a pleasure for the children, but the distance was such that it was shared amongst neighbours, each taking turns to go in for provisions for themselves as well as others. One wagon or cart could carry enough top-up supplies for two or three neighbours. Once or twice a year a longer trek was made to the bigger towns of Roma or Mitchell. Those trips meant an overnight camp in the townships before returning the next day. The Barlow children had to take it in turns of going to the 'big smoke' as the family cart couldn't carry all six children as well as bring the required supplies back with them. Usually Matthew and John would take it in turns to drive the cart along with 2 children each trip. Occasionally Mary would go in with John while Matthew and

Charles were left at Burton to take care of the children. This trip was usually extended an extra day as they both took the opportunity to kick their heels up and stay in the hotel for a couple of nights. It was their holiday, their chance to escape the constant worry for a few precious days. Perhaps a new dress, a few meals, a few wines, a little romance, a luxurious hot bath at the hotel and time to renew their relationship.

The weeks passed and Will waited for the weekly mail delivery from the passing Cobb and Co. coach on route from Roma to Springsure and Emerald, via Injune. John had told him that it would probably take a month or more but Will was so looking forward to their project that he'd run out to meet the drivers every Tuesday. He told them what it was that he was waiting for and each week the drivers would keep their eyes out for the young lad waiting by the gate.

Two months rolled by and the drivers were so saddened by Will's weekly disappointment that they promised him they would ask around and see what they could find out for him.

A few more weeks passed and the Cobb and Co driver arrived with a number of maps from different areas of Queensland and New South Wales. Still nothing arrived from Brisbane so Will and John began to piece together the river systems themselves with the maps generously collected the Cobb and Co. driver.

Finally, the Surveyor office maps arrived for the Queensland region and information on what other maps would be required from the New South Wales Surveyor's Office to make their project complete.

By then Will's project had become a Cobb and Co driver's project and as the word spread on the 'bush telegraph', maps and drawings came in from other drivers and farmers throughout Queensland and New South Wales. Will even received a map, along with a good luck letter from a Victorian farmer who lived at Echuca on the River Murray. He wrote to young Will saying that he had heard of the young boy's project from the captain of a riverboat, who had heard it from a farmer at Wentworth, who had heard of it from a Cobb and Co driver. The bush telegraph by then had stretched over a thousand miles.

Within three months of starting the project, a collection of official and unofficial maps (mud maps as they were called) and drawings of the rivers, roads and towns of eastern Australia were sitting on an old wooden table in the Barlow's barn. Farmers, drovers, riverboat captains, storekeepers, Cobb and Co. drivers and many others had helped supply them. In addition, there were the official maps from the surveyors in Brisbane and from those out on the road. There was so much information that John was unsure of how to piece it all together. Matthew finally came up with a solution.

'We should whitewash one of the outside walls of the barn' he suggested, 'then we could paint a huge outline of Eastern Australia and charcoal on it all the information young Will and his new friends have gathered.'
Will excitedly thought it was a terrific idea also. 'Do you think Father will let us do it though?' he asked.
Matthew 24, the eldest in the family, told young Will that he would speak to their father that evening over supper. To Will's joy, when the subject was raised that night over potato soup and baked beans, the rest of the family thought it a great idea also. With the whole family supporting Will, their father John had no other option but to agree, which he did willingly. 'Lovely idea', he said, 'help take our minds of the bleeding drought, besides the barn could sure use a lick of paint.'

So began a project that would keep every member of the

family, along with a number of neighbours, and one very friendly Cobb and Co driver, occupying their spare time for weeks to come.

The first job was to whitewash the sidewall. John purchased some paint from Roma and a few neighbours pitched in some half-filled cans left over from previous projects. Local farmers had a liking for small white washed picket fences surrounding their homesteads. It added a little bit of colour, neatness and order to there sometimes drab looking slab huts and wooden homes. The timber was very dry from the on-going drought and required a few coats to get a good seal over it.

Then using a number of different coloured paints, they painted lines on the wall to represent the outline of Eastern Australia. Then the maps were put together inside the barn and with great skill the images were duplicated onto the outside wall with charcoal sticks, roads, tracks, rivers and towns, even mountain ranges. Some of the larger homesteads and properties were added last. Everyone involved had a job to do. Someone marked out the roads, others added the rivers, and so it went. The hardest job of all was trying to keep everything in proportion, as the wall was much larger than the maps arranged inside the barn. Charles, the second eldest son, seemed to be the best at it. Perhaps a draftsman or architect in the making. The troupe would mark lines on the wall with chalk, often having to wash it off again when things just wouldn't fit together.

The farm chores still had to be attended to, but after that was done, every spare moment of time went into the wall. It became the biggest event in the district at that time. Everyone talked about it. Each weekend, as the wall took shape, more and more people turned up to help or just to look at what the Barlows were doing. Campfires were lit, billys were boiled, and it didn't take long before they'd roll up their sleeves and do their bit as well. No point standing back watching. Saturdays would see people roll in throughout the day. Sundays was an after lunch event as church services came first with most.

Finally, about four months after Will and John had sat under that big old gum tree; the Barlow's, along with over twenty neighbours and friends, stood back and admired the finished work. One side of their rough wooden barn was now a giant map of Eastern Australia, from South Australia, through Victoria, New South Wales and Queensland right up to Cape York Peninsula. Although there was little information from the far north, as it was still pretty much unsettled, the map did include every major town and the complete river systems of inland eastern Australia, from Townsville to Adelaide.

Through all the work and effort, Will's original question was finally answered. The little creek that ran through their property slowly made it's way into the Balonne River, which in turn met up with the Maranoa. From there, it flowed south to become the Culgoa River and then eventually became the Darling River north of Bourke. The Darling meandered through outback New South Wales, over barren plains, around mountain ranges, slowly giving lifesaving water to far out stations and townships until eventually, near the Victorian and New South Wales border, at the small settlement of Wentworth it ran into the mighty Murray River. It carried the flows of all those rivers and creeks along with the Murray Rivers own waters from the snow covered ranges of the Snowy Mountains. The waters from the little property known as Burton Downs in Central Western Queensland reached the sea in South Australia to the south of Adelaide at the river port of Goolwa. One of the world's great river flows, an epic journey from raindrops to ocean waves, thousands of miles away, a journey that could take over six months.

The wall was truly an impressive effort. They had gathered so much information that when word reached the Governments of both Queensland and New South Wales about it, both sent representatives to the humble Barlow property to make copies of the information that had been compiled to compare and even add to their own maps at the time. The Government officials also took photographs of the wall, which were taken back to both Sydney and Brisbane and once there they made their way into copies of local newspapers and gazettes. The barn wall and the story of young Will of Burton Downs became very interesting reading, for a short time at least. It read 'The Boy from the bush with a Grand Plan'. He had captured the imagination of many a reader in the big cities, which was quite a thrill for Injune.

In 1884 most of inland eastern Australia had been explored and roughly mapped, but the information sent by farmers, drivers, drovers, stock-hands, riverboat captains, storekeepers and others, helped fill in some blank spaces here and there and helped correct some mistakes in the existing mapping.

The Queensland Government decided to pay the Barlows for the valuable information the project had provided. They presented, to a surprised and delighted John Barlow and his family, a bank cheque for 50 pounds for services rendered to Australia.

Fifty pounds in the 1880's was a lot of money. It was indeed a timely gift for it would help keep them in food and provisions for quite some time. However, the drought was still with them and although the 50 pounds was extremely welcoming, it would not put water into the creeks, rivers and dams and without the water, their cattle, along with their livelihood, would rapidly fade and die.

The 'Australia Wall' had been a good diversion for everyone, including John himself, but now that it was finished it was time to get back to reality, time to go back to the worries of the drought and the struggle to keep their livestock from perishing. If the cattle died, the family would not be able to stay on at Burton Downs. They needed good rain and they needed it soon.

John had spoken to Matthew on a number of occasions about what he thought they could do to keep the family on the farm, but there was no clear resolution to the problem. Matthew felt they should discuss the matter with the whole family over supper, after all, he said, 'look what the last family get-together produced.'

Over the next few weeks, evening meal times also became family discussion time on what they thought could be done to keep the property from going under. They were losing cattle to the drought and things were getting increasingly worse, and nothing positive was coming forward from their talks.

Then one morning, young Will came running into the shed. His father had been working all morning forging horseshoes in the hot coals over a blacksmith's fire. Still stoking the fire, he looked up with surprise when Will ran in.

'Is everything all right there Will?' he asked, wiping sweat from his forehead with his black sooty hands.

'There's dust over the hill. Is it Tuesday?' he asked. Tuesdays was when the Cobb and Co coach passed their property and of late it would almost always stop with letters and notes for Will about his project. There was a time when the coach would rarely stop with mail but over the past months it had stopped every week with more news.

'No' replied John looking past his son to the doorway

and farmyard beyond, 'today's Friday.'

John put his poker back down in the fire, took his leather apron off and the two walked towards the doorway together. Once outside in the sunlight John looked to the south-west, to the track from Mitchell and sure enough, there was a cloud of dust rising above the nearby hill.

'Who could it be then Father?' asked Will excitedly.

'Perhaps it's just someone travelling north.'

It was a large cloud of dust and travelers on that road were usually only on horseback. This had to be a wagon, John thought, only a wagon pulled by a number of horses could kick up that amount of dust.

'Can we go up to the gate and watch them go past?' Will asked.

'I can't see why not, I could use a break from that hot work in the shed' John replied as they both looked out towards the rising dust cloud.

'Shall I get Matthew and Charles and the girls?'

'No let's not make too big a fuss. We'll just walk up ourselves.'

They headed off together along the track that led to the gateway on their property. It was a walk of about half a mile.

'You've got black all over your face, Father,' said Will in a knowledgeable tone.

John wiped his face with his shirtsleeve.

'Yes dirty work, forging over a blacksmith's fire. But it's a job that has to be done or the horses will be useless to us.'

'Do all horses have to have shoes Father? he asked as they strolled towards the gate. He didn't get an answer.

Mary was hanging clothes out to dry when she noticed John and Will heading towards the gate. 'Where are you young boys going then?' she called.

'Will saw dust over the hill. We're just going for a stroll to see who is passing.'

Mary looked towards the hill in question, 'It may be Cobb and Co, Will,' she yelled, knowing he looked forward to the stage-coaches arrival each week.

'No, mother' he called back with the authority of a mature person, 'today is Friday.'

'So it is Will, so it is.'

Mary had stopped hanging the clothes out and the girls, who had been playing nearby, also heard the conversation and had now joined their mother.

It was as if everyone at Burton Downs had stopped to see who was coming down the road, on 'that' very day, in 'that' little part of the world. It seemed as if everyone sensed something unusual was about to happen.

As it turned out, it was old Joe the Hawker. Old Joe travelled the countryside alone in an old canvas covered wagon filled to bursting point with pots, pans, utensils, fabrics, cottons, tools, tobacco, whisky and anything else that isolated outback farmers might wish to purchase from a wandering old hawker.

Although there was a quiet feeling amongst them that morning that something was special, no one was to know that the arrival of Joe the hawker was to change their peacefully happy existence at Burton Downs forever.

The old wagon rattled over the hill and down to where Will and John were waiting by the two very tall upright posts that was their gateway. 'Has it been a year already, Joe?' was Johns greeting, remembering that old Joe usually made his way to Burton Downs about every 12 months.

'Actually it's been about 18 months. This old fella's slowin' down with age,' Old Joe replied.

The two men laughed.

Old Joe was an elderly man with a face that was hardened by a lifetime of outback travel. His face was like a roadmap itself. He had a face full of grey whiskers and an old felt hat that sat back on his head. He had long eye brow hairs that were on a journey of their own, apparently all in different directions. His eyes were red from the dust. An old pipe hung from the corner of his mouth and his teeth were stained brown. He spoke slowly in a tone that spelt experience. This was a man who had seen so much, but a man who kept it all inside. He could have been fifty years old, or he could have been ninety. His face reflected the harsh land.

'Climb aboard young fella, and I'll give you a ride up to the house.'

Will looked at his father for approval and upon receiving a nod of the head, climbed up to sit with Old Joe. The horses immediately lurched in action with the speed of a turtle crossing a road. The noise from the old wagon was foreign to Will, all those pots and pans, as well as other metal tools and utensils, all banging and clanging together. Somehow though, they had a rhythm, like they had been practicing for years, as they had, a million dusty miles, all swaying in time. Clanging out a tune for the old Hawker and keeping him company during those lonely hours on the road.

John walked alongside the wagon chatting to Joe all the way back to the homestead where Mary and the girls were waiting.

It was Mary's turn to greet the old weather beaten wanderer, 'Hello Joe, and what new goodies do you bring this year?' she asked with a hint of excitement in her voice, even though she would know, due to the drought, they would not be able to purchase much, if anything at all. However, she may well have hoped that some small part of the fifty-pound gift from the Government might make its way out and into old Joe's kitty, in exchange for some new material or provisions. She could hope.

Old Joe went straight into his regular spiel, 'Well madam, I've got the usual pots and pans as well as some fine new fabrics from Paris - fine enough to delight any fair maidens eye.'

The girls chattered excitedly at the thought of new fabrics from which their mother could make fine new dresses for them all.

Old Joe continued chatting away about all the new products he had for sale making his way to his big finale.

'And finally, I have newspapers from ole Brisbane Town, barely a month old. They carry news from England and news of riches found lying on the ground way out in the far western parts of New South Wales, near the South Australian border.'

He knew the way to get the women excited, was to offer them fine fabrics from Paris. The men were more interested in farm implements, guns, bullets, bridles and saddles, but he knew that talk of riches lying on the ground would prick everyone's ears up.

'Some boundary rider has stumbled upon a hill of ore near a location known as Broken Hill. One thinks we shall hear more of this broken hill in the future, for they say it will be the richest of mineral bearing regions in Australia. There is even talk of gold and silver. It is said you can see the dust clouds from miners heading west, rising so high you can follow them all the way to Broken Hill. Tis a story for the ages. Farmers are walking off their selections and trekking west. Dreams, riches and failures will surely follow. Me thinks this old war horse will just keep plodding me path and leave the goldfields for the young-ens. I've seen it all before'

The talking and trading went on for about an hour until it was time to stop for lunch. After lunch came the handing over of the money for goods purchased, then Old Joe climbed back onto his wagon and headed north towards the next property. He left the Barlows a few pounds shorter, but richer with new fabric for the ladies, and news of the outside world for the men.

As time passed Mary Barlow was kept busy making dresses and scarves for the girls, shirts and trousers for the men. All took their turn at reading the newspaper from Brisbane with great interest, men first girls later. News from the outside world was a rare thing at Burton Downs. News about England, about cattle prices and of course about the new discoveries of gold and other precious metal that seemed to be being discovered all over the land. Such discoveries had fortune hunters from all corners of the world rushing to Australia and opening up previously unused land.

The boys read, and then talked about the latest of these discoveries, Broken Hill, with excitement. The paper said that a young boundary rider on a large western New South Wales sheep property called Mt.Gipps Station had stumbled over a lump of what he thought was tin.

What young Charles Rasp actually discovered that day was the world's largest single deposit of Silver and Iron Ore. Also scattered around the region was large amounts of Gold and Zinc.

The area was said to be harsh terrain and was at the southern end of the rugged Barrier Range just outside the South Australian border. Captain Charles Sturt had discovered the district some 40 years before and upon sighting an odd broken shaped hill just aside from a group of pinnacle shaped hills named them Broken Hill, and The Pinnacles. He wrote in his journal that the area was scorching hot by day and freezing cold by night and according that the area was 'very isolated and extremely desolate'. Yet some 40years later the youthful boundary rider, Charles Rasp, was to turn that isolated, desolate land into the talk of the world.

Miners, traders, ex-farmers, horse traders, conmen, working ladies and even the odd bushrangers were said to be pouring into the district. Hundreds of miles of rough unforgiving country from the nearest townships of Wilcannia on the Darling to the east, Wentworth to the south and Burra to the west broke hearts and backs as hundreds push forth to 'stake their claims'. To the north lay the unknown. Land that had rarely been trekked, certainly not settled. The land north belonged to a few nomadic aboriginal tribes, eagles, galahs and kangaroos.

The stampede, as it fast became, helped small traders along the way to become large traders overnight, if they could get supplies in. Everything had to be carried in on horseback or in wagons over open virgin country. Horses and wagons were sold to prospectors on the way to the diggings, only to be bought back cheaply on their way back out. The goods were then re-sold to the next person heading to The Hill, and so it went. In some cases, it was reported that goods were sold to travelers, stolen back within days and then sold off again, wild times, wild people, riches at your feet, or so the paper said. The young boundary rider, Charles Rasp had unwittingly changed the face of that region forever. The paper had made it all sound so inviting, so exciting, to the imaginings of two young restless boys stuck on a small farm in outback Queensland.

Matthew read the paper over and over again and every time he read it, Broken Hill and all its riches loomed bigger and bigger. Then one night over supper, a few weeks after the visit from the old hawker, Matthew raised what he thought was a possible solution to their problem of the drought and their dying cattle. He proposed that he, along with his younger brother Charles, should take some of their cattle to the new mining town of Broken Hill and sell them there.

'With so many miners pouring into the area there is sure to be a big demand for fresh meat. We could expect to get top money for the cattle, being that the supply to a remote area like that would be slow. We stay here and pray for rain or we do something positive now and survive.'

There was total silence at the table. Matthew looked up at his father and was greeted with a slight frown.

He continued, 'No rail, and no real roads. Once the local cattle have been sold and slaughtered someone could make a fortune by bringing fresh supplies in,' Matthew added, trying hard to convince his father.

'If we do nothing', Matthew added, 'the cattle will soon be worthless, nothing more than rotting carcasses on the ground.'

He looked around the table for some sign of support, but none was forthcoming, so he continued anyway.

'It would take us no more than about six months or so to go down and come back again and if we travel during the winter months we'd be back before the summer heat sets in. Do we really have a choice?'

It seemed like a good idea; in reality, it seemed like the only idea. No one would want to see Matthew and Charles leaving home on such a dangerous trek but what choice did they really have. Rain might not come until the next summer. Do nothing and the cattle would surely die and along with them, their futures at Barton Downs.

After some open discussion between Matthew, Charles and their parents, John agreed to think on it some more. He ended the discussion by adding that if he should decide to agree, then he would lead the party down himself, to look after his boys as well as their cattle. Matthew saw that as a positive sign that his father had quietly agreed to the idea.

Over the next few days discussions were held informally between John and Mary and at times Matthew and Charles were brought into some of those discussions. Finally one night over supper John addressed the whole family.

'After much thought,' he said with the firm authority befitting the head of a family. 'I have decided,' he paused a while and then looked over at his two sons.

'No... should I say... WE have decided... that the only hope of surviving this drought is to sell most of the cattle before they do in fact perish.'

He continued, 'Cattle prices in Brisbane are low because of too many poor cattle on the market and I believe Matthew's idea has considerable merit. Better prices should be found away from traditional markets.'

He paused again, as he looked around the table at his children, knowing that his decision would take him away from them for between 4 and 6 months and leave Mary to battle alone in the bush with the young ones.

'Matthew's idea was a good one and he, along with Charles and myself, will take most of the cattle to sell in Broken Hill.'

Mary was not all that keen on the plan. She had heard of the tough life that miners and diggers had to endure in their pursuit of riches and she didn't want her sons subjected to those hardships and dangers. However, both Matthew and Charles were adamant. They wanted to try their luck in Broken Hill. To them it was the adventure of a lifetime.

John went on, 'If the journey is too arduous we will change our course and head for Dubbo and sell the cattle there. Prices will not be as high, but I will not risk lives or cattle in the pursuit of mere money alone.'

He concluded by looking at his youngest boy and said, 'Young Will here, well his wall will show us the way to go. We will follow his map down south. I am proud of my boys in their thought and planning. Without their fortitude we would probably perish along with our cattle. The future lies with them and their ideas and I take responsibility to help them fulfill them'.

With that decision, the Barlow family had gone from being cattlemen to becoming drovers as well, and were probably about to risk all that they had worked so hard and so long for, on one last roll of the dice. It was almost a case of all or nothing. However, with the drought getting worse as each week passed, it was agreed that it was the best and probably the only option available to them.

The very next morning, after an early breakfast, John, Matthew and Charles and young Will, went to the barn wall. They spent most of the morning going over the 'map' as well as all the other information they had received and finally settled on their most probable route. They were very aware that things could be very different when they got out on the track. Therefore, with that in mind, they could only select a possible route. Young Will looked on with pride. They would copy the wall on drafts of paper to take on their journey

The plan was quite simple, head west until they reached Havelock Station on the Maranoa River then south along the river to the small town of Mitchell. From there, they would follow the Maranoa all the way down, past its junction with the Balonne River, to the township of St. George. Then they would take their first rest, re-stock with provisions before heading out to meet up with the Culgoa River and follow it south-west to the town of Bourke.

Near Bourke, the Culgoa River became known as the Darling River and they would follow it all the way down to Wilcannia. After another short break, they would continue along the Darling until it ran into the Menindee Lakes, south east of their destination. The last part of the journey they would have to leave the safety of the river systems and set out north-west until they reached Broken Hill. By following the rivers as much as possible, they concluded that they'd never be too far from water and food for the cattle, as well as for themselves. In addition, there were more existing cattle and sheep stations along the river system, which would mean they would be closer to help should they need it at any stage.

John calculated they should get to Broken Hill in around four to four and a half months, all being well, and the return trip, without the cattle to slow them down, should only take around four to six weeks. His prediction confirming the six to seven month journey that Matthew had estimated earlier.

The Journey 1884

About three weeks later, in the autumn of 1884, with the weather turning cooler, John, and the boys spent two days herding one hundred and fifty six head of cattle together in the creek paddock. They were in the final stages of getting ready for their journey south. Once there, they selected the strongest for the journey, deciding to leave the weakest behind, some to feed the remaining family, some to trade should they need provisions and some because they simply weren't strong enough.

Mary was still apprehensive about the family having to split up for such a lengthy period of time. She had never been away from John more than a few days before and she held some fears about the children's health and safety. What if something went wrong? However she knew she would have to stay and that was that.

Seventeen-year-old son Thomas, and fifteen-year-old daughter Lucy, would help Mary run the farm and look after the two youngest, Will and Sarah. Left behind also, would be about forty head of cattle, including two young bulls. That stock, should they survive, would be used to re-establish a herd when the men returned.
Of the forty left behind, some would be slaughtered to keep the family supplied with fresh meat for the six months that the men would be away.

It was arranged that when help was needed around the farm, a neighbour, Henry Williamson would come over to assist. His payment would be half of any cattle slaughtered while the boys were away. Mary didn't fancy the job of the slaughtering, gutting and breaking up a beast, so it was arranged that any killing and carving up would be left to Henry.

So there it was, a plan to rescue the Barlows and their property, Burton Downs from that terrible drought of the 1880's. All being well, they would rebuild their stock numbers through the late eighties and by 1890, they should be bigger and stronger than ever.

They were ready. They rested for two more days and went over and over their plans. Then early one morning, John and the two boys said their farewells to Mary and the other children and rode up to the top of the hill that overlooked their little valley. It was to be the first of many hills they were to ride over. The start of what they knew would be the longest journey of their lives.

John and the boys paused at the top to look back at the children chasing them up the hill, and at Mary, standing in front of their homestead. Time seemed to stand still for that moment. The sun had just crept over the horizon on a typically crisp autumn morning in outback Queensland. Galahs were squawking in the gum trees above. A little coil of smoke could be seen above the chimney of their small, but adequate farmhouse. It just hung there in the cool air. There was freshness in the air and all seemed right in the world.

Mary waved at the three men mounted on their horses. It must have been a sad moment for her indeed. She was powerless to stop three of her loved ones from journeying far away and to be facing many a danger ahead. Her heart dearly wanted them to stay, but she knew they must go. Their futures depended on it.

The three sat there on the horses for a moment or two, each with their own thoughts of what they were leaving behind and of what awaited them in the near future. John broke the silence of the moment with a stern harsh voice, 'Well, come on boys, we've got some cattle to get to Broken Hill.'

With a final wave good-bye, they turned their horses away from all they knew and loved, and headed off. The two younger children Will and Sarah continued on their chase up the hill for a while but it wasn't long before their energy ran out and they were left stranded half way. They stood there for a while looking at the empty hilltop. Mary had tears in her eyes as suddenly the three horsemen wheeled around and disappeared over the hill in a few short seconds. It was as if the countryside had just swallowed them up. As the two children slowly began the walk back down to the homestead, Mary fell to her knees on the dry, dusty, Queensland earth and prayed for their safe return.

Day One Of Many

It was a tense first day for everyone. The boys were keen to get on the trail, but John was understandably concerned about leaving Mary and the children. Back at the homestead, the remaining children were a little cranky. They had not wanted to stay behind. The thought of a cattle drove, sleeping under the stars, campfire food and travelling to new places was far more enticing than chores around the property. Meanwhile, Mary tried hard to show a brave face, but on more than one occasion, a tear or two was seen to be rolling down her aging cheeks. She tried hard to keep everyone busy, especially herself.

The men had provisions enough to last them to at least St. George. It included canvas water containers, dried preserved food, cooking utensils and extra clothing. All the extras had been loaded onto four packhorses. The packhorses had all been tied together, along with two spare horses. The cattle had been penned up in a small paddock a few miles from the homestead, and John and the boys headed straight there. They rounded up the herd and within an hour were heading west south-west, leaving Burton Downs behind in a cloud of dry Queensland dust.

The going was tough at first, not the countryside itself, but rather the lifestyle. They weren't used to their new type of life, that of a drover. They'd lived a fairly soft life at Burton Downs. A big day back there would have meant five or six hours on horseback, mustering cattle or riding fences, but now it was up to twelve hours a day in the saddle, and it was day after day, after day.

After the first week though, they began to settle into

their new roles and as each day passed they were finding the going that much easier. They also found that each day they were travelling longer distances. They were sliding into a routine, each with his role to play. Once they stopped for the night it wasn't all lay back and rest time. Someone had to set up camp, while someone else organised firewood, while the third would get a campfire started and a much-earned meal under way. During the long nights, they would take it in turns of riding around the herd, keeping the cattle quiet and keeping an eye out for dingoes. They'd seen some close enough to make John and the boys aware of their presence. A dingo attack on a weakened calf might cause a stampede and that was the last thing they wanted.

If the cattle were restless at night, they soon learnt that the best way to settle them was an old drover's trick, sing to them. They all felt a bit silly at first singing to the cattle but again as time went by, it all became quite a routine. Each of the men would take a three-hour turn in the saddle keeping an eye out for the prowling dingoes and watching and singing to the herd.

To get a new day under way they would rise before first light, stoke up the campfire, heat up the billy and cook breakfast. All going well, they would be saddled up and moving the cattle out around about the same time the sun would be presenting itself on the eastern horizon.

Most days they'd have a small lunch break, usually determined by the movement of the cattle and the local terrain, and then push on until late afternoon. They would stop about a half hour before dark, around 5ish, giving themselves enough time for one of them to gather wood for the all night fire while the other two would set up camp.

Their nightly camps consisted of a couple of canvas

covers slung up over trees or scrub bushes to protect them from the cold night air and against the cool evening winds that sometimes blew in from the west. They had a tent with them, but they would only put it up if the weather looked like turning bad and rain was imminent. A raging fire was never far away.

One afternoon, as grey storm clouds gathered in the west, they decided to stop early and put up the tent and as had been expected, later that evening, rain began to fall. As the rain got heavier, the men settled in for a long night perched beneath the canvas, with the noise of the rain thundering above them.

Charles thought it funny that back home, the rain would have been a blessing, but out here, the bleedin' rain meant it'd be tough and miserable travelling for the next few days. He could think of nothing worse than riding for hours in cold wet clothing.

They talked into the night, about funny times and good times they could remember about rain. The young men had not seen a lot of rain in their lifetime. John had more stories to tell. They hoped that the rain would head north and ease the burden on all the farmers in the districts they had passed through, and especially for their own family struggling from lack of it back on Burton.

All districts, even if caught in the grip of a severe drought, received some rainfall from time to time. Sometimes it might rain lightly all day or all night, but rarely was it enough to get the rivers running or enough for grass and crops to grow again. The grasses of Central Queensland had long ago turned brown and yielded very little nutrition for the hungry cattle. Rain out here was liquid gold. Generally speaking, the ground was so dry and the sun so hot that they would need a few good storms or weeks of light rainfall for it to have any real impact.

Still it didn't stop the three of them from quietly wishing for the rain to make its way north to Burton Downs. John felt that good solid constant rain might even allow them to change their plans and head home again, something the boys had mixed feelings about. Not so John, he would have headed home the very next day if he thought the cattle would survive back on Burton. Home was home and it would always take a lot for him to leave it, after all that's where his beloved Mary and the rest of his children were, and he was missing them terribly already.

However by the time the sun rose the next morning the rain had stopped, the clouds had cleared, and it was back to the long trek ahead.

As soon as they had finished with breakfast that morning, Matthew rode out to scout ahead. From time to time one of them would ride out ahead of the mob, looking for an open path through the scrub and around the hills. Flat open ground made for better going, so they were constantly on the lookout for easier routes to take.

On this particular morning, he would have to be on the lookout for flowing creeks or slippery mud flats, anything that represented a possible problem in moving the cattle through. Within a few hours, Matthew returned with the news that the route ahead was clear and so they stepped up the pace in a south-westerly direction.

After eight days of droving, the men reached their first real signpost, Havelock Station. For three men on their first outing, they had done well to move 150 head of cattle through rough and largely unfamiliar ground. In fact, compared to a fully experienced drove team, they hadn't gone far at all in those eight days, but they were learning fast and getting better at it by the day. They not only had to get used to a different life pattern, but they had to learn how to handle cattle on the track. Fattening them up in a fenced yard at Burton was a far cry from keeping them moving through unknown territory. They had to learn to deal with it all, so too did the cattle.

At Havelock Station, they would link up with the dry Maranoa River and their first sighting of other humans since they'd left home. It was good to sit around a campfire that night talking with the folk from Havelock. The men exchanged ideas, plans, dreams, yarns and many a joke.

'You had any rain out your way?' one of the men asked the Barlows.

'Not enough to help out, nothing good in months'.

'So did you lose many head back on your property?'

'No not really, but another three or four months like this and we'll be in big trouble. That's why we decided on droving the mob to market,' John told them.

John enjoyed the night tremendously. He always enjoyed talking with other cattlemen, and it was something that he rarely had the chance to do. In his life back on Burton, he might get to occasionally talk to a neighbour or two. Perhaps he would get the opportunity for a 10 minute chat to the Cobb and Co. drivers, if they ever had need to stop on their route north or south past Burton Downs.

'It's good to chat with others,' said John, as he tossed some logs onto an already raging campfire. Occasionally we get into Mitchell for supplies and it's always good to throw down an ale or two with some of the locals. It's good to hear of the problems others face, you learn a lot from that I think.'

'Yes you're right,' was the reply.

It wasn't long before one of the Havelock station-hands brought out a harmonica and a few songs got tossed around the flickering light as the night wore on. Songs were sung, bush

29

poems recited, and many a tale of good times and bad times got
passed around.

Oh the campfire flickered
As the night crept in
And the cold air was burnt away
Oh the flames were bright
Against the darkening sky
As the stars replaced the day

Oh the firewood crackled
And the flames licked o
As it keeps the cold at bay
And the billy boiled
Like a dear old friend
As the heat did cometh our way

Now this untamed bush
We call our own
Is where we want to be
With a really good brew
And a hearty beef stew
This campfire's a friend to me

It's our mate, it's our lover,
While we live in the bush
A treasure it is for sure
And to sit in its glow
In this proud land we know
Truly leaves you wanting for more

Dawn came around again to find a number of bodies still lying around the campfire. An early breakfast was attended to and after some fond farewells and plenty of hand shaking, the men of Havelock Station and the men of Barlows parted company. John, along with and his two sons wondering what lay ahead, and the men of Havelock a little envious of the adventure about to unfold for the men from Burton Downs.

The dust was again stirred by the mob of cattle as they turned and headed due south, following the Maranoa River towards the fast growing township of Mitchell. More days passed until before them lay the tiny township of Mitchell.

The first thing John and his two sons noticed, as they approached the township, was a new railway bridge being built over the river. A train line from the east had reached Mitchell only two years before and with it had come traders, jobs and a number of new settlers. They were looking for their place in the sun, a place to create a new life. Finally, for the first time, the bridge would link the vast areas to the west with the east-coast and the trading hub of Brisbane. These were exciting times for Mitchell.

The new bridge was right in the middle of the town, so John and the boys stopped for a while to marvel at the construction that was going on. It was indeed a beehive of activity. Instead of the traditional old wooden pylons, concrete ones were being buried deep into the dry creek-bed. They were told by one of the workers, that they were in fact the first concrete pylons ever to be set in Queensland. They had happened upon a piece of Queensland history in the making.

They settled the mob down, and that night they enjoyed the company of men who had built bridges all over the world. The boys sat around the campfire and listened in awe at the tales that was being freely thrown around. To listen to those worldly men certainly gave them a thirst for travel and adventure. To their amazement and pride, most of the men around the campfire that night, agreed that what the Barlows were in fact doing, was truly an adventure of great proportions itself. Many of those present wishing they could tag along for the ride also.

John knew it, but he doubted that the boys had thought too much about it, only that it had to be done in order to save the farm, and that was that. John was glad they had camped with the bridge builders that night, for he believed it had taught the boys things about the world out there that he knew he never could. He could see excitement in his son's eyes when they realised that a big world awaited them. The world was an adventure just waiting for two young men to tackle. Life on Burton would never be the same again for Matthew and Charles. If John hadn't fully realised it before then, he certainly did that night.

Another wonderful night passed and the next day saw John sending a letter to Mary, while the boys mixed and mingled with the bridge builders and the local town folk.

Two days later, full of pride and self-confidence, the Barlow men were on the road again. They headed the mob south, following the Maranoa through reasonably flat, bushy country. Their next stop would be the township of St.George, but that was a long way ahead. Now at least though they had a ready-made map to follow the Maranoa.

For most of the trek to that point, they had been going overland and navigating by the sun and an old compass, but for the next thousand miles or so, they would follow the inland water flow of Central Australia. The rivers by their very nature twist and turn as they find flat ground to flow through, so the men had to try to work out routes that might shorten their travel distances. For this they relied on young Will's maps and some local knowledge gained wherever possible, and travel overland between the bends and curves of the river. In other words, they used the rivers as guides but tried to plot a straighter and shorter course, as the crow flies, between the bends. This meant that someone would have to regularly ride ahead to try and find a straight route between watering stops. Sometimes they would leave the safety of the river for days at a time before they would again link up with the muddy life giving waters of the outback.

The section from Mitchell to St.George was tough going. The countryside was full of low scrub bush and they had to back check through the scrub constantly for straying cattle. When the ground was flat and open, they could travel between fifteen to twenty miles (24 to 32klm) on a good day. Some days, because of thick scrub or hilly terrain, they wouldn't travel half that distance. In real terms they probably travelled a lot further.

John decided that after leaving Mitchell, they would stop and rest each seventh day. He knew a break would do them good. A day also to check on their gear and take care of the stock and horses, so, as it had been back at Burton Downs, Sundays became their day of rest. It was the day they would set up a proper camp. Put up their tent, wash their clothes, re-shoe any horses that may require attention and treat any cuts the horses may have sustained while riding through the scrub. It was also the day when they had the time to cook up a proper meal, like a big, healthy hearty stew. The weekly stews were generally made tastier by the inclusion of a freshly slaughtered rabbit or possum.

Thus, Friday and Saturday became the days to keep an eye out for stray rabbits or possums to shoot at night in readiness for the Sunday stew. If they couldn't find a rabbit or possum, then snake or lizard would do almost as well. Once mixed in with the other ingredients for the stews, it was hard to tell what the source of meat was anyway, they all tasted pretty much the same. Just some were tougher than others. The nutritional value of fresh meat was important in keeping the men fit and healthy out there.

Kangaroos and wallabies abounded in the bush, and there was no shortage of them. However, they chose not to shoot them as they would only use a small portion for their meal, the rest of the carcass would have to be left behind to rot. John had been brought up with the motto, 'waste not-want not,' and that type of waste just didn't seem right to him, so they looked out for smaller animals. Also from time to time, the odd koala would be seen in treetops, but Charles, the youngest of the party, liked the furry little creatures too much and made the others promise not to shoot them for their meals unless it was an absolute emergency.

About half way between Mitchell and St.George, they passed through a region where they experienced a strange feeling, a sense that someone or something was watching them. The horses were restless for a night or two, so too were the mob of cattle.
Matthew was the first to mention the strange feeling, 'Hell, I don't like this place, Dad. The hair on the back of my neck is standing up.'
Charles was quick to comment also, 'My horse has been spooked for a while now. What do you think it is?'
John, being a typical bushman, was very superstitious about strange feelings. It was the middle of the day and he had heard dingoes howling in the distance, something that was odd indeed. Dingoes generally hunted at night. This was a strange place and he knew it.
'Perhaps there's an aboriginal burial place nearby,' he

commented as he kept a tight rein on his horse, as it was hell bent on shaking its head from side to side and whinnying constantly.

'I don't like this place one little bit,' said a very pensive Charles, 'Let's just keep moving. Let's just get away from here as quickly as we can?'
John chimed in again, 'I'm with you Charles, let's get down the track a ways. I feel like someone's walking on my grave around here.'

They pushed on but the feeling stayed with them all day long. Finally, very hungry and tired, they stopped for the night. The first thing they did, before they set-up camp, was to put leg ropes on the horses. Usually they would just tie them on long ropes, but they too were spooked. Then they built a number of large bonfires, perhaps in the belief that the large fires would keep the demons away.

That night the wind howled through the trees. Somewhere out there in the cold night, the dingoes howled also. The horses whinnied constantly and the cattle were restless to the point of a possible stampede. It was not a pleasant experience riding the mob that night trying to keep them quiet. The wind in the trees, half moonlight and fast flowing clouds all helped to paint pictures of ghosts dancing in the scrub. It was a long, long night indeed for everyone.

What sleep they had was disturbed time and time again and they were more than happy to break camp early next morning and push on without any breakfast. By the middle of that day, they felt easier and it was agreed by all that the feeling had passed. Whatever it was, they had left it behind them.

'We should avoid that area on our way back,' John told the boys when they stopped that night. 'We'll work around it; I'm not going through there again. Someone dancing on someone's grave for sure, it ain't good.' He went on, 'did you notice there were no other animals around there. I never saw one.'

Bushmen are very superstitious men by nature, and a bad feeling or a bad spirit, was something to be avoided wherever possible.

The one good thing they noticed as they travelled further down the Maranoa was that the water holes in the riverbed were getting bigger and more frequent. Just a few days later, the waterholes linked up and the Maranoa had become a river again.

'Now there's a sight to behold,' said John, as he looked at the water, 'if only the old creek back home could look like this again, I'd be one happy man.'

It had been a long time since the creek at Burton Downs had its share of water.

One morning, Charles went to scout ahead, and a short time later he came racing back down the track.

Bringing his horse to a halt in a small cloud of dust, he told the others the reason for his excitement, 'There's a big town just a couple of hills over. People everywhere, biggest town I ever saw. It's got to be twice the size of Mitchell at least.'

John replied in a calm voice, 'That'll be St.George.'

Matthew had been aware for a few days that they must be getting close to St. George. The track they were following was well used and was getting wider, always a sure sign of a town ahead.

'You don't mind if I ride ahead with Charles for a look do you Father?'

'Go ahead, I'll settle the cattle down here for the night.' replied John, 'but stay out of trouble,' he added as they swung their horses towards the township. It had been weeks and the boys were eager to see people again.

CHAPTER TWO

Nundooka Station. South-west Queensland 1994

After four years of heartbreaking drought, the likes of which had not been seen for decades, the autumn of 1994 saw the rains finally come to the parched, ancient, western Queensland landscape. It was largely due to the monsoon trough of Northern Australia, which had drifted south in the late summer, bringing plenty of moisture with it.

El Nino, a weather pattern that controls weather across both sides of the Pacific Ocean, or so the modern meteorologists assured us, had been playing up and the heartland of Queensland's farming communities had suffered badly.

Droughts had come and gone before throughout history, but this part of south-western Queensland had seen more than its fair share. They had wreaked havoc on crops and livestock, that was to be expected, but this time, the drought coincided with a downturn in the economy of not only Australia, but across the Western world.

Money was very tight, and the banking institutions that had freely lent money in the previous decades, were now rightly or wrongly foreclosing and sending farmers and their families from their beloved land, and changing their lifestyles forever. Generations of landowners were left with no-where to go, with no other skills, very little money and worst of all, with badly broken spirits.

The tension, heartbreak and personal devastation that was being created by the banks and the drought, was tearing families, and in some cases, whole communities apart.

The south-west district of Queensland is centred on the modern town of Roma and lies about five hundred kilometres (300miles) west of Brisbane. Mitchell, a much smaller township, is a further eighty kilometres (50 miles) west and the cotton-producing town of St.George is two hundred kilometres (130 miles) to the south of Mitchell. The country inside the triangle formed by linking these three townships is said to be among the harshest and toughest land in Queensland.

The land is generally flat. The occasional rise of small hills and with odd clumps of rugged ranges scattered throughout the district. Much of it is covered with large areas of almost impassable dense scrub. The odd cluster of giant gums, set mainly near the water holes stand like sentinels guarding the precious waters, that is, when there is water in those holes. Just to the east of the connecting road between Mitchell and St.George, is a fairly rugged range of hills. Mt. Inviting, at three hundred metres above sea level, is the tallest point.

North of Mitchell, it is even more rugged with the Chesterton Ranges about a hundred and fifty kilometres away, and nearby is the very scenic Carnarvon Gorge, the highlight of the Carnarvon National Park.

The whole area between Carnarvon and St.George, including the Roma and Mitchell districts, had been caught up in the prolonged drought with all its associated dramas. Without exception, the whole district had suffered dramatically.

Then quite suddenly, in the months of February and March, in the latter part of the summer, the 'great drought' finally broke and the rains came back to that parched corner of the world. Two cyclones, about three weeks apart, crossed the coastline, one to the north of Rockhampton and the other up in the Gulf of Carpentaria. Both quickly becoming rain depressions and began drifting south-west and south respectively, dumping large amounts of rain over the arid inland of Queensland.

After those good, steady, soaking rains, the communities were at least breathing easier in the knowledge that their livestock would survive, and that major crops could be planted during the autumn and winter months, something that hadn't happened for a number of years. They would be happy knowing that within the next six months at least, money would begin to flow through the townships of rural Queensland as surely as the rainwater flowed down the once dry and cracked riverbeds and waterholes. The rains generally brought with them some flooding in low-lying areas, but after the years and years of drought, a little too much water was looked upon as a blessing, not a curse.

Danny was just ten years old, the year the rains returned, and to a child of that age, the coming of the rains meant a whole new period of fun times ahead. Rivers, creeks and dams, that were once empty and lifeless, would soon become swimming holes to play in. They would in no time at all be alive with tadpoles, yabbies and fish, and that meant pole fishing, yabby netting and tadpole catching excursions ahead.

All the yarns that old 'Poppy', Danny's grandfather, had told him about the good old days when Poppy and Danny's dad, fished the mighty Maranoa River for large catches of everything from Murray Cod to Yellowbelly, would soon become reality for him also. All his short life he'd heard terrific stories about the trips to the favourite waterholes and the catches of freshwater fish and big, fat, juicy yabbies that once caught were boiled in a billy on the banks and eaten almost as soon as they had been taken from the water.

The stories of his mother's legendary fresh fish patties, would soon present themselves as reality and being so much better than the ones she made with fish out of a tin can. Danny had heard all about eating freshly grilled fish for breakfast. He'd listened to the tales of fish and potato patty sandwiches for lunch, and about yabbies cooked to perfection on the barbeque, then put with a fresh salad and eaten out on the front verandah for dinner as a western sunset lit the skies. Heaven surely was yabbies at sunset.

It all sounded pretty good to young Danny. He couldn't wait for those days to come. After years of eating beef stews and lamb chops and in tough times, the odd bit of kangaroo steak, the fish thing sounded pretty darn good. His Poppy had always assured him that the stories were completely true and when the time came to go fishing, they would feast for weeks at a time. As his grandfather always said, 'make hay while the sun shines'. He would have to wait a few months yet though. The fish needed time to grow fat on all the insects and bugs the rains would bring.

Funny thing, Mother Nature, that suddenly, after years of no rain, a once empty waterhole or creek-bed can produce tiny little fish that eventually grow big and fat. Fish eggs that had lain dormant in the sandy bottom suddenly hatch and the cycle of life begins again. It's a cycle that has adapted to the harshness of outback Australia very well over millions of years.

Danny could hardly wait for that day when he could go catch fish with his grandfather, like the big ones he'd heard so much about. For that matter he'd just love to catch a fish, any fish, even a tiny one would do. He couldn't ever remember going fishing, although his Mum assured him that he had on a number of occasions when he was still a toddler. It all sounded terrific to him.

Meanwhile, while he waited for the fish to hatch and grow, there would still be water in the river, and in the creeks and dams. To a young country farm boy, that meant swimming, diving and perhaps even building a raft like his hero, Huckleberry Finn, whom he'd read about in a book from the school library. He always loved that story. He'd read the book three times. It was without a doubt his favourite.

The coming of the rain meant that when the sporting elite from Mitchell State School went to Roma for the annual regional sports day, country versus townies day they called it, instead of dust, dirt, and rocks, that had been the norm over the past number of years, there would be green grass covering the oval. No more skinned knees and grazed elbows, just grass stains on clothing that mothers would have to contend with later. Still, better grass stains than blood stains any day.

Although Danny lived out of town on a sheep producing property, he still went to school in Mitchell, and every kid around the local area looked forward to the once a year sports day. They trained for it for months ahead. They planned their school activities around the big event. The kids from the bush just loved trying to 'stick it' to the townies from Roma, not to mention the fact that it was a day away from school with all their mates. Danny was looking forward to it enormously. The breaking of the drought had put a smile or everyone's face. There was new hope in the air. It was indeed a great time to be a kid.

The best thing of all about the rain returning was that it meant young Danny's father would be coming home again soon. Even better still, he would be coming home happy, like it used to be before the drought brought so many hardships for all of them. The way it had seemed to Danny was that when times were good, when money was plentiful, when the grasses grew high, everyone seemed to be so deliriously happy. It hadn't been like that for a long while. His 'Poppy' had told him that it used to be like that all the time. He also reassured him that it would be like that again now that Mother Nature had smiled down on their little part of the world.

The family farm, or station, as they are called in outback Australia, was called 'Nundooka' and by local standards, at 20,000 hectares, was a relatively small property. It was located just off the road between Mitchell and St.George, about eighty, dusty, bumpy kilometre's south of Mitchell. At the last count, they had around 1500 Sheep, 100 cows, (some for milk purposes only) a couple of pigs, a pet Emu, and five working sheep dogs along with ten horses.

Danny Richards, along with his mum, Annie, his dad, Lucas, and his grandfather, Rufus John, known to the family as 'Poppy', had lived on Nundooka all their lives. His grandmother, Mary Ma, had died about 9 years before, when Danny was a baby, so he couldn't remember her. He only knew her from photos, and the thing's people had told him about her. They were all very good things. Rufus John, 'Poppy', had never really got over the death of his lifetime mate, but, as the saying goes, life goes on, and the silver haired old man now spent a lot of his time with Danny.

Nundooka was also situated near the banks of the mighty Maranoa River, one of Queensland's great inland rivers, and that made their part of the world very special. Well that was according to Poppy and his dad and they should know, they knew everything that was important.

For a long time, under the existing drought conditions, there had been almost no feed for the sheep on Nundooka. The property was heavily in debt, and he knew that if things got any worse, there was every possibility they could lose it to the bankers and their auctioneers. Lucas was forced into taking most of their sheep to graze along the edges of the roads, the long paddock, as it is known out bush. Better that than them surely dying from hunger in the barren paddocks of Nundooka. He had no choice; he simply had to keep the sheep alive until the rains returned and the markets improved.

A drought in Australia doesn't mean there is no rain; it just means the rainfall in a certain area is well below the average annual rainfall. Often the brief showers or storms are not enough to produce worthwhile grass growth in the paddocks, but would be enough to produce good supplies of grass on the roadsides. The roadways and subsequent edges of the roads are the property of the Local Councils and Governments. To people on the land they are known as the Long Paddock. When rains do come, the water runs off the roadway surface and into the ditches on the side of the roads, which act like small dams. Around these pools of water, grass grows long and lush, before eventually the water evaporates away again. Long after paddocks have been eaten out, green pick can still be found along those edges.

From the day Danny's father left to travel 'the long paddock', Poppy had been the most important person in the young boy's life. His mother was so consumed with everyday life on the farm that she just couldn't find much time for Danny. Well not the amount of time a mother would like to spend with her child. Life seemed to be passing her by so quickly and she was concerned she was getting old before her time. Danny did everything with his Poppy, including looking after the stock that had been left behind on Nundooka, as well as his own daily chores.

As time went by and the drought worsened, more and more farmers were forced into taking their sheep or cattle into the long paddock. That meant Danny's father had to go further and further from home in his search for patches of grass that hadn't been eaten out by other struggling farmers doing the same thing. The struggle to find more roadside feed became an all-consuming struggle. Lucas found he was thinking less and less of home and his family, and more and more, his only thoughts were of his 'new' family, the mob of about a thousand sheep, his two horses and three working dogs.

Before he left, Lucas decided that Nundooka could still feed about five hundred sheep and the hundred or so cattle he ran, so he left them behind to graze on the little grass left, while he took the rest on the road. There was no point in trying to sell the stock, their condition was poor and the market prices were even poorer. To beat of the bankers he had to keep the sheep alive, whatever it took.

In his first few months away, Lucas had returned home on his rusty, old motorbike regularly, but after about six months on the road, he was that far from Nundooka, he rarely rode home. He just didn't have enough money left for petrol for the round trip, plus the fact that he never felt comfortable leaving all those sheep on their own, even if it was for only a day or two.

He had set out in the early part of 1993. By the middle of the autumn of 1994, Lucas had been in the Long Paddock for a little over a year. He, like all the others in the area, prayed for rain on a daily basis.

Sad Times
4.45p.m, Friday, March 8, 1994.
Nundooka Station. Mail Stop MS227, via Mitchell. Queensland.

Danny had arrived home as usual on the school bus at about 4.15. Soon after, he sat under his favourite old tree at the front of the house and ate his afternoon tea. He sat there for a while thinking. His dad hadn't been home for a visit for nearly three months. It had been so long since he'd seen him he could barely remember what he looked like any more.

He had a dream once, that his father had come home dressed in a new suit, driving a new red car and he didn't know who it was, he didn't recognise him. The dream troubled Danny.

He sat there squeezing his eyes closed tight, trying really hard to find an image of his father, but as hard as he tried he couldn't remember what he looked like.

Then he had a scary thought, he didn't know if he wanted him to come home anyway. Over the past year, whenever his mum and dad did get together, they always argued and fought. He hated it when they argued. They argued about money, about sheep, and about the cost of food. They argued about his mother going into town. Wasting money on petrol, his father had said, although Danny couldn't figure out how his dad knew she went into town anyhow.

'You only need to go shopping once a month,' Danny overheard him saying. 'If I ever find out you're seeing '… At that point his Poppy walked in on the conversation and there it ended, with Danny unsure what that particular argument was all about.

One time, Danny thought that his dad was going to hit his mum. He was really angry with her, but they saw Danny watching them, so he just yelled at her instead. After that argument, Danny remembered he ran over to the shed and hid. The shed, and the big old tree, were Danny's favourite places to go when he needed to go somewhere on his own.

That afternoon in March, he sat there thinking. They always used to be happy and laughing. He remembered that they used to hug each other all the time and when they all went shopping into town they would walk along together holding hands. He remembered thinking that he'd never hold hands with a girl, unless it was his mum, but he always liked to watch them doing it.

Danny was sure he would have missed his father a lot more than he did if his grandfather had not been around. His Poppy had become more like his dad to him. He was always there, always laughing and telling jokes or singing old songs. He loved to tell stories about the War. Danny sat under his tree in the cool afternoon shade and thought that one day he'd write a book about his Poppy's stories, especially those war ones they both loved so much. He hated writing stories at school, but then there was something special about his Poppy's stories. The stories he had to write for school were always about boring subjects. They never let him write about the subjects that HE wanted to write about. Danny never knew whether all those old stories were true or not. His dad said that Poppy made them up as he went along, but they sure sounded real to Danny.

Time slipped by under that big old tree, just thinking about the good times, when out of nowhere a thought entered his head, he hadn't seen his Poppy that morning or that afternoon either. Maybe he'd slept in. He liked to sleep in sometimes. He always said that it was old age. You were allowed to sleep in when you got old, 'it went with the territory', he'd say. Perhaps he used to just lie there thinking about those old stories. Danny knew that the old man loved telling those stories, just as much as he loved hearing them.

He hadn't seen his Poppy or his Mum when he got home from school that afternoon. Mind you, he hadn't exactly gone looking for them. When he got off the bus he just felt like sitting alone for a while. Funny though, he thought, his mum was usually there with afternoon tea ready for him as soon as he walked in the door. She must have been in town or something.

That was it, he thought, and Poppy probably went in with her. Still it was odd, for if she did go into town, she was always back home before the bus pulled up.

Danny was content just sitting there alone, when he heard a noise behind him. It startled him. His immediate thought was that it might be a snake. He spun around quickly and was happy to see that it was just his mother.

She looked at him for a moment without saying anything, and he could tell straight away that something was wrong, her face very pale. She didn't look too good, he thought, a bit crook looking. Her eyes were red and puffy. He knew she had been crying. His first thought was that his dad might be home and they'd been arguing again. Something caught his attention and he looked down at her hands. They were shaking, not a lot, but enough for him to notice.

She made a funny noise, like she was clearing her throat. When he looked up to her eyes again, he saw a single tear flow from the bottom of her eye. He watched it as it slowly made its way down her cheek and drop off the side of her chin. Then there was another one.

He was a bit confused, but he also knew that he was about to hear something that was not going to be good. He took a deep breath, like he was bracing himself for what was to come.

For sure his dad was home and they'd been arguing again, he thought. It looked like they'd had a real big fight this time. Maybe his dad wasn't coming home ever again. Another thought entered his head, what if there'd been an accident on the road somewhere. Mum always used to say to him, 'You be careful out there. There are some real idiots on the roads these days.'

Perhaps a car had hit his father. One being driven by one of those idiots she'd warned him about. Danny always heard about bad accidents at school. Someone always knew about them and it seemed like everyone loved to hear about who had died, or who had been injured, and stuff like that. Maybe it was going to be his dad they'd all be talking about tomorrow.

Then suddenly his mind just stopped and went clear. Perhaps he stopped his mind thinking because he didn't like what it was thinking about. Just like when you're having a bad dream, and you wake yourself up, because it gets too scary.

Then for a brief moment, there was nothing in his mind. Everything suddenly went still and quiet. Then he wished his Mum would say something, anything.

'What's wrong Mum? he asked.

He looked up into her red eyes and the moment seemed to last for ages, then finally her lips began to move and his focus went down to them. Her chin and lips trembled together as she began to say something through the tears.

'Danny, I've got some bad news.'

She paused again and cleared her throat, her voice was odd, but he remembered thinking 'get on with it Mum'. What she said next he heard very clearly. He would remember her words clearly for the rest of his life.

'Danny, Poppy's dead', she whimpered.

Danny's mind tried to focus on what his mother had just said - 'Poppy's dead.'

What did she mean Poppy's dead?

Did it mean his Poppy was now in heaven? What did that mean? Suddenly images began to flash through his head. He remembered thinking about heaven and big gates propped on puffy white clouds. Heaven! Then he remembered his beautiful Poppy telling him stories of fishing and of himself watching him pick his teeth after a meal with a toothpick. He always did that. Funny things were rushing into his head.

His Poppy's dead. What exactly did that mean? He couldn't grasp the idea clearly.

Then his mother reached out and gave him a hug. He remembered hearing her crying as they stood beneath his favourite tree. He didn't think it would ever be his favourite tree again.

Our Poppy, no, his Poppy, was dead. It kept going over and over in his mind, as they stood there for ages hugging each other. He knew that his mum understood what it all meant. However, he still didn't understand fully. His head was spinning with thoughts and emotions. He understood the words all right, but he just couldn't image what every day would be like without his Poppy around. He was always around, always. At that moment though, he wished he could be hugging his Poppy too. He had a feeling that he just wanted to get on his horse and ride away. He just couldn't stop the images of his Poppy flashing in and out of his head.

'Poppy's dead,' he said, half thinking out loud. 'Poppy's gone to the angels. I was just talking to him yesterday, how could he be dead so soon.'
His mother heard his whisperings, 'I know dear. It's hard for me to imagine also.'

'But I don't want my Poppy dead. He can't be dead. Dead is what cows do, or horses when they got old, but not to people we love.'

'Sadly Danny, sooner or later we all go to heaven.'

'What have I done wrong?' he blurted out, sounding very much like he was beginning to panic a bit. 'The priest at church always said if you did bad things God would punish you. What have I done that was so wrong that God would take my Poppy away.'

'No darling. It isn't anything to do with you. Poppy was

just old and God wanted him to go up there. It has nothing to do with you.'

'So why is Poppy dead? Why has God taken him away from us?'

Then Danny began to wonder if it was his mum's fault for arguing with his dad so much, or his dad's fault for never being home when they needed him. He needed him now and where was he. His head was racing again. However, it didn't matter what he thought, his Poppy was dead.

He didn't want to cry. He felt like he wanted to, but his dad had always said that boys don't cry, so he didn't. He wished he had cried right then, for it might have made him feel better, then and later. He didn't cry, he just stayed there hugging his mum for ages, while she cried enough for both of them.

Over the next few days, people came to visit and to stay at their property. They came from everywhere, friends, cousins, uncles, aunts, nieces and nephews, all of them sad and most of them crying and crying and crying. Danny never did like to see other people crying, and nothing over the next few days was to change his opinion on the matter. In fact, it probably made it worse. He should have cried with them, but he didn't. Men don't cry, his dad said so.

He remembered there were heaps and heaps of flowers. Firstly, they were put in neat looking vases, until there were no vases left. Then they were put in jam tins and cut off plastic milk bottles and in the end in plain old plastic buckets. There were flowers everywhere. He'd never seen so many flowers in his whole life before. He liked the flowers though because his Poppy had told him once that his 'Nana' loved flowers, especially red ones, she always loved red ones. He looked lovingly at all the red ones and thought of his Poppy. He personally liked the pink ones, but he would never tell

ANYONE that, for fear of being called a sissy. Pink was a girl's colour, or so all his mates said.

The dining table was full of cheese dips of every colour and taste. In addition, there were sweet biscuits, dry biscuits, home-made cakes, red onions, green onions, cheese and gherkins on little sticks. There was lots of food and drinks. It seemed like everyone who came, brought flowers, cheese dip, homemade biscuits and bottles and bottles of Coke, Fanta or Lemonade. Every now and then one of the men would bring in a large bottle of whisky or a carton of beer. The men brought the alcohol and the women brought the food and soft drinks. He wondered why that was, because they all ate and drank anyhow.

Danny remembered that was the only good part about those couple of days, lots of food and hardly any of the adults eating it. The older people just sort of picked a bit here and there. His cousins and he just kept pigging out, and all that Coke and lemonade to drink. For a small period of time, he forgot about his Poppy. Well that wasn't exactly true, but all those kids to play with and all the yummies to eat sure helped a lot.

After a few days, everyone got into their cars and they followed each other into town. There were about thirty cars, including Utes, and four wheel drives, all heading down the road to Mitchell one behind each other. They headed straight to the local church in the main street, the one just near Danny's school. He hadn't been to church since his cousin Maggie got married about a year before. He didn't like going to church much, nor did his Poppy. Whenever Poppy had gone to church, he would nod off to sleep.

When everyone was finally there, they walked in and sat down. Danny noticed THAT right up at the front of the church was a coffin and people were walking up and looking in.

'What's in the coffin Mum?' he asked, hoping to hear her

say flowers or something like that.

'Your Poppy dear,' she answered.

'You mean my dead Poppy?'

'Yes dear that's the way they do it. People like to say their good-byes this way.'

'But he's dead! Isn't he in heaven already?'

'His spirit is darling, but his body is still here.'

'Do I have to look Mum? He asked in a somewhat horrified voice.

'No dear,' she answered, 'not if you don't choose to, it's up to each person to decide for themself. Some people like to say goodbye this way. Others choose just to remember them as they were.'

'What are you going to do, Mum?' he asked.

'What do you think I should do Danny?'

'I don't know, but I don't think I want to go up there.'

'Then perhaps I'll just stay here with you. Is that O.K?

Danny sat there for a while, still feeling confused by the whole scene in front of him. It still didn't seem to make much sense. There, right in front of him in the Mitchell Lutheran Church, people were lining up to see his Poppy's dead body. At that somewhat frustrating moment though, he was finally starting to fully understand his Mum's words from a few days before, when she said Poppy's dead. He was gone forever.

He felt horrible. He was in a church full of friends and relatives but he felt really sad and alone. For one awkward moment he thought he was going to spew up all the food he'd eaten over the past couple of days. His stomach was turning over, and over. He was so overtaken with sadness at seeing the coffin up the front at the altar and to know that his Poppy was lying in it, dead. He couldn't go up and look, even though he knew he was going to heaven next and he'd never ever see him again, never, ever. He just didn't want to see a dead body. The thought of it scared him too much.

One good thing did happen that day though. Danny's father came home. It had taken two days for the message to get to him that his father, Poppy, had died, and when he did hear the bad news, he jumped straight onto his rusty old trail bike and rode straight to the church.

Danny was really happy to see him again. He looked very thin in the face when he arrived and he'd grown a beard since the last time he'd seen him. Danny thought he looked heaps older with a beard.

His dad walked in, dressed in a suit. Danny knew he must have stopped off at their home on the way past to get all dressed up like he was. He also knew that his mum wouldn't be very impressed if he'd turned up in his dirty, smelly old work clothes.

He looked for them as he walked down the middle of the aisle.

They didn't hug. They always hugged when his dad came home before. He guessed it was because of all the sadness for his Poppy, that they didn't hug this time. He thought his dad probably felt embarrassed in front of all those people.

Not long after the funeral the arguing started again. It went on and off for most of the night. Danny remembered thinking that his Poppy would have told them to stop arguing if he was still there. Whenever Danny tried to say something, his dad would just tell him to shut up and butt out of grown-ups business.

He didn't understand much of what they were fighting about, but the name Robert kept coming up. His mum just kept saying that it was hard being alone, that a woman needed someone fussing over them every now and then. Again Danny felt confused, he'd always thought that he and his Poppy did that, fussed over her, but for some reason, that wasn't enough.

He wished his Poppy were there at that moment. He wanted to talk to his grandfather. He was feeling frustrated and a little scared about his mum and dad fighting again, especially now. He realised he wasn't ever going to be there again. He was on his way to heaven and that Nundooka, without his beloved grandfather, was going to be a strange place for some time to come. It would just be him and his mum now.

His father had told them that because of the rain in the district of late that he was slowly making his way back home along the roads. Soon he'd be home for good. He hated the fighting and arguing. His Poppy had made Nundooka a fun place to live, with lots of laughter, lots of stories, lots of fun. Nundooka was going to be a very different place now without him.

The next morning Danny's father got on his motorbike and rode off again, back to his sheep and the long paddock.

CHAPTER THREE

St. George 1884

The Barlow's had been on the trail for only six weeks when they reached St. George. For a team of beginners, they had learnt fast and had made good time.

John settled the cattle down on a common just north of the town and headed in to stock up on provisions, and also to find the boys, who had gone ahead.

There was a sign on the edge of town. He stopped to read it. 'St. George is built on the spot where explorer Thomas Mitchell camped on the 23rd April 1846. In the land of our fair Queen the 23rd of April is celebrated as St. George's Day. It is from this occasion our friendly town was named. All law-abiding persons are welcome within.'

The township had done well for itself in its short forty-year life. He headed straight for the Post Office and sure enough, as they had planned, there was a letter waiting from Mary. He caught up with the boys and headed off to a wooden bench in the Town Square. John opened the letter and read out loud.

'Everyone is well and we all send our love. We all miss you enormously. The farm is fine although there has been next to no rain. A week after you left, we had some good falls but nothing useful since. Sarah found a large snake in the barn. Will cut his leg when he fell chasing a small whippy around the house paddock. It was nothing serious, although his screaming concerned me at first. Poor dear, I think the blood from the cut scared him. We received the letter you sent from Mitchell. It sounds very much like you have a long journey ahead still. Our thoughts are forever with you. Please write at every opportunity for we crave news about your progress. Henry Wainright, (their neighbour) has been over at least once a week and has been very helpful around the property. He is, as you have always said, a great neighbour.'

The letter went on about people who had called in seeking news of their progress. 'From time to time, we get news from the Cobb and Co. drivers of a sighting of you and the mob and Will is quick to locate you on his wall of maps.' The letter finished with the usual well wishes and they all prayed for a safe return.

There was a second letter folded inside the main letter. It was a personal letter with private words from Mary to John. It was obvious that she was missing him terribly, but she knew what her boys were doing had to be done. She tried to show John her strength and patience in her letters.

They had been together for nearly thirty years and the separation was very painful for her. However, she promised to be brave and strong and to spend all her 'spare hours' with the children, to help her forget how much she missed her 'men'.

The letters made John homesick. Not so the boys though, by now they were happy doing what they were doing. They were natural drovers and life on the road was agreeing with them. A whole new world was unfolding before them, and they loved it.

Matthew had wanted to strike out and travel for some time. He felt he had out grown Burton. Charles had been more apprehensive at first and it took time before he got over missing his home, but by the time they reached St.George, he was in his element and enjoying every moment of it.

The cattle were still in reasonably good condition. Since

leaving Burton Downs, they had fed on good grasses. All was going according to the plan.

After a break of three days, they headed out again. Half a day's ride from St.George, the Maranoa flowed into the Culgoa River and then meandered off in a sou-westerly direction.

The landscape was changing somewhat. The countryside was flatter. Gone now were the rolling hills that slowed the early part of the trip. There was now more open ground, a sign of what was to lie ahead of them. Gone too was most of the low scrub bush that had made the going tougher. In its place, towering above them, were the far more traditional Australian gum trees.

Their journey so far had been nearly perfect. With the exception of that spooky day and night they had spent between Mitchell and St. George. The horses were doing a fine job bearing up to their loads. Along the way they'd only lost two calves to a dingo pack and two mature-aged steers that had wandered off and been lost in the scrubby bush land somewhere. All in all, the trip was rolling along quite smoothly. They'd learnt so much since they'd left home. The boys were now confident to tackle just about anything that lay ahead of them. John, being older and more experienced on the ways of the bush, was considerably more cautious. He knew there was still a long way to go.

Late one afternoon, just a few days out of St.George as the men were setting up for the night, a stranger cautiously rode towards their campsite. When he got close enough he called out and asking politely if he could join them. Charles had just lit a fire and had set the Billy up to boil water for a brew.

'Please join us, Sir, my son is preparing a Will of tea and you are welcome to a cup as soon as it's boiled,' said John.

Matthew made his way across to his still saddled horse and pretended to be unsaddling it. In reality, he had gone there to be close to his rifle in the event that the stranger wasn't friendly. Bushrangers and vagabonds were known to be everywhere and one could not be too careful.

The stranger introduced himself, 'My name is George Lamwith. I'm a cattle breeder. In fact, this is part of my property you're travelling through right now.'

John looked at him with some apprehension. 'I'm pleased to meet you George. I'm John Barlow, and these are my sons, Matthew and Charles. I hope you have no problem with us passing through your land.'

'No, not at all John, I had heard you were heading down this way, on route to Broken Hill I believe.'

John now feeling more comfortable with this intrusion, replied, 'Our stock was dying in the drought up north, we really had no other options than to take them south to market.'

'I think what you and your boys are doing is very commendable. I see it as a very smart business venture and apart from welcoming you to my part of the world, there is another reason for my visit tonight. I have a proposition for you and your boys.'

He paused as John passed him a mug of the steaming hot tea.

'Sugar?' asked John.

'Two please.'

George took the old tin mug from John, ' No point in beating round the bush, I'll get straight to the point. If you would be interested in taking 80 head of my cattle to Broken Hill with you,' he said in a very forthright manner, 'I'll be prepared to pay you a healthy percentage of the sale price as payment for your efforts.'

John looked across at the boys who were expressionless at that point.

George continued, 'I'll send one of the men in my employ, my wife's brother Benny, along for the journey. He could help with the extra cattle and he'll also be my security.'
John jumped in sternly, 'Sir, I am an honest man.'

'I'm by no means accusing you of being anything else John, but you must understand that I need to be assured that you will look after my cattle as if you would your own,' added George apologetically.
John paused and took a sip of piping hot tea from his old tin mug. George blew into his mug, to cool it somewhat, and then took a sip also. The boys, who had been listening quietly to every word, seemed to be caught up in the moment as they also took sips from their mugs.

A few moments later, John looked back up to his visitor, 'Go on, George, you have our attention.'

George continued, 'When you arrive in Broken Hill, and you sell my cattle along with your own, you will receive two bills of sale and two credit notes for my mob. One with be drawn up for 70% of the sale price and will be made out in the name of George Lamwith of Bungunnia Station. The other credit note, for 30%, will be made out in your name sir. It's that simple.'

John pondered the offer for a moment, 'Seems to me, even with your man along for the journey, you still take an enormous risk. There is no assurance that we won't run into more drought, bushrangers, bushfires, stampedes, anything could happen out there,' replied John with concern in his voice.

'My cattle, like yours, will probably perish here if the drought continues. We too have had precious little rain. I am only proposing to send a small part of my herd with you, sort of a trial run. I will remain here to take care of the rest. Sure it's a gamble, but not as big a gamble as you are taking, Sir. I consider that if you are prepared to gamble your future on this venture, then my risk is considerably smaller and in relatively safe hands. You have far more to lose than I, and that is my assurance.'

John listened intently as George continued, 'I'd heard you were coming from the stock agent in St.George some time ago. He had heard of your journey from a stock agent in Mitchell. So, I made some inquiries about you while you were heading down and all our information was the same, that you were a very honest and trusting man. We have heard all about your young son's wall of maps, in fact, we even sent him some information on our district. Word spreads out here. You three, along with young Will, are quite famous. Your reputations precede you.'

Matthew and Charles sat quietly listening to the conversation between the two older men as George continued. 'We agreed that if you could get this far without any major problems, then chances are that you could get all the way, and let's face it, if you do get to Broken Hill, the rewards should be handsome indeed. A good price is hard to get in these tough times. I cannot take my own cattle to market there, so getting you to take some of mine along seemed like a fairly good proposition. A gamble it is sure enough, but then all of us who make our living from the land are forced to take gambles from time to time.'

John reached over, lifted the billy from the fire and topped his mug up again. Steam rose from the hot brew. He looked back at George and with a gesture, offered him a refill. He reached out with his mug and John carefully filled it again.

'Two sugars wasn't it?' asked John.

'Thanks.'

The two men went through the ritual of blowing into the mugs again. Then, almost in unison, they proceeded to take careful sips.

'Well, what do you think?' asked George.

A few moments passed, then John answered, 'I'll discuss your proposal with the boys tonight, and perhaps we can talk again in the morning. They are a part of this venture and it would not be proper to make a decision without their input.'

'I'd have expected nothing less of you John. We'll leave all business talk until tomorrow then.'

All four chatted on for a while about rain and droughts, the usual things you would expect to hear over a campfire between cattlemen.

Just on nightfall, as George had made light of his second mug of tea, he bid them good night and rode out of their campsite promising to return early next morning with some freshly made scones for breakfast and looking hopefully towards a positive answer.

John, Matthew and Charles watched George ride off and then, as if one, all sat back down and stared into the fire, almost as if they were looking for an answer in the flames.

After some minutes, Matthew broke the silence, 'I think it's a bloody good idea,' he said in a very positive tone. 'Bloody good idea' he repeated.

Silence fell on the campsite again and again the three of them stared blankly at the crackling fire.

Then John looked up at the younger Charles and asked, 'What do you think Charlie?'

Charles thought for a moment, then offered his reply, 'Seems like a good idea to me also, but you're the boss Father. I'll go along with whatever you two think.'

With that he looked back into the crackling fire and the three returned to their deep thoughts.

Matthew spoke with authority, 'Well, we're already going that way. With an extra man along it shouldn't be any harder than it already is.' He looked up at his father for a response. There was none.

John was still staring into the flames. Matthew went on, 'Might slow us down a bit though, eighty extra cattle.' He followed by answering his own question, 'It shouldn't take that much longer though, maybe an extra week or so, and we've got time. He probed for another answer, 'what do you think Dad?'

John looked up at Matthew, 'I think you're right son, maybe an extra week or two, but then as you say, we have the time.'

They didn't leave it there though, they discussed George's proposal at length well into the night. George seemed a nice enough bloke. He was just a battler like they were, perhaps a little better off than them, but a battler nonetheless. As Matthew had said earlier, they were already going to Broken Hill, and now they would get a cut of the price of George's cattle for their trouble. It seemed like a sound enough business arrangement. Then there was the question of whether the proposal was enough. Perhaps it was too much, how would they know. After considerable debate, they finally decided that if George was prepared to offer a 70/30 split, then it wasn't too little, which then begged the question, was it enough? Should they go for more?

Charles opened up that discussion in earnest when he asked his father, 'How would you go about asking for more money?'

John thought about it for a few moments and then answered, 'You're right, Charlie, I don't think I'd know what to say. What about you Matthew, could you do the dealing for us? I've never liked that sort of thing. Your mother always handled those situations.'

Matthew looked into his father's eyes and without a hint of concern answered, 'I can deal with that. I think we should at least try for a better price. I believe Mr. Lamwith would be expecting us to negotiate.'

'Do you think so Matthew?'

'Yes dad, just think about it, would you offer top price straight up.'

'No I suppose not.'

'If you were prepared to accept say 60/40, would you say it straight out. I think not. He's a businessman, and he's expecting to pay more, maybe hoping we're new at this business and we'll accept his offer, but I believe he is prepared for a counter offer. Let's not disappoint the man.'

They talked on into the night and after more hot cups of tea from the old Will and a hearty meal, they decided to take George up on his offer and agreed that Matthew should try to get terms of 65/35. If George came back with a counter offer, then they would be better off by a small margin at least. They wanted to act like businessmen; well Matthew did at least.

That night, they all bedded down under a full moon, feeling quite happy with how their original decision to 'drove' cattle to Broken Hill seemed to be turning out well.

They remained in camp the next morning, enjoying the break from the early morning starts that had been their ritual since leaving Burton, and waited for George to return. Sure enough, about two hours after first light, George rode in again. This time he had his wife, Mabel, and her brother Benny with him.

Mabel was every bit an outback farmers wife. She was dressed in plain clothing with a big leather belt wrapped around her mid-section. Her hair was pinned back in a bun, as was the practical style for out there. She looked like she'd had a hard life, but still had that typical friendly outback style and manner. Her face was lit with a big broad beaming smile.

Benny also, was a bushy through and through. Rough unshaven face, a holed and battered hat that should have been retired ten years before, and something that had once resembled a cigarette, hanging from his lips. He too knew hard times, and it showed on his weather-beaten, leathery skinned face.

The two groups sat and chatted again, over yet another billy of hot strong tea. This day though, there was a treat in store, some freshly baked scones that Mabel had made that very morning. Charlie was the only one not there that morning, he was out on his horse checking the cattle.

'We discussed your offer in detail last night,' said Matthew with a positive air. 'It was indeed an interesting offer and we thank you for it. However, to get straight to it, we all felt that with such a long way still to go and a lot of possible unforeseen problems to address, we felt that perhaps 30/70 didn't quite reflect the risks we may face. It is one thing to lose our own, but the extra care needed to protect another's was considerable. We felt 35/65 would be a better figure to adequately compensate us for our efforts and concerns.'

George looked at Matthew eye to eye, 'I can see you're learning fast young man. You'll make a good businessman one day.'

'Perhaps that day is today.'

'Perhaps it is. Tell you what, let's split it three ways. I take two parts, you fine folk, take one.'

'Thirty three percent?' asked Matthew.

'Indeed, young man, thirty three percent.'

Matthew looked across at his father, and raised his eyebrows. Almost immediately John nodded his head ever so slightly.

He looked back at George, 'George, you have a deal, thirty three percent is acceptable to us.'

Men did deals in the 1880's in simple fashion and this deal was no exception, it was all over with quickly, no frills. The men shook hands, and that was that.

Mabel knew immediately that the dealing was done, 'Warm scones anybody?'

No one needed to be asked a second time, the fresh home-baked scones smelt a delight.

The two families had struck up a good friendship in the short time they had been together. The two men, indeed the two families, had a lot in common. They talked at length about the hardships of living out there in the bushland of Australia, and of their dreams for the future.

Mabel could only listen to so much of the men's talk, so around mid-morning she left and headed back to her homestead. George followed a few hours later just a little after lunch. The Barlows, having to wait on George's cattle, spent the rest of the day checking on their gear and just quietly caring for the mob. That night they slept under the stars by an open fire, very satisfied with their day's negotiations and enjoying another break from their normal daily routines.

Next morning, as had been arranged, John met up with George and helped pick out eighty of the strongest looking cattle from one of his holding paddocks. There was no point in picking out weak cows and steers; they needed to be healthy enough to survive the long trek ahead. When that had been done, George got Benny and another stationhand to lead the cattle over to an area near the Barlow's camp and settled them down there. Matthew and Charles then joined their father and George and they together proceeded with another head count, just to do a final check of the numbers before the two mobs were run together.

Finally, in the early afternoon the two herds were linked together to form one big mob, numbering some two hundred and thirty head. Late that afternoon, after another chat, over yet another billy of tea, the men parted company. George leaving with a promise from John that he'd send the money to him in about three or four months.

In a short space of time, the inexperienced Barlows, had gone from being just plain old small time cattle breeders, into becoming experienced drovers, and now they had become entrepreneurs as well. They had every right to feel proud of themselves that night, and they did.

First light next morning and the Barlows, along with Benny, continued on with their amazing journey. They continued south along the Culgoa River. The waterway was getting deeper and wider as it joined up with a number of other small rivers and creeks flowing in from the eastern slopes of New South Wales and the vast western plains of Queensland.

It was apparent to them that the area to the east had seen recent rains. The creeks and rivers from the north however were carrying far less water. It was obvious that Queensland was still held in the grip of that terrible drought of the 1880's.

Water in the river was plentiful and grass around it was green and lush. However, as little as a mile away from the riverbank, the land was hopelessly dry and barren. The tree-lined riverbanks, covered in dark wet mud and tall green grasses, took on a whole new appearance, a dry barren vista of grey covered saltbush plains that stretched out to the horizon.

The noise of hundreds of birds, of all sizes and colours, screeching and squawking as they nestled in the trees, faded away quickly if one moved inland and away from the slow flowing life rich river. Then, as you returned to the lush waterway again, the noises and colours almost magically re-appeared. It was a strange and harsh world that they ventured through, yet all agreed, it was extremely beautiful as well.

They pushed steadily south-west. As they went, they scouted ahead trying to speed their progress by finding ways of cutting across the open plains between the river bends that snaked their way through the ancient land, but it was not always possible. Young Will's maps of the areas helped somewhat, but in some sections, they simply had to follow the river itself. On those occasions, progress could be frustratingly slow, as at times they found themselves almost heading in the wrong direction.

Most good days they were making around fifteen to eighteen miles progress, but, at the end of some days, they would be nearer to their destination by only half that distance. In spite of that, they knew that sticking to the river was their only choice. It was still their safest option. To leave the safety of the river and head directly inland towards Broken Hill would be extremely perilous, and so they continued the daily routine of scouting ahead looking for safe ways to shorten the journey.

Eventually, the Culgoa River joined forces with the Barwon River from the north. Soon after that, the Bogan River flowed in from the east and the New England Ranges. At that point, where the Bogan River joined the southern flow, about twenty-five miles north of the inland town of Bourke, the collective waterways became known as the Darling River.

What a grand sight it must have been to the weary travelers, way out there in the middle of that barren land, three mighty rivers coming together. They might have wondered why that point had been chosen by Mother Nature to become the birthplace of one of the world's greatest rivers, the Darling. With such a flow of water heading inland, it would be easy to understand why early explorers believed that Australia had a giant inland lake or sea. In fact, the waters weren't heading inland at all, but rather they were generally heading south. The Great Dividing Range, which runs the whole length of eastern Australia, from the south, right up through to the north, blocked the water from flowing eastward to the coast. Therefore, any rain that fell on the western slopes of those mountains, firstly flowed westward, but then eventually turned in a more southerly direction. One by one, the small creeks spilled off the mountains and became rivers as they flowed into each other, until finally hundreds of miles inland, they produced one magnificent watercourse.

As the men stood looking at the birthplace of that great river, their appreciation and respect for their homeland country grew even greater. They were on a journey of discovery, and they knew it was becoming a very special time in all their lives. The previously small confines of Burton Downs had opened up to present to them Australia's mighty inland, the 'outback' as it is affectionately known. Impressive, scary, bold, exciting, dangerous, alive, this was truly the adventure of their lives. The small confines of their home had opened up to present Australia's mighty inland, or outback, as it was so affectionately called.

CHAPTER FOUR

Jock's Flight
7a.m.Wednesday 13th March. 1994
Toowoomba, Queensland.

March the 13th started out like any other day for Jock Miller. Jock was the owner / operator of Toowoomba Air Freight Services. He was also very much a creature of habit, which would see him up every morning at 6a.m. A light breakfast with his wife and three children, a hot morning shower, a quick read of the headlines of the local paper, the 'Toowoomba Chronicle', then he'd jump in his little four-cylinder Toyota and drive to the local airport, just a few kilometres away.

Once there, he'd go straight to his modest little office, which was situated on the side of Hangar 1A and at 8am sharp, he would begin another working day. Firstly he'd check for messages on his answering machine, and then for any faxes that may have come in overnight. Usually there were none. Not that Jock's business wasn't successful, it was in a modest way. It was just that most contact and calls were made after 9am when other business's opened up for the day. The mornings that Jock had a pre-arranged early flight were different of course. On those occasions he could be in the air as early as 5am, on route to wherever it was that the job was taking him. If however, he had no bookings, then the morning routine would follow its usual procedures. After the calls and faxes had been checked, the kettle would go on and he'd settle in to read the rest of the local newspaper.

Around 8.30 Jock would wander out of his office and into Hangar 1A. Inside the hangar were a number of small commercial and private light aircraft. One of those was a Beechcraft Baron Twin Engine, six-seater aircraft with the name Toowoomba Air Freight Services painted on the side. That plane was Jock's pride and joy.

Jock had been a small time commercial pilot for just on 10 years. He had worked for a number of different companies all over Australia. Finally one day, he decided that it was time to take his wife, Mary, and their children and head back to his home town of Toowoomba. His family hadn't known what a settled home-life was like and now that the kids were old enough for schooling, he and Mary felt it was time to plant roots somewhere, for the sake of their kids educations. Jock also made the decision, with Mary's support, that they would try their hand at a commercial freight and passenger charter service of their own. He was tired of flying for other owners all over outback Australia. It was time to become a boss himself. So Jock and Mary leased a second hand plane, and an office at the airport, and launched Toowoomba Air Freight Services.

When Jock arrived at work that morning, sitting on his desk, beneath the fax machine, was an urgent message from the Jackson Oil Fields. He torn the paper from the machine and read it. The message seemed simple enough, 'Please contact the Maintenance Manager at Jackson as soon as you get in - urgent you do so.'

The Jackson Oil Fields are about three hundred kilometres south west of Charleville, in a very arid part of the Australian inland and about eight hundred kilometres due west of Toowoomba.

Jock immediately picked up his phone and rang them. He knew the Maintenance Manager out there very well; he was an old friend. The two men had worked together previously in Papua New Guinea and had kept in touch ever since. When his old friend heard that Jock had started his own charter and freight business, he had tried, whenever possible, to pass work his way. Also he knew full well that he could always rely on Jock to get the job done on time, with very little fuss.

Jock was told that Jackson's major underground pump had broken down and the back-up unit had also failed. Storm clouds were on the horizon and Coopers Creek along with the nearby Wilson River were already overflowing from previous heavy rains further to the north. The pumps at Jackson were needed to keep any unwanted underground water flows under control. If the shafts filled with water from another downpour of rain it could set the Oil fields production back months. They would not only have to clear the shafts of the flooding, but it would take expensive valuable maintenance time to repair any damaged equipment underground. The pumps were critical to a good continuing operation.

He was told the much-needed parts should be available in Toowoomba, and his instructions were to pick them up and fly them direct to Jackson. Jock realised the urgency and knew that his old friend was relying on him to come through. He also knew that if he got the job done quickly, there could be the bonus of more work to follow in the future. He had transported supplies and people all over the region since he'd started his charter business, but this was by far the most important job he had been called upon to do. This one job, done correctly, could ensure the future of his business for a long time to come.

Jock hopped back in his car and went straight around to the Machinery Supplier in South Toowoomba, the one his mate in Jackson asked him to check with first. He had no luck there, they were out of those particular parts. The supplier had a quick look on his computer and told Jock that the parts were only available in Brisbane. They told him they could get the parts up on overnight transport and they could be there early the next morning.

Jock immediately rang Jackson and gave them the news. The reply was simple, fly straight to Brisbane, get the parts and fly them out urgently, repeat urgently. They weren't concerned with the cost, there was more rain on the way and that spelt trouble. Jock understood. He put the phone down and asked the supplier to check again. Was there any other supplier around town who had the parts? After a few minutes with his face buried in the screen of the computer, the trader looked up at Jock repeating what he'd said earlier. Brisbane was the only place in the south-east corner of Queensland that had the parts in question. They got on the phone again and rang the main supplier in Brisbane for confirmation that the parts were there. They arranged for the parts to be waiting for Jock when he arrived in Brisbane. They all appreciated the urgency. Jackson Oil Fields was a good customer to everyone associated with the mining industry.

He rang Mary and told her the story and told her he'd be away for at least two days. He asked her to get some of his clothes together, along with his toothbrush, a shaver and deodorant. Then could she meet him at the airport hangar as soon as she could get there, and finally could she organise a thermos of hot coffee and some sandwiches for the flight.

He immediately drove back to the airport and set about preparing the plane for the flight.
Shortly after, Mary arrived. He told her of the plan, which was simple enough. Fly down to Brisbane, get the parts and then fly them straight out to Jackson. He'd stay there overnight and fly back sometime the next morning, unless he could get some

return work, a back-load. With a touch of luck, he might be able to fly some staff back for their break. Jackson's staff were flown out on a fourteen-day shift, then they were flown back home (usually Brisbane) for five or six days off. Normally they used another Charter Company for those passenger flights, but Jock was hopeful, that if he was already there, they might use him instead. Sometimes Company Executives were flown in or out to Sydney, and what a bonus it would be if he could score a trip down to Sydney.

By 9.15a.m, Jock had fuelled up and was ready to go. He applied for and received clearance to take off from the Toowoomba Control Tower under the call sign, Delta Tango 104. Not long after, with both the engines screaming at full throttle. His take off was perfect.

Toowoomba airport is situated high on the edge of an escarpment on top of the Great Dividing Range. Jock climbed to 2000 feet and then turned eastward towards Brisbane. In a short time he flew out over the escarpment and down into the Brisbane Valley. He had taken many a tourist for joy flights over this area before. It was truly spectacular flying. The rugged mountains and the sprawling plains below, leading all the way to the Pacific Ocean some 150klms away and visible on the eastern horizon.

It was a perfect morning for flying. Not a sign of the storm clouds Jackson had spoken of, but then why should there be, Jackson Oil Fields was eight hundred kilometres away in western Queensland.

The flight to Brisbane started uneventfully. In fact it was very peaceful up there, the sky was clear, the air was very still over the Brisbane Valley, 'The Queensland Salad Bowl' as it is known, looked lush and green after good recent rains. Jock could clearly see the patchwork formation of the fields below.

He could see the main highway leading to Brisbane beneath him. It was quite full of cars and trucks of all sizes heading in both directions. They looked like matchbox toys in a child's playground.

He relaxed and took a moment to ponder his lifestyle. All was good. His passion for flying was now his full-time job. He was working from his home-town again, after years in far-away places. Business was good. Well, good enough to believe that the future was something to look forward to. His reputation was spreading with more work coming his way every month. Most importantly his family was together and had roots firmly planted in one place. Life couldn't get any better, he thought, as he flew east on that glorious March morning.

Then, in the middle of his pleasant daydreaming, for one brief moment, he thought he felt a misfire in one of the engines. Instinctively, his attention turned back to the plane. He scanned the panel of gauges in front of him looking for something out of the ordinary. His body tensed slightly. He listened to the pulse of the plane. The pilot and plane became one. He flew on cautiously listening for any hiccup in the plane's engine. A few minutes passed and everything sounded and felt OK.

He decided that when he got to Archerfield Airport in Brisbane, he'd get a mechanic to take a look over his little 'baby', just to be sure. It would be a long flight out to Jackson and with an approaching storm front, he could not be too careful. All being well, he would only get held up by perhaps an hour or so. Being every inch a professional pilot, he knew that prevention was better than a disaster later. First rule of good flying, good take offs should always be balanced out with equally good landings.

He stayed alert for the rest of the journey to Brisbane, listening closely to his engines and watching the gauges. All seemed to be running smoothly again. Perhaps it was nothing more than some small impurity in the fuel and the carburetors had cleared it out without any problem.

Jock could see Brisbane getting closer. He began making his descent when he was over Ipswich. Shortly after, Delta Tango 104 landed safely at Archerfield Airport at precisely 10.27a.m. Once on the ground, under instructions from Air Traffic Control, he taxied the plane to a holding area. He then walked straight over to the airport's main workshop area to look for a mechanic to get his engines checked out.

It posed no problem, another of his old mates, a man named Benny, worked at Archerfield and he was happy to look at his plane as soon as the engines cooled down. He was told there had been some dirty aviation fuel around, and that he should be able to look over the plane, clean the carburetors, and have him back in the air again in about an hour. With that arranged, Jock's next task was to go to the main office and check if the parts had arrived for him, as had been arranged from Toowoomba. He'd then grab something to eat, check the latest weather reports out west from the control tower, log in his flight plan and be back in the air and on his way by around midday.

Well, all good plans can go wrong. The parts were there all right but when he returned to check on his plane there was a delay. An electrical part in the engine would have to be replaced. Jock jumped in a taxi and went over to the electrical supplier, who was only a few suburbs away. He bought the part he needed and was back at Archerfield just before 1o'clock. An hour later he got the all clear from Benny. She was ready to fly.

During the delay, Jock had rung Jackson Oil Fields to tell them he had the part and all was well. He hoped to arrive out there between 7 and 8 p.m. He asked if they could arrange for lights at their landing strip to guide him in. Jackson's airstrip was a daylight field, but in emergencies they could land a plane with a few quick arrangements. Most outback properties and small towns have landing strips, and in the event of an after-dark landing, the strip could be lit with headlights from cars, tractors, lanterns or spot fires if they had too. Most bush strips can't afford lighting so that was the outback way of doing it. Jock had landed at night in the bush many times before. It was never any real problem.

He checked the weather again, and made sure that he had the part for Jackson safely on board. He'd hate to forget that. Soon after, he was roaring down the runway. This time he would be heading west for Jackson.

Delta Tango 104 was airborne at 2.40p.m. It was a little later than he had first planned, so he decided that he'd fly direct, no wasting any more time with stopovers anywhere. He wanted to make up time. The news on the approaching weather front wasn't ideal, but flying rarely was. To Jock it was all part of the challenge. That's what flying up there in the clouds was all about to him, the freedom and the challenge.

He headed west, directly into the afternoon sun. Within minutes he was flying back over Ipswich and then out over the 'Salad Bowl', until he could see the mountains fast approaching and way up on top he could see his beloved home town coming into view.

He flew over Toowoomba at about 3.30p.m. He looked down and thought to himself that Mary would have just picked the kids up from school. About now, he thought, they'd all be sitting around the kitchen table having afternoon tea, biscuits and chocolate flavoured milk. Mary would be having her usual cup of herbal tea. The kids might even be wondering where their dad was. He knew where he was. He would soon be almost directly above them, at 8,000 feet.

He decided he'd contact air traffic control at the airport. He would try and get them to patch him through to the phone at his home, so he could say hello to the family. If they were able to, he could talk to them from the radio in the plane.

He called the Control Tower. They asked him to give them a moment to set it up. The next voice he heard was Mary's.

'Where are you dear?' she asked.

'Almost above you at about 8,000ft,' he replied.

He heard Mary yell out to the kids to go out and look up and see if they could see their 'daddy'. Jock informed her that he was just a little west of the city. He could faintly hear the kids yelling back that they could see his plane above them. Mary felt a small tingle go down her spine. How proud she was of him.

'Are they still watching?' he asked.

There was a short pause as Mary looked outside to the children.

Eventually the reply came, 'Yes dear.'

'Tell them to keep watching and I'll give them a wave,' and with that he waved the wing tips from side to side.

'He waved Mummy. We saw him wave,' they yelled from just outside the back door.

'They saw it dear. They'll talk about that for days..... We love you .... You be careful now, I heard on the 3o'clock news that there's a few bad storms out that way,' Mary stressed.

'I'll be OK. You know me. Besides, I flew in Papua New Guinea for two years remember, and nothing's as bad as the storms you get up there, don't worry. I'm a good pilot. I can survive anything.'

They chatted on for a few minutes longer until the Toowoomba Control Tower cut in on their conversation and said they had to terminate the call as another plane was requesting landing instructions. The last thing Jock heard was his wife's soft loving voice, say 'I love you sweetheart, do be careful.'

He felt good. It was great being able to be part of their afternoon tea, even if it was for just a moment and from 8000 feet above them. The pleasant moment passed, and then it was back to the job at hand. Getting the parts to Jackson through the storm front and bad weather ahead of him was his main priority now. He corrected his course, checked the instruments in front of him. Then he looked up at the growing cloudbank ahead. Nothing to worry about just yet, he thought. It had been such a hectic day. He'd been on the go since 7 a.m. that morning, and he believed he'd earned a bit of rest time. It was time to flick on the auto-pilot. Time to regain his thoughts and settle in to the flight, and to pour a mug of coffee from the thermos Mary had so lovingly made for him earlier that morning and have a bite to eat. After that, he thought, he'd check the position of that weather front with Roma Air Control.

His flight west was proving to be a bit bumpy, due to the air being pushed ahead of the storm front. But nothing to be alarmed about, he'd expected that. The flight path took him west north-west over Dalby, on past Miles, then due west to Roma and over Charleville, basically following the Warrego Highway. From Charleville he'd head south-west to the Jackson Oil Fields.

He was a few hours behind time. The headwinds were so strong he couldn't hope to make up much time against them on his current flight plan.

Somewhere near Dalby, Jock made an out-of- character decision to change his flight plan. Instead of following the Warrego Highway all the way to Charleville, he decided he would fly due west over Surat and straight on to Jackson. The storm front was moving north-east, so the change of flight plan would hopefully see him miss the storm altogether, at the very least he would only run into the southern edge of it.

He could make up some time by flying due west and by missing the main brunt of the storm and that way he could get the parts to Jackson a little earlier, perhaps even before darkness had set in.

He must have been getting very weary up there alone. Perhaps with auto pilot on he had nodded off for a moment or two. Maybe he just simply forgot, or maybe he thought he had done it. Jock was generally an extremely thorough person when it came to flying, but for some reason he didn't radio Roma or Brisbane of the change in his flight plan.

He was now heading due west, in a straight line to Jackson, and flying over open ground. However, everyone else still believed, according to his flight plan, that he was following the highway to Roma and Charleville. By now he was flying over fifty kilometres south of his original flight plan and moving further away from it each minute he was in the air.

Normally on a flight of that length he would take a break by landing at Roma or Charleville for an hour or so, but this trip was urgent and he was behind schedule. His change of plans didn't allow for any stop-overs. Jock needed the work and his reputation of 'getting the job done' was important to the survival of his small charter business. He felt it was worth the risk of flying straight through and so he pushed on.

Around 6.30 p.m., had it been a clear day, he should have been able to see the lights of Roma ahead to his right. But Roma had been hidden behind low clouds blowing in ahead of the storm. It was perhaps sixty or seventy kilometres away, yet still he didn't think to notify them of his change of flight plan. He'd been watching the lightning ahead for some time, and perhaps that had preoccupied his thoughts. He flew on, now a touch south of due west

He'd flown through many storms before, especially in Papua New Guinea. He knew to treat them with respect, keep your mind on the job and in a half an hour or so you'd fly right out the other side safely, he thought to himself.

The storm had moved a little south in the last hour or so. Suddenly his change of flight plan hadn't helped. Now he was about to fly right into the teeth of it and it was looking more and more like it was going to be a bad one. Below him the ground was hidden under a blanket of grey cloud, above them and ahead they were black and reaching high into the darkening skies. Also, the head winds were growing in strength all the time. He had been off auto-pilot for some time and was now working hard at holding the plane steady.

About ten minutes later, the storm, and Delta Tango 104, met each other about 8000 feet above the Queensland bush. The plane tossed and bounced with each up or down draught that it ran into. Lightning was flashing all around as his engines roared at maximum capacity. Jock's knuckles turned white from holding the joystick. He could feel that this was going to be a bad one, a monster. The plane was being tossed around like a balloon. Jock's heart was racing.

'Keep your cool', he thought to himself. 'It's a bad one, but you'll be out the other side soon enough and then it should be clear air all the way to Jackson'.

He'd been buffeted and belted by the storm for about ten minutes when out of the blackness, a bolt of lightning hit Delta Tango 104. It brought with it a deafeningly loud bang. The plane shuddered violently. Jock felt a moment of pure panic when he thought his heart had jumped right out of his chest. He fought hard to hold the plane and also to regain his composure.

Once he'd done both his next thought was 'Damage Control'. Check out the plane and see what damage, if any, had occurred. He looked across at the wings first. His mind was racing. The wings looked okay; no noticeable damage there to the eye. Both the engines were still roaring flat out and that was a good thing indeed. To lose engine power in this storm could be catastrophic.

Next he looked down at the control panel. 'Damn it', he called out loud. The panel had suddenly gone completely blank, no lights anywhere. All the gauges were out! There was nothing! He leaned forward and looked closely. The lightning outside the cockpit window threw an eerie light over his small world, but it was not enough to read the instruments clearly. The sudden surge of power from the lightning strike had apparently blown all the on-board electrical circuits. More than likely the instruments were damaged as well, but he couldn't tell. Also, he couldn't tell if he was flying straight, not a good situation to be in when in the middle of such a savage storm. He desperately needed to keep the wings straight, but what was straight. He was pretty much flying blind.

He did know his altitude though. This model of Beechcraft had an old style altimeter that ran separately from the main electrical system. With the lightning throwing light onto the gauges from time to time, he could just make out that he was at 7000feet and slowly descending.

'Keep your cool'! He said out loud to himself.
A few seconds later he repeated himself, trying to stay on top of his growing fear, 'Keep your cool'!

'Don't panic! You know what you're doing'! A few seconds, and a number of deep breaths later, he regained his composure and started thinking clearly about his position.

If he kept flying west, the way he was going, he'd fly straight through the storm, nothing had happened to change that. Once through the storm, he could then try and find Charleville, which should be ahead of him to the north-west. But then again, he thought, if he missed Charleville, without instruments and in the growing darkness, he'd have nowhere safe to land. Then another thought entered his mind, perhaps he should turn back towards Roma and hopefully land safely ahead of the storm. If that didn't work, if the storm had already reached Roma, he could turn east until he outran it and found somewhere safe to land like Miles, Chinchilla, or Dalby, even fly back to Toowoomba, if he had to. He had enough petrol to fly there and back again. Was it better to fly with the storm or continue struggling into it with no instruments?

He fought to hold the joystick as the powerful winds tossed him around. Then he decided that his best plan, without any instruments, was to head back to where he had more options for a safe landing. He'd turn north and back towards Roma and the Warrego Highway immediately.

The radio was his next thought. He'd call Roma Tower and inform them of his situation. He automatically reached down for the radio's switch and flicked it on. To his great relief, a single red light came on, followed by a crackle in his headphones.

He grabbed the microphone with one hand and made the call, 'Delta Tango 104 to Roma Control. Over.'

It was difficult enough trying to hold the plane with two hands, almost impossible with one. He quickly put the mike back down on his lap and grabbed the joystick with both hands again.

He waited a few moments then repeated the procedure, 'Delta Tango 104 to Roma Control. Over.'

Jock listened anxiously for a return call signal. Nothing but static from the storm came back through the headphones. He tried a third time and still there was no reply.

At that point Jock tried hard to convince himself that receiving no answer, was not a serious problem. Roma was only a small airport. The night operator might be out for a moment. He could be boiling the kettle, going to the loo or even on a phone call. Small country airfields are relatively casual places when there were no planes around. With the storm closing in, the air space around Roma was more than likely cleared by now. He couldn't expect the operator to be sitting there vigilantly waiting for that one-in-a-million call of someone in trouble.

Jock figured the operator would be back shortly and he would try again soon. There was no need for an emergency distress call yet. He would only be putting out a warning and that could wait another couple of minutes if it had to.

He realised he was 7,000 feet above Terra Firma in a black void, lit only occasionally by the almost blinding flash of lightning. The plane had taken a pounding in the storm and when the lightning hit, it might well have tossed him off course and having no instruments didn't help his situation one little bit. He was a little disorientated, after all the tension and excitement of the past few minutes. A sudden uncharacteristic panic attack hit him and a wave of fear surged through his body.

'Come on Jock, this isn't that bad, get yourself together.' East was behind him, if he was still heading due west. His mind was racing.

'Slow down. Think man, think. Bring the bloody plane around and head for Roma. It's that simple,' he told himself. He thought about Mary and the kids back home and slowly started to calm himself down.

'Okay, now execute the plan,' he told himself.

Jock began to bank the little Beechcraft to the right, towards Roma. Calm yourself, he kept saying. Keep your cool boy. Stay on top of it. This is not a big deal. You've seen worse days than this one before.

Jock had always had a good sense of direction but he knew he'd have to dig deep now if he was going to get back on the ground safely. He decided that once he was heading north, he'd descend to about 3000feet, where it would be easier to see the lights of Roma. If he couldn't spot Roma, he should at least find the highway, and from there, car lights would guide him to safety.

He fought hard with the joystick to bring the plane around. He was about half way through the turn, when another loud BANG exploded in his ears. The plane seemed to jump, almost as a reaction to his body wanting to jump at the suddenness of the deafening noise.

How was his luck, he had been hit by lightning a second time.

Then just as suddenly the plane dropped hard and veered away to the left. He looked out the cockpit window and saw a trail of flame behind the engine on the left wing. He realised immediately that it was the engine that had been hit by the lightning and also knew it was well and truly out of action.

Jock fought hard to regain control of the plane and at the same time trying to keep a sense of direction, when to his horror, the plane shuddered again. This wasn't the shudder of an up-draught from the storm. This was different. He quick look out the other side of the plane and he could see engine number two spluttering. Within seconds, it had died also.

In the bat of an eyelid he had been thrust into a serious life-threatening situation. He was now almost certainly going to crash. No engines and in the teeth of a wild Queensland storm. He knew instantly that he was in real trouble, big trouble. Now he had every reason to panic, but this time he kept his calm.

He was fighting hard to regain some control over his tiny battered plane, but, as you could expect with no engine power, it didn't respond very well. Thank goodness he'd had his seat belt pulled up tight, for the little plane was now being tossed around like a cork on a raging sea.

He knew he was going down, and he knew he needed to get a Mayday call out urgently before it was too late. However, to get to the microphone, meant he had to take one hand off the controls. It would be a dangerous move, but he knew he had to do it. He looked down to where the mike was still sitting on his lap. He waited for some easing in the howling wind, a pocket of calmer air, and when he thought the time was right, he snatched down and grabbed it.

Releasing one hand from the joystick control meant he had to compensate with the other. He didn't have enough strength, and the plane dived sharply into the wind. He dropped the microphone back on his lap and with two hands back on the joystick fought to pull the Beechcraft out of the dangerous dive.

How was he going to get out a Mayday call. He could feel sweat on his forehead and dripping from his armpits. Lightning continued to flash all around him. He regained some composure.

Suddenly a thought jumped into his head, 'did I notify Roma of my change of flight plan?' He struggled on, trying to hold the plane airborne and trying to think. 'If I didn't, they'll be way off the mark with their search.'

He knew he had to get a call out or no-one would know where he was, not that he knew for sure himself. He was going down and all he could think was that if he could get at least one call out that would at least put a search party in the right area. All air traffic control and Mary knew, was that he was following the highway west.

He quickly reached down and snatched up the microphone. With it still in his hand he grabbed the joystick again. Now at least he had the microphone at his grasp. While still fighting to keep the nose of the plane up, he leant forward, pushed the button down on the top of the microphone.

'Mayday! Mayday! Delta Tango 104, Mayday!'
With the utmost urgency he repeated the call,

'Delta Tango 104 Mayday, Mayday.'

'I'm going down, 100 k's south of Roma. Repeat, off course and going down. No Engines, no instruments.'

A sudden blast of turbulence rocked the plane and he was smashed into the microphone and joystick splitting his lip open. Within seconds he could taste blood in his mouth. He reeled back away from the joystick. He spat some blood from his mouth, composed himself and leaned forward one more time.

'Mayday, Delta Tango 104, Mayday!'

'I'm going down. Repeat, I'm going down.'
The time was 7.04 p.m.

The Mayday Call
Wednesday March 13th 7.04pm

In Roma, Bill Reynolds, night duty officer at the Roma Airport was just climbing the last few stairs back into the tower when he heard what he thought was a Mayday call. He'd just stepped outside for a quick cigarette and to watch the lightning show to the south of him. He raced the last few steps and ran towards his control panel just in time to hear another call crackle over his speakers,

'Delta Tango 104, going down, repeat going down'.
He grabbed his microphone from the table and acknowledged

the call.

'Caller in distress, this is Roma Tower, come in.'

He tried to sound calm and professional, but in truth his heart was already pounding.

He strained his ears for a reply but there was nothing but static coming back through the speakers.

'Caller in distress, this is Roma, come in please.'

He looked out the window and searched in the darkness of space for a sound, but again there was nothing.

Oh no, he thought. I've lost them.

'Caller in distress, acknowledge please ...... acknowledge please.'

Still there was nothing, just the noisy crackle of static being generated by the storm to his south.

He listened intently, his heart slowly getting back to something like normal, but now with a strong feeling that this was his moment and he had to rise to the occasion. Lives were at stake here, real lives; real people now depended on his actions.

His training clicked into gear. He flicked the button on his microphone again and slowly and precisely he put out another call, 'This is Roma Control Tower. Can anyone on this frequency acknowledge a Mayday call?'

He listened for a few seconds and then over the airwaves came a clear, cool, calm voice.

'Roma Tower this is Qantas 245, bound for Mt. Isa at 31,000feet, over.'

'Qantas 245, Receiving you, over.'

'Roma Tower, we confirm a Mayday call, over.'

'Qantas 245. Did the Mayday give a position, over?'

'He may have Roma, it was not a clear call. We have a storm on our radar to your south and it is tossing up a lot of static. All we heard was his call sign, Delta Tango 104, over.'

'Qantas 245, what is your E.T.A. in Mt. Isa? Over'

'Roma tower, E.T.A. is twenty hundred hours (8 p.m.) Over.'

'Thank you Qantas 245. We'll get back to you if equired. Out.'

Bill immediately changed radio frequency and called Air Traffic Control in Brisbane with the news that he had an emergency on his hands. He had a reported mayday and a confirmation from Qantas 245. The message was from Delta Tango 104. He was going down. Bill also reported to Brisbane that the location of the downed craft was unknown.

Brisbane acknowledged, and told him to get all available emergency staff on active alert. Then he should arrange an immediate meeting of appropriate emergency personnel. He was also advised to get assistance in the tower as soon as possible and to proceed with continuous calls in an active frequency search pattern.

Wednesday 7.10 p.m.

After receiving the call from Bill Reynolds in Roma, the staff at Brisbane Air Traffic Control also swung into full disaster alert. By the call signal they immediately knew that it was a small plane, nevertheless it was a craft down, and as yet, they had no idea of how many lives were in danger.

All the appropriate authorities were notified. The next job was to find out just exactly who Delta Tango 104 was. They could then work out where he was from, and even more importantly from his flight plan, approximately where he might be.

A quick scan of the computer database told them the plane, Delta Tango 104, was based in Toowoomba and registered as Toowoomba Air Freight Services. All flight plans, when registered, are sent through to Brisbane. The appropriate operator was immediately contacted for details on Delta Tango 104's flight plan. Toowoomba Airport was contacted to see if they had any updated information on the pilot, the plane or its possible where-abouts.

Toowoomba couldn't tell them any more than they already knew, except that he had passed overhead at 3.30 p.m. on schedule and in accordance with his flight plan.

Things started to move more quickly from then on. As the minutes ticked by, more and more personnel got involved in the preparation for a search.

Toowoomba Tower identified the owner as Jock Miller. Now at least they had a name to put to the emergency caller. They were instructed to contact Jock's wife, to notify her of the call, and to see if she had any information that they may not. Toowoomba Tower immediately rang Mary and notified her that Jock's plane might be down somewhere in the Roma area. They told her they had received a Mayday call from him and that an official search would be getting under way immediately.

Mary was shocked and a panic feeling ran through her body. Their sympathetic words of reassurance fell on deaf ears. The fact was real. Jock had sent a Mayday call. Her thoughts recalled his call to her earlier in the day and how happy he sounded doing what he loved best. A horrible realization passed through her that he had crashed and would be out there either injured very badly or even worse. She tried to stay calm to give the tower any helpful information she could all the while feeling very anxious indeed. They asked her if she knew of any possible changes to Jock's scheduled flight plan. Toowoomba tower knew that she was probably the last person to talk to him, when they'd patched him through around 3.30 that afternoon.

Toowoomba Control didn't want Brisbane Air Traffic to know they'd allowed Jock to chat with Mary over the air, so that part of the conversation was left out when they reported back. What they'd done was officially a bit of a no-no, and they didn't think Brisbane needed to know about it.

The time was now 7.18p.m and no word had been heard from Delta Tango 104 in the 14 minutes since the last and only call, despite Roma's continued attempts. It must now be assumed that Jock Miller's plane had indeed crashed.

Information from Toowoomba about Jock's flight plan, his departure time from Archerfield and that he had checked in as he passed over Toowoomba at about 3.30p.m. Had the Roma Emergency team calculating that Jock should have been somewhere between Roma and Charleville.

The storm was measured at being 250 kilometres wide and 100 kilometres deep and up to a height of 40,000 ft. A low pressure had developed into a storm just south of Charleville and intensified as it rolled slowly east, right into Jock Miller's path. In a very short space of time the storm had grown into a monster and Jock was believed to have run straight into the northern part of it.

The emergency services believed that there were three options available to Jock when he realised just how big the storm had become. Either he flew straight into it in the hope he would to pass through it quickly, not aware of its sudden development into a severe storm. Also he may have flown to the north of his original flight path hoping to avoid the turbulence. Alternatively, he may have headed south for the same reason, to get away from the storm. They had received no reports of him landing safely anywhere in the district. Besides the Mayday call pretty much ruled out a safe landing somewhere. There was no talk of him looking for a place to land. The call heard by the

Qantas pilots was clear, 'He was going down.'

The fact that Qantas 245 picked up his call about five hundred kilometres north of Roma, when en route to Mt. Isa, probably meant Jock had tried to fly around the storm to the north. However the southern route theory couldn't be totally discarded as a possibility. It was however less likely, as the Qantas pilot had said the message was relatively strong and clear. The part about them also reporting heavy static was left out. The storm around 7.00pm had been moving east-sou-east, instead of north-east, as earlier predicted, which lent support to the northern flight path theory.

An Emergency Command Post was set up at Roma Airport within an hour of the message being received. By then most of the storm had passed through the Roma district and was now tracking east-nor-east, towards Dalby.

The district Police, State Emergency Services (SES), Lions, Apex, local Council Members, along with half a dozen local pilots and the local helicopter service, had by then, been notified. By 10.30pm most had arrived or contacted the Command Post for further instructions. Also arrangements were being made in Toowoomba to fly Mary to Roma at first light.

A meeting held at 10.45p.m, with all concerned parties, had decided they wouldn't be able to see much until daylight. It was decided to spend the night working out how best to use their resources to maximise their search during daylight hours. A number of those at the command post manned the phones and called people throughout the district asking if they'd heard anything at all. The response was generally the same. The thunderous noise generated by the storm had hidden any sound of a plane or a possible crash. No one had seen or heard anything.

As the night wore on, preparation for the morning search

continued in earnest.

Thursday March 14 saw the sunrise at 5.42a.m, and by then all of the ten planes and three helicopters that were available were in the air searching.

The news was flashed out over the local ABC radio and the local commercial station 4ZR, about the possible crash of a plane in the Roma to Charleville districts. The two radio stations were calling for anyone who may have seen or heard anything during the night, to notify their local Police station immediately.

There was always the chance that it had been a hoax call. It had been known that certain persons had made fake calls in the past. Jock Miller had a solid reputation. However, there was always the possibility that it wasn't Jock Miller who made the call. For now though, they would treat this as a serious situation, unless told otherwise.

The Jackson Oil Field was contacted at first light to see if they had seen or heard from Jock during the night. They hadn't. They were asked to call Roma Command if he did happen to show up. There was always the outside chance that he'd landed somewhere, and then taken off again after the storm had passed, unaware that there was a search for him in progress. If his radio were out, he wouldn't know if his Mayday call had been heard or not. Without a working radio he wouldn't be able to cancel the call, so he may have headed straight for Jackson after daylight. Most of the emergency crew at the Roma command post believed that it was wishful thinking to believe that Jock might just have turned up at Jackson unscathed. Still, every possibility had to be looked at.

No useful information came forward from the public during the morning. Like those who had been phoned during the night, the noise of the storm's thunder and associated downpour of rain had presumably drowned out any noise of Jock's plane roaring through the night. The little that did come forward had Jock still on course with his flight plan up until about Miles. From there on he would have been hidden by low cloud preceding the storm.

After that, nothing! No one had seen or heard anything. The plane had all but disappeared into thin air. Jock had flown out of Brisbane air space and off the radar screens long before the storm had hit. Toowoomba and Roma weren't equipped with radar but rather, like most country airfields, were radio contact only. They were there simply to monitor the arrival or departure of local traffic and if Jock didn't radio in they wouldn't even know he was in their district.

By lunchtime, a very anxious and concerned Mary Miller arrived in Roma. She was taken straight to the Emergency H.Q and briefed on the latest situation.

By then, it had been decided the search area would take in the area between Charleville in the west, St.George in the south, Springsure in the north, and just in case Jock turned back, the search would extend back to Miles. It was an enormous area to have to cover and they knew that they would have to rely heavily on air support, as well as from the public, their eyes on the ground. The radio stations were again contacted with the latest updates, and they immediately started broadcasting half-hourly bulletins, asking the public to be vigilant and to report anything unusual immediately.

The morning wore on and no news was coming back from the air search or from those on the ground. A few spot fires were reported here and there, but when checked, they were found to be small grass or tree fires probably caused by a lightning strike the night before.

Midday came and went and still there was no good news. No

bad news either.

Then, out of the blue, at 12.26p.m, a radio on one of the desks at search headquarters that was still tuned on to Jock's last known frequency crackled into life. At the main communications desk, the radio operator screamed out for everyone in the room to be quiet. He thought he'd heard something on Jock's frequency.

They immediately switched on a tape recorder, one that had been set up earlier to record anything that might come in over the radio. A recording may pick up a clue that the listener may miss at the time. Also it had been known for pranksters to make calls in the past and in the event of that happening, a recorded message could be used later to identify such a dangerous nuisance caller.

Deathly silence descended on the room as everyone stared at the radio set sitting on the table. Seconds seemed like hours. Then the radio crackled again. A muffled noise could be heard for about twenty seconds and then nothing again.

The radio operator swung into action calling back to Delta Tango 104, searching for a response - There was none!

Silence again descended on the room. That little black box sitting on the table, the one that held the secret to the mystery of Delta Tango 104, sat silent again.

The Police Inspector grabbed the tape out of the small recorder. 'Stick another tape in there,' he said, as he headed for another, bigger, tape deck.

The radio operator replaced that tape with a new one and then continued calling, 'Delta Tango 104 come in, over.' Still there was nothing.

The Police Inspector played the tape on the bigger machine, over and over, louder, and louder. By now twenty or so people had gathered around, trying to work out if the call was from Jock, or more importantly what had been said.

The voice on the recording was very unclear. No one could work out exactly what had been mumbled. The voice sounded very weak and soft. They were sure about the call sign though. They could hear enough to recognise that it was from Delta Tango 104, but the rest of the message was very faint and almost inaudible.

It was however agreed, by everyone in the room, that the call was genuine. It was the first piece of positive news since the storm. The Police Inspector declared to all those present, that Jock was alive. A collective cheer went up around the room. Other than Mary, not one soul there knew him personally, but the camaraderie felt in those situations was united. The voice sounded very weak though. It was concluded also that he sounded injured, perhaps badly. Time was their enemy. They had to find him, and fast.

The important thing though, was they had received a call from Jock. However, they still didn't know where to start looking.

They needed to clear up the message to try and work out what the rest of it said. What did he say, did he give a clue to where he was. The second part of the message was very faint.

One of the local Apex members, who had been called upon earlier in the day, was a young musician, John Green. 'Johnno', as he was known in the district, had done a lot of work at the radio station over the years. He was a bit of a whiz at writing and recording jingles. Johnno suggested that if he ran the tape through some of the sound equipment at the radio station's recording studio, they might be able to 'clean up' the sound enough to hear it better.

It was worth a try.

Hope had entered the room with that muffled call.

Mary called her home in Toowoomba to tell her mother, who

had been called in to care for the children and was waiting anxiously with them for any news.

Everyone's spirits had risen at the knowledge that he was still alive at least.

Within an hour, Johnno was back from the recording studio with more good news. He put a tape in the tape deck and pushed the play button.

'Delta tango 104 - Mayday - Mayday' - then there was a lengthy pause. That was the first part of the message they had figured out earlier.

Then the good news, 'Near a red hill - repeat, a red hill - I'm injured, send help - badly broken leg - send help immediately.'

The tape deck went quiet.

A discussion followed where it was presumed that Jock, probably weakened from his ordeal, was unable to continue. Perhaps he'd received head injuries, as well as the broken leg he spoke of. He might have been unconscious from the time of the crash, and may have regained consciousness about 12.30pm, just long enough to make the second Mayday call. He could just barely make-out some background noises.

Well at least it was good news. Jock was still alive.

The bad news was that they still didn't know where he was. Also, the radio sounded weak, and if it was still switched on, then it could be expected that pretty soon the batteries would be completely flattened. If the plane's batteries did go flat, all chance of radio communication would certainly fade and their hopes of finding Jock in time would be set back enormously.

However, they did have a clue, a red hill. It was the only thing they had to work on.

So the question was thrown around the headquarters, what did he mean by a red hill? Where was this red hill?

They set about investigating immediately. More detailed

area maps were obtained from the local Council offices and scanned by half a dozen men. Was it the name of a hill, or an area, was it a property name, or was it some geological feature out there in the bush somewhere?

Geologists were called in from two local mining companies along with their geological maps.

All maps were studied and studied and studied again. Where was this 'Red Hill'?

In the early hours of the morning, the experts reached somewhat of a consensus. The theory was that the plane probably went down in an area north of Roma, near the Chesterton Ranges, just south of Mt. Ogilvie, which was known as Hillside. There, the iron oxide in the ground, also known as red oxide, gave off a reddish-copper colour. Usually the earth in that area was covered with grasses and low scrub. But if a bush fire had swept through that area in the past 3 or 4 months, it would have reduced the ground cover. Then all that was needed was some good rain, and the ground surface could have been washed clean, making it possible to see the iron oxide surface. All of that should give the ground a reddish colour.

Looking further they discovered that the Chesterton region had indeed had a number of substantial bush fires through it during the drought. Also the area had received plenty of rain in the past month or so making the conditions perfect for the red oxide surface to show through. That had to be it.

There was no property, station, township or area known as Red Hill. It had to be the red oxide theory. It was agreed then that Jock had come down somewhere near the Chesterton ranges. Well at least that was the most likely scenario with the information they had at hand.

However, a couple of the locals disagreed They came up with a theory that at sunset the night before, with the storm behind it, might have given of a strange glow, leaving an imprint on the pilot's mind. It had been a particularly spectacular sunset. Perhaps he was delirious and the Red Hill could have been anything or anywhere. Maybe it had nothing to do with reality or the crisis he was in.

It was agreed that he had to be badly injured. No way could he have landed safely out there in the grips of such a savage storm in such harsh terrain without sustaining injuries. In a plane crash the most likely injuries would be to the head. He had every reason to be disorientated and incoherent. A knock to the head could see him imagining all kinds of things.

Nevertheless, the vast majority in the radio room made the decision, that over the next few days, most of them would concentrate on the 'official' area, that being the northern sector around the Hillside region, just to the south of the Chesterton Range. They would go mainly with the red oxide theory.

The downed pilot's wife, Mary Miller, who was in the room at the time that decision was made, quietly disagreed. She had a feeling her husband would have stayed on course and was within a 50klm radius of Mitchell. She knew he wouldn't have panicked and she believed he would have stayed with his flight plan. She also believed there might have been a chance that he tried to turn around and follow the highway back to Roma. She was sure they were looking in the wrong area. To her, Hillside just seemed too far from his designated flight plan. It was also further north than he needed to be if he tried to fly around the storm front. But she was told quite emphatically that there was no 'Red Hill' around the Roma or Mitchell areas. He had to be north around Hillside.

The following two days of intense searching of the Hillside region and into the Chesterton Ranges uncovered nothing. Finally, on the morning of the fourth day after the storm, it was decided to break up into groups and expand the search to a one hundred kilometre radius around Roma.

In the meantime Mary was growing more and more concerned for Jock's wellbeing. She knew he was tough, but so too were the conditions he was being asked to survive in. The injuries that he briefly mentioned in his second Mayday call were expected to be quite severe and she was concerned that he may not be able to help his own recovery out there. He knew first aid procedures well, but that would only be of use to him if he were in good enough condition to be able to use them.

She couldn't live with the thought that he was out there in extreme pain. She kept telling herself that he was tough. That he was a fighter and that he would never give up. She imagined in her mind, that he was waiting for her to come and rescue him. She was also becoming more and more frustrated by the 'official' notion that he was north of Roma. She didn't know why, but as each day passed she grew more and more certain that he was to the south or west of Mitchell. Woman's instincts she put it down to, but she just knew he was alive and waiting for help to arrive.

The search continued, mainly in the northern, eastern and western sectors. It was still believed that with the storm at its worse to the south of Roma, Jock would have avoided that inhospitable region at all cost.

On Tuesday March 19, at 6pm, the search for Jock Miller was officially scaled back. Jock hadn't been sighted since the previous Wednesday six days earlier, and nothing more had been heard from him so it was very probable that he was dead. No sighting had been made of his plane, Delta Tango 104.

It was as if he had simply disappeared from the face of the earth. Surely he would have been seriously injured in the crash and in that arid part of Australia it would be a miracle if he could have survived for that long, alone and injured. As concerned as they still were, the reality was that the cost could no longer justify the means. People had to get back to their regular jobs and business's. Life had to go on and someone had to make the decision to get back to it

A one hundred kilometre radius in the Queensland outback was a big area to get lost in. They could search for months and still not find any trace of Jock or his plane.

Under the pressure of Mary's insistence, it was decided to keep one chopper in the air for a few more days and two crews on the ground in 4WD vehicles. The 4WDs would concentrate on the accessible areas, like roads and bush tracks, in particular along bush tracks and fence lines. The chopper would search the areas around the ranges and gullies, areas that the ground crews couldn't reach.

Mary was still sure they had searched in all the wrong places, and so unofficially, she and one of Jock's mates from Toowoomba, decided to search on, forever if they had to. They borrowed a 4WD and searched the area that Mary still felt Jock had come down in, an area around Mt. Inviting. She hadn't given up hope. She had to believe Jock was still alive out there somewhere. She couldn't image life without him, and for her it was totally unacceptable to think of their kids without a father! She simply refused to believe he was dead, so now that the search had been drastically scaled down, she was going to follow her instincts and search in more depth to the south.

While the official search party's 4WDs continued to search in an arch around Roma, Mary arranged to take her borrowed 4WD and follow her heart south. Through the local news services, local property owners were still being encouraged to be watchful for any sign of wreckage from Jock's plane. Even a burnt out area of bush-land, or something as simple as a dying tree, might hold the answer to its whereabouts. The crash and possible explosion might have started a scrub fire, although it was generally accepted that the rain that night would have snuffed out any grass fire almost as soon as it started. Still, stranger things had happened. It was like looking for a needle in a haystack, and she knew it.

Mary kept reminding herself of the story of the Stinson plane crash. Way back in the 1930's, a plane had disappeared on route from Brisbane to Sydney. A man named Bernard O'Reilly found a burnt out area of the Lamington Plateau, in the southern highlands of Queensland. Against all odds and after trekking for days through wilderness, O'Reilly found the wreckage of the plane. The official search for the Stinson had been conducted hundreds of kilometres to the south-east, well away from where O'Reilly had found it. He also found two men alive, well beyond when they should have been dead.

Mary knew that Jock had been inspired by the story and had often mentioned the toughness and heroism of not only O'Reilly, but of the two survivors involved in the tragedy. Jock always said that he was impressed by the fact that O'Reilly never lost hope, nor did the two survivors. Mary took strength from the story. It was her crutch, and there was no way she was going to lose hope either.

The 'official' searchers believed they would have to get very lucky now. Most of them felt they were only looking for a dead body anyway, but they pushed on, if only to get an answer to the riddle.

Mary was the only truly confident person left. She alone was positive he had survived somehow. That he was still alive out there somewhere. She knew her man, she knew her Jock. He'd never give up, he was a fighter, a survivor. Somehow he'd find a way of staying alive until help reached him. He should have water, she was certain of that. There was always plenty on board the plane. Also, he was a natural bushman. If he wasn't critically injured, she knew he would know where to find more food and water. She knew her husband well, and she was extremely confident he could survive for a long period while waiting to be found. The only question was just how bad were his injuries?

Her love for him, as well as her obligation to their children, drove her on. She'd promised them that she would bring their daddy back home. For Mary, there simply weren't enough daylight hours to search in. She'd go all night if she only could. Even when darkness forced her back to Mitchell, she'd continue chasing up any new information that might have come in. She spoke to the locals over and over again. She hounded the police, and the other searchers for any clue they may have overlooked. She followed up every possibility. She harassed the local radio station to keep Jock's story alive. Someone had to find something one day.

Everyone admired her tenacity. She just wouldn't accept the word 'no' as an option. Most thought that if Jock was as stubborn about dying as Mary was of finding him, then he could probably survive out there. But the reality was that he had been in a plane crash and had been missing without trace for over a week now in some of Queensland's harshest country. As much as they hoped, for Mary's sake, that Jock would be found alive, most believed the end result would be a different story.

CHAPTER FIVE

Bourke and Beyond 1884

Just a little over four weeks after leaving St George, the drovers headed their mob of cattle over a small hill. There before them, nestled on the treed banks of the Darling River, were streets lined with cottages all in neat little rows. Bourke in the winter of 84 was a bustling little township of around four hundred people. It was a bee-hive of activity, horses and carts, children playing in the gutters and all the way down to the river, where a number of river-boats were being loaded or unloaded by hard working bronzed muscular men.

They learnt later that this tiny oasis in outback New South Wales was first known as Fort Bourke, and established in the mid 1830's after explorer Thomas Mitchell had camped there on an expedition north. Charles Sturt was believed to have been the first white man in the area, when he passed through in 1829, six years before Thomas Mitchell set up camp on the very same riverbanks the Barlows were looking down on now. Over the years, pioneers followed the explorer's tracks heading north along the Darling River from Victoria, forging settlements along the way. Paddle steamers followed soon after with supplies to maintain the lives of those settling in the dry inland of Australia. Because of the nature of the river system, Fort Bourke was as far as the great paddle steamers of the 1800's could navigate, thus the soon to be renamed Bourke, was a very important river port as well as a bustling little town.

The Barlows decided on a few days rest. One of John's first stops was at the Postal Office, as he had done in St.George, to send a telegram home to the rest of the family.

'All well in Bourke. Stop. Love from all here. Stop. Letter following. Stop. John.' He asked if any mail had arrived for J. Barlow and Sons. Sure enough, there was a letter waiting from Burton Downs.

It was a simple letter. In it Mary wrote that there was still no sign of rain and the family was fine and all healthy. She added that they were missing them dearly. The part about them all being well was good news, not so the part about no rain, but then again, he had expected no less, he could only hope the drought had broken.

There had been some signs of rain in the areas they had passed through and John had hoped that the inclement weather had made its way north. If their venture were to be successful, it would only get them out of financial despair if the drought were to break back at Burton Downs as well. Without good steady rain, the money from the drove would run out in a few short years and the Barlows would again be struggling and in danger again of losing their property. Water was the true key to success on the land, water was like gold out there, and John knew it only too well.

When he left the Post Office, he sat himself down under an old river red gum on the banks of the Darling, and spent some quiet time penning the letter he had promised he would.

Later that day he sold a few head of cattle to the local butcher, and with the money they sat down to a good meal and a drink or three at the rather rowdy Bourke Hotel.

Also while there, he stocked up on provisions, and walked around town just enjoying the company of other people for a change. He loved his sons like any father should, but he also enjoyed chatting with older folk, about the types of things that older people talk about.

Next morning, after a good night's sleep, John walked along the riverbank. There were piles of timber and wool bales stacked up twice as high as a man could stand. The timber had been brought in by the riverboats, and the wool was stacked in readiness for the next boat to take them to other ports and towns far afield. One old local he met told him the Darling was reasonably low with water and had been for some time. Even so, the riverboats had continued to bring trade up and down all season long.

While he sat talking to the old-timer, he noticed there was a small punt, taking people from one side of the river to the other. He could also see long wooden slides on the town side of the riverbank. The river levels rose and fell with the seasonal rains, and the slides were apparently used to get freight down to the boats and to haul provisions back up when the river was low. As the slides weren't being used commercially at that time, a dozen or so of the local children were having a great time sliding down them and into the muddy water below. Sitting there watching the young ones having such a good time took his thoughts back to Burton Downs and to young Will. What a grand time he would have if were there with them. The young ones back at Burton would not have seen so much water in their whole lives

He spotted a couple of lads sitting further up-stream fishing. He said farewell to the old man and headed over towards them.

'No boats around this time of year lads?'
They looked up lazily, sized him up, and then one of them slowly replied, 'Just missed one mister. Headed south a day or so back.'

'Are you expecting any more in soon?'

'Think there's one due next week some time.'

'And the fish are they biting?'

'Every now and then, when they've got nothing better to do we get the odd Murray Cod. Best fishing after the paddlers have stirred up the water.'

He sat talking with them a while longer until eventually Matt and Charles joined him.

'Wanna do some fishing too? One of the boys asked, 'we got another line here.'

Matt and Charles thought it a great idea, and took up a wooden rod, put a worm on the hook and sat with the young locals and fished the Darling with them. John got out his paper and pencil and continued with his letter to Mary.

'Catch anything? He asked the boys when the boys approached him about an hour later.

'Not a nibble,' Charles answered.

John went on, 'Got me a feeling that I want to get on that little punt down there and see Bourke from the other side. You boys want to join me?'

Matt and Charles were happier heading back into town to look at the young women from the hotel window. John handed the man a coin and slowly crossed to the other bank.

'You wanna go back also mister?' asked the punt-man.

'Later perhaps! When do you return?'

'Be about an hour, mister.'

'That would be just fine Sir.'

John found a tree to lean back on and sat for that hour finishing his letter, sitting in peace and gazing back across at Bourke.

The trip from St. George had taken four weeks, with the

loss of about six head of cattle. A few young ones had died along the way from dingo attacks at night. Most had simply been lost in the scrub, just wandering away to become feral animals.

John was aware that the next part of the journey, from Bourke to Wilcannia, would be the longest stretch they would have away from civilisation. He took time gathering as much information as he could about this next section. He spoke with locals, with workers down on the riverbank, also with farm workers he met in the hotel and of course, he spoke in depth with the local constable of police. He was getting wiser as the journey went on. He knew that the best help he could summons was knowledge and information supplied by the locals. After all, it was their land they would be travelling through and no one knows the bush better than the men and women who live and breathe it every day. It's a part of their soul. John prepared well and when he was ready, he went and found Benny and the four continued their journey.

The nights were getting longer and colder the further they travelled south. The cooler temperatures during the day, was now making the journey easier. The cattle too seemed to be into the routine. They appeared to sense when the men were ready to head out each morning.

However, they weren't making as much ground each day. First light each morning was later and each afternoon they would have to set camp earlier before the sun settled in the west. Also now, they had to pitch a tent most afternoons to help keep warm during the colder nights, and all of those campsite preparations took up precious daylight hours. When they first set out on the journey, they had around thirteen hours of good daylight to travel in. That was now down to around eleven hours, and getting less as the weeks rolled by. Still, John told the boys whenever they complained about the cold, better the cooler days of winter than the scorching heat of an Australian summer. The journey they were undertaking would be almost impossible in the heat of the long summer months.

One night, during their evening meal, Charles brought up the subject of their slower pace, 'We don't seem to be getting as far each day Father.'

'I have noticed Charles,' he replied.

'Is that going to be a problem?' Charles asked.

'I don't think so, son, I had expected it. I think we're doing well. So long as we don't run into any trouble, we'll be well home before the summer heat returns.'

Matthew joined the conversation, 'Shall I get the maps out and we'll take a look at what's ahead.'

The men studied young Will's maps by the light of a raging campfire and talked about what may lay ahead.

'It looks like the river doesn't know how to run in a straight line,' said Charles.

'Well,' John answered, 'if these maps are anywhere near true, then I think we've passed the worst of it. Also, the cattle don't need as much water now, so we may be able to find some shortcuts around those bends.'

So far they had only left the river for a day or so at a time, but there did appear to be sections ahead where they could leave the river according to their maps.

Benny, who had been sitting quietly sipping on a mug of tea, decided to enter the conversation. 'We can cut across ground in a number of places, but we'll have to rely on a compass to keep us heading in the right direction.'

'Have you travelled through this country before?' John asked him. Knowing that if they strayed too far from the Darling, got lost or even delayed and couldn't link up with the river again, and they would not only be endangering themselves, but they could severely weaken a large number of the cattle.

The river not only provided them with much needed water, it also produced bird and animal life, which provided fresh meat for their diet. Fresh food was important if they were to maintain their strength. The river helped to make the journey more pleasant; not that anyone expected a pleasant trip.

'I've been part of the way down to Wilcannia, Benny replied.'

At that point he reached over and pointed to a spot on the map, 'They found underground water here at a place called Kallara Station. An artesian bore they called it. They reckon there could be artesian water under most of inland Australia. Imagine that, an ocean of water down there.'

'I read about that in a newspaper some time back,' said John. 'It sounded like a bit of a tall story to me. Can't imagine how it got there or how you'd get it out of the ground if it was true.'

Benny responded immediately, 'I know a fella who's seen it. He was there about a year ago. Fair dinkum fella he was too. Wouldn't lie about a thing like that.

He pointed to the map again. 'About here, I think he said, followed it down to Kallara. That's where he said he had seen the bore. Water was gushing out of the ground, hot water too it was, like a grand old fountain back in London Town.'

He paused briefly looking at the maps, and then continued, 'It could take days off the journey if we cut through to Kallara, got some water and then picked up the river again further south.'

The heat was not a problem, it was still winter, but if they didn't get to Broken Hill before late spring, the summer heat might well be a danger on the return journey home.

The four men sat and studied the maps, and after some further discussion they decided it looked like a pretty good idea. Matthew was still a little concerned,

'Dad do you think the cattle can travel for that length of time without water?'

'It's still cool enough during the day, and the grounds flat and easy travelling, so the cattle shouldn't get too tuckered out,' added John with a certain confidence in his voice. 'Looking at these maps, about half way to Kallara the river cuts back to the west and it looks like the river and the creek are only about a day's ride apart.' John continued, pointing to the map in front of him,

'If the going gets tough and the cattle look like they aren't doing too well, then we'll head straight back to the Darling.'

John looked around at the others for confirmation. 'Agreed then?' he asked.

Benny and Matthew agreed to the plan. Charles said nothing; he felt that he wasn't old enough to enter into the decision making yet.

John looked at him, 'Have you got a problem with the plan Charles?'

'No,' he replied sheepishly.

'Well?' asked John, still looking for a response to his earlier question.

There was silence as the others realised that for the first time John was asking Charles for an opinion on something of significant importance. It was like he was finally acknowledging the young Barlow's manhood.

Charles looked slowly at the three men in turn and in particular to his father. Then, with all the calmness of a seasoned bushman, he casually replied, 'I think it's a sound idea, it will save us time and as you say, if something goes wrong we can head back east to the Darling in less than no time.'

Aware now that he had their full attention, he continued, 'Besides, I'd like to see this artesian bore water for myself. If the inland has more of it, then it might be the future for all of us out here, and it would be good to know how to get it out of the ground. Perhaps Burton Downs has artesian water. I'd hate to think we were sitting on a whole lot of it and never knew. We could be sitting on top of an inland-sea, while we go broke from no rain.'

The men all nodded in silence and approval. Charles knew that his maiden speech as an adult had been accepted and it made him proud. So for now they would push on down the river. About three days on, where the Warrego joined the Darling from the north, they should come across that small creek, heading south-west. From there it was on to new discoveries. The next morning they headed out with renewed excitement.

Encounter on the Darling River

Early one afternoon, about a week out from Bourke, they were surprised by the strange and haunting sound of a riverboat whistle in the distance. To John and the boys it was a sound they had not heard for a long, long time. In fact, not since they had travelled to Brisbane Town some ten years earlier, where they'd watched in amazement at the paddle steamers moving up and down the Brisbane River.

It was such an unusual sound to hear way out there in the middle of 'no-where'. It was a hollow echo that seemed to travel great distances in the cold winter air. It was a sound the cattle hadn't heard before, and it startled them somewhat. Realising that the cattle could become restless quickly and fearing that another blast from the paddle steamers horn might spook them into a stampede. John called out to the others to try and keep them calm.

He thought it best to stop the mob and wait there for the paddle steamer to pass them. They could band the cattle tightly together and keeping them bunched up would make it easier to keep them quiet. If they were on the move, it would be harder from stopping them rushing into the bush. If they weren't careful they could spend days trying to round them up again. Another long blast was heard away to the south. The cattle paid no attention to it this time.

'Charles,' he called across the mob, 'the three of us can keep them settled here, how about you get a fire going and cook us some tucker. Keep your horse ready, just in case they start to move.'

While John, Matthew and Benny rode quietly around the mob, singing and talking to them, Charles got the fire under way and slung a billy of water over it.

Charles had watched children back in Bourke netting tasty looking little yabbies and thought now was as good time as any to try his luck at trapping some. What better breakfast than a handful of freshly caught and cooked yabbies.

While the others kept the mob quiet, he got some rotting flesh from an old roo carcass and placed it in a small net he had brought back in Bourke. To his joy, the local yabbies must have been a hungry lot, for in just a short time he had a reasonable feed of a dozen or so of the little nippers.

Charles reset the net, threw it back in to the muddy water and headed back to the fire. He threw some more wood on, the poured the boiling billy-water into a bigger pot and threw the yabbies in as well. Then he added a few vegetables and sat down fully satisfied with his small effort. He could just imagine the surprise on the faces of the others when they ventured in for a well-earned feed, to be presented with such a culinary delight.

'Tuckers up,' he called to them.

John told Matthew to ride in and get a feed, 'And send Charles out here to take your place.'

'What slop have you stewed up this afternoon?' Matthew asked as he rode into the makeshift camp.

'Not much, you don't deserve anything special,' he replied in a cheeky tone.

Matthew dismounted and walked over towards the campfire. 'Smells alright whatever it is.'

'Fresh yabbies, brother dear, get your choppers into a few of these little beauties,' he said as he handed a bowl of freshly cooked yabbies floating in a watery mix of almost fresh vegetables, including some mushrooms found by the riverbank.

'I'm impressed little brother, I'm impressed.

Charles rode out and joined the others and not long after Matthew rode back out also.

'Good tucker? Benny asked, 'I could eat me horse.'

'You may have to,' replied Matthew, 'it would sure taste better than the slop Charlie has stewed up or us.'

He looked across at Charles and gave him a wink. 'That's a bit rough Matthew, you guys didn't give me much time to get it ready, what do you expect.'

Benny rode off towards the campsite.

'Is it that bad?' asked John. Both his sons laughed out loud.

'What's the joke boys?'

'No joke dad, you'll see when you get in there. We was just having some fun with Benny.'

'I caught some fresh yabbies and cooked them up. They was lovely eating, we just wanted to have some fun with Benny.'

'Yabbies hey?'

'And tasty ones at that dad.'

Again they were interrupted by another haunting whistle blast. The cattle hardly murmured.

Shortly after, to their absolute joy, they were treated to the sight of a riverboat steaming around a bend, not a half a mile away. The rare sight of a paddle steamer making its way up the Darling River in the middle of no-where simply mesmerised them. It was one of those magic moments in life, one that would be remembered forever. Out there, in the middle of the Australian wilderness, a paddle steamer, proudly puffing smoke from the small funnel, and creating a wonderful flip-flop sound, the kind that only the paddles of a riverboat can make as it plods though still waters.

The boat slowly made its way towards them. As it neared they could see as the paddles leapt out of the water on the final part of their circular action, they threw small droplets into the air; droplets that captured the sun and shone back at them like diamonds. The four men stood and watched in total silence.

The Captain, who by now was quite visible in the wheelhouse, had also spotted the men and their cattle. He stepped out from the wheelhouse on to the open deck and waved at them. Almost straight away the paddles stopped turning and the boat began slowing moving towards the bank.

'He's stopping,' said Charles. 'We'll get a chance to look at her up close, maybe they'll even let us go on board.'

As the beautifully crafted timber boat slowed, the captain looked for a clearing on the riverbank and steered towards it. Then suddenly the paddles erupted into action again, startling the men on the bank. This time though, they rotated the other way, backwards. The boat slowed until it almost halted. Another man, standing on the bow, threw a rope towards the bank. Matthew and Charles ran across, picked it up and immediately started pulling the boat towards them. When the boat was within a few metres, the man on the bow called to them.

'Tie us up to a one of those old river gums, mate.'

It had looked small as it rounded the bend, but up close it was truly a large and impressive vessel. They wondered how such a large boat could handle the many twists and turns in the river, not to mention how the captain could avoid snags and floating debris that drifted throughout the river system.

The skipper called out from on board, introducing himself as Captain Kirkwood, of the Barrumba Queen. Soon after, a gangplank was thrown out and rested between the boat and the riverbank.

Once secured, the skipper dutifully invited the drovers aboard. 'Come aboard gentleman. Tis a fine ship and tis equally fine to extend our hospitality.'

He introduced his three-man crew to them, and after a short tour of the boat, the Barlows and the Captain, settled down on the foredeck for some refreshments.

'Saw you from a ways back. Sawdust rising from the land and figured it must be something like drovers on the move. Mind you, I did get a surprise to see you way up here. I've seen a few mobs being driven to sale further down in Victoria, but never up this high.'

John replied, 'Guess you think we're a little crazy?'

'Don't know you to be able to make that conclusion. You must have your reasons. Anyways, thought we'd stop and say

G'day. Give us a chance to stock up on firewood for the old boilers and ask about conditions and water levels up ahead. It's safer to stop when others are around. A riverboat is just as much a target for bushrangers as anyone. When we stop, that is. While we're moving down river, or anchored at night in the middle of the river, we're pretty much safe enough, but once we tied up to the banks, it makes us an easy target also. Sometimes they stalk us for days.'

The men sat and listened, while they enjoyed the refreshments

'I could see you boys had a large number of cattle, too many to steal without word passing along the river, so I assumed you was genuine folk and this would be a safe place to stop and top up with wood. There's safety in numbers, as they say.'

'We're glad you see it that way, Captain Kirkwood, and may I say the pleasure is all ours. I'm sure the boys have enjoyed having a look around your beautiful boat.'

With mouths full of food the boys all mumbled back their approval.

The captain could see the boys were enjoying his friendly gesture of food on the foredeck.

'One of the few luxuries we have on this boat is the food cooked by 'Cookie-Sun', our Chinese cook. I'll introduce him to you later, when he comes up.'

They sat in the shade and talked for ages. He told John and the boys, that this particular riverboat carried food and provisions to the towns and stations along the Darling. They journeyed from Echuca, on the River Murray, all the way along the Darling, to Bourke. That was if there was enough water in the river to get that far up. On the return journey back down the river, they would pick up bales of wool, salted animal hides and occasionally passengers from the same townships and stations, all the way back down to Echuca again. There the wool would be graded and sorted and then shipped overland to Melbourne and then on to countries all over the world.

He also told them that on their last few trips up, they had shipped iron and steel to Bourke, as well as the usual provisions. The iron and steel was being used to build the new railway bridge over the Darling River in readiness for the arrival of the railway track from Nyngan, to the south east of Bourke. Oddly though, he said, by carrying the steel to help build the railway they were in fact slowly putting themselves out of business. The railway would be a quicker more cost effective way of getting supplies to the outback, and once the rail link was opened, the paddle steamers would no longer be needed and would quickly die out as a viable means of transportation.

The men talked and talked, as if they were old friends seeing each other for the first time in a long, long while. Good company was hard to find out there and John had missed the companionship of someone his own age and this wonderful old river captain was good company, and they reveled in each other's company.

More tea was served along with some freshly made apple pies. 'Can I borrow your boys for a few hours?' the skipper asked John.

'What did you have in mind for them?'

'A bit of honest toil, if they can find themselves up to it. It'd help me out a quite a deal if they could.'

Soon after Matthew, Charles, Benny and two of the crew, trudged off into the bush to gather firewood to fuel the riverboat's insatiable steam engines, while the two older men talked on. During their conversation, the captain warned John to be careful and wary of any travelers they happened to come across out there.

'We don't usually stop to talk to strangers, too risky these days, but when I saw the cattle I was pretty certain you were drovers and not thieves or vagabonds.'

He lifted his coat up at the side to expose a firearm and added, 'But one should never take too many chances out here. There is many a thief and murderer hiding away in these parts just waiting for a naive traveler or dreamer to pass their way.'

'Sorry,' he added, looking towards the pistol, 'but that's the way it is out here. One can't afford to take any chance or you may not live to see another sunrise.'

'We have hardly seen a soul since we left Queensland,' said John.

The old salt got a pipe from his pocket and began packing it down with tobacco. 'Since the big strike in Broken Hill, there's been a lot of unsavory looking ruffians around the riverbanks and along the bush tracks. The further south you go the worse it gets. Bad men with bad intentions everywhere I'm afraid.'

John listened intently as the captain continued.

'Just be vigilant. They look for unsuspecting travelers to bail up. Money, jewelry, food, horses, and I've even heard that one poor soul was killed for no more than a pair of new boots he was standing in.'

He paused to sip at his tea and to look up at John, perhaps looking for a reaction.

'Unfortunately, all too often they get rid of the evidence by killing the poor unwitting traveler and disposing of their bodies. There truly is some evil men around.'

'You make it sound rather frightening. Perhaps we've been lucky, but we haven't seen a soul,' John replied.

'Trust me when I say, from here on be well on your guard or you may be sorry. We've pulled bodies out of the river downstream before, and we have had to bury them on the riverbank, never even knowing their names. Just left them lying beneath a blank cross. Trust me John Barlow, be careful.'

That part of their conversation ended there. Then, when the old captain finally finished packing his pipe, he lit it up with a few puffs and leaned back in the deck chair and didn't say another word for ages. John took in the moment enjoying the serenity of the Darling. As the afternoon sun began to sink below the tree line, and the cool air slowly crept into their world, another day drew nearer its inevitable end.

The younger men worked on until dark, collecting wood and returning it to the riverbank, and piling it by the riverbank. They seemed to enjoy the physical labour as they took it in turns of chopping the wood to a storable size. It was good for them to do something different for a change, and to yarn with the others as they worked.

Cookie-Sun, complimented the hard day's work with a delightfully tasting meal, after which the men settled down around a large campfire on the riverbank and talked well into the night.

The men of the rivers were interested in listening to the tales of the drovers and equally the Barlows were keen to hear more tales from the riverboat men. The boys quietly wished they could spend more time with each other, to hear more tales of life from their different worlds, but the drovers knew that they had already lost valuable time. This would have to be the last time they could sit by a raging fire with these most interesting men.

Next morning, after sharing the results of Cookie-Sun's early start, John and the boys helped the crew load the rather

large pile of chopped firewood on board the boat. By mid-morning, with the storage bunker in the engine room now almost full, they again sat on the fore deck and enjoyed bush tea. Again Cookie-Sun showed his worth. This time serving them with freshly baked scones covered in a golden bush honey.
Finally, Captain Kirkwood interrupted the morning's second feast.

'It's been a pleasure John, and I thank you and your boys for the help with the firewood. If you're ever around the river just ask after me, someone will always know where I'm travelling. Perhaps the boys might like to journey with me sometime. It would be my pleasure to show them my mighty rivers.'

'And you too captain,' John replied, 'if you're ever up our way,' he interrupted himself with a small laugh, 'I suppose not, the rivers up our way aren't big enough to float a dingy, and not wishing to sound rude, but I can't see you on a horse somehow.'

'Rode one once,' he answered, 'still got the bruise on me butt 30 years later. I like the soft folds of a river beneath me, but I thank you for the offer.'

The men shook hands and as the Barlows walked off across the gangplank, Cookie-Sun came running on deck, 'You take, you take,' he yelled at them, 'Cookie-Sun's best apple pie, just like mother make. You guys, nice fella, you see Cookie-Sun again, I cook you plenty more apple pie.'

He hand them a large apple pie wrapped in some calico cloth and with that one of the crew pulled the gangplank back on board. Charles and Matthew released the fore and aft ropes from the gum trees, and the riverboat ever so slowly drifted away from the bank.
When the boat was clear of the edge by a few metres, the captain fired up the engines and the giant paddles slowly began

their rhythmical rotation.

'God speed and a safe journey,' the captain yelled to the Barlows, as the boat began to move forward under the motion of its paddles.

It was a wonderful sight watching that splendid craft slowly steaming away. It's huge blades flapping at the muddy waters, enclosed by magnificent greyish-green Rivergums standing guard over the whole vista. Then to watch it disappear around the next bend until it was gone from view, visually swallowed up by the solitude of the outback, as if it had never been there at all.

For some minutes the men continued to listen to the flip-flop splashing sound of the paddles growing ever fainter until that too was gone. Just as they were preparing to re commence their own journey and as if to reassure the men that it was all real, that they would never be too far away, the captain gave a long blast on the steamer's whistle. The drovers looked back up the river again, in the direction of the sound, and like it were the final act in a play, looked at each other and smiled.

Suddenly she had never been there at all. It had become like a romantic mirage, just another fleeting moment in the course of a long, long journey.

Silence engulfed the river again. Like a blanket pulled slowly down over reality. Well for a moment at least, until suddenly the squawk of the native parrots returned and all that was left was the river, the noisy birds and the journey ahead.

As the riverboat moved north towards Bourke, and its date with the future, the Barlows and Benny packed up their camp. Then, with an ear-piercing crack of a bull-whip, Matthew got the mob moving south again..

It was indeed a strange land of contrasts, John thought,

as he rode on that day. Even though Queensland had been in a severe drought, water was still plentiful in this part of the Darling River system, thanks to good summer rainfall over the New England region. The waters were wide enough and deep enough to allow a riverboat up and down with relative ease. Yet, just a few hundred yards inland from the river it was an extremely contrasting picture. Hardship seemed to invade this landscape everywhere. No rain also meant, no water, except for that which slowly meandered down the river. The gums took on a dull greyish colour and the leaves drooped sadly downward, vastly different from the posture of those along the Darling. The mud of the riverbanks and overflows suddenly dried and turned to dust. Red dust, that lifted from the ground and blew into the air at the slightest hint of a breeze or a passing animal. The happy chatter of birds in the Rivergums was gone also, replaced by the offensive squawk of the scavenging crows, picking and fighting over every dead carcass.

Kangaroos, wombats, emus, dingoes, parrots, and galahs were in abundance along the river's edge. They had seen them in the hundreds, if not thousands, but a few miles away from the river only the odd lizard or snake was seen scampering for cover. There were almost as many dead carcasses to be seen rotting on the ground as live ones seen searching for feed and grasses to survive on. Then, suddenly and miraculously as you returned to the safety of the river, the dry arid desert transformed back into a land of plenty again. Just a small corridor of happy abundance skirts the inland rivers of Australia. The rest of our vast land is a dry, barren, harsh place, where death is more a daily reality than is life.

The drovers were witnessing Australia at its best and its utmost worst. It is a land of great distances, and of vast changes. It is also a land of great beauty and as the men rode on towards their ultimate destination, Broken Hill, they began to appreciate the wilderness more and more. It had a tragedy all its own. A life and death struggle, but also a beauty within it. It had a soul, a beating heart and the river was its blood flow.

CHAPTER SIX

Jock's Plight
Wednesday March 13th. 7.04p.m. 1994

> 'Delta Tango 104 Mayday.'
> 'Delta Tango 104 Mayday.'
> 'No instruments.'
> 'I'm going down - I'm going down.'

In that last terrifying moment Jock knew he was about to crash. There was not a thing he could do about it anymore. The fact was he was going to crash and death loomed as a reality. The violent fight between the storm and his plane was over. The storm had won. The fight to survive the impact was only moments away.

He dropped the microphone in his lap and tried to concentrate on his battle with the joystick. He needed desperately to keep some sort of control over the plane. He had to find a way to survive what was about to happen to him. He braced himself mentally. He felt sweat drip from beneath his armpit. The ground was about to invade his life in the worst possible way. It had always been a standard saying amongst fellow pilots, that good landings should equal good takeoffs. That was not going to happen to Jock this time though. This was not going to be a good safe landing, no matter which way he looked at it. He tried to focus on the reality of the situation.

Suddenly Jock thought he spotted something ahead in the darkness. Then in a flash that something was clearly visible. Trees screamed towards him at over a hundred kilometres an hour. This is it, he thought. He held his breath and braced his body.

'This is it,' he screamed at the top of his voice. 'This is the day, the place, the moment.'

He heard the sound of the trees smashing into the wings of his plane, ripping and tearing at the thin aluminum skin, the sound of bolts being torn from their mountings. Also the terrifying sounds of branches and leaves slapping against the windscreen. He held on for dear life, and then, an almighty impact, like someone had hit him in the face with a baseball bat.

The next thing Jock felt was the heat of the sun beating down on his face. He slowly opened his eyes to a blinding light. He could taste blood in his mouth. It was daylight. The blinding light was in fact the sun.

Where am I, he thought? What happened? He couldn't remember a thing.

The sun was directly in his eyes. It was terribly bright. It hurt. In fact he hurt all over.

Why am I looking into the sun?

He couldn't move, he was held down by something that wouldn't let him go. He felt trapped. He moved his head carefully and slowly to one side. It was extremely painful, but he continued to move it anyway. He could still taste the blood in his mouth. He didn't like the taste one little bit. It was awful. His mouth hurt. His forehead hurt. His ribs and his legs hurt. Just about every part of his body hurt. He felt like he'd been inside a cement truck for hours being tossed around.

He moved his body slightly, and then he moved his head a bit more, then his body again, then his neck and head again. Slowly but painfully he was getting more and more movement. He didn't feel quite so trapped.

He sensed the sun wasn't as blinding now. It had gone behind a band of clouds. He began to make out forms in front of him, blurred forms. The smashed and broken instrument panel came into view as his eyes slowly began to focus again. He couldn't recognise it at first. What is this thing he thought? Where am I? Why am I in pain? He was confused about the taste of blood in his mouth. He couldn't understand any of it. He tried to spit some blood out, but it hurt his mouth, so he thought it best to put up with the taste for now. He rested for a while, looking at the instrument panel and still trying to work out what it was and what it all meant.

Slowly, things began to come back to him, little flashes, little bits at a time. He remembered the storm and the lightning. He felt so tired. Then he felt faint. He knew he didn't want to pass out, so he tried again to try and free his body. His leg was hurting more now, and his head was still pounding. The clouds had gone and the sun was hot on the top of his head again. He was still aware of the taste of blood in his mouth, which helped remind him of the reality of the situation that he was in trouble.

'Oh for a drink of water to get rid of this taste of blood', he thought. Then he remembered he always carried a water bottle on his right side. He reached down for it. He was surprised when he realised that his right hand was free, and sure enough, there it was, a water bottle. He was pleased that he had remembered the water bottle it assured him that his memory was coming back to him. He washed away the taste of blood and enjoyed the cool refreshing water. It felt good in his mouth. It hurt somewhat but at the same time it was like it was bringing relief to his situation.

He looked at the instrument panel again and stared at it until finally it started to make some sense.

A plane ..... It was the instrument panel of a plane. He

was in a small plane. He was in the pilot's seat.

Then suddenly he felt very nauseous again, his head began to spin and he blacked out again.

Sometime later he regained consciousness. By then the hot sun was directly overhead. He was still in a lot of pain. His head felt like someone was inside trying to get out with a SledgeHammer. His leg too was searing with extreme pain.

'Water! Water' he told himself, 'keep up the fluids, he must keep up the fluids.' If he had dehydrated from the heat of the sun, he'd be dead in no time at all.

He drank again from the water bottle. Each small sip of water seemed to help clear his muddled head. He looked down at the instrument panel again. This time it made more sense to him. He saw the radio microphone amongst the smashed panel. It looked like it was all right, sitting there in its cradle. He put down the water bottle, reached out with his right hand and picked up the microphone. He felt dizzy again. He put the microphone down in his lap. At that very moment he remembered doing the same thing in the darkness of a storm, but he couldn't remember anymore. His memories just weren't quite there yet. Tantalisingly close, he could feel it, but not quite there. He reached out for the radio switch and despite the pain that ran through his body with the movement he flicked it on.

His leg was giving him extreme pain, it must surely be broken, he thought. The pain was too great to be anything else. He felt light-headed again.

He immediately realised there was no crackling sound that was usually associated with turning the radio on. Perhaps the speaker was damaged, he thought. It wasn't as important to receive a message, but it was critical that he got one out.

Jock raised the microphone from his lap. Again he felt a wave of dizziness wash through his body. He was having trouble clearing his mind. He knew it was going to take all his effort, but he had to get out a Mayday call. If he were going to survive this situation, then he would need help urgently.

One of the troubles he was facing was that he didn't know where he was. A Mayday call wouldn't mean much without a location for the rescuers to focus in on. He looked back down at the instrument panel, but most of the gauges had been badly damaged in the crash. He had nothing there that would give him a bearing, a location. He remembered they'd been knocked out by the lightning strikes. Bit by bit his memory was coming back.

He looked around hoping to spot a landmark of some kind, something that would help his rescuers identify his location. He didn't know how long he could hold on out there in the oppressive heat. Outside the smashed cockpit of his once beautiful plane, he could only see gum trees and bushes. There were certainly plenty of them. He wondered whether the bush would hide his location.

Suddenly he felt faint again. He tried very hard to focus and told himself over and over that he wasn't going to pass out. He had to get a Mayday call out and he had to do it soon. He tried taking a few deep breaths, but his ribs hurt.

In front of him was a rock wall, to his left he could see a clear patch of ground, to his right there was nothing but gum trees, and then more gum trees.

Then, through slightly blurred eyes, he thought he spotted something. It was a fair distance away, perhaps a kilometre or two, but there was something red out there for sure. What was it though? He still couldn't focus properly. He strained his eyes, but they still wouldn't give him a clear image.

He could make out a hillside partly covered in something red. Perhaps it was red soil. Then he thought, no, it was too brightly coloured to be soil. Perhaps it was bushes or wild flowers of some kind.   He tried to focus on that hillside. Definitely red, strong red colour, he thought, but what was it? His eyes were letting him down. A red hill, surely someone would recognise or understand what it was that he could see and be able to locate the spot on a map. It was all he could focus on through his blurred vision and he knew he had to go with it. He was fearful that he might pass out again at any time. He knew he was weak. Time was the enemy now.

He pushed the button on the microphone and tried to raise it from his lap. He felt a wave of light-headedness come over him. 'Get the message out quickly. It might be your last chance', he thought, frustrated at not being able to control his situation. He raised the microphone to a position just in front of his mouth.

'Delta tango 104 - Mayday.'
He felt nauseous. He knew he was going to either pass out again, or he was going to vomit. He had no strength left. He could barely talk.

'Mayday - Mayday – a red hill – I see a red hill - I'm injured, send help - injured -
With all his energy now spent, Jock passed out again.

When Jock regained consciousness for the second time, the first thing he noticed was that the sun was behind him. He strained to look over his shoulder and saw that it was very low in the sky. It was much cooler now as well. He realised then that he was facing east, he had regained some of his memory and he realised now that he might be facing towards Toowoomba, towards home and his beloved Mary and his two beautiful children. He took that as a positive omen.

He knew they'd be extremely worried about him by now. He made a promise to himself at that moment, that for his family he would get out of this alive. He was not afraid of dying but he was very concerned about the pain Mary and the children would suffer if he did. 'As sure as dust storms in a drought,' he told himself he was going to survive this ordeal.

How on earth did he survive, he thought? The wings had been ripped away and the state of the front part of the plane was horrific. Pain racked his body. He knew that he was in a desperate predicament, one that was going to need careful planning if he was to get through it.

First thing was to put out another Mayday call. He remembered making a radio call, but he wasn't sure how much of it he had actually transmitted before he passed out. That was if the radio had even worked at all.

'Of course it did,' he told himself, trying hard to stay positive. 'Of course it did.' In his situation the more calls, the more information he could get out, the sooner his rescuers could find him.

He could see the red hill more clearly now. It was very distinctive indeed. That was his mark that was his focus point they'd find him for sure if he could let them know about the red hill.

Jock reached down and picked up the microphone from his lap, and then leaned forward to turn the radio switch on. It was already on. He realised at that moment, that when he passed out earlier, he must have left the radio on. Even if the radio was working when he tried to get the earlier call out, the batteries were now hopelessly flat.

He felt shattered. He realised that his last link to the outside world was now gone. All he had to hope for now was that his earlier message got through and that someone would know what and where the red hill was. He knew in his heart that the batteries were well and truly dead, but he had to try. He had to believe that he'd given himself every possible chance. Perhaps there was some small charge left to get one more message out, so he pushed the button down on the microphone anyway.

'Red hill, red hill, if anyone can hear this, I'm near a red hill facing east.'

Realistically, his only hope was that someone heard his first mayday call and was responding to it at that very moment. So after calling a number of times, he carefully leaned forward, switched the radio off, and methodically placed the microphone back in its cradle.

Jock also had to face the realisation that he was alone out there, wherever there was, and it could be a long time before someone stumbled across him in that harsh land. He knew there would be a search mounted for him, but they mightn't realise that he'd changed his flight plan. He knew it would be like looking for a needle in a haystack. Did the radio work; did they get his messages? Did they know about the red hill?

He wanted to believe that at least one of the messages got through, but he also knew he had to prepare himself for a long wait if it hadn't. They would know he was down. It was almost 24 hours, and he would have been reported missing between Toowoomba and Jackson. His first Mayday should have got out, but he only had time enough to report he was going down, not where. In his second message he reported the red hill, but he wasn't sure whether that message got out at all, besides, what would 'near a red hill' tell them anyway. He didn't even know where he was, so he couldn't expect them to know yet either. He had to rely on luck again, that someone saw or heard him go down, or that someone would stumble across him out there.

Survival... that's what it was all about now. It was up to him. If they came for him in the next few days that would be wonderful, but if they didn't, he would have to survive out there until he was well enough and fit enough to get back alone.

He thought of Mary and his children. He had always wanted to settle back in Toowoomba and since he had, life had been just great, well at least until now. He would survive this ordeal, he told himself. His time wasn't up yet. He had things he still wanted to do. He wanted to watch his kids grow up and one day he wanted to take Mary and show her 'his' view of Australia, the way he loved it, from the air, as well as from the ground. At some time in the future, they had planned to take three months holiday and fly around Australia. That was his dream, their dream, and he was going to hang on to it. He wasn't ready to die yet. It wasn't an option. He had to learn how to get through this situation. He told himself that everything he did from now on must be aimed towards surviving. He simply had to, for his family and his dreams.

The Bus Ride
Thursday 14th March.
The day after Jock flew out of Toowoomba

It had been almost a week since Danny's grandfather, 'Poppy', had died. It had been a tough week, but somehow they all managed to get through it. His mother had struggled the most. She cried when he left for school and had red eyes when he got home again. He wanted to stay home with her, but she insisted that 'life must go on', and so it did.

Danny climbed aboard the school bus that morning for the usual morning trip to the Mitchell State School, about 80klms away. He was a bright student, not a genius by any means, but smart enough to be comfortable at school. His teachers had often written in his half-yearly report cards that

'Danny was a pleasure to have in the class.'

Five mornings a week, Danny's mother would drive him down to the main Mitchell road, a few kilometres away, and there they'd wait until the school bus arrived at about 7.25a.m. He would climb aboard the bus and wave good-bye to his mother through the windows. At about half past eight, he'd arrive at school, along with the twenty-three other kids who would also be picked up along the way.

Danny was the seventh to be picked up on the morning run, and the seventeenth to be dropped off on the home run each afternoon. It was the same trip he'd done so many times before, without anything exciting ever happening. Except for the day that Johnny Madison put a green tree frog down Caitlan Fenwick-Jackson's back. That had everyone laughing that morning. Well, all but Caitlan that was, she hated frogs and Johnny knew it all too well. She was so angry that she dobbed him in to his teacher when they got to school and he was given detention at lunchtime for a whole week.

Everyone had to endure a lengthy speech from the principal on verbally abusing and bullying of others. However he, along with everyone else, thought it was worth it, because Caitlin Fenwick-Jackson had always thought she was too good to be sitting on the bus with the likes of them. She needed to be brought down a peg or two, and Johnny achieved his goal that morning, much to the delight of all.

Danny boarded the bus as usual, waved goodbye to his mother, and the bus rattled off towards Mitchell. However this particular trip was going to be a little bit different from all the others before. About fifteen kilometres down the road, excitement filled the bus when a police car was seen screaming towards them with its red and blue lights flashing. To a bus full of country kids, bored with their usually mundane ride to school, it looked very impressive indeed. The bus was filled with commotion as the driver slowed down.

The police car came to a halt right in the middle of the road. The dust settled enough to show two big burly policemen getting out. One signaled to the bus driver to pull over and stop.

'Wow!' Danny thought, 'this is cool'. Perhaps there was a bad car crash up ahead, or even a local bank robbery, or a murderer on the loose. If it was a bad accident, he really didn't want to know or see. It was surely too early for a bank robbery, and perish the thought a murderer might be on the loose. He waited somewhat nervously as the two giant figures in blue approached the bus door. Those on board couldn't wait to hear what all the fuss was about, and Danny couldn't have known that what he was about to hear would eventually change his life, and the lives of his family, in the strangest of ways.

The bus driver opened the side door, and one of the police officers stepped inside. He took off his cap and spoke quietly to the driver; then he turned to the children and in a loud booming voice called out to them to settle down and be quiet.

He paused for a moment, like the headmaster always does before he addresses a school assembly, waiting for the last voice to fall silent.

'Did any of you children see or hear an aero-plane in your area last night?' he asked.
A hum of mumbling broke out which continued for a minute or so as the kids asked one another.
The policeman waited a few minutes and then he continued, 'we received an emergency call from a light plane around 7p.m last night, during that big storm that blew through. The pilot reported that his engines had failed and he was going to crash. We have heard nothing more from him since then.'

The word crash brought about another instant buzz from

the kids, this one much louder though. The policeman waited until they'd settled again and then he continued,

'By the strength of the radio signal, we're told the plane could be anywhere between Charleville, St. George, Roma and Springsure in the north. He may have been flying through this area, or maybe not. We really don't know. So if anyone here heard or saw anything last night we would like to know about it now please.'

There was stony silence on the bus. It went with some innocent head shaking, the kind that is usually associated with the 'it wasn't me sir, I didn't do it' look.

The man in blue went on to say that they would be contacting as many people as possible in the area, to see if they had heard or seen anything unusual at all. He also added that they wouldn't be able to speak to everyone in the area, so they needed the kid's co-operation and help.

'Firstly you can help by keeping a look out through the windows,' he said, 'for anything unusual, anything at all, the plane, some wreckage, or even signs of a grass fire. If you see anything that is different or unusual, tell the bus driver, and he can report it to us. Now,' he continued, 'one other thing, when you get home this afternoon, I want you all to talk to your parents about it as well. They might have seen or heard something that you didn't. We want everyone to be vigilant, because, out here in the bush, a plane could almost disappear. We could be looking for days, even weeks, in such a large area.'
Finally he looked sternly at the kids.

'It's up to everyone to help us find this plane and the pilot, before it's too late,' he paused. 'Keep your eyes and ears open for anything at all. The pilot could die out here very quickly if we don't find him. He needs your help if he's going to survive.'

Someone called out from the back of the bus, 'Is he still alive?'

'We don't know, but we are remaining hopeful.'

The police officer put his cap back on, thanked the children for their attention, climbed down from the bus, got back into the police car and drove off in a southerly direction with lights blazing away.

The kids clambered over to one side of the bus and watched as the police car sped past them. Then they all turned and watched out the back window as the car disappeared behind a cloud of dust. The bus driver waited a moment or two then politely ordered everyone back into their seats and they continued on their way to school.

On the way to school, they saw kangaroos, emus, rusty old car bodies, millions of trees and hundreds of empty soft drink cans and beer bottles, but not one of them saw a crashed plane.

Mitchell had never had a plane crash before, and all the talk at school that day was about nothing else. Everyone had heard something. The rumour machine was running at full speed. Some said they saw the plane in the sky that night, although they weren't believed because the night of the storm had been moonless and very dark. One boy even said the pilot was alive. That he, the pilot, had stayed at his place that night, and had flown out the next morning after first having breakfast with them. Someone else reported that story to the headmaster, and after a phone call to the boy's parents, it was revealed that it was a made-up story, a little bit of a porky. Needless to say the boy in question got into quite a deal of trouble from his parents, and the headmaster, for lying.

The bus trip home that afternoon was much the same, with everyone on the bus straining to see something, anything that might be a lead.

Friday was a buzz at school again, with the news from the day before, about the pilot getting out a message. It managed to keep the story hot on the list of main topics. By Friday afternoon, there was still no sign of the plane or the pilot, even though search parties had been sent out in all directions.

On his way home that Friday afternoon, Danny wondered if his father would have heard the news yet. He was still a fair way south of them, in the 'long paddock' with their sheep. The Police probably weren't looking down that far and more than likely no one would have passed the news on to him. He also thought of his 'Poppy'. He wondered what he would have done to help in the search. 'He could have found the plane for sure,' Danny thought. 'He was a real good bushman. He would have known exactly where to look for the plane.'

He tried to think like his grandfather. How would he find that plane? Where would he begin to search for it? But his grandfather wasn't there and the truth was that Danny had no idea what his 'Poppy' would have done.

He decided that he'd ride around Nundooka himself and look around for any sign of them over the weekend. He spent most of the Saturday and Sunday riding his horse around looking for the plane or its pilot. He thought if he could find the pilot alive, he'd be a hero. The headmaster would call him up on parade one day, and he would tell the whole school the story of how he found the plane crash. What a hero he would be. The whole school would clap and cheer him. Wouldn't that be cool, he thought to himself as he rode around Nundooka.

First, he headed out towards the rusty old windmill in the bottom paddock. It took him nearly all morning to get out there, but he just had this feeling that was the place to start seriously looking. It was about a twelve-kilometre ride. He went out along the dry creek and then skirted around Blacksnake Hill. It was a nice ride that he'd done many times before. After the recent rain, there were a lot of wildflowers. They were everywhere, more than he had ever seen before. Perhaps, without the sheep on the property to eat them, they had flourished.

He also noticed that the trees too, looked greener and taller. During the drought, the trees seemed to lose that lovely green colour and the leaves would hang down looking rather sad, perhaps making them appear smaller. The trees and the countryside looked so much better after the rains, he thought to himself as he rode on. He had spent many hours riding around with his grandfather. He had taught Danny how to appreciate the bush.

There were a lot of kangaroos around, 'whippies' as Poppy had always called them. They loved watching them bounding about in their mobs, tall, free and proud to be Australian icons.

He also saw families of emus grazing together on the flats, as well as goannas sitting perched up in trees looking down on him as he rode beneath. He was always a little worried by the goannas when he was on horseback.

He leaned forward at one stage, patted his horse on the neck, and spoke to him, 'I bet they'd know if that crashed plane was around here, those goanna's know everything that's happening out here'.

The countryside was indeed looking good. There were snakes around as well. It was still too early for them to hibernate. Winter was a few months away. He knew to be very careful around snakes. They could spook his horse and throw him off. It would be a long walk home without a horse, so he kept a vigilant eye out for snakes, as well as signs of a crashed plane.

Danny's sport's day jitters
Monday 7a.m.

After searching all weekend around Nundooka without any luck, Danny caught the Monday morning school bus with growing excitement. This was going to be a special week. This was school sports week. He expected all the school chatter would be about the upcoming sports days, but instead most of the talk was still about the missing plane and whether or not the pilot could still be alive. Everyone still had a theory, like he had been eaten by dingoes, or he was seen in Roma at the pub drinking, and then there was the one where the legendary Australian bunyip had taken him back to his cave and eaten him. Danny never did work out whether the bunyip one was meant to be a joke or serious. He hoped it was a joke, because he liked the girl who told it. He just hated the thought that she might be that dumb as to believe her own story. Still, holding hands with her behind the sports shed was put on hold for a little bit longer. Time to summon the courage and ask her back there, but also time to figure out if she was 'fair dinkum'. There was a lot of 'my dad said' or 'Uncle Joe reckons' still flying around. Everyone had an opinion.

Danny's mind was more focused on the annual District's School Sports Carnival, to be held the next day in Roma. To his amazement it was almost un-mentioned.

The 'country versus townies' sports day was also the stuff of myth and legend. Everyone looked forward to that one special day in March. They planned for it, they trained for it, they prepared for it, and they wanted more than anything to beat the 'Townies' from Roma at the big event. Every town within 300 kilometres had a team and it was always 'us' versus 'the Roma townies'.

However, on this Monday morning, the very day before Sports Day 94, the talk was all still about Jock and his plane, 'Delta Tango 104'. Every boy in the district had been out looking for the plane throughout the weekend. They all wanted to be the one who found him. Some went alone; others went out in groups on their little 'adventures' into the bush. They went out on horseback, on motorbikes, in motorised buggies and some just rode their BMX's or mountain bikes. To the boys' amazement, even some girls joined in the searching. To find Jock would elevate one immediately to the status of an instant hero, and it seemed every kid in and around Mitchell had been on a mission to solve the mystery of the missing pilot and plane.

All day long, between classes, the kids talked about Jock as if they'd known him all their lives. The chatter didn't stop when they boarded the bus to go home. No one talked of the usual pre-Sports Day nervous butterflies in the stomach, just about Jock and the plane. It was as if sports day almost didn't exist.

That afternoon, Annie, Danny's mother, got a phone call from a friendly neighbour who lived about 60 kilometres down the road. The word was that Lucas, Danny's dad, was well and truly on his way back to Nundooka, and would probably be home by the weekend. Lucas had asked if they wouldn't mind calling home for him and giving Annie and Danny the news. He'd made good ground in the previous week or so, and was well ahead of time.

They were going to help Lucas put the mob into one of their paddocks. He wanted to leave them there for a day or so and surprise Danny by driving down to Roma and watch him run in the school sports day carnival.

The bus pulled to a halt as usual and when Annie told

him the news, he was over the moon with joy.

'Perhaps when Dad gets home we could go look for the missing pilot together.'

'I'm sure your dad would love to. It would give him a chance to take a look around the property and see if there's any work needing catching up on.'

'You mean busted fences and stuff?'

'I'm sure there's a few out there. Heaps of feral goats around at the moment, they like to run through fences, rather than around them.'

'Dad hates feral goats, hey Mum?'

'Yes he does Danny. They just do so much damage.'

'He always said he'd take me shooting one day, he did', Danny mumbled.

'I think he meant when you're a bit older Danny, well I hope he did', Mum snapped.

'I can handle a 22 Mum!'

'I hate guns and although I know they're a pest, I still hate the thought of someone shooting those poor creatures', she said.

'But we kill some of our sheep to eat', Danny added.

'That's a little different though. That's just for food, no other reason. Anyway, are you getting excited about tomorrow?'

'I sure am, Mum but I think I'm the only one who is. Everyone's still going on about the plane crash at school.'

'You might just be surprised at who else is getting excited about the sports day also', Mum smiled.

'I'm gunna run real fast tomorrow. You just wait and see. I'm gunna run so Poppy would be proud of me.'

That night, Danny began to feel the nerves of impending sports day excitement. He also thought a lot about his grandfather. It would be sad that he wouldn't be there at this year's big day.

He'd quietly hoped that his dad might be at there with them, seeing that his Poppy wouldn't be now.

'Some kid's parents don't even bother going at all,' he thought, 'at least Mum will be there.'

Thoughts of the sports day ahead, the missing pilot and his plane, his father getting home soon, and just missing his dear Poppy, seemed to fill his head. Finally, after tossing and turning for ages that night, he fell into a deep sleep.

Tuesday 5.30 a.m.

Dawn broke next morning to a lovely clear blue sky. A beaut day for school sports events, he thought, someone must have ordered it especially for him. He rubbed the sleep from his eyes, as the hint of a cool breeze blew over the hill from the west and in through his bedroom window, the best kind of morning to be waking up to, one with the promise of greater things ahead.

Danny usually rose early. He was never one for sleeping in. Well except for the occasional cold morning in mid-winter. Those zero degree mornings when the doona traps you beneath it for a little more time and just won't let you go.

Almost the moment his eyes were open he was out of bed. It was his morning chore to feed the chickens before school and collect any eggs left in the chook house the day before. The chooks stayed in the run all day, yet it amazed him that every morning there would be two eggs under the bush on the outside of their fenced area. He never saw any chickens outside, but sure as the sun comes up every morning, there were two eggs in that exact same spot. Poppy had always teased him that it was the fairies playing games at night with the chickens. They must have been getting out somehow, but he never could work it out. His Poppy once said that some things weren't meant to have a logical reason, they just happened, and Danny was happy to agree with him, whatever it meant.

Danny called out to 'Legs' the family's pet Emu. The emu came loping in from the paddock down behind the shed. 'Legs' couldn't jump the fence so he found a spot where the fence wire was very loose and just ducked his head and at full speed just fell through it. Danny got a laugh every time the emu ran through that fence. It looked like his legs just folded up beneath him, just like an airplane after taking off. The funny part was that his legs never folded in time, and he would nosedive out the other side. The rusty old wire fence had long given up the battle of keeping the galloping Emu at bay, and just yielded to the inevitable onslaught.

Legs had been their family pet ever since the day Danny's father had brought this tiny, scrawny, featherless bird home. He found it wandering alone, and after looking around the area, he had found the tiny Emu's mother dead by the side of the road. It had been hit by a car or a truck. Lucas brought the young Emu home and the whole family took care of it until he was fully-grown. They decided it would be the right thing if they released him, but Legs had different ideas. He ran as far as the next paddock, where he stopped, picked at the grass for a while, looked around at the homestead in the distance, and then just slowly wandered back. He hadn't ventured beyond that paddock since.

The paddock that he now called home was known to Danny's family as the 'house paddock', and Legs shared it with the six house cows, two pet pigs and with five working sheep dogs. Only two of the sheep dogs were there however, the other three were out helping Lucas in the 'long paddock'.

Danny took the eggs he'd collected that morning back to the kitchen, where he wrote the date on each one with a pencil, T19, (Tuesday the 19th). Chook eggs were at their best after a couple of days, and at their worst after about two weeks, so the best way to keep track of the eggs age, was to write the date on each one. There were six eggs that morning, including the mystic two that the fairies had hidden under the bushes.

He had breakfast a little earlier that morning, because they had to drive the extra distance to Roma for the sport's day carnival. The trip would take about a half an hour longer than it would normally take on the bus to Mitchell, so they left home at around 7:15.

The drive to Roma took about an hour and a half. They took the back road that morning. It was a dirt road that bypassed Mitchell and picked up the main bitumen highway about half way to Roma. They could keep an eye out for the crashed plane and it's pilot on the way. Annie, like most people, believed that the experts were right. She believed that if the pilot was still alive, he certainly wasn't in their area. He would have flown further north, she had always said. It simply made more sense. But Annie had no problems with doing what Danny had asked, about taking the back road for a change.

They played 'I spy' for a while, then Danny talked about how good it would be when his dad came home for good. His mother tried to explain that it might take some time for everyone to get used to living with each other again, after being apart for so long. She explained that even though the drought had broken, they were still under a big financial burden. Sheep prices were very low and they still owed the Bank a large amount of money. Money they had borrowed for living expenses while Lucas was away. It was called an overdraft, and they would need to pay it

144

back within the next few years if they were going to survive on the land.

Danny understood all that, they had discussed such things many times before. Annie had always tried to involve him in everything to do with the property. The hope was that one-day Danny would take over the property from them, and he would need to know just what to expect from it.

Danny felt his mother was trying to prepare him for when his dad got home again for other reasons. That maybe the arguments might return. She just told him that grown-ups were put under enormous pressures in their lives, and sometimes that boiled over.

He enjoyed being a kid. He just missed his dad some times, and he especially missed his Poppy. He knew his mum and dad still loved each other, he thought they'd just forgotten how to show it.

They arrived at Roma in good time. The track had been dry and dusty, but generally it was in better condition than she had expected. Annie decided they'd head for McDonalds and have some pancakes with that yummy syrup, just as an added treat.

'What your dad doesn't know certainly won't hurt him. This is our little secret,' she told him.

Lucas didn't like wasting money, as he put it, on takeaway foods. Truth was, he had been struggling on the property for so long, that he had forgotten that sometimes those little treats were very rewarding to them all.

After breakfast at Maccas, they headed for the school car park. They made their way down to the oval and found their school's designated area. The host school in Roma always provided large awnings for each school to congregate under. This year the Mitchell School had been given a red, white and blue awning, with Roma Toyota, printed on the roof.

The kids enjoyed running through their semi-final heats in the morning, while the mothers, along with the odd father or two, sat around talking, drinking tea and coffee, and catching up on 'the good old times', as they put it. There was, as expected, plenty of talk about the missing plane, and not unlike the kids of the district, most of the adults had an opinion. Their theories weren't as way out as the kids, but most agreed that the search would now be for a dead body, no longer for a living person.

After an early break for lunch, the real action began. Eventually, it got to down to Danny's age group.

A deep voice boomed out over the loudspeaker, 'Runners in the under 11, 200-metre final, to the starting line please.'

'That's me,' thought Danny, as he nervously headed towards the far end of the oval. He waved to his mother as he jogged past the Roma Toyota awning.

'Good luck, Danny,' she called, which only added to his growing nervousness. He loved all sport, and in particular he loved running, but he hated that nervous sick feeling he got just before the start of a race.

'Under 11 Boys,' said the booming voice, followed by a momentary pause.

'On your marks - get set -'

'Steady,' he said in a quiet, but nevertheless, stern voice. Then came the loud bang of the starter's gun and Danny's legs took over. He ran as fast as those legs could carry him down the straight to glory. He heard the crowd as he passed each team's tent. He couldn't make out anything, other than a loud roar, but it lifted him to greater things. He powered on and on. He could see the people behind the finishing line jumping and yelling as the runners got closer. He saw the yellow line tape strung across the track. He was getting close now, and he thought he was up there near the front, but it was hard to tell. He just kept looking straight ahead and running hard, because that's what he had been told to do

A lady in a big white floppy hat walked towards him. He thought to himself, 'Did I win? No I couldn't have, someone else pulled the tape away, the winner always pulls the tape away!'

'Young man,' she said in a very proper manner. Danny began to get excited. Perhaps he was wrong. Perhaps he had won.

'Congratulations young man,' she said, 'you ran 3rd.'

'Third Mum, I came third, I got a bronze', he said when all the fuss died down.

'Third is very good Danny. I'm really, really proud of you.'

The Long Paddock

Lucas Richards had been in 'the long paddock' for over a year. Each night he had slept under the stars, or in an old tent he carried with him. He had cooked his meals on open campfires or in his camp-oven. He had withstood searing heat in the summer months, bitter cold winds in the winter, and bush flies that harassed him constantly. He had washed himself in dirty coloured boreholes, and at rusty old windmill troughs. He had been lunged at by startled snakes, watched seasons come and go and lived with dust in his mouth for most of that time, certainly for longer than he wished to remember.

He'd travelled 'the long paddock' looking for roadside grass and when he found some he would set up camp in that area for sometimes up to a month watching over his grazing sheep. When that patch of life-giving food for his sheep had been consumed, he would push on to the next substantial patch and do it all over again. Perhaps it would be just a few kilometres down the road, or a half a day's push, or maybe it would be many, many kilometres away taking days to reach.

He had to do it. He didn't want to. God knows he'd rather have been at home on Nundooka, but he had no other choice. To keep his farm, he had to keep his stock alive, and to do that he had to be out there in the long paddock. True country styled dedication and commitment. He'd watch the skies for rain clouds or heat storms and remember where it had fallen, knowing that in a few week's that area should provide rich new grass for his sheep to graze on.

There were times when Council road-workers would pull up and give him locations of where he'd be able to find feed. Lucas would then have to make the decision, would he move his sheep to that area and risk another farmer with a mob beating him there, or would he stay and graze out where he was. Pushing them too hard could weaken them very quickly.

There were so many other struggling sheep and cattle breeders out there on the long paddock, that it was almost a 'cat and mouse' situation, first in, best dressed, as the saying goes.
Lucas had never wanted to deprive other country folk of their right to survive, but he knew he had to keep his own sheep alive and healthy, if he was to keep his farm away from the ever-present Bank Manager and those dreaded loan repayments.

Finally, when the drought-breaking rains arrived around Nundooka, Lucas turned his mob of sheep around and had been making his way back home ever since. He knew he couldn't push too hard, for the sake of his sheep. He chose the shortest route he could, and each day, edged closer and closer to home. In the year and a bit he'd been on the road, he'd usually travel small distances at a time, then rest before moving on again. It had been a snail's pace at times, but that suited the sheep.

However, on the return trek it was a delicate balance between his want to get home quickly, and not pushing the sheep to hard. His mob held the key to the future of Nundooka and he knew it all too well.

Lucas grew more and more anxious and as the days went by, he felt more and more homesick. He had received the message about his father's death (Poppy), while still on the track north of Bollon. The local police constable received a phone call from Annie and brought the sad news out to him. At the time he was only about 70 kilometres from home, but the message had taken a couple of days to reach him. With permission from the manager on nearby Hillsborough Station, he left the sheep in a vacant paddock and headed home for the funeral, on his old motor bike.

It is never easy losing a loved one, but Lucas found it even more distressing because of his absence at the time of his father's death. Also, after the funeral, he didn't have time to stay and grieve with his family and friends. He would have loved to stay another day or two, but he knew he had to get back to the sheep.

Lucas never really felt lonely on the road. Sure he missed his family, but there was always so much to do, it occupied his time and thoughts. However, the days after the funeral, he felt extremely lonely out there. He longed for some human company. His mind kept taking him home, and more and more, he'd catch himself remembering the good times growing up as a child on Nundooka.

When he was a child, his father had taken him everywhere with him. They had been inseparable, and he remembered them clearly as wonderful times. He was taken droving and he'd always be there for the round ups. He used to help out with the wool classing, after the sheep had been shorn in the shearing sheds each year. He'd also watched in horror as the young rams were castrated, and all the sheep were mules'd.

Mulesing was an operation performed by a hired expert. The men would flip the sheep on its back on a special table, and then they'd hook the sheep's back legs under two clasps so that the sheep's rear end was exposed. Then with an extremely sharp knife, he'd slice the skin and wool away from around the sheep's backside. It was cut off to stop the sheep from getting fly blown with maggots down there, a situation that if left untreated could be life-threatening to the sheep. As a child, Lucas had never liked that part, but it had to be done. Now as an adult it was simply part of his job.

Going to school hadn't been as important back when he was a child. Lucas would inherit the property one-day, so it was expected that he spend as much time as possible learning the skills a farmer and sheep breeder would need to make good on the land. Those skills, passed on by his father, were deemed more important in the early 1960's than a traditional education in the schools. Most of what he learnt in the way of reading and writing his mother taught him. Although times were changing rapidly, the 60's in Australia still relied heavily on the wealth from the land.

Lucas had very fond memories of his childhood though. He remembered that times were hard. Seasons too were predictable back then, with plenty of good rain, green grass, water in the dams and bores, and the mighty Maranoa River flowed steadily inland. He swam, or fished in the Maranoa almost daily. The river was such a large part of his life back then.
He felt sorry that Danny had never experienced those wonderful times. It was so different now. To Danny, the Maranoa was a dried up old creek bed that rarely had water in it, let alone

enough to catch a fish or a yabby. Mickey played down in the sandy riverbed, but it was nothing like it was when Lucas was his age.

He promised himself there and then, that when he got back home, he would show Danny some good times, like the ones he had as a boy. Nundooka was a beautiful place and he vowed to make sure that Danny realised that as well. He was going to spend as much time as possible with him in the future. He'd been away too long and he had missed out on a big piece of his son's childhood. Their Poppy's death had made him stop and think about his own life, as well as Danny's. He also vowed to himself, to try and find more time getting his marriage to Annie back in shape.

He understood now that women, as well as men, needed someone. Annie had often said that everyone needs someone to fuss over to make them feel wanted and loved. He knew he hadn't done that in a real long time. He promised himself that things were going to be different when he got back. No more arguments. He was going to try and be more tolerant and not get so upset by small trivial things, as he had in the past. He realised that Annie and Danny, had been living through tough times, just as much as he had. He should never have taken his daily frustrations out on them. He knew that now.

Early that Tuesday morning in March, Lucas was moving his sheep along the road, east of Abbieglassie, barely 50 kilometres from Nundooka, when his friend Reg pulled up in his Landcruiser. He had organised with Lucas the day before to look out for the sheep for the day, giving him some time to drive to Roma and watch Danny run in the sport's carnival. In return, he would pick up some machinery parts and provisions Reg had been waiting on and bring them back later that afternoon.

So Lucas headed off to Roma in the borrowed

Landcruiser, thankful of the chance to see Danny run in his race. It was time to start to put into practice what he recently promised himself he would.

The drive to Roma was a pleasant change. The comfort of sitting in a car again, listening to the radio again and watching the world fly by. He'd lost his portable radio on the track months before, so he hadn't heard radio in a while. He listened in to the hourly news broadcast and was intrigued to hear the reporter mention the lost plane and pilot.

'That's nearly a week since that bloody storm,' he said back to the radio. 'Poor buggar's surely dead by now. The dingo's would have made a meal of him.'

He glanced out the window at the passing scrub. 'Poor bastard, you could lose a bloody army out there in that bush, and not find 'em for years. Poor bastard.'

As he drove one of his favourite songs came on the radio, 'Needles and Pins', by the Searchers. Automatically he found himself singing along with the words.

'Needles and Pins-za, because of all my pride - the tears I tried to hide - Needles and Pins-za.'

All the frustration's and hardships of the past year seemed to pour out through his vocal chords. He sang along at the top of his voice, oblivious to the world outside.

'Hey, I thought I was smart, I won her heart. Didn't think I'd see, she wise to him not me.'

Kangaroos stopped nibbling on the grass and looked up bewildered when they heard the strange noise briefly enter their world. The Emu's stopped running and looked around perplexed. Snakes slithered into undergrowth, as birds scattered from their lofty perches. Lucas singing at full pitch was not a sound to look forward too. Indeed it could peel paint from walls.

When the song finished he chuckled to himself. The

song had taken him back to the time when he and Annie had driven all the way down to Brisbane, to one of the RSL Clubs, the Kedron-Wavell, if he remembered rightly, just to watch the Searchers sing that song, their song. They were the days when he was young and free. So much had changed since that carefree time. Had they appreciated those times when they were theirs to enjoy. Oh to turn back the clock to those wonderful days. They had done what they wanted, when they wanted. Truth was, they probably hadn't, but it seemed that way now as he looked back through a world full of complexities.

As he drove on, he found the words going over and over in his mind. Because of all my pride, the tears I tried to hide, hey I thought I was smart, I won her heart. He kept thinking about those words. That was half of his trouble, he thought, pride. He had been pretty pig-headed at times and his pride had taken a beating of late, what with the drought and the long paddock. The struggle to survive had become all-consuming. There seemed to be no time for anything else. With the farm struggling of late, he had felt so inadequate. He just didn't have the money or the inclination any more to do something impetuous, like jump in the car and take Annie to Brisbane, like they had to see the Searchers all those years ago. They used to have a lot of fun back then, but it was true to say that they also had good seasons and plenty of money in their pockets.

Since the drought, things just weren't the same as they used to be. It was that pride of his that had convinced him to go on the road, the long paddock. If he had sold half their stock, they could have survived until good seasons came around again, but his damned pride wouldn't allow him to do that. In times of drought, poor quality stock would be dumped on an already overloaded market. He didn't want others to see him as someone not providing for his family, and to sell at a cheap price, as it was back then, would have dented his damned country pride

Was it that stubborn pride also, that was driving him and Annie apart. She had never liked the idea of him going away in the first place. She had undoubtedly been lonely without him, but then it seemed that whenever he did come home, he just wanted to argue and didn't understand why. He realised that he had changed. He had become uncaring of her feelings he believed it was because of the worry of the farm. No wonder she wanted to spend more and more time in Mitchell. He had been a bit of a bastard of late. His damned pride was shutting her out to the point where she had to find friendship elsewhere.

They'd known Robert for years and years, since school days in fact. He was a good guy. Why did he ever think otherwise? Instead of arguing about the time Annie was spending in Mitchell, he should have been thanking Robert for being there when she needed someone.

He realised he hadn't been there for her over the last few years and he wasn't very proud of himself because of it. He'd been hiding himself, along with his pride, out there on the road, away from the world he was scared to face. Things had to change, and he knew it. His father had spoken to him about it a few months before, but Lucas had brushed him away. Since the funeral he realised he owed Annie and Danny much more time in the future. Maybe a bit of a holiday would help to get them back on track as a marriage and family.

'I'll start today', he said to himself, 'right now, bugger the pride thing. Pride is about love and family, not bloody sheep.'

He found the school grounds and parked the borrowed vehicle in the car park.

'Under 11 girls, on your marks.'
He realised the boys would be next and he wouldn't have time to get down to the oval in time for Danny's event, so to get a better

view of the running track, he climbed up onto the roof rack on the Landcruiser.

He had just clambered atop the vehicle when he heard the voice boom across the open ground, ' Under 11 Boys, take your marks. He felt a bit silly standing on the roof of the vehicle looking down at the oval. A little like a penny-less boy peering over the fence at a footy game, watching from afar.

He remembered his old school days and felt a bit of that nervous anticipation return to his stomach, the type you get just before a race, and he knew Danny would be feeling it also. He heard the bang of the starter's gun. He watched as the eight little bodies hurtled down the track. He could hear the crowd cheering louder and louder as the runners crossed the finishing line. He had a reasonable view of the finish line and felt proud when he realised Danny had at least run a place. He watched as a teacher walked over to his son and handed him a green sash. Lucas tried to remember what the green sash meant.

Third, wasn't it? He asked himself. 'Third was good!' He was running against finalists from all around the south-west district, so third was admirable.

After a minute of feeling pleased with Danny's effort, Lucas made his way down to the oval. He saw Annie standing with a group of other mothers, and headed over to her.
Annie looked up and saw him coming. She was pleased he'd made it to the sports day, for Danny's sake, she was also happy to see him herself.

'Did you see the race dear?' she asked, as he got closer.
He answered and Annie knew from his voice that he was happy. She hadn't heard that in his voice for quite some time.

He continued, 'He was great wasn't he. He's a good kid that one. We did something right when we had him?'

They hugged but the moment was interrupted by one of

the other mothers suggesting they should head over to the presentation area if they wanted to see Danny receive his medal.

'In third place,' the announcer said, 'Danny Richards, Mitchell State School.'

Danny was popular at his school and beyond, so much so that he received more applause than the first and second placed runners did. Lucas felt proud. It took him back to when he had come second in a similar event at Dalby. He could clearly remember the look on his old Poppy's face when he stood on the winner's rostrum all those years ago, and finally he understood what 'that' look meant. It was the look of a 'proud as punch' father.

As Danny stepped onto the right hand side of the winner's rostrum, he looked around to where he thought his mother would be standing, and couldn't believe his eyes when he saw his dad standing there as well. His face beamed, and then out of sheer joy he punched the air. The next thing he knew there was a finger wiping a tear away from his cheek, and a warm and loving voice saying, 'He's missed you so much dear.'

When the lunch break came, the three of them, along with dozens of other families, sat under a large shady tree on the outer edge of the oval and ate sandwiches together. It was the first time they had done that as a family in a long while.

Danny ran in two more team events for the Mitchell State School before Sport's Day 94 drew to a close. He ran in the 100m and 400m relays, in which they finished out of a place in both events. There were no more medals for Danny that day, but it didn't matter to them for it had been a special day indeed.

As the events came to a close, Danny asked if it was ok if he drove home with his dad. So at around 2.15 that afternoon, Lucas and Danny headed off to get the machinery parts for Reg before driving home in the borrowed Toyota Landcruiser. Annie headed for Nundooka in the family car, happy to be driving home alone. She knew how important it was for Danny and Lucas to spend time together.

On the drive back, the two talked and talked, until it seemed like there was nothing more in the world to talk about. School, Nundooka, sheep, Poppy, girls, future dreams, and even Jock's plane got a bit of a mention as well. Then Lucas suddenly dropped a bombshell on him.

'How bout you come out with me and you can help me bring the sheep home. It'll only take another four or five days to get them back to Nundooka, maybe less with you helping. What do you say then? Drovers together hey!'

Danny was dumbfounded. In the whole time his father had been away, he had never once asked him to come out and help.

'Wow, yeah, that'd be cool, but do you think Mum will let me? I'd have to miss some days at school.'

'You leave your mother to me,' he replied, 'and a few days away from school won't hurt. We'll ask your teacher for extra homework when you go back.'

Danny knew they'd be camping out under the stars, and he loved that idea. That was if it was dry, but even if it rained they'd put up the old tent. Either way it sounded terrific. He knew that each night they would build a campfire and there'd be plenty of time sitting around just listening to stories like the ones that his grandfather used to tell. Poppy's stories were often about campfires and sitting around them for hours telling endless tales of fishing, and droving, and tales like chasing wild pigs through the scrub. His grandfather always referred to it as 'back in the good old days.'

Danny imagined it would be the same for him and his Dad, now they could make their own 'good old days.'

He knew the campfires would be great, and he also loved

riding his horse and droving sheep, so he knew he was in for a terrific few days. To him, that sounded about as good as it could get. He'd missed his Poppy so badly since his death; time with his Dad would help him forget for a while.

'What about school Dad, you sure I won't get into trouble not going?' He sounded worried.

'Oh I think your teachers and mates can live without you for the rest of the week,' smiled Lucas.

'But my medal, they'll call me up on parade and make a big fuss and stuff.'

'You'd enjoy that, wouldn't you?' Lucas agreed.

'Yeah. It'll be cool as,' grinned Danny.

'O.K. then. We'll stay at Nundooka tonight and I'll take you and your mum into Mitchell first thing tomorrow. We'll do the parade thing and get some photos. Your mum and I can do some shopping, and then about lunchtime, we can pick you up from school and head home early. How's that sound?'

Danny's day just got better and better!
'Sounds really good to me! Do you think mum will go along with it though?'

'Like I said before, you leave your mother to me.'
He paused for a while as Danny took it all in, and then added, 'We'll spend the rest of the week bringing the sheep home, just like your grandpa and I used to do.'

Danny was thrilled. Third place at the big Sports day with his mum and dad watching; now four or five days on the road, camping out at night and mustering sheep by day. He couldn't wish for anything more.

'Dad?'

'Yeah?' answered Lucas.

'This has been a terrific day, the best day in my whole life so far.'

'Yeah, it's been great hasn't it,' agreed Lucas.

'I just wish Poppy was here too.'

'I think he is Danny - If there is a heaven, then I'm sure he's sitting on a cloud looking down on us right now.'

'Do you believe all that stuff Dad, you know the stuff about heaven and clouds and angels and all that.'

'Well, to be honest Danny, I'm not a hundred percent sure, but it does sound good, don't you think?'

'Yeah, I can just imagine Poppy sitting on the edge of a cloud waving at us right now.'

Lucas pulled the vehicle to a halt by the side of the road and got out. Danny got out as well. Lucas looked at a band of big thunder-headed clouds building in the west and asked, 'which cloud do you think he's sitting on?'

Danny pointed skyward, 'That big white one there Dad, I think he's on that one.'

They both looked at the cloud he was pointing at, and then looked at each other and laughed.

The rest of the drive home to Nundooka was all about what they'd do together on the road. At one stage Danny remembered Jock and the crashed plane. He told his father the whole story, as he knew it, and then asked if he could ride off some time to look for it.

'I don't think it's around our district,' Lucas replied, 'I heard it was further north.'

'You never know. Mum said he could be down this way,' Danny replied eagerly, 'and they haven't found him where they've been looking, so he could be down here.'

Lucas couldn't see any harm in Danny doing a bit of searching, although he thought it would be futile. Danny was a good young horseman and he knew his way around in the bush,

'As long as you don't ride off too far, I suppose it'll be all right.'

'Thanks Dad,' he replied, looking over at his dad with a big smile on his face.

'No problems, Danny, no problems.'

By the time they got back to Nundooka, those big thunder-heads had turned black and were looking threatening indeed.

'Batten down the hatches Danny,' Lucas told him as he drove the vehicle into the shed, 'This looks like a bit of a blow coming through.'

CHAPTER SEVEN

The poet in the Bush

After leaving the chance encounter with the riverboat behind them, the Barlows pushed on for another week, until one day, just east of the Thoolabool Ranges, about half way between Bourke and Wilcannia, the men from Burton Downs came across a lone boundary rider.

Being a boundary rider out in those parts was about as lonely as it gets, and it would be fair to say that he was happy to see the drovers.

'Name's Bobby Bright, but me cobbers just call me Bandicoot, big nose an all. Do you mind if I ride a long for a while? Bit bleedin' lonely out here.'

Bandicoot sported the biggest moustache you would ever be likely to see. He also wore a huge brimmed battered old hat and rode on a big black mare that must have stood 17 hands tall and all that for a man who stood no more than about 5'4" tall.

'Good campsite ahead. I camped there last time out,' he told them in his husky voice, 'Tilpa Overflow, they call it, the coolest, clearest water for hundreds of miles, and good swimming hole too. A feast of great yabbies, big as wombats, just waiting to be caught. I'll show you the way.'

John was a little wary after what the riverboat captain had said. However he felt with the four of them, it should be safe enough, but just to be sure he asked Bandicoot a few questions about the district. A bushranger or cattle thief might have some knowledge of the area he worked in, but not as intimately as a boundary rider would. A boundary rider should know the land like the back of his hand.

'What say you're a bushranger trying to lead us into a trap?' John questioned half jokingly.

'No sir, I lived out this way for nine, no, maybe ten years gone. I know the land like it's my own. This is all part of the Kallara Station, that I work for.'

John looked at him leaning over the horn on his saddle, 'If you know the land so well, then tell me about the river. Tell me what's back up stream about 50 miles or so.'

Bandicoot gave John an almost perfect description of every bend in the river, every waterhole, every river crossing and every hill of note. He also told John where he should have taken the cattle to save time and energy.

'And what's ahead?' John asked.
Again Bandicoot prattled on about every hill and bend in the river for miles ahead. One thing for sure about him, he could certainly talk. Nevertheless John was just being careful, even though he was hugely impressed by the man.

'I'm John Barlow, from Burton Downs, nor-east of Mitchell, up Queensland way. These are my boys, Matthew and Charles, and this is Benny, from Bungunnia Station near St.George. Sorry about the questions, but you can't be too careful out here.'

'That's all right. I guess you have to be careful.'
Bandicoot continued, 'Bungunnia Station hey. Well tell me, how is old George Lamwith these days.'
Benny cut in immediately, 'You know George?'

'I worked there once for about a year. Let me see', he took off his battered old hat and wiped the sweat from his forehead with the sleeve of his shirt, and then replaced his hat on his head.

162

'Must be near on twelve years back. Year of seventy-two or maybe seventy-three it must have been. Wild country back then it was. We helped him to build a barn, then added another room to his old hut. From memory he was working on a dam when I left.'

He paused again briefly to swat some flies away from his face and then continued, 'Best cook in Australia is old Mabel. Best roast meals a man ever tasted. She still in good health?'

Benny replied, 'Sure is. Made of good stock that one. Mabel is me sister.'

'Good to hear, and how's old George. Tough man to work for, tough man.'

'George is fine too', Benny replied.

'How long you been working there then Benny?' Bandicoot continued.

About five years was the reply.

Benny felt an explanation was needed, 'I had a spread out near Ivanhoe, sheep and cattle, mainly sheep. Drought of Seventy-Eight hit me hard, it was the last straw. What grass the drought didn't kill, those flamin' rabbits ate, left nothing but dust. Break your heart it would. I went on the wallaby track for a while till George and Mabel gave me somewhere to settle again.'

The rest of the men listened intently and Benny continued.

'I only intended staying a year or so. Then about a year back, George said if I want to stay on, the property could be all mine when his time came to go to God. Being they have no kids and all, so long as I took care of Mabel. Well she's me sister isn't she, so that was an easy decision to make. I stayed.'

'I didn't know that Benny,' added Matthew, 'I thought you were just a station-hand there.'

'Well I guess I am now. The past don't matter for much anyways. And what of you Bandicoot, why did you leave?'

'No reason, sometimes you're just ready to move on. Well, truth have it, I didn't get on that well with George. He's a hard man to please. Not like Mabel though, she was always so humble. Took good care of me she did.'

'Where did you go to then? After you left George's place, I mean,' Matthew asked.

'Drifted around some, up and down the Darling, even got down as far as Melbourne once, but couldn't handle all the people and noise. Was heading up north again but needed a job and a feed and somehow ended up here.'

The men could have sat in the sun and talked forever. 'Where's this waterhole Bandicoot?' asked John. 'Perhaps we can talk more once we're there.'

They got the mob moving again and Bandicoot showed them the way to the campsite he'd spoken about. When they got there, it was almost a stampede for the water. The cattle wanted a drink and the men just wanted a cool dip in the refreshing waters. With that out of the way, John and Matthew settled the cattle down and set up camp for the night, Bandicoot showed Charles and Benny how to catch a feed of yabbies for supper. Not that Charles needed teaching; he had a hand for it already.

The men talked on, warmed by a blazing campfire and full to the brim with the fattest juiciest yabbies they'd ever tasted. They also sipped on copious mugs of black tea sweetened with bush honey and spiced up with a touch of rum. They felt like kings of the world. In the years to come, the tough times on the track would be washed away, but they'd remember good times like these.

Bandicoot told them about an artesian bore that had been drilled at Kallara.

'What's an artesian bore?' John asked.

'Underground water, so much you can hardly believe it. Shoots out of the ground some 20 feet into the air, almost boiling hot it is, like one of them fancy fountains down in Melbourne Town. The experts from over Sydney-way reckon there could be millions of gallons of water down there. Just got to find it and tap into it.'

'Millions of gallons?' queried Benny.

'Sounds hard to believe I know, way out here 'n all. You have to see such a thing to believe it. I'll take you to Kallara homestead if you want.'

'Is it far?' asked John.

'Two days down river, the bores a half days ride west of there. You can meet my boss man, and he'll take you down to the borehole himself. Proud as punch of the thing he is. Proud like it's a newborn son. Twenty feet into the air, never stops, just keeps on coming, such a wonder to see, it is.'

Hangovers, from the Irish coffee slowed their start the next morning.

Three days later the drovers were amazed to be standing near an artesian bore. Everything that Bandicoot had told them was true. Out in the middle of the driest continent on earth was a fountain of steamy hot water shooting 20 feet into the air. It had apparently been doing so for months and it was now believed that there was enough water down there to go on flowing for a hundred years or more.

The Kallara station-hands had dug away enough area to create a large dam, which was growing daily. The water on the outsides of the dam had cooled enough for animals and humans to drink from and after an invitation from the Kallara's owner;

John drove the cattle down to the water's edge.

They were told that experts from the Governments departments of many states had been to Kallara and most felt that much of inland Australia could have artesian water below its surface. If that was the case, the inland of Australia could well be relieved of the ravages of future droughts.

What early explorers had searched for, the great inland-sea, was in fact there all along. Not on the surface though, as they had first thought, but beneath the surface hidden from view. An ocean of life giving waters just waiting to be tapped and used. With new information and industrial knowledge, add some finance and hard work, it was felt that artesian bores could be drilled on properties throughout the outback.

Wealth came to some lucky ones who found gold, but John sensed that an even greater wealth could be achieved if they could tap into this underground ocean. The Barlows got as much information as they possibly could from the men at Kallara and after a lengthy hot bath in the bore, Bandicoot gave them directions back to the river.

The four left Kallara Station feeling like new men and with a new hope of what could be achieved with some persistence and luck in the outback. If they could find the life-giving water back in Queensland, their futures could be assured. They believed they had a good future in breeding cattle, but they needed water. If Burton Downs had no artesian water, they could search elsewhere and once it was found, make a new home by the bores. Mother Nature was fickle. Hoping for good seasonal rains was unpredictable and this was a better way for sure. This was the way to prosperity in the years ahead. This was the future for the outback.

They pushed on taking the mob down the route Bandicoot had laid out for them and it wasn't long before they reached their next milestone, the small inland river port of Wilcannia.

It had taken the men just five weeks to drive their cattle from St.George. They had made good time. They'd spent some enjoyable time with the paddle steamer captain and his crew, as well as the valuable detour Bandicoot had taken them to Kallara station and the artesian bore. Apart from that, it had been an almost uneventful journey through some rather unforgiving countryside.

John was content with the thought they had made the right decision, not only to move and sell the cattle before the drought took them, but more particularly with his decision to follow the Darling inland instead of more traditional stock routes to a market. They were over half way to Broken Hill and there had been no major problems thus far.

The weather had remained dry, although they did run into a couple of days where light rain had fallen. Well it had been more of a drizzle, than anything else. More importantly, they had gained valuable knowledge on a range of things, knowledge that would surely help them in the future.

The further south they went the more it looked like good rains had fallen recently. In the previous week or so, they had come across outcrops of fresh green grass for the cattle to pick on. Keeping the cattle fit and well fed was paramount to getting them through to Broken Hill in good condition. Solid, healthy cattle meant a good price when it came time to sell. Considering the length of the journey so far the cattle were still in pretty good shape.

The country they had been passing through was still

fairly flat, with most trees growing along the river. Inland was dry, red, dusty earth with the odd covering of low greyish saltbush, and the occasional stand of thin wiry trees here and there. Wildflowers were beginning to bloom in small clumps, sometimes in the most unlikely and forbidding places.

Nature presented herself to be full of surprises, especially out there in the Australian wilderness, and just when they thought they'd seen it all, she would show them something new. Wildflowers in the desert certainly fell into that category. The one flower they saw, albeit rarely, that they all agreed was the most spectacular, was a bright red pea-shaped flower with a black eye in its centre. This spectacular flower grew from a thin greyish green spindly looking shrub that grew close to the ground for protection. The contrast of the bright red and black flower against the pale colour of the shrub was brilliant at its best. The 'outback' was putting on quite a show for the four drovers the further south they travelled.

At Wilcannia, like at townships before, they left the cattle on the outskirts of town and spent the best part of the following day stocking up on provisions from the local traders, fresh and otherwise.

John had a chat to the others about hiring two extra men, for added security in this last and most dangerous section, from Wilcannia to Menindee Lakes, and then on to Broken Hill itself. They all agreed, so John discussed the idea with the local police constable. He knew of two men, that he was sure could be trusted. One was a cook named Alfred and the other Jimmy, a stockman. Both men were keen to get to Broken Hill. The constable also advised them to tell anyone who asked that they were going overland to Broken Hill, and not to tell anyone of their planned route, not a soul.

'The bush telegraph' he said, 'is notorious for getting information into the wrong hands. I'll notify the constable in Menindee and in Broken Hill of your route.'

'From here on' he added, 'be extremely vigilant, there are a number of known villains in the district and it seems like more are arriving each day. It's a long way to the 'Hill' and once you leave Wilcannia you're pretty much on your own.'

The constable continued as John listened intently, 'Tell anyone who asks that you're heading along the river to Culpaulin, then due west to Wilsons Well, Worungil Tank, then on to Little Topar. They'll believe that, it's the shortest route to Broken Hill, the one used by most on horseback. It's on that track that we're having nearly all of our problems. The Menindee route is longer, but there are more properties along the river, safer if you stay near settlements. I'll give you directions to the stations, and if you check in with them, we'll know where you are and that you're travelling safe.'

With a crack of their whips, the men got the cattle heading south towards Culpaulin. There, instead of turning west, they kept going south towards Bililla Station, then made their way through Burraroo, Viewmont and Windale stations, and eventually to the small township of Menindee. Apart from the odd station stockmen occasionally seen in the distance, not another soul did they see.

The men had learnt well the skills of droving in the months since they had left Queensland. Now, after months on the 'the wallaby track', they were on time to get to Broken Hill, and then to beat the summer heat home again. More importantly, from a business point of view, the cattle were in reasonably good condition. In fact, they were in better shape than when they were back on Burton Downs. They'd expected some kind of trouble along the way, but so far they'd had none. It was a little unnerving though, almost as if it was too good to be true. It all seemed too easy, and John felt edgy. He remained vigilant.

The township of Menindee is situated near the banks of Lake Menindee, the largest of a series of inland fresh water lakes that were filled every few years by the northern rains. The town consisted of a few traders and a pub, always a pub, along a small dusty street. There were a number of small dwellings either side of the businesses, beyond that was a small church and the local police constable's house, which doubled as a police station. Out the back was a small lock-up with a rusty iron door that didn't look like it had been used that often, an encouraging sign indeed, John thought.

A little south of the township, the Darling River, when in flood, would break it's banks and spill into the flood plains and forming into Lake Menindee, Lake Cawndilla, Kangaroo Lake, and eventually into Lake Tandou. The Darling continued on southward from there, until eventually flowing into the majestic Murray River. The overflow waters of the lakes system remained to become a haven for animal and bird life. There had been times during the great drought of the 1870's, when the lakes had almost dried up. Only small pools of water had remained. The once wet, muddy banks, left dried and cracked. Governments had already discussed plans about one-day in the future damming the lakes and thus being able to control the flow of waters into and out of the system better. If the dream were to be fulfilled, generations to come would never again want for fresh water.

Before they had set out, young Will, whilst gathering the information for his famous 'barn wall map, had shown a keen interest in history. So after the first brush with the new bridge and the history of Mitchell, Matthew had been writing a journal of sorts. Each place he travelled through, he made it his hobby to document as much of the local historical facts as time allowed. If nothing else, he knew that when they got back to Burton Downs, young Will, and probably the rest of the family, would enjoy listening to Matthew's history journal.

Tiny Menindee was strong on natural history, and with some vision, Matthew noted that one-day big things were possible for the area. Gold finds always petered out, but if something could be done to keep the water in those lakes, they would prove more value in time than any gold rush could. He believed that in the future, Menindee would harbour a large flourishing community. Perhaps this could become the inland-sea that early explorers believed existed in inland Australia.

The drovers meanwhile had followed the river and as much as possible kept away from the tracks, stopping only for a few hours at each of the stations. The going was easy over flat, open ground. The cold westerly's of August were easing off, and they knew that the warmer spring wasn't far away. The trouble was with spring moving in on them, they knew that the summer's heat wasn't far away either. Western New South Wales was not a place they wanted to be in the summer heat, so they pushed on, their goal now truly in sight. Also the days were longer now, which allowed them more time to forge ahead.

John checked in with the local Menindee police constable and got as much information as he could. Within hours they were again heading south. The word they deliberately spread around town was that they were moving the mob down the Darling, all the way to Wentworth and to the Victorian markets.

Five miles out they turned due west and crossed a small creek that connected Menindee Lake with Lake Cawndilla. Out of sight, they stayed on the western banks of Lake Cawndilla, fattening the cattle on the lush green pick that surrounded the lake. They knew of two watering holes between Menindee and Stephens Creek, so their plan was to head for each of the known waterholes, rest a day and then push on again. Time was still their biggest enemy. They also knew that around the waterholes they were most vulnerable to attack. So the time spent there, although essential to the health of the cattle, was also a potential problem. After three days at Lake Cawndilla, they headed out.

This was the final part of their journey and potentially was going to be the most hazardous. This was where finally they would leave the Darling behind and set out over true desert country. Mile after mile of stony desert flats, with the occasional covering of grey saltbush. This was unforgiving, harsh, tough, uncompromising land.

They were aware that they would have to carry extra water for themselves, so they had quietly purchased three extra horses back at Wilcannia. At the lakes the spare horses had been loaded to the hilt with water bags. For the first time on their long journey, they could no longer rely on river water to sustain them. For the first time on their journey, John was hoping to see rain clouds overhead. Good rain could not only provide additional drinking water, but also help settle dust kicked up by the moving cattle mob.

The police constable back at Wilcannia, had advised them to keep away from the known tracks wherever possible, it would be harder going but safer in the long run.
He also said that another danger could be the dust in the region. In such dry conditions, their cattle would throw a large cloud of the reddish bulldust into the air. Such a cloud could be seen for miles, alerting any would-be bushrangers or cattle duffers of their whereabouts.

They decided, on the advice given to them by police that they would travel in short stages during the day. They'd push them for a number of hours, then take a few hours break, then a shorter push during the middle of the day and then again a few hours before dusk. That way the clouds of dust could be mistaken for small dust storms, or 'willy-willies' as they were known out there, rather than if they drove the herd all day. The constable had told them of a couple of horse dealers who had taken the same route, using the same tactics, just a few months earlier, and he'd heard down the track that they got through without any mishaps.

Having to stop a moving herd three times a day would not be an easy task, but they would heed the local policeman's advice, after all, he should know best. This was his country.

If they went due west from Lake Cawndilla they would eventually pick up the mainly dry, Stephens Creek. That would lead them close to Broken Hill. They had been told the tracks closer to Broken Hill were where most of the robberies had taken place. Apparently some travelers, who had set out from Wilcannia or Menindee, were never seen or heard of again.

At least with a cook on the team now, they would have time for a couple of pretty good meals each day. The boys predicted that the Menindee to Broken Hill push, would take them around 3 weeks, and it wasn't long before they all settled into their new routine.

They would sleep light each night and each morning they would rise before first light and set off straight away. They would push the mob hard in the cool mornings and then would stop around 9ish for a couple of hours and tuck into a fully cooked meal. Around 11am they would set out again for about 3 hours. Another break and then the final run at about 4pm when they'd push on until the sun sank over the western horizon. On moonlit nights they could even push on for a few hours more. No time for tents now, it was just a raging campfire, an easy feed and a sleep under the stars.

The inland desert sunsets were truly spectacular and would light the skies and horizon until as late as seven o'clock some evenings. The beautiful dull light of dusk seemed to last forever out there in the outback. Early mornings and late afternoons were undoubtedly the best time of the day to travel. It was much cooler, and the cloud of dust rising behind them was not as noticeable in the dim light.

The Wandering Writer

One night, about ten days out from Menindee, the men were camped near the base of a small hill that rose about one hundred feet from the dusty desert floor. They camped on the eastern side of the hill to protect themselves from the cool evening winds that sometimes sprang up unannounced. Matthew had been looking after the cattle on the first watch, when he heard a noise somewhere off in the distance. He quietly rode back into camp, woke his father with the news that he was sure he'd heard a horse neighing out to the north of them. He was west of their camp at the time and was sure the neighing hadn't been from one of their horses. It was always a possibility that the desert was playing tricks on his hearing, perhaps the sound had bounced off the little hill, giving a false idea of the direction, but he didn't think so. He was certain the noise he'd heard had come from a northerly direction, away from the campsite.

John quietly woke the others. A quick count was made of their own tethered horses to make sure one hadn't got free and wondered off. They were all there. A sudden fear rushed through the camp. Who or what was it?

Immediately some thought the worst. Perhaps it was bushrangers who had seen the dust trail and were closing in for the kill. Perhaps they were sneaking in under the cover of darkness with intentions of surprising them in their sleep. Perhaps it was an illusion or just a wild brumby. They had seen camels out there, left to turn feral, or perhaps, this was just a horse left to fend alone out there.

They quickly put out the campfire and a tense night followed when no one slept a wink. They sat together in the cold darkness, wondering, worrying, and straining their ears for any hint of a sound, be it human or otherwise. They took it in turns of sitting atop the small hill, hoping for an early warning, should trouble come calling.

It was a long night that eventually gave way to light on the eastern horizon. With the growing eastern light, the desert slowly took on a familiar appearance. Firstly trees were silhouetted in the distance. Then their shapes became clearer, more defined, colours reappeared in the form of leaves and bark. Then animals and birds were becoming visible, starting to go about their own morning routines. The sky slowly changed colours as the sun looked to jump into the sky from where ever it goes at night. At least now they could see if there were any dangers in the near vicinity, instead of relying solely on their hearing.

They were quietly discussing sending a party to scout to the north, when they heard the sound of a horse in the distance. This time it was clear. All ears strained trying to locate its position, but all was silent again.

'Could anyone work out where it came from?' asked John, taking on the role of a general with his troops.

Benny shook his head in the negative, but replied in the

positive, 'North, I think, a couple of miles off maybe.'

'Just one horse?' asked John.

Matthew joined the debate, 'Just one. I'm sure.'

'Maybe a lone traveler,' Charles added.

'Let's hope so,' added John, trying to sound cool and calm.

The men stared at the northern horizon and tried mentally to ready themselves for any approaching danger.

John interrupted the moment of silence in a whisper, 'Matt.'

'Yeah,' he whispered back.

'You, me, and Benny, we'll ride out, the rest can stay here and look after the cattle. No one do anything stupid, stay calm and alert,' ordered John.

In the meantime, Charles had walked up the small hill that had been their comfort during the night, to look out over the surrounding desert. Suddenly, a man appeared from behind some trees, about a mile and a half to the north-east, and riding slowly towards their camp.

Charles ran part of the way back down the hill, then squatted down, cupped his hands around his mouth, and called to those below somewhat cautiously, 'I see him.'

'Where?' asked Matt, looking up at Charles crouching on higher ground.

'Nor-east, about a mile or two,' replied Charles, pointing in that direction,

'How many?'

'Just the one, I think,' a slight pause, 'well that's all I can see.'

'Did he see you?'

'Don't think so.'

There were a few moments of quiet while John thought about

what they should do. Then he looked towards Charles, 'Go check if there's still just the one rider?'

Charles scrambled back up the rise and peered carefully over the top.

He looked back towards the camp and raised one finger to the sky.

'What should we do,' asked Matthew, looking to his father for guidance.

'Play it safe, Matt. Let's take no chances.'

John called to Charles, 'Wave him in.'

He paused again for a moment, still trying to think out the situation, and then spoke to Matthew.

'You and Benny cover our backs, just in case it's a trap of some kind. I'll meet the rider with Charles.'

John reached for his rifle, which he kept stored in a sheath on the side of his saddlebag, and checked to see if it was loaded. Benny looked over anxiously when he heard the noise of the gun being readied.

John knew there was no way of knowing if other riders were hiding in nearby bush, waiting to attack when their guard was lowered. He handed the gun to Matthew and pointed towards some low bushes just south of the campsite.

'Stay hidden over there. Benny, you go with him and watch our backs. Matt, you make sure to cover us with the rifle I'll call you back in when I think it's safe. Take a water bottle with you. You could be there for a while.

Benny grabbed his water bottle from over his saddle and the two headed towards a small clump of bushes. John, still concerned about the situation, called out to them again, 'Remember, stay under cover, until I give you the all clear. Better be safe than sorry.'

Matthew knew exactly what his father was asking him

and Benny to do, and so they set about finding a hiding spot from where they could watch the campsite from most directions.

John took a revolver from his saddlebag and stuck it in the belt of his pants. He then turned to the two men who'd joined them in Wilcannia, 'If this turns bad, you two get the hell out of here. I don't expect you to stand and fight with us. These aren't your cattle.'

With that, he walked two horses up to where Charles was watching the incoming rider.

'He doesn't look too good, Father, he's crouching over in his saddle. He might be sick or injured or something.'

'Be alert Charles,' said John, as he joined him on the side of the hill, 'It could be a trick. Let's be careful here.'

The rider approached slowly, looking up but still crouching over his horse slightly. When he was within calling distance, he leaned back in the saddle, stopped his horse, and called out to John and Charles on the hill, 'Sorry to trouble you chaps', he said in a prim and proper English voice, 'but I could use some help here.'

'Are you alone?'

The rider nodded, 'Yes Sir, I most certainly am.' He continued, 'I was cruelly robbed, Sir, some twenty or so miles back down the track, by some villainous highwaymen. As I said, can I trouble you for some aid?'

John asked the rider to come in slowly, and as he got closer to them, it became obvious from the blood around his face, that he was injured.

'He looks bad Father, his face I mean.'

'Yes he does, but we stay on our guard just the same.'

John and Charles rode out to meet him and Charles helped to hold him upright in his saddle, as they brought him into camp. The other men then helped him down from his horse and sat him down under a small tree.

'Tea and damper is all we can offer at the moment.'

'Tea sounds wonderful. Thank you kind sirs. Could a weary traveler trouble you for a shot of whisky in it also, if you could so manage?'

'I think we can manage that, for medicinal purposes of course.'

'Precisely sir, you read my mind.'

One of the men lit a campfire and when it was blazing away, threw on the billy. The cook mixed up a quick damper and threw it in a camp-oven, enough for an early breakfast.

Charles tended to the stranger, wiping the blood away from his face, and cleaning his wounds with some of the whisky.

With the blood wiped away and it obvious they were real wounds, John asked him his name.

'Richard Fairclough, sir, from Bristol, England, on a journey to see the world.'

'State your business out here, Mr. Fairclough?'

'Richard, please. I am a writer, in search of stories of adventure and life, for the purpose of writing my next novel.'

Benny joined in, 'Seems like you've found a story or two to write about then.'

'Indeed I have. I hadn't intended to live them quite as vividly as I have though. It's a touch wilder out here than I had wished for.'

'So, Richard, how did you get those injuries. What happened?' John inquired.

So while the billy boiled and the damper cooked over the fire, Richard Fairclough, writer, and obvious storyteller of Bristol, England, began to tell his own real life tale.

He had been visiting the newly booming mining town of

Broken Hill, in search of characters for his book, when he decided it was time to head back to the civilised world in Sydney Town. He went on to say he was bailed up and robbed by a group of undesirables, three in all, about 25 miles along the track to Wilcannia. He said he had been warned about travelling alone, but he was an adventurer, a novelist in search of a good story. He needed to travel alone, to feel the spirit of the land, as he put it.

The 'undesirables' had taken his money belt and all his provisions, but he had somehow talked them into leaving him with his old nag of a horse, and a small amount of water. The man was a very good talker, a good storyteller and quite the charmer. He even asked the bandits if he could include them in the wonderful tale he was going to write when he got back to Sydney Town.

He was perhaps a touch naive, but indeed not a stupid man. He well knew he'd been extremely lucky they hadn't killed him, let alone leave him with his horse and water, so he decided to return to Broken Hill and report the incident to the local police. He knew their next victim might not be as lucky as he was.

Over a cup of black hot billy tea he continued with his story. He explained that he'd had a small amount of money hidden in the stitching around the edges of his horse's saddle blanket. Had the thieves taken his old nag he would have been penniless, but luck had been on his side that day, he was alive and armed with a real life adventure to write about.

The police in Broken Hill told him there was very little they could do, but added that they would send a patrol into that region in the next week or so. They also said that he was a very fortunate man to have run into robbers who weren't intent on killing their victim. The only reports they had received back in

'The Hill' over the previous few months, was that of dead bodies rotting out there on the track.

Lucky indeed, but the adventures of Richard Fairclough of Bristol, weren't over with.

They say lightning never strikes twice in the same place, and if you follow that theory, he would be safe to continue the journey the same way he had before. With that thought in his head, he purchased more provisions with the little cash he had hidden and set out for Wilcannia again. He hadn't travelled far, when he thought twice about the proverb. If the bushrangers were doing well in that area, how silly would it be for him to ride straight back into them? He decided to take a different route, this time, he would follow Stephens Creek to the Lakes and then he would wait in Menindee for the next paddle steamer heading north and get passage on it to Bourke. If there were no northbound steamers available, then he would follow the river south to Wentworth, then take passage on a riverboat heading east along the Murray River and eventually make his way back overland from there to Sydney.

However, Richard Fairclough still had bad luck sitting firmly on his shoulders. Two days out from Broken Hill, along the Stephens Creek, he was bailed up again. This time there were two robbers, and they weren't at all impressed with the little amount of food and money that he was carrying, not to mention the tale of woe he offered or the story of him being a writer. This time his charming manner fell on deaf ears.

He sensed that he was in grave danger, so he decided his best chance was to make a run for it. His horse wasn't young or particularly fit, but he looked in better shape than the 'bag of bones' the robbers were riding. He thought he had a fair chance of outriding them. He took a tight grip on the reins and dug his heels into his horse's girth and rode straight at the bushrangers waving his hands in the air, screaming like a wild banshee.

The robbers, and more particularly their horses, were caught by surprise at his sudden action, and both of the horses reared into the air on their hind legs, throwing their riders to the ground. Then, after a few moments, in which they regained their mounts and composure, the scruffy looking bushrangers set out after him. Because of his quick action, Richard Fairclough of Bristol, England, was now a half a mile or so out in front of them, and leaving a cloud of dust behind him.

After a fairly short chase, where he thought they were slowly getting the better of his old nag, he spotted some hilly terrain. He knew that the only chance of escaping with his life was to get into the hills and somehow lose them up there. Down on the open plains, there was simply nowhere to hide, and he didn't know how long the old nag would run before it would probably drop down dead beneath him. He rode into the hills.

He paused in his storytelling for a moment. He was feeling light headed and dizzy, so John leaned over and topped up his mug. Richard sipped on the hot tea laced with whisky, or more to the point hot whisky laced with tea, and regained his composure. Then in his own time he continued with his story.

The next thing he remembered was waking up in darkness. He was lying prostrate on the ground with plenty of aches and pains, and a very, very sore head. He crawled under a rocky ledge in a small gully and hid there for the rest of that night and half way into the next day, too scared to come out into the open. Suddenly, he noticed his horse walking back down the gully towards him as if nothing had happened at all. Not sure whether it was the robbers setting a trap for him, hoping he would come out of hiding to grab the horse, so he lay still and quiet for a while longer, trying to work out what to do next when the horse made that decision for him. It walked straight up to where he was lying and just stood there looking at him, as if to say, 'Well, what are we waiting for. Let's get out of here.'

Let's go indeed, he thought, and with that, he took the horse by the reins and very quietly walked out of that gully forever.

By this time, he had every one of the drovers hanging on his every word, for not only was he a writer of some note, if you could believe him, he was truly, a darn good storyteller. Everyone, that is except for Matthew and Benny, who were still off in the distance hiding uncomfortably behind a clump of bushes. They were still waiting on a signal from John to tell them all was well. Finally, after an hour or so, he signaled to them to come in. He introduced the boys to Richard and quickly told them the story thus far.

Richard Fairclough then continued with his amazing story.

After he had escaped from the gully, he rode for most of the next day, not sure which way he was going or where he was. He was quite lost when he saw a cloud of dust in the distance. He thought that it was probably a stagecoach and decided to head in that direction. He hoped that humans would be somehow connected with the dust trail and that should mean safety again. Well at least he hoped it did. He didn't believe he could be that unlucky a third time.

After riding in the direction of the dust cloud for a few more hours, it suddenly stopped and he again felt cautious. He decided to keep heading in that direction and a little later to his joy he saw a dust cloud rising above the plains. Then, just before night set in, he could just make out that the dust was being whipped up by a mob of cattle. Finally, he thought, he had made the right decision and he would try and seek refuge there. Slowly, and very carefully, in the failing light, he rode on. Then suddenly, shining in the distance like a beacon in the darkness, was a large campfire. The ground was slightly hilly and as he rode on, the campfire would rise into view at the top of the small hills and then disappear again as he rode down into the gullies. Then suddenly, when he reached the top of the next hill, the welcoming glow was gone for good this time. He searched for it with a somewhat sinking feeling. Again he felt terribly lost and alone, but he thought the best thing to do was to wait until first light. He knew he was close and in the morning light he was sure he would be able to find the cattle. He bedded down for the night, safe in the knowledge that just over the next few hills, lay the hope of safety.

Richard apologised to the drovers when he was told how he had unintentionally frightened them out of their previous night's sleep. He added though, that the very closeness of his presence, which had brought them such a restless night, had in fact allowed him to sleep like a baby all night long.

'It will make a wonderful tale for one of my books. Don't you think?' he asked, as chunks of the freshly baked damper dipped in bush honey were passed around.

After listening for a while, John was convinced that Richard Fairclough's story was factual enough. The writer in him had probably glorified the events somewhat, but John knew that he posed no danger to them or their mob of cattle

John told him they were heading for Broken Hill and over the remaining damper he invited Richard Fairclough, writer and storyteller of Bristol, England, to join them if he so wished. He could pay his way by helping with the mob by day and perhaps entertaining them at night with some of his stories and writings. He may have been heading for Sydney, but the best John and the boys could offer at this stage, was safe passage back to Broken Hill. He would have to decide what to do from there, perhaps, John suggested, he could ride out to Bourke with them after the cattle had been sold.

Although he was not keen on returning to Broken Hill, it was the best offer he'd had in weeks. He accepted graciously, and for the third time in less than a month, Richard Fairclough was heading back to Broken Hill.

Around noon, they again headed out in a west-north-westerly direction, and pushed on until dark, trying to make up for time lost that morning.

A few days later they reached the banks of the dry creek-bed known locally as Stephens Creek. From there, they would set out on the last and most perilous part of their epic journey. They knew that Stephens Creek would lead them straight towards Broken Hill, but it would also take them ever closer to danger. The thieves and bushrangers that preyed on travelers in and out of the rich diggings like vultures and crows over a dead or dying carcass, abounded in such areas.

From here on in, it was decided that they put an extra man on watch each night, an outrider just to be on the safe side. If Richard Fairclough had been bailed up by two different bands of villains near Broken Hill, then they should not take the last part of their journey too lightly.

One day as they followed the Stephens Creek northward, they noticed storm clouds in the north-west sky. It was hard to tell just where the storms were likely to pass, but John felt it best to settle the cattle down anyway. A thunderous storm could easily spook the mob and the last thing they wanted now was a 'rush'. (The drover's term for a stampede)

They set up tents that night for the first time in a long while, in anticipation of a wet night ahead. They lit their campfires just above the banks of the dry creek bed and settled the cattle down for the night. As darkness fell they could see the storm lighting the sky more clearly. The worst of the storm appeared to be passing over a range of hills much further north of their campsite, but they knew they could still expect to get some rain.

That night, out there in the total darkness of the outback, the lightning forked relentlessly across the night sky, putting on a spectacular show.

Every available man was out on horseback trying to keep the cattle close together and as quiet, and as calm as they could possibly keep them. The storm began to drift more their way, and the lightning got brighter and the thunder grew louder, as the storm moved closer. The men worked hard to keep the mob bunched up, terrified that a rush was imminent and they themselves could get caught under the thundering hooves of more than a hundred terrified cattle.

About two hours after dark, the storm hit them in earnest with strong winds, lightning, thunder and a huge downpour of rain. It reminded the Barlows of the type of summer storms they used to get back in Queensland. It only lasted about 20 minutes, before it passed over and headed east towards Menindee, leaving them with another spectacular lightning show after it passed. The back view of a summer storm sometimes holds more appeal than the onset. Perhaps it is just that it can be enjoyed more, knowing the danger has passed.

Back at camp the wind had torn at their tent flaps leaving everything, including their bedding, well and truly drenched. They knew they were in for another uncomfortable night without much sleep. At least, they were comforted in the knowledge that the mob had stayed quiet and they had not been caught up in a stampede. If that had happened, they knew they would have spent the next few days searching for the scattered cattle.

With the storm passed and the mob quiet, the men set about tidying up the camp. They built a large bonfire in the creek bed, around which they hung their wet clothes and bedding, in the hope that they could dry them out enough to get some useful sleep later that night.

By about midnight, many hours after the storm had passed, its glow barely visible away to the east, the men finally settled down to some much-needed sleep on the creek bank. They left the huge campfire blazing in the middle of the creek-bed.

Benny and Richard Fairclough were watching over the cattle, when they heard a rumbling noise coming from the north, from the direction of the small ranges. Within a few minutes, the noise had grown much louder and they were growing more and more concerned about it. Neither man knew just what was causing the roar, but it was obviously getting closer. They decided to wake the others.

Richard headed into camp to alert the others, while Benny rode up along the creek bed to see if he could see what was causing the noise. Once awake, the drovers stood by the banks of the dry creek, in the glow of the crackling bonfire, totally bewildered as to the nature of the noise.

Suddenly Benny raced out of the darkness, 'Get outa the creek! Get away from the creek!' They didn't have to be told twice, the tone in Benny's voice was enough to send a cold chill through them. 'Water! bloody mountains of water coming our way fast. Get out, get out.'

They scrambled up and back from the creek bank and watched as Benny rode out of the darkness followed closely by a mass of water perhaps five or six feet high. He suddenly pulled his horse out of the creek bed and up the bank as the wall of water raced passed them all, sweeping away everything in its path.

Within a few minutes, the bone-dry creek bed was replaced with a raging river, by now about ten feet deep, that sounded like an earthquake as it rumbled passed them ripping and tearing at everything in its way.

'Secure the horses,' John yelled over the roar.

Charles grabbed the horses and led them back a safe distance and secured them to trees. The others tried also to grab whatever they could and pulled it back from the edge. The raging water rose that high that it began to spill over the top of the creek and sweep away whatever the men couldn't carry from their campsite.

Stephens Creek, only minutes before had been totally dry, was now a devastating torrent that lasted for about fifteen minutes. Then it started to slowly recede, until eventually it settled down, leaving only a gentle flowing stream, a few yards wide and a few feet deep.

There wasn't much they could do in the darkness. The cattle were all over the place and most of the provisions, utensils, and camping gear, were somewhere down stream in that raging torrent. Eventually they realised there was very little they could do in the darkness, so they settled down again for the night, this time about a quarter of a mile inland from the creek bed. They slept using saddles as pillows and saddle blankets covering them in a vain bid to keep warm in their wet clothes. It was to be a very long, cold and wet night with very little sleep.

As dawn brought light and eventually some warmth to the area, it exposed the amount of damage that had been done a few hours earlier. The water had almost stopped running but the creek bed itself was now somewhat deeper and wider than when they last saw it in the light of the day before. The watery torrent had left debris lying on the creek bed as well as wrapped around tree trunks lining the banks.

Where they'd left their gear the night before to dry out by the fire, was now covered with three large and somewhat broken gum trees. Those magnificent gums hadn't survived the onslaught of the rushing water and had fallen into the creek and been left covered in debris. Included in the debris were the carcasses of a number of animals that hadn't been as lucky as the men had.

'Wild night,' said Richard, in a laconic way, 'Exactly what do you suppose brought that on us?'
The men looked around at each other, wondering who would be first to offer an opinion.

'Some sort of dam burst,' replied Benny. 'I reckon a build-up of water from the storm got held up by a dam of some sorts somewhere. Perhaps fallen trees in the creek bed, making a sort of dam. Water backed up until the dam gave way and before you know it, you're looking at a wall of water roaring at you. Saw it once before, down Ivanhoe way. Scary business, if it's coming your way.'

It had indeed been a fearsome sight, and frightening to think that if Benny hadn't warned them, some of them may have been caught up in that torrent and died right there in the middle of no-where, along with those poor unfortunate animals. They were lucky to have escaped unscathed.

The Barlow boys headed out early to look for the cattle, and were very happy to find them quietly grazing together about a mile from the creek campsite. Again they were lucky, the cattle could have scattered for miles in all directions, but after being on the road for so long, they just stuck together in a mob.

It was hard to tell if all the cattle were there, so John decided to leave them for the moment, quietly grazing. They could do some sort of a head count later. With the cattle safe, the men went on a search to try and recover the remains of their camping gear and personal belongings. Matthew stayed by the mob while most of the others rode down-stream to see what they could recover.

Their ride along the creek bank revealed that a number of cattle had been lost to the raging waters. They must have gone down into the creek bed during the night and been swept away when the wall of water hit. A number of carcasses were found lying grotesquely tangled amongst the debris and fallen trees, and there was no way of knowing how many others might have been wash further downstream in that fast rushing water. It would be difficult to do an exact head count out there, they might not find out how many cattle had been lost until they got to Broken Hill.

Over the next few hours they found a few strays wandering around aimlessly, so the rest of the day was spent looking for more.

Eventually ten cattle carcasses were found in all, along with a number of dead native animals. Nearly all their provisions had been lost, except for the odd item they found along the creek bed. That included a few pots and pans, and a couple of very wet blankets they had laid out by the bonfire to dry earlier.

To their amazement, one of the blankets they found hanging in the branch of a small tree didn't appear to be one of theirs. No-one recognised it, and they could only hope that it had been left in the creek-bed at some other time, by some other traveler. The alternative to that scenario was that someone else might be camping nearby. Perhaps bushrangers or cattle duffers lurking nearby watching, and waiting for what they see as the right moment to pounce. Even some poor unfortunate traveler might have been asleep in the creek bed somewhere and the torrent had caught him unawares.

It was decided immediately that two armed men should proceed north up the creek for a way carefully checking things out. The blanket could quite simply been left behind by others, or it could be from another camp further upstream. The flood may have surprised them also, and those people may be in trouble and need assistance. One way or the other it needed to be checked out.

Charles and Benny were picked and rode of along the creek bank northward with instructions to take no chances. Do not approach any strangers, until they were sure it was safe to do so.

The two men didn't return that night which led to concerns about their safety. Another dilemma rose, would they now send out another party to look for them, or wait and see what the morning brought forth. To everyone's relief, early that morning, the two rode boldly back into camp. They reported that they had seen and found nothing, and decided to sleep a few miles upstream from the main camp to keep an eye and an ear out for any nighttime movement.

It seemed to them like the closer they all got to Broken Hill, the more dramas they encountered. The bulk of their journey south from Queensland had been quite uneventful, but now as they neared their goal, every day seemed to produce another problem. With still about a week's droving before they reached Broken Hill and having lost nearly all of their food supply to the raging waters, John knew they would have to live off the land as much as possible. They carved up one of the dead cows and ate well for a day or so, but in the outback heat, fresh meat went bad rapidly. It was case of eat it or leave it.

Charles got quite adventurous and tried to make some

beef jerky by laying small strips of beef in the sun, but found it only a beacon for every fly in the vicinity. The beef jerky idea died very quickly when the fly infested meat very quickly revealed a healthy batch of wriggling maggots. In reality, the maggots may have been nutritional, but the thought never entered his head, a maggot was a maggot, and certainly not a culinary delight

In the days remaining, until they reached Broken Hill, they would hunt for kangaroos, wombats, goannas, or whatever wandered unsuspectingly into their path. If all else failed they still had more than two hundred head or cattle to keep them from dying of hunger. Fresh water was not a problem, even though most of the raging torrent had gone, the creek now contained many pools of fresh, albeit muddy, water. All their salt and spices had been lost along with their small supplies of dried vegetables, so from here on in, it would be cooked meat with no extra trimmings.

It was pleasing though to think that they were only about seven days from their destination, it would have been far more unpleasant if they had lost their supplies earlier in their journey. The thought of weeks and weeks of 'roughing it' would not have been good for morale.

The next seven days passed quietly and without any major incident, until finally late one morning, Broken Hill lay just ten or so miles ahead of them. John sent Matthew in to make contact with the local Police to let them know they were just outside town. He was to inform them that they expected to be in town within the next 24 hours, and he was also to arrange for a holding yard for the cattle.

Late that afternoon he arrived back, with the news that Broken Hill was only about a half a days ride ahead. They would have to leave Stephens Creek and head due west for the last eight or so miles. Matthew arranged to be met by five or six riders to help them get the mob into a holding yard used previously for horses. The yard was on the southern outskirts of town.

The drovers stopped that night, for the last time on the banks of Stephens Creek and at first light the next morning stirred the cattle and headed west. They met the escort of stockmen as arranged and by mid-afternoon the cattle were safely penned up.

The Barlows, along with Benny, rode into 'The Hill' proud men that day. The two from Wilcannia and Richard Fairclough rode in as somewhat relieved men to have arrived safely. After just under 19 weeks travelling overland, they had finally arrived at their destination safe and well, and with over 200 head of cattle still in pretty good condition. They'd done it, and in doing so saved Burton Downs from going under.

CHAPTER EIGHT

Jock's continuing battle
South Western Queensland.
6a.m, Wednesday March 20th. 1994

This was the seventh day since his plane had gone down in that storm and he thought to himself that all things considered, he'd done well. The night times were the hardest, but he had survived seven long dark ones so far, and he hoped the worst was over. He knew he could cope with his situation, if he had to, for a while longer yet. His leg was a problem and he was still putting up with a fair amount of pain, especially at night, but as each day and night passed, so the pain was slowly easing. His injuries were still too severe to think of trying to walk out of there. Besides, he still had no idea where he was. To leave the wreckage might lead him into more trouble and further away from help, instead of towards it. His broken leg would be too painful to put much strain on it, but then the longer he stayed, the greater the chance of a serious infection setting in to his wounds. He had to stay with the wreckage for a while longer. He knew at that stage he still had to rely on others finding him.

Away to his north was that peculiar 'red hill'. It still represented his best hope of discovery. It was the only bright colour on an otherwise drab landscape and he looked at it often. He estimated that it was about one and a half kilometres away, but he still wasn't sure what it was. Between him and that red hill, was a flat, scrubby area with a small hill rising from the plains. Beyond that was another hill and it was on that higher hill that Jock could see the blaze of red colour.

Red Oxide can make the earth look a reddish colour. He'd seen red oxide country from the air before, but that was more of a dullish, dirty coloured reddish brown. This was a brighter colour, more like some kind of wild flowers. He would have loved to just get up and walk over and see what it was up close, but he knew his leg needed more time to heal. The hill now occupied his mind more often. One day he'd get over there but for now it was a case of surviving, the hill would have to wait.

Jock knew that Mary would search for him forever if she had to. So he knew if he kept himself alive, sooner or later someone would find him. She was his big hope, and he believed in her totally. He knew that without a dead body to prove his death, Mary would not lose hope and faith. He would be the same, if something had happened to her.

'Stay alive!' he kept telling himself, 'Stay hopeful and stay alive! She'll find me.'
He knew that he had to remain focused on the mission before him. Everything he did must be for that purpose and that purpose only, to stay alive until they found him. He also believed that luck was still on his side, that it hadn't deserted him just yet. After all, he had survived a plane crash. He'd made a bad decision by flying off course, and he had paid a price for that error in judgment, but luck had put him safely on the ground when most others would have perhaps died in a firey crash.

He needed to believe that the Mayday call had been picked up. Even if his message didn't get out they would still be searching for his missing plane. But where were they? Quite obviously they were looking in the wrong areas. But he believed that every day they looked elsewhere, brought them closer to the day when they'd be searching his area. He had to be ready. He had to stay vigilant for any sound.

During the first few days as Jock had laid there waiting for help to arrive, he had pieced together what he thought had happened and how he had been lucky enough to survive the crash. His recollections were that the plane had lost altitude fast. He slowed the plane's air speed before it hit the ground. A fast impact would have probably killed him outright. The only way to slow his descent was to raise the nose of the plane, point it back up into the wind, and let the wind and the upward motion slow down his speed. The risk was that he might have stalled the plane, and would literally fall out of the sky. Another problem that faced him was in the darkness, he hadn't known exactly where the ground was and he didn't want to hit the ground tail first. If that had happened, the tail would have ripped off on impact, and the front of the plane would surely have flipped over and over and he'd never survive that type of impact.

His best chance was to hit the ground evenly. Just like a normal landing, only with the wheels still up. Then the plane's fuselage would skid across the surface, slowing it down, until eventually, the plane would have pulled up safely. The theory was to land safely in complete darkness, in pouring rain, on flat ground, with no trees or large rocks in his way. The reality was that he didn't see anything in front or below him and had absolutely no idea of what he was about to land on. He could have slammed straight into the side of a hill or a great big gum tree.

Had he attempted to land with wheels down, they might have dug in and the plane would have surely flipped over. No engines meant no braking system, and the least amount of movement along the ground the better; less targets to hit. He was in the hands of God, fate or luck, whichever one of the three you believe in. Jock believed in all of them.

Three times during those final few minutes he had pulled the little Beechcraft's nose up into the wind, and each time, as expected, it had slowed him down. He had held the nose up until just before the point of stalling and then pointed it down again to get above stall speed. Then suddenly he had seen a flash of something below him. It had to be the ground.

Once more, he pulled the nose back up, slowed down then leveled out just before impact and just hoped and prayed everything was on his side.

The plane had slammed down on a flat, almost treeless area. It skidded over the ground and through small spindly scrub for about 20metres before the left wing had hit a big old gum tree. It had spun the plane around slowing its forward motion. The plane had finally come to rest in a stand of low bushes just a few metres from the side of a rocky outcrop. One beautiful big old gum tree that had probably stood proudly for over a hundred years had stopped him from slamming into that rock wall and certain death.

Fate had played a part in it by coming to rest in a pretty good position. He had a number of large trees around him which helped to shade him from the blazing sun. He also had quite a number of low scrub bushes around him protecting him from the cold winds that blew in at nights. The down side being that the gum trees and the bushes had made it very difficult to be spotted from the air, or for that matter, from the ground.

Jock kept trying to piece together what had happened after the crash. He remembered when he regained consciousness for the second time, he'd left the radio switched on and in doing so had flattened the battery. Any last hope of getting another message out had gone. At that point, he knew that he was on his own until help arrived.

The days ahead would not be easy ones. He knew he had to somehow get out of the smashed cabin and set up some sort of a camp on the ground, using what was left of his Beechcraft for cover against the elements.

To get out of the cabin he would have to clear away as much of the debris from inside the shattered cabin as he possibly could. The instrument panel was literally in his lap, broken glass was all over the place and ripped and torn aluminium framework and wiring was everywhere. Pieces of twisted aluminium from the canopy were hanging menacingly around his face, and around his legs, the engine mountings had been pushed back putting pressure on his shins and ankles. It wasn't going to be an easy job. He knew to get out safely he would have to take his time and work through it bit by bit.

The damage to his leg was going to make any movements extremely difficult, but he knew he had to somehow put up with the pain.

The first few days were the toughest and most painful, but thankfully, no infections set in on any of his wounds. He made a quiet prediction to himself, that his rescuers would probably take three or four days to get to him now after redirecting their search efforts, so he started planning for that.

Most of the first day after the crash, he had drifted in and out of consciousness still sitting in the cabin. He spent what he could of the second day, clearing away the debris from his body and from around his injured legs. It was slow and painful work. There were times when he thought that he might just stay where he was, but then he thought, to survive for any period he needed to get out of the wrecked cockpit.

By early Friday evening he was just about ready to try and get out of the cockpit and onto the ground just a metre or so below him. He was exhausted from the pain and the struggle to get clear, so he decided to try and get some sleep that night and tackle the painful task of getting out early the next morning.

Hunger slowly returned to him. Jock remembered the lunchbox and thermos that Mary had so lovingly prepared for him back in Toowoomba. He'd pushed them in to a large pocket that was attached to the inside of the door. He reached down into the crumpled side of the plane. He found the thermos first and sipped the coffee straight from the flask. Even though it was cold, it tasted great. Then he found the lunchbox and slowly delighted on some of the two day-old sandwiches and home made cake. He couldn't eat much. His ribs were too sore. So he just picked away at the food a bit at a time, as he continued trying too clear wreckage away.

He thought about Jackson. He hoped they weren't having any problems without the pumping parts he was meant to be flying to them. He felt bad about letting them down, but there was nothing he could do about that now. It all seemed so long ago, so much had happened since he'd found the fax from Jackson and took off for Brisbane. Yet on the other hand it was all so vivid in his mind.

In the distance, between the gum trees and clumps of scrub, he could see that red hill. Wild flowers in bloom, yeah, must be wild flowers, he thought, too bright to be anything else. He remembered seeing them the day before and vaguely remembered saying something about it when he made his one and only radio call before the batteries died on him. That red hill was the only real landmark in his line of vision. Everywhere else was just trees and scrub. It stood out like a beacon and he thought that someone would know where it was. That was, of course, if someone had received his message.

That night was not a good night for Jock. He tried to get some sleep but he drifted off from time to time. The cooler night air made all his injuries ache badly, especially his leg. Nights were the worst...cold, lonely and painful but he kept telling himself that this was about as bad as it would get, and if he could just get through the night, he'd be OK.

The next morning the skies were clear and the air crisp, typical of an autumn morning out in that western part of Queensland. It was a Saturday. Well at least he thought it probably was. Jock had always liked Saturdays. That was the day he could be a full-time family man. Since he'd settled back in Toowoomba, after all the years travelling around as a charter pilot, he had come to look forward to Saturdays very much. Generally it would include a trip to Grand Central Plaza, the local shopping mall, as well as the usual run around to the kid's sporting events, cricket, soccer, netball, gymnastics, depending on the season. It was always a busy day, but always a fun day.

He knew there'd be no sport and no shopping for his family in Toowoomba this Saturday. He knew Mary would be nearby somewhere, close he hoped, helping in his search and that was a comforting thought. Their kids might be here also, or, Mary might have left them with their grandmother back in Toowoomba. That somehow made the situation a lot more tolerable. He just hoped, wherever they were, that they weren't worrying too much.

He nibbled on some breakfast, in the form of Mary's fine sandwiches and then told himself it was time to deal with the business at hand. It was time to try and get out of the wreck and on to the ground. Then he could try and fix his injuries and set up a camp as best he could. He knew that getting out of the plane with a broken leg was not going to be easy and was certainly going to be painful. He prepared himself with positive thoughts about his family, and their futures.

After part of Thursday, and most of Friday, clearing the wreckage away, the actual act of getting out took no more than a few seconds.

He steeled himself for the effort and the pain that was just ahead by screaming out as loud as he could. Then with all his fortitude and courage he lifted his torso up with his arms and with every ounce of his strength he threw his body to his left.

The damaged side panel of the cockpit door simply crumpled beneath his weight and a second later he thumped to the ground in unbelievable pain. He'd never felt pain like it before. Tears ran down his face. Like anyone in intense pain, he gritted his teeth together as hard as he could and hung on with determination until the pain slowly began easing, enough at least that he could think clearly again.

He was concerned he'd done more damage to his broken leg. It sure felt like it, he thought, as he lay there still grimacing in pain. He lay on the ground in a prostate position, too scared to move for fearing the excruciating pain would return, but he was no longer trapped in the wreckage. He was on the ground and that was a win for him.

Around the middle of the day, Jock realised that he had either passed out, or had slept for some time, either way he was pleased that the pain was somewhat more bearable now. Aware also that it was a warning from his body. It was injured and it needed to be cared for.

He became aware of how thirsty he was. He'd been lying there in the heat of the day for a number of hours. When he made the move out of the cockpit, he'd left the coffee flask behind. He didn't think of it at the time. He had been fully concentrating on getting out, not what to take with him. As it so happened that when he fell out of the plane the thermos had dropped out also and was on the ground just a short distance away. He reached over and grabbed it, then drank the last few drops it had to offer. He realised right then that he needed to find water, and sooner rather than later. He had also finished the sandwiches and cakes while still in the plane, so food too was on his 'find soon' list.

He needed to find food and water from somewhere soon. Using strips of his torn clothing, he bandaged the worst of the cuts as best he could. It would have to do for the moment, but the further he went the more he realised he needed the first aid kit in the wrecked plane. Infections could become a serious matter, so he really needed to get back into the plane. Also there would be some food and water in the emergency packs tucked away in a special compartment just behind the wings. He twisted around to see just where he had to get to. The wings had been torn off by the landing impact, and the external compartment door to the emergency packs was on the other side of the plane, so he couldn't see whether they were still there.

He threw the empty thermos over his head in the direction that he would soon follow. Then slowly he began to drag his broken body towards the back of the fuselage. The pain in his leg was almost unbearable, so much so that he could only drag himself a small distance at a time, then he'd have to wait until the pain eased, and then try again. Finally he got past the section where the wings had once been. The whole journey of around three metres took him well over an hour, and on more than one occasion he thought he was going to pass out from the pain.

The back of the plane had come to rest on a rock and it was propping the plane's body up high enough to allow Jock room to slide under it.

He tucked the empty thermos under his arm, and dragged himself under, being careful not to cut himself on the twisted strips of underbelly of his once beautiful Beechcraft. He got to the other side and rested. Even the smallest of tasks seemed to take up so much energy. He lay there for a while with his eyes closed waiting for the pain to ease and wondering whether the toll might be more than his body could take.

'Survive' he told himself as he lay there, 'this is about survival and at all costs, I WILL SURVIVE'.

So, with his focus now back in place, the next problem was that the door to the emergency compartment was jammed up against the very rock that the plane was resting on. He snaked his body around to get a clearer look at the area. Luck again had played a part. Back underneath there was one small section of the undercarriage that had a gash in it. He couldn't understand why he hadn't noticed it as he pulled himself under just a few moments earlier.

He twisted his body back around and slid under the plane again until he was above the tear and then put his hand up into the gaping hole to see what he could reach.

He pulled out everything he could feel including the rescue pack, a torch, some plastic sheeting, the first aid kit, a waterproof hat and a jacket rolled up in a small bag. He could also feel the large plastic water container that he always carried in there. He immediately realised that it was too large to pull through the gash in the bodywork, but he knew the small amount of water in the emergency pack would only last a day or so. Slowly bit-by-bit he wriggled and worked it into a position directly over the hole.

The container, like most of its kind, had a screw top lid, which, in his situation, was not accessible.

Jock opened the rescue pack and found a small screwdriver with which he could punch a hole in the bottom of the container. The next problem was how to plug the hole up again when he'd filled the flask. He looked through the pack again and found a small pencil. He thought he could use it as a removable plug, but he would need something to stop the pencil from popping back out under the pressure of the water above it. In the first aid part of the rescue pack he found a small container with an eye drop solution in it, and inside that was a little rubber squeeze plunger.

He removed the rubber from it and stretched it over the end of the pencil. Then he stabbed a hole into the water container with the screwdriver and after a few more digs at enlarging and rounding it, he pushed the rubber-covered end of the pencil up into the hole. He lost a little water in the time it took to create it, but thereafter it worked amazingly well. Hardly a drop leaked out, the rubber was holding the pencil in place perfectly and the pencil was filling the hole. 'Job well done', he thought, as he filled the thermos with water.

He didn't like the idea of staying under the plane. It was a bit too claustrophobic for his liking, so he pushed and wriggled his way back to the other side again.

He'd been so occupied under the fuselage that he hadn't felt the pain in his leg, but now that he'd completed his mission, the pain returned. He rested awhile. An hour passed before the pain eased, and as it did he realised that his appetite was returning.

It had been almost three days since he'd had his last full meal, but even so, he could manage only a small amount of the food from the emergency pack. He drank a small soft pack of glucose-enriched fluid.

He hoped that help was only hours or at worse a couple of days away, but he also knew that he could be out there in the bush for longer. He'd have to think about a plan to ration what food and water he had left, but with a bit of sustenance in his body, Jock decided the next urgent task was to survey his injuries in more detail. He knew that if he were to control the situation he was in, firstly he'd have to make some kind of a splint for his broken leg. The sooner he immobilised the fractured part, the better his chances would become.

There were plenty of broken tree branches, as well as some loose pieces of plane wreckage lying about, so it didn't take long for him to fashion a splint for his leg. He tied some electrical wiring around his ankle and then got a number of pieces of debris and branches about the same length and tucked them in the wiring. Then he got another piece of wire and laid it under his upper thigh. He moved two splint lengths under his thigh but between the wire and his skin. He then positioned a few more lengths on the top of his thigh. Then he tied the upper wire around the splint pieces and pulled them in tight and then positioned one more on each side of his legs. He worked away at the whole thing until he had all 6 pieces firmly in place and tightly bound. It was a good job done, he thought to himself as he looked over his work. He was happy in the belief that with the leg secured by the splint, then the pain should subside considerably over the next few days.

The next few days passed quietly as Jock got into a daily pattern of eating, napping and tending as best he could to his injuries. His main priority still was the welfare of his body. He also listened out intently for noises that may herald the arrival of rescuers, but there was only the sound of the bush, the birds and insects, no man made sounds, well not yet at least.

He believed that his leg was probably broken in two

places. He also thought he quite possibly had a few broken ribs. He was also aware of some type of neck injury, perhaps from whiplash when the plane spun around after hitting the old gum tree. His neck was getting stiffer as the days went by. There was little pain, just stiffening.

He thought of lighting a signal fire but his injuries stopped him from moving too far and gathering enough firewood. Besides what if the scrub around him caught alight, he wouldn't be able to get away in time and risking being badly burnt, if not worse.

So, at least for the moment, he was safe and warm in his 'cosy' little part of the world. His biggest problem was that no one would know where he was. He would still be very hard to spot from the air or ground. His best hope was that red hill, as long as his message had been received. If so, the search parties had a target at least. If worse came to worse and he hadn't been found within about two weeks, he believed his leg would have healed enough to try walking out himself. He would set about fashioning a set of crutches later. Crutches also would allow him to get into the clearing and start a signal fire without endangering himself. He felt comforted in the thought that at least he had options if a rescue party couldn't find him. He had plans and plans kept his mind in a positive frame. In the meantime his one aim was to stay healthy.

In the many hours he spent laying in the shade of the fuselage, he thought about home and family. He took great comfort in the thought that they would be out there searching for him. He worried that Mary would be upset and under a lot of stress not knowing his fate, but he consoled himself with the thought that if he stayed alive and healthy, then both their ordeals one day soon would be over. His toughness and her persistence would see them through it.

Surely it was only a matter of time and a bit of luck until someone found him. There had been no planes overhead, which meant they were searching elsewhere, so he knew now that it might take some time to find him. He began to plan his survival in every detail, firstly by rationing his food and water.

He estimated it would be about two weeks before his leg was in good enough shape to be able to get down to the clearing each day and start a signal fire.

He had a good supply of water in the emergency compartment of the plane. Also the plane's engine cooling system might still have water in it, not the type of water you'd choose to drink each day, but still if he needed it, there should be some there.

He decided to try and supplement his water supply each day by using an old bushman's technique. He dug a hole in the ground and placed his plastic lunch box in the bottom of the hole. Then he laid a piece of plastic sheet into the hole, with an opening in the middle at the bottom. Each day, he'd break off small pieces of grass, weeds and scrub bush, and he'd put it in the hole. Then over the top of all of that he'd place more plastic sheets, like a lid over it. The principle works on evaporation. The daytime heat draws the moisture out of the plants, leaves and bushes. It tries to evaporate, but because it's trapped under the plastic cover, it reforms as droplets of water on the inside of the top sheet. When the droplets are big enough gravity takes over and fall onto the lower sheet and eventually down through the tiny hole at the bottom and end up in his plastic lunch box.

Each morning Jock would put more 'fresh' leaves and plants into the trap and each evening he drew about a quarter of a cup of water from the lunch box. With the water he had and what he got from the bushman's trap, he knew he had enough water to stay alive for months. With that done he turned his attention to food. That was going to present itself as more of a problem. The emergency pack didn't hold that much, it was only meant as a seven-day survival pack, but what it did have was highly nutritional. He could stretch his food supply out to maybe ten or twelve days, but he needed to find more food in the bush, if he was going to survive for a lengthy period. He believed in his heart that they would find him in a few days but he was a smart enough bushman to know that a lengthy stay might be a very real possibility.

As the days ticked by he began to think more and more about how to supplement his shrinking food rations. Thinking about the equipment he had available to him from the plane, Jock used his bush sense and came up with a plan, a crazy one maybe, but if nothing else, it would help take his mind off other things. He remembered he had a small telescopic fishing rod on board the plane, and a casting net. He also had a portable single-burner stove fuelled by kerosene. He'd always been a mad keen fisherman and always carried a rod and line. You just never knew when time would allow a mad keen fisherman to wet a line, he had told Mary.

He'd seen a number of small lizards scurrying around the place, including one large goanna who wandered by from time to time. He decided to try and lure a lizard close enough that he could throw the fish net over it and then cook it on the kerosene stove. They should taste alright he thought, after all, the Australian Aborigines had eaten them as part of their diet for nearly forty thousand years.

So his plan was put into action. He would first catch a grasshopper, hook it on the fishing line and then cast the bait out. If a lizard got hooked, he had himself a feed straight away. If it didn't, there was always the possibility that he could slowly reel the line in, hopefully with the lizard following, and when it was close enough, he would drop the net over it and dinner would be on the plate soon after.

He smiled to himself. If someone had told him such a story in a hotel bar, he'd think they were drunk. It all sounded a bit crazy, but it was worth a try. If nothing else he thought, it would occupy him for a while and take his mind of the pain and loneliness. These were desperate times, besides, it was the only thing he had going for him. He couldn't go chasing them, so the next best thing was to get them to come to him. Fish in a river, lizard on the ground, same principle, it could work, he told himself.

Anyway if his 'fishing trip' didn't provide food, there was always a Prickly Pear bush in an emergency. Mary had bought him a book on bush tucker a few years before and he remembered reading that the prickly pear bush was a member of the cactus family that was imported into Australia from the Americas as an exotic fruit producing plant. The plant thrived in the dry inland of Australia until it became such a big problem that an eradication program had to be started. The cochineal beetle, which is also used for food colouring, and the Cactoblastis moths were imported and set loose to control the Prickly Pear plant. Since the release of the insects, along with a ban on growing the plant, most of the pesky cactus was killed off, albeit there were still some areas where it survived. On the top of a nearby hill, standing like soldiers guarding over him, Jock could see a clump of Prickly Pears covered with tiny red fruit. Just the very thing a crashed pilot needs as a reserve supply of food.

They were still too far to get to yet, but in a week or two, when his injuries were healed enough, and if the searchers still hadn't found him he might be able to get over to them if need be. Apparently the Prickly Pear's tiny fruit was quite pleasant to eat. He'd also read that the inside pulp, which didn't taste too pleasant, could provide nutrients and moisture, enough to keep him alive if things got desperate. The down side was they are covered in vicious little needles that inject themselves into the skin and are quite painful. Still, he thought, it may never get to that. Thank goodness for that bush tucker book Mary had given him.

Jock was pleased at least, that he still had a clear mind with which to keep on top of the situation at hand. When thoughts of panic that he may not be found crept into his head, he desperately tried thinking of more positive things.

He got the fishing tackle from the plane wreck and set about hooking up the line. He put on two hooks, along with a small sinker. Almost the same rig he would use to fish with. The second hook was just a little further up the line, the idea being that if the first didn't get one, the second just might.

His first real attempt at 'fishing' for lizards seemed a bit silly to say the least.
The principle was that lizards ate insects, so Jock caught a small grasshopper, put it on the hook, cast the line out, and waited for a passing lizard to be tempted. Just like fishing for Yellow Belly in an outback river or dam, the only thing missing was the water.

He chuckled to himself as he sat patiently waiting, 'Lizard fishing. Now there's a new craze. That could take off. Come to the outback of Australia and go lizard fishing with Jock, your local lizard-fishing expert.' Suddenly the chuckle became a full bellied laugh as he imagined the Greenies up in arms about the damage to the environment and 'Save the Lizard' bumper stickers on sale at every petrol station. His laughter was cut short, when the pain from his sore ribs suddenly kicked in.

Time passed, a few hours at least, before he saw his first

lizard. The lizard was quietly, cautiously creeping towards the grasshopper and the awaiting trap. It was a small dragon lizard, but apparently not a hungry one, as it just walked straight past the little grasshopper that was being sacrificed in the name of Jock's survival.

'Perhaps he should try a larger grasshopper,' he thought. 'A bigger temptation might get a better result.'

So Jock set his eagle eye to look for a bigger hopper. He spotted one, and at the very moment that Jock lunged at it with his hands, the fishing rod jerked and started moving around.

He grabbed the rod, and then looked up to where the first bait had been lying in wait. He was surprised to see the small dragon lizard had returned, and was now jumping around madly hooked on the line by his back foot.

The lizard must have quietly returned and been checking out the bait on the end of the line and was probably startled by the noise of Jock trying to catch another grasshopper. When the lizard turned to run away he must have snared his foot in the second fishhook. Jock's crazy idea had worked. He now had a way of hunting for food without hurting his broken leg.

'My goodness', he thought to himself, 'after all I've been through, luck's still on my side.'

He carefully reeled the lizard in then quickly hit it on the head with the handle of the screwdriver. A feeling of sadness passed over him, as he felt sorry for the little lizard. Oddly though, he hadn't felt any sorrow for the grasshopper. He supposed that was because they were considered a pest in rural Australia, but lizards were not. They were cute and no harm to anyone. However these were desperate times and the primitive nature of things in the wild had to take over. He did what he thought he had to do to survive. He vowed to himself there and then, that he would only ever kill an animal, if and when he needed to.

He skinned and gutted the lizard. Then he got out his little cooker and cooked and then dined on fresh meat for the first time in a while. In fact he was dining on fresh lizard for the first time in his life, and it was very tasty, not unlike chicken. Perhaps it was a little stronger, but certainly edible.

As the days went by, Jock became quite sharp at luring lizards to his line. Mostly the lizards won and scampered away with a free feed, but he got lucky enough times to justify his efforts

On one occasion, he put some of a lizard's intestines on to the hook and then cast it out. He wanted to see if any other creatures were interested. He ended up having to scare a fox away, so he decided not to use that type of bait again. He didn't like the idea of foxes sneaking around his campsite; so from then he decided he'd stick to his proven mix of grasshoppers and lizards. The incident made him aware that he shouldn't leave food scraps lying around, for fear of attracting more foxes or dingoes to his area. They may well turn out to be a threat to his safety, so from then on any skin, bones or intestines were buried.

There was an abundance of kangaroos and emus out in that region after the recent good summer rains.

'Funny', he thought, 'you hardly see a kangaroo during a drought, then after some rain they seem to be everywhere, full of energy and bounding all over the countryside'.

Perhaps they were doing what he was being forced to do, by staying in one place and conserving their own energy to increase their chances of survival. 'If only I had a rifle', he thought, 'I could survive out here for months.'

The next few days passed in much the same manner. His life was now into a set routine. He was waiting patiently for one of two things to happen. Firstly, that help would arrive, or secondly, that his leg would heal enough for him to be able to walk out to safety. So he rested his wounds, ate from the ration pack, plus the occasional lizard when he felt the need for fresh food, and drank water from the bushman's hole as well as from the supply he still had in the back of the plane. Life wasn't too bad. Well at least he felt he was safe and he had enough food and water until someone found him.

One morning he woke to a small, but pleasant little surprise. His water trap had attracted the attention of a small turtle. It must have crawled under the plastic during the night or early that morning and had made itself quite at home. He smiled to himself as he watched it drink its fill and then ever so slowly walk out of the hole, passing Jock as if he wasn't even there and wandering off into the bush from where he must have come. How cheeky is that he thought as he watched the little creature disappear from view.

Unbelievably, the very next morning, and much to Jock's delight, the little turtle returned and the same ritual followed.

'Well, at least I'm not alone,' he thought. 'Something knows where I am, even if it doesn't acknowledge me.'

From then on, each morning he would check the water trap to see if his little friend had returned and sure enough, each morning it would be there. Jock looked forward to the morning visits. It gave him a warm feeling inside, a feeling that life goes on, and like the turtle, he should make the best of what life presents.

He'd been quite amazed at how many different kinds of animals made their way past him each day, but the turtle was the only one to 'enter his space'. The others walked, ran, hopped or slithered past, generally at a safe distance, but the turtle came right into Jock's camp and made himself at home. The little turtle gave him hope, and in a strange way, it gave him friendship.

Mary searches on
Thursday, 21st of March 6.00 a.m. (The eighth day)

Mary had fought every inch of the way with Government officials and State Rescue services personnel to keep the search for Jock active. Initially they had searched the area to the north west of Roma, in the Chesterton range district. After no success up there, they shifted the search to an area reaching 250klms west, 100klms east, and 50klms north and south of Roma. They still believed he had followed his flight path and was somewhere close to the main highway west.

She was becoming more and more concerned that Jock had come down further to the south of Mitchell. She had a gut feeling, but no one would listen, so she decided to concentrate her own personal search in that region. She asked her mother to drive the children out to join her. She didn't really want them around all the drama that was unfolding, but she felt they might feel better being close to their mother during this stressful time. She also felt it might help her 'keep it together' as well.

The owners of the motel in Mitchell had helped by putting Mary, the children, and her mother up in two of their motel rooms and were feeding them, morning, noon, and night, all free of charge. There was no doubting the generosity of many of these country folk. When the chips were down, they lent a helping hand, wherever they could. To Mary they were inspirational. With so much love afforded her, she just knew there would be a positive outcome, however long it took.

Jock's best mate, Roger, had also arrived in Mitchell and had joined Mary in her search. The two left the motel each morning in a loaned Toyota Landcruiser, and began searching along tracks and in creek beds to the south. Wherever the four-wheel drive went, they went. They stopped at every farmhouse getting as much information as they could from the local farmers.

The questions were always the same. Had they seen or heard anything unusual, and could they please check their properties for any sign of Jock and his plane. He had to be out there somewhere and the more people looking the sooner he would be found. She told them all she believed if he had survived the crash he would still be alive and waiting for help to arrive. She told them that Jock was a survivor and that he would find a way of staying alive for as long as he had to. 'Keep looking', she pleaded to each and every one of them, 'PLEASE keep looking.'

She and Roger were fed everywhere they stopped and would be sent off on their journey with more scones, cakes and sandwiches than they could ever hope to eat, and always with her thermos full of piping hot tea.

The word 'no' didn't belong in their language. If only she could convince the search officials to expand their search further south. It was almost as if they were thinking just what would a woman know about such things. They simply wouldn't listen to her.

Mary and Roger continued their search each day until after sunset and the darkness made it impossible to continue safely and then and only then, would they return to Mitchell. Roger would call the search and rescue headquarters in Roma from the motel in Mitchell, to get the latest updates. Then, after he'd passed on the news, or generally the lack of it, he'd head off to see the local Police officer in the hope that something useful may have come in from the locals.

Mary's mother Alice tried to keep the children active

during the day by taking them to the library or out sightseeing. On one occasion they spent the whole day as a guest on a nearby farm. The children had a ball, they rode on tractors, watched the cows being milked, and went searching for chicken eggs in the hayshed. For every egg they found they were given a lolly in exchange. They had a wonderful time and couldn't wait to tell Mary all about it when she returned that night. Mary was buoyed by the belief that the children seemed quite unaffected by the drama going on around them.

Mary also questioned locals about the 'red hill' that Jock mentioned in his Mayday call, but all were baffled. A few old locals mentioned occasionally seeing wild red flowers with black centres growing in the scrub after a few good seasons of rain. Sadly though, not one of them could remember where they'd seen them, and to say there was enough to turn a whole hill red, would only be a bush tale. But it was a clue, something different, and worth looking into.

She went to the local library and did some research on native Australian flowers and the nearest thing she could find was Sturt's Desert Pea. It was a native Australian plant that produced a brilliant red flower with a jet-black seedpod in its centre. They were rarely seen in Queensland, more a native of desert areas of New South Wales and Southern and Western Australia, but it was the only native outback flower with a bright red and black colouring together.

One old timer, who lived alone in an old two-room shack just outside Mitchell, told Mary that he once heard an old tale about a remote area to the south that had plenty of 'them flowers' growing wild. 'Some said it was dead drover's blood that coloured them flowers' he told her, 'and that the area was haunted, a spooky place to be avoided.'

As the story went, there was an old drover's trail that

headed through that region. 'About a hundred years ago,' he told Mary. 'Some drovers took a mob of cattle down into New South Wales. It was around the time that gold and silver had been discovered at Broken Hill, and miners were pouring in from all over the world. On their way back to Queensland a few of them disappeared.

One of the many explanations, the old man said, was that they might have been attacked by a pack of dingoes. They had always been a problem in that area. Even today there were many sightings of dingoes.

'More than likely,' he added, 'their horses being spooked by the dingoes and ran off with their food and water supplies. Eventually the men would have perished out there with no-one ever knowing where they were, or what happened to them.'

He was happy to tell her the other stories he'd heard, if she wanted, but he believed most were just rubbish yarns told by drunkards. He did add that there had been yarns of unmarked gravesites and ghost horses riding at night, but again, they were stories told over many ales at the local pub, and couldn't be taken too seriously. The true story, if there was one, had never been recorded, and the old stories were surrounded in myth. No one knew for sure if the drover's story was fact or fiction, and no one had seen the red flowers for many years. The old-timer remembered that the hill was close to the Maranoa, but he wasn't exactly sure where. It was pretty isolated down there, he told Mary, and parts were very dense with low, thick, scrub.

Mary, by now, was just about ready to believe anything, she was running out of ideas, so she decided to go to the local newspaper and Council offices, and try and find any information whatsoever on the 'missing drovers' story.

Her time and effort appeared wasted, for no record of the incident at either office was found. She decided to try the local library. The Librarian, Miss Abercrombie, spent a number of hours with Mary and eventually located an old book of short stories and poems. In 1953 the Show Society had run a competition for local writers and poets, and the following year had put an anthology together to celebrate 50 years of agricultural shows in the district.

The book had a number of short stories, a couple of good local yarns, one or two small fiction stories, dozens of poems and even the words to a song. As to be expected from such a small town project, there were good ones, bad ones and others somewhere in between. It had probably sold enough copies to cover its costs, but that would have been about all for it was definitely not a literary classic.

Mary looked through the index and found what she thought she was looking for on page 46. It was a poem called 'The Tale of the Missing Drovers'. She found herself a quiet corner of the library and read the poem. It made interesting reading. She read through it a few times trying to absorb the words.

She read......

The Tale of the Missing Drovers

From the North, these desperate men had come,
Droving cattle on a southern run.
Riding horseback, singing song,
The land harsh and the trail long.

They headed south for six months more,
To reach the land of silver ore.
They made their fortune with cattle sold,

Then turned for home all proud and bold.

Packs of dingoes they did see,
Frightened now, their horses flee.
The drovers perished in summer heat,
Sixty miles north of two rivers meet

Now ghostly horses ride at night
With thunder hooves in terror flight
Blood red flowers mark this place
Where drovers perish without a face

No trace be found, they died alone
Far from loved ones, far from home,
And every year the red flowers bloom,
And mark this spot of saddened gloom.'

Author uncertain. Poem submitted by T.Wilson

Was it fact or fiction? That was the question on Mary's mind. Did the story produce the poem or was it a case of a poem creating the story. Well it was something at least and anything was better than nothing. It fitted with the old man's tale.

She studied the words, 'Sixty miles north of the two rivers meet,' and 'every year the red flowers bloom'. Was the poem a map to Jock's red hill?

She sat there for a half an hour or so, going over and over the poem. She called Miss Abercrombie over and read it to her. After more chat, they eventually decided that it was worth pursuing. The librarian got out a map of the south-west district of Queensland and they studied it closely. The only notable rivers in the region were the Maranoa and the Balonne, and they both met thirty kilometres north of St. George.

Where the two rivers meet ...... sixty miles north from where the two rivers meet, or a hundred kilometres in today's measures. That would have the 'red flowers blooming' in the middle of nowhere. It was a hundred and thirty kilometres north of St.George and eighty kilometres south of Mitchell. A little further south than where Mary thought Jock might be, but an area that hadn't yet been searched. It was a very real possibility.

Miss Abercrombie found a much earlier map of the region in the back room. The map was considered fragile, and had been filed away rather than have the public damage it any more. They found markings on it of a number of old stock routes, and sure enough one of the stock routes ran from Emerald in the north, down through Springsure, around the Carnavon Gorge to the Merivale River. Then it continued on to the Maranoa and then through Mitchell and down to where it ran into the Balonne north of St.George.

Where the two rivers meet. From St. George the stock route loosely followed the Culgoa River to the south-west. Mary got out an early map of New South Wales and found the Culgoa River and followed its flow until it ran into the Darling River at Bourke. It then flowed down to Wilcannia, and Broken Hill was only a hundred and twenty miles, or two hundred kilometres to the west. The stock route then headed on to where the Darling meets the Murray and from there it split south to Melbourne and west to Adelaide.

'If I were a Queensland drover', Mary said to the librarian, 'and was trying to get to Broken Hill, that surely would be the quickest and safest way to get there, following the rivers'.

Mary got her notebook out and scribbled down the clues.

What did she have thus far?

The tale of some drovers heading south towards Broken Hill. Then apparently getting lost and dying somewhere on their return on a stock route between St. George and Mitchell. She also had the local stories of wild red flowers and unmarked graves.

Why red flowers, she thought. Stories abounded of red poppies growing wild in the battlefields of France and Belgium where soldiers died in World War One. Could this be something similar?

It all seemed to fit with what she'd been told. The story seemed to be heading in the right direction at least. Miss Abercrombie was growing in support for the story as well.

But what of the bit about, '60 miles north of the two rivers meet'. No one had ever found the drovers, so was that a guess, an estimate of where they had probably disappeared. Perhaps the unknown author had found the graves and not told anyone, just simply written it into the poem. Was the red hill something to do with someone finding some human bones? Perhaps planting flowers at that site and since then growing wild, spreading up or down the hillside. It made a lot of sense, yet on the other hand it made none.

Mary returned to the motel and discussed her findings with her mother and Roger. To her utter joy they agreed with her. They both believed it was worthy of spending some time looking into.

Later that afternoon, Roger drove Mary to the rescue headquarters in Roma. There she presented her theories and research to the search coordinators, but the look on their faces when Mary told them the story, was another story indeed. She remembered them saying something about her being under a great deal of stress, and that they couldn't spend money on searching out an old bushman's tale. It was painfully obvious they didn't agree with her.

'We're on our own again, Roger. They didn't want to know did they?'

'Nothing new Mary', Roger agreed. 'No problems, we'll do our own thing. End result is if we find Jock, then who cares who was right and who was wrong. Let them follow their old die-hard theories, we'll take the gamble. Let Jock be the winner.'

'Thank you dear Roger, you've been a tower of strength to me and I love you dearly for it. True friends are hard to find. I'm glad you're ours.'

'Keep that up Mary and you'll have us both in tears.'

'Maybe a good cry wouldn't hurt either of us', said Mary.

'Speak for yourself, men aren't supposed to cry', Roger added.

'Oh right, Mister Macho.'

Instead of a good cry, they both ended up having a good old laugh together.

They returned to Mitchell that night, with about the same amount of official support they had when they set out, very little to none.

Back in the motel room, they went over the maps and the poem again and again. Were they not seeing something here? Or perhaps they were seeing too much of nothing! Mary looked for more clues.

Submitted by T.Wilson, the poem said.

Maybe that was a better clue. Who was T.Wilson? If they found him or her, maybe they could get more of the story behind the poem. At least they could try and get an answer to some of the questions.

Did T.Wilson write the poem? What did T.Wilson know? Was the poem based on fact or fiction? The most important question regarding the writer, was if he or she were still alive?

Someone had to know who T.Wilson was. First, Mary checked the local phone book, but there was no listing. She rang the mayor at his home and he kindly went and unlocked the Council Chambers and helped her search there, but there was no current record of a T.Wilson in the district. The mayor informed her, that in 1965 there had been a massive flood through Mitchell and most of the early town records had been lost. She left there disappointed yet again.

Next morning, Mary rang the current Show Society's Secretary. She knew nothing also. The articles in the book had been submitted over fifty years before. However, during the conversation, she did suggest that T.Wilson might be a woman, and if so, may have married and changed her name.

Dead-end again! How frustrating it was. Finding the writer of a poem that was at least fifty years old could take years itself, and time was running out for Jock.

That Thursday was the first day that Mary hadn't physically been out searching for Jock, instead she had spent the whole day trying to find more about the story of the missing drovers.

Suddenly there was a loud clap of thunder. She had been so involved in her mission that she was totally unaware of the storm clouds gathering around her. Moments later there was a large downpour of rain, as a wild storm blew over the Mitchell area.

Roger still believed in her totally, and agreed to carry on

the search for as long as it took, no matter where she wanted to look. That night they talked it over and both decided to give the poem at least one shot.

So, first thing next morning, the ninth day of the search , the two friends left Mitchell and headed down the dusty St.George road towards the place known to the poet as, 'Sixty miles north of the two rivers meet'. They'd been down the road before, but this time they wanted to look at an area further south. They drove past quite a few properties and homesteads, including one that had an old red milk can for a mailbox with the name Nundooka painted on it in white. There was quite a deal of debris lying across the road from the storm the previous day, and Roger had to drive carefully to avoid fallen trees and branches.

A little over an hour's drive from Mitchell they came across a man and his young son leading a large mob of sheep north along the road. They stopped briefly to allow the sheep to pass their vehicle and Mary asked the man if he knew of the whereabouts of any red hills, possibly an outcrop of wild red flowers. The man seemed surprised and a little confused at her questions and shook his head, 'Sorry,' he replied to her questions.

'Have you heard anything about Missing Drovers? A few old-timers back in Mitchell said some drovers were supposed to have perished in this area a little over a hundred years ago.'

'I remember my father telling me something like that when I was a kid,' replied the man, 'but that was a long time back.'

'We'd always thought it was just an old yarn, probably made up by someone telling tales around an old campfire. You know what it's like,' he answered.

'Anything you remember would be useful, anything at

all?' Mary asked.

'We don't sit around campfires talking any more, not since television,' he added, 'so *you* forget these things. I'll probably remember it one day when I'm in the shower or something. Sorry!'
Mary nodded back to him, unsure if he appreciated her urgency.

'Bad storm yesterday,' he added, trying to be polite. 'I can feel another one in the air. You be careful this afternoon. They can blow up pretty quickly out here.'

The man looked like he wanted to get on with his work, so she bid them farewell and they drove off heading south again. She had been watching the vehicle speedo reading and about eight kilometres further down the road, about a hundred kilometres from Mitchell, Mary asked Roger to stop.

'This is about it, sixty miles north of where the two rivers meet.'

She got out of the vehicle and surveyed the area to the east of them. It was fairly flat ground, covered in low bushy scrub and not too far off she could see some low hills rising above the tree line. Roger joined her and asked her if she had seen something out there.

'No,' replied Mary, 'and we probably won't. People drive up and down this road every day and no one reported seeing anything. The man and the boy probably passed by here and they didn't see anything.'

Roger knew exactly what she was getting at, 'You mean, if we're going to find him, we'll have to get off this road and go bush.'

'Exactly,' she said looking back out in an easterly direction. 'No point driving up and down roads that have been checked out before,' Mary said, 'It's time to take a chance and head into the bush. Maybe we'll get lucky and find that red hill.'

'We need some luck,' he replied, knowing that it was more like searching for the last crab on the ocean floor.

'Don't you quit on me know, Roger,' she said with a touch of frustration in her voice.
'You know better than that, but let's be realistic. This is a needle in a hay stack.'

She knew it, but she really didn't need to hear it from Roger.

They both got back into the vehicle. Roger engaged the four-wheel drive control and without a second thought turned the Landcruiser east and drove straight into that harsh lonely region.

'He's close by,' she said to Roger, 'I can just feel it.'
Within a few hundred metres the bush had swallowed them up. They had disappeared into a wall of thick scrub and they started to understand why Jock hadn't been found. It was like an African jungle out there, he could be ten metres either side of them and they'd never see him. They could have already driven straight past him and not known.

'Keep heading east,' she told Roger, 'we are close, I know it, he's out here somewhere, I just know it.'

'What-ever you say Mary. I'll go with this womanly instinct thing. My mother was freaky with that sort of stuff.'

Slowly the vehicle made its way inland. They had to work their way around all types of obstacles, massive gum trees, fallen trees, branches, rocky outcrops, and dense scrub. Just about everything but wild red flowers and crashed planes.

'Do you think it's worth tooting the horn out here, perhaps Jock might hear it.'

'Anything's worth a go,' he replied.

They plugged away heading east. The wild life was plentiful, even though the area was not long out of a serious drought. There were plenty of green weeds and grasses on the ground, and a lot of birds. Every time Roger tooted the horn, hundreds would fly out of the trees in fright. Kangaroos, wallabies and emus were everywhere. The country was not good farming land but it was certainly alive with native creatures.

They slowly made their way east for about 2 hours, before stopping for a rest and a re-think. They estimated they were about ten kilometres inland and approximately north of the point where the two rivers ran in to one. Sadly they had still seen nothing to indicate that Jock might be out that way. No plane debris, no red hill, nor any burnt trees that may indicate a fire from a downed plane, nothing but bush.

Hope again faded. They decided to head back towards the Mitchell-St.George road.

They took a slightly more west-north-west direction, trying to cover new ground. About two and a half hours later they reached the main road. Nothing! They drove back towards Mitchell in silence, only broken occasionally by the soft weeping sounds of a woman losing hope. The day had been a long and draining one.

CHAPTER NINE

Broken Hill, the Silver City

On the 10 of September, in the year of 1884, John Barlow, along with his two sons, Matthew and Charles, Benny from Bungunnia Station, Richard Fairclough, writer from Bristol, England, and a few others, rode proudly into the rough, tough, dirty township known as Broken Hill. They had with them over two hundred cattle.

They had all made it through the epic journey safe and well, quite a notable feat in itself. The journey had taken just a little under 19 weeks and for a farmer and his two sons, who had never driven cattle further than about fifty miles before, they had made good time. They had lost no more than seventeen head of stock during the one thousand mile, five-month journey. They'd had only two bad experiences during the journey. One was in the first month, when they passed through an area that seemed to unnerve everyone, including the cattle. It was a ghostly experience, that all agreed was most unpleasant. The other was in the final stages when they were nearly caught up in a flash flood that ripped down Stephens Creek. Generally speaking, the trip had run very smoothly. They had met some amazing characters and seen some remarkable things. If they included the eighty cattle that joined them at Bungunnia Station, then they had in fact arrived with more cattle than they had set out with.

Another oddity in their journey was the fact that they had also collected humans along the way. Benny had joined them in May at Bungunnia. Then in August, Jimmy the stockman and

Alfred the cook, joined them at Wilcannia, and soon after, the last addition to their group, Richard Fairclough, writer-adventurer, from Bristol, England, whom they had found wandering the bush after a fair share of bad luck.

They could look back over wonderful memories of Mitchell and the bridge builders, of the riverboat encounter, its wonderful crew, and seeing Australia's first artesian bore and the amazing Menindee Lakes. But best of all they had passed safely through some of Australia's most beautiful outback country, along some of her great rivers, the Maranoa, the Balonne, the Culgoa and finally the mighty Darling itself.

They hadn't run out of food or water at any stage, although after the flooded creek episode, they had to change their diets somewhat. They didn't run into any robbers or murderers, albeit they had come across poor unlucky Richard Fairclough, who had been on the wrong end of more than his own share of robbers and vagabonds. They had not been lost at any stage, despite travelling through some of Australia's harshest and most desolate regions. Surely the most hazardous part of their odyssey was over; they had made Broken Hill safely.

A trader by the name of Preston, who'd heard about the cattle drive, rode out and met up with them on the outskirts of the township. Along with him were half a dozen stockmen whom he had employed. He formally introduced himself to John and the boys, and negotiated with John to act as their agent. Then Preston arranged to meet with John again after the cattle had been penned up safely in the makeshift holding yards and a full head count had been completed. Preston told John that he had arranged with a number of local businessmen to buy the cattle and to graze them on a nearby piece of privately owned land until such time as they would be needed.

John was a little surprised at how organised Preston was. He didn't know if anyone was even aware they were coming, let alone anyone interested in buying the whole mob.

The Barlows had always believed the venture to be somewhat of a necessary gamble and when they reached Broken Hill, it may take them some weeks, perhaps even months, to find buyers or agents prepared to buy the cattle. Preston was indeed unexpected, but nevertheless an enormous relief to them. Apparently, word reached Preston through the police constable in Wilcannia, although the exact route was not passed on. The expected arrival time was also a bit vague. Enough detail however for Preston to act on and make preparations for the arrival of the mob.

The men took the cattle to the holding yards, where they completed a head count: 122 steers, 76 cows and 15 calves, a total of 213 head.

Thirteen cattle were set aside immediately, to be sold to the newly opened butcher shop. That was done to give John and the crew some much needed cash to enjoy some of what Broken Hill had to offer. John also owed money to the two men who helped them on the Wilcannia to Broken Hill section.

John, who had experienced hard times before in his own life, didn't want to see Richard left penniless, so he invited him to join them for an ale or two or three. His intention was to offer him a small sum of money privately. He didn't want to leave a poor man so down on his luck.

No haggling or bartering took place at the holding yards, for right up front Preston offered John a very good price, a price that John had no hesitation in accepting. The price was more than enough to set them up for many years to come.

After the initial cash payment for the thirteen cattle sold

to the butcher, no more money changed hands between John and Preston. Two bills of sale were drawn up for the remaining two hundred head and signed. Soon after, a telegram was sent to John's bank in Mitchell. There arrangements were made for money from Preston's account in Sydney to be moved across to John's account and the next day a telegram was sent back to Broken Hill confirming the arrangements. The other bill of sale was wired on to George Lamwith's bank in St.George. It was for his share of the Bungunnia cattle, as per the agreement with the Barlows, less the cost of the cattle lost on route. John and George had agreed back at Bungunnia that any cattle lost on route would be deducted at the end on a one-third/two third basis. One third of the cattle lost would be deemed to be George's and two thirds lost would be deemed to be the Barlows.

With the business all done within a day, the drovers headed for a ramshackle building known as one of the local pubs, where John met up with Richard Fairclough. He bought them all a warm beer and then took Richard aside for a quiet chat.

'Richard, I can't see you left out in the cold, so to speak, so I've an offer for you- and I shan't take no as an acceptable answer.'

Richard put his mug of cool ale down on the roughly cut wooden table and looked into John's eyes hoping to get a glimpse somehow of what he might be about to propose.

John raised his mug and took a small sip and then placed it back down, 'I have ten pounds set aside for you.'

'Really' replied Richard, trying to sound like he was about to enter into an arrangement with his agent back in Bristol, 'and why have you done that my new found friend?'

'You are going to need some money to get you back to

Sydney.'

'That is very generous of you John, but accepting charity is not one of my family's strong points.'

'Not charity, my friend, a business loan, shall we call it?' Richard took another drink from the battered old pewter mug that came with the ale.

'You have my attention Sir. Please do go on.'

'When we leave Broken Hill in a few days, we would like you to accompany us back to Bourke. From there you can get the Cobb and Co. back to Sydney. Sometime after your arrival there, you will, I have no doubt, establish yourself as a writer of some note.'

Richard interrupted, 'You sound sure of the future and of my untested talents.'

'You survived two robberies out here. I am a great believer in fate, and I believe it is destiny that you have come this far, so we will help destiny get you back safely to continue on your path.'

'And how will I pay you back fine Sir?'

John swatted a fly from his face and explained, 'When you have successfully published your first novel, as I am sure you will, I would appreciate that the Barlow family be mentioned, and I ask that you send a personally signed copy to me and my family at Burton Downs.'

'That's it?'

'Richard, I'd gladly just give you the money, but I know you'd be too pig-headed to accept. So that's the deal. Do you accept?'

'I'll do more than that John Barlow. This brutal land was built on the flotsam and jetsam from the far-flung backwaters of this earth. But you and the boys Sir are fine Australian stock, and you cut powerful figures indeed. I already have a few characters in mind, built around you and the boys. A writer is blessed to find good wholesome men, with such pride and integrity. Good stock makes for good characters'.

Richard stood up, took his mug of ale in his hand and raised it above his head, 'John you are one fine gentleman, and not only do I thank you for your generous offer, but I happily accept all your terms and conditions. When do we leave this God forsaken den of thieves?'

John also stood and raised his mug to meet Richard's. 'We'll leave for Bourke in a few days; after we have rested a while.'

Richard took a swill from his mug, wiped the froth from his lips and offered one more toast, 'To destiny, my dear new friend, to destiny.'

John raised his mug in reply and repeated, 'To Destiny.'

The two men drank their ale and talked amid the noise and bustle going on around them, until finally John excused himself and headed for the telegraph office. He wrote a short message and had it sent to Mary via the Postal Office in Mitchell, informing her of their safe arrival and about the banking arrangements in Mitchell.

'Arrived safe. Stop. All well. Stop
Home in 6 weeks. Stop
Money Mitchell Bank 10 days. Stop
Love John and boys. Stop.'

After so long away he knew money on the way would be welcome news back home. He knew the money he'd left behind must be exhausted by now. He also sent a telegram to the Mitchell Bank, briefly telling the manager of the sale in case something delayed the transfer of money while they were on the return journey. If there should be a problem they could sort it out without his consent, so Mary could draw on the account funds as soon as needed.

Finally with all the business attended to and most of the cash money temporarily deposited in a safe at the police station, John and the boys headed over to the nearest thing to accommodation that Broken Hill presented, Margaret's Board and Bathhouse. It comprised of a dozen or more canvas tents of various shapes and sizes. The largest tent was set up for the sale of 'sly grog'. The local inn keeper carted ale and spirits in from Sydney, but Margaret specialised in locally made moonshine, Bathtub Gin, as it was also known. Because of the unknown ingredients and alcoholic content, it was sometimes said to drive a man to the brink of madness with its consumption, but then no one really cared about health issues in a wild town like Broken Hill. Margaret's moonshine was more popular than the legal brews, simply because it was cheaper, and that was all most of the miners cared about. The local police seemed to turn a blind eye to the sale of it. Perhaps they had an arrangement with Margaret for payment in some form or other to look the other way, an arrangement well known in Australia back then.

Two other rather large tents were used to serve hot meals twice a day. Breakfast was served from around 5am, and then an evening meal was served from 5pm onwards. Behind the food tents were smaller tents, each containing an old bathtub filled with steaming hot water from an old engine boiler. Along with the water came plenty of bars of locally produced soap to help wash away the dust and sweat of the outback. For an extra fee a woman could be arranged to bathe you.

Beyond the bathing tents, were lines of accommodation tents, probably about 50 or more, all complete with above ground stretchers and straw mattresses, quite a luxury way out there.

There was a wide variety of characters hanging around Margaret's establishments, and just about everything and anything could be bought or sold there, whether it be legal or illegal, nobody cared that much.

John bought the boys a hot meal and a mug of the crudely produced moonshine to wash down the food, or at the very least to help their stomach acids break down the food. Then they luxuriated in a steaming hot bath, and finally John checked them into a three-man tent for three nights.

Over the next three days, while John was restocking for the journey back to Burton Downs, the boys, along with Benny and the flamboyant Richard Fairclough, took in all that the bustling township of Broken Hill had to offer. They wandered around the diggings, to the southern and western ends of town. They wandered through the makeshift stores and businesses that were springing up everywhere. It didn't take long for them to appreciate the hardships that the miners and fortune seekers had to endure in their quest for riches or simply those trying to squeeze out a living in this new territory.

The boys knew that most of the miners had little or no hope of ever getting rich, and that the few that did probably wouldn't live long enough to enjoy it. Miners drank hard and fought often. As well as that, they ran the risk that if they did strike it rich, someone was likely to rob them, or worse, for their newly found wealth. The only people making any money out of Broken Hill in those early days were the storekeepers and the entrepreneurs. Very few, perhaps only those like Margaret with her Board and Bathhouse, or Preston, the man who had arranged the sale of the Barlow's cattle, would ever leave 'the hill' with nice little nest eggs. Most would eventually leave as they had arrived, almost penniless and more than likely broken in spirit.

Most miners lived in the most appalling of conditions out near the main diggings. Few lived in the 'better' conditions at Margaret's, and even fewer were busily building houses on the eastern side of town, away from all the riffraff.

In no time at all, it was obvious to the Barlows that everyone had to eat, and they realised they would be better off being cattlemen and drovers than hoping to survive in such a desperate environment as this one. The two boys knew their father had just made a pretty penny selling the cattle, as well as the commission he made from the sale of George Lamwith's stock. The very same cattle that would have probably died of starvation back on their property in Queensland. They both decided that their futures lay in breeding their own cattle, as well as from time to time droving cattle, there's and others, to markets, wherever they were. They could be breeders, drovers and agents, all in the one business. That left only one question remaining to be answered, where?

Burton Downs was subject to severe droughts, so they would have to look for a property perhaps nearer to the coast where the rainfall was better. At the very least it would need to be a property closer to permanent water where the risk of severe drought conditions was not so great. Perhaps closer to one of the mighty rivers they had followed down from Queensland. Rivers like the Culgoa, or the Darling, better still, if they could find, and set up an artesian bore somewhere, then they would be set for life. Water was to be their strike and the cattle their gold.

During their time in Broken Hill they talked over their ideas with John. He wasn't all that keen on the droving side of things as he felt it too hard a life for an old timer like himself, it was definitely a young man's profession. He added that he thought the boys were more than capable of doing the droving on their own, employing some extra riders to help. In general though, he felt it was a good plan, one that would give them more than a better chance of succeeding as cattle breeders in the future. John would remain at Burton Downs and added that he could partner them financially towards setting up on a small property of their choosing. He suggested that they run a few head of cattle and even a small mob of sheep on the property, and drove cattle for themselves and others in the cooler winter months. He believed too that their futures lay in diversifying, not putting all their eggs in the one basket. This was a New World now, Australia was opening up and there was a good future in it for a couple of smart young men prepared to work hard at it.

The boys had been thinking more down the lines of the whole family setting up a new venture, but the suggestion of going it alone was more than they could have dreamed for. If they could find suitable land, perhaps within a few hundred miles of Burton, they could then help each other out in droughts by moving stock from one property to the other. The boys liked the country around the Culgoa River south of St.George and John agreed that it had good prospects for the future. They also felt that he needed to expand his own interests by looking for land to the west of Burton, nearer the Maranoa, where he could be assured of a more reliable water supply. Perhaps he could stock a Maranoa property with sheep and that would help in the plan to diversify for the future. They could keep Burton Downs for cattle and multiple properties would hedge them against drought and harsh years. They could slowly stock their own property with money made from droving.

John was impressed and told them, 'You've been thinking about this for a while have you'?

'Well actually, it was Charles who first brought up the subject. We were just waiting to see how things panned out when we got here.'

Charles joined in; 'It was the artesian water that got me thinking. If we can be near permanent water, we can't fail.'

'You're dead right,' John added.

'We started talking about our own place back then and the droving suits us well.'

John was a proud father. His boys had developed into fine young men, 'It sure has been a learning experience, hasn't it boys?'

Matthew continued, 'Preston's got it all figured out also. We do all the hard work and with some forward planning he made money from your dream. Smart man that one, you've got to admire him.'

'We thought that when we head home,' Charles added, ' Matthew stay in St.George a while and talk up some business for us for next autumn. Perhaps look around for a property that might be for sale.'

'A fine idea, Charles. A fine idea! George Lamwith will be pleased with the results, so I'm sure you can count on him again and when the word spreads you'll be overrun with business. You boys think you can do it without me, this old body might not be able to handle another trek like this one.'

'You've taught us well Father. We'll do just fine alone.'

'Well then, go and enjoy yourselves while you can. We'll have time enough to talk it over on the ride home.'

The Return Journey 1884

Three days was more than enough for the Barlows to realise that Broken Hill didn't have anything more to offer than it had already given, so the plan was set to leave the Hill early the next morning.

A final telegram was sent home, telling Mary they were on their way back. One more hot bath, one more comfortable night sleeping on a straw mattress at Margaret's Board and Bathhouse and they'd be on the trail again.

Benny was found in one of the tents, very much hung over and looking decidedly ill after a session on the Bathtub Gin. Richard Fairclough was also found trying to charm the local 'ladies of the night' for a free daytime encounter. They too were smart business ladies, they loved his tales of the world, but unless his hand went into his pocket for money, they were listening only.

That last night they dined together at the hotel on the finest rump steaks, Barlow beef of course, along with what the cook called, 'almost' fresh vegetables.

Over their meal they discussed the journey homeward. John told them he felt rather uneasy about leaving Broken Hill all stocked up with food and water, as well as the cash he had left over in the police constables safe. He also felt that word might have gone around the district, that they had sold more than two hundred head of cattle. Most people back then, didn't trust banks and were quite prepared to carry cash with them, believing that a rifle was as good as any bank, so therefore it could be presumed that they were carrying a great deal of money with them.

Thieves wouldn't know that the money had been arranged through the bank in Cobar, so John felt the most dangerous part of their journey would again be from Broken Hill to Wilcannia, and in particular the first fifty to a hundred miles out. If anyone were planning a robbery, there would be plenty of places for a successful ambush out there.

It was decided by all, that they would tell anyone, and everyone, before they set out, that they were heading west into

South Australia. They would be travelling down to Adelaide and then on to Melbourne and Sydney by boat. That way any bushrangers or band of thieves would expect them to leave heading west on route to Adelaide, some three hundred miles down a well-used trail.

The most likely place for an ambush would be near the South Australian border around the small settlement of Cockburn. It would be far enough away from the police and easy enough to hide out in the hills around there after such a robbery. So they spent plenty of time telling anyone who would listen that they were heading west in the next day or so.

The secret plan was that the very next morning they would head westward for half a day. Then about half way to Cockburn they would turn north and into the rugged Barrier Ranges for cover and protection. Once there, they could find high ground overlooking the plains from where they would keep an eye out for anyone trailing them, and then turn northward in the protection of the ranges. When they felt it safe, they would come out of the hills and head overland in a north-easterly direction towards the artesian bores at Kallara, then on to Bourke, totally bypassing any known Wilcannia routes.

The great danger was that if they got lost or injured no one would even know they were out there. But they had taken many risks before travelling in the wilderness, and they had prevailed, so why should it be any different this time. Summer heat was another big danger, but it hadn't quite set in. They had time. It would be easy once they reached Bourke and the rivers. It was just the overland section to Bourke where the lack of water would be their greatest concern.

John was confident they could get to Bourke in about three weeks without the cattle to slow them down. There they could see Richard safely on a Cobb and Co. stagecoach for

Sydney and continue north themselves, leaving Benny at Bungunnia Station on the way through.

It had some risks, but then, the whole idea of the trip from Burton Downs to Broken Hill had plenty of risks. They had strength in numbers, there would be five men on the return journey and they would be able to travel much faster on horseback than they had been able to on the journey down. If danger presented itself, at least they wouldn't have to stay with a mob of cattle, they could high tail it away and lay low somewhere until all was safe again.

Benny knew of a station owner about a hundred miles north along the Tibooburra road. He was sure they could buy fresh horses and water there if they needed to. He'd worked with this man many years before, and he'd since heard that he had taken a family out there to set up a property himself. As far as he understood he was still there. The property was called Packsaddle, and he had a fair idea of its location. It was just what John needed to hear. He was concerned they would get slowed down too much by carrying enough food and water through the ranges to get them back to Bourke. The news of Benny's friend meant they could ride lighter, and move easier through the Ranges. Once at Packsaddle, they might be able to buy some packhorses and travel more comfortably to the artesian bores at Kallara. At the very least it would be a place to rest for a while. However, that was further down the track, there first concern was to get clear of Broken Hill and into the relative safety of the rugged Barrier Ranges.

They left the next morning at 4am in darkness. They had with them two spare horses loaded with provisions and two packhorses loaded with canvas and pigskin water bags. They headed west quickly but cautiously, for most of that first morning. Then early in the afternoon, when they were sure that no one was on their tail, they turned north-east behind a row of small hills leading to the main Barrier Range. They sat there behind the hills watching the Adelaide trail for a few hours, and then rode north into the rugged ranges. They rode on in the moonlit night for a number of hours before finally stopping to set up camp in a small gully.

John decided they should set up two camps. One camp with a small fire and some bedding laid out around it. They also left a number of horses tied up to a tree within sight of the campfire. This was to be a false camp, in the event that they had been followed out of town and 'bushwhacked', while they slept. They actually camped in the darkness about a half a mile away, each taking turns at sitting watch over the false camp.

It was a cold night and without a fire to keep them warm, no one slept too well. They still may have been followed during the day and might have seen them set up the false camp. Unlikely, but still anything was possible. They still harboured fears of being attacked in their sleep. It was a long, long night.

Just before first light, they carefully approached the false camp, still nervous about being attacked. The camp was exactly how they had left it the night before and the men felt at ease for the moment. The whole of that day they took it in turns of watching the plains below from the top of the gully while the rest caught up on much needed sleep. That night feeling better about their safety, all got some more sleep as the night wore on. At dawn next morning they quickly packed their gear up, loaded it all back on the packhorses and set out without breakfast, wanting to get as far away as possible from the danger area. John changed direction again, and headed due north, deeper into the very rough and rugged ranges.

The Barrier Range was a wild untamed wilderness in the spring of 1884. It was for that very reason that John chose to go there, the protection its ruggedness provided. The travelling would be slow for a while, but he only planned on staying in the ranges for a few more days.

They headed slowly north for three days. It was rougher country than he had expected. It's harshness was in fact its beauty. This was truly the wild heart of Australia. The hills were full of huge gum trees towering above them. The gullies, where the water cascaded through after rain, were an abundance of wild flowers of every colour and shape. The region was a haven for kangaroos. There were plenty of big reds and even bigger greys, some standing over two metres tall. Also there were dozens of different types of smaller rock wallabies. The odd wild rabbit could be seen bounding around. Rabbits hadn't taken over the north-west part of New South Wales yet, not like they had further south, but there were enough around to suggest that they may one day be a problem. They were tempted to shoot some for fresh food, but John was still concerned about any noise that might draw attention to their whereabouts. The ranges also produced an abundance of bird life, parrots of every colour, tiny multi coloured budgerigars and literally millions of pink and grey galahs abounded. There were giant black cockatoos and the smaller cockatiels, and the magnificent king of the skies, the giant Australian eagle.

The Barrier Range was a beautiful region indeed, a true natural wilderness. But John knew that sooner or later they would have to leave its beauty and cover, and get back on to the open plains and start heading east north-east towards the Darling River.

They pushed on slowly by day through the harsh terrain and at night slept around small fires deep in the gullies. From time to time they would top a ridge and see below them the magnificent plains to the west and to the east. It all looked so peaceful and harmless down there, but they knew the ranges still provided much needed cover and protection, for the time being at least.

When John was finally sure that no one was following them, and they were sufficiently clear of Broken Hill, they rode out of the rugged hills and made their way back down to the sweeping plains stretching far over the horizon to the east.

At first, when they came out of the ranges, they were a little disorientated, but Benny, the true bushman that he was, didn't take long to work out where he thought they were.

Once down on the flat desert-like plains, they came across clumps of a very unusual wild flower, a red and black beauty known as Sturt's Desert Pea. Charles loved them from the very first time he saw them, and he kept an eye out for them every time they went near rocky terrain. He'd first seen the flower in Broken Hill, growing out the back of Margaret's Board and Bathhouse. In his eye it was the most beautiful of all the wildflowers. A flame red flower, shaped like a pixie's ear, with a pure black eye in the middle, set atop pale coloured greyish-green foliage. The stark contrast between the red and black seemed to emulate the harsh contrasts of this wildly, beautiful land. The plant itself, if not in flower, would blend so well with it surrounds that he could hardly notice it, nature's way of protecting it no doubt. After the rains came, it would blossom into full flower and send forth its seed to grow again when the next rains came, thus completing nature's cycle. That timeless cycle had been repeated again and again over millions of years, and in this ancient land, only the timing of the rains altered the pattern.

Charles set about collecting seedpods from the plant whenever he could. He made sure not to take all the seeds, so they could survive into the future. He intended taking the seeds home to his mother in Queensland, as a gift from their journey. He knew they'd look impressive in his mother's front garden and it could live on as a reminder of their epic journey. He wrapped them carefully in a red and white handkerchief and carried them in his packsaddles with all the care necessary to protect this gift to his mother.

Benny found the way to Packsaddle, and was pleased to find his old friend still there and doing well for himself. The men spent a few days there unwinding, and for the first time since they'd left the 'hill', slept peacefully in the stockman's quarters. They purchased extra provisions and an extra packhorse from him, enough to get them through to Kallara.

Two days after arriving at Packsaddle, they headed out north-east again, safe in the belief that any would-be robbers were far, far, behind them now.

From time to time they came across signs of other human activity, old campfires or discarded equipment. Sometimes in the distance a flickering light, perhaps a campfire or a settlement or station, but they chose to avoid any further human contact.

They set their camps at night in dry creek beds. Setting camp in a creek bed is usually thought of as being a dangerous thing to do, as the wall of water they'd encountered in Stephens Creek attested to. However, setting up down in a creek bed would afford them enough cover to have an open campfire each night and not be spotted, so they took the chance. Besides, having left the Barrier Ranges behind them, the chances of rain cascading down on them was not much of a threat any more. The creeks out there in the open plains rarely saw much water at all. Any rainfall in the Barrier ranges would take a day or more to reach them, so they felt less of a threat from water than they did from bad men or cold nights.

Each man would take a two-hour watch at night, and a few of the horses were left a few hundred yards or so up the creek-beds, with bells tied around their necks and hobbles on their legs. It was an old bushman's tale they'd heard of on the road. The horses would sense the danger of an oncoming storm or even a bushfire long before they would. The horse's restlessness and eventual panic would get bells ringing, thus alerting the sleeping campsite in time to react to the impending danger.

For a little less than two weeks they pushed north-east. By now they were feeling a great deal more comfortable about getting home safely. They rode out early each morning and pushed hard until the sun got too hot above them, and then they'd find a shady spot to rest, generally under coolabah trees around the many dry creek beds they encountered. By mid-afternoon, after a number of hour's rest and a good feed, they'd ride on until darkness forced them into finding a place to camp for the night, and so it went.

One night they lost two horses when something or someone spooked them and they broke clear of their tethers. By the time they heard the bells ringing and got to where they had left the horses, two had disappeared into the darkness.

They had seen signs of aboriginal campsites in the area, but had not seen any yet. Another restless night followed, although they were certain that aborigines or wild animals more than likely spooked the horses, also the threat of bushrangers, made for another worrying night.

Part of the next morning they searched for the two runaways, but without any luck. However, they did see more signs that aborigines were in the area. Although aborigines had no use for horses, they had been known to sneak into camps and release them in the hope, it was thought, that 'the white fellas' wouldn't come back that way again. Perhaps in hard times the horses would make an easy meal for a tribe of hungry families. Whatever the case, the horses were never seen again, and neither did they come across any nomadic desert wanderers.

Finally they reached the banks of the Darling and were comfortable in the belief that the most dangerous part of the return journey was behind them. The Darling was such a refreshing site after two weeks in the hot dry stony desert; it was like running into an old friend out there in the wilderness.

Three weeks had passed since they had left Broken Hill and they were travelling well. They were about a hundred and fifty miles north of Wilcannia, and immediately set a course for Kallara Station and the artesian bores, and renewed their friendship with old Bandicoot, albeit only for a day. From there they retraced their tracks back up the Darling until they reached Bourke in mid-October.

The nights were still cool enough, but the days were heating up dramatically. John was glad that they were less than a month away from home. He didn't like the idea of travelling out in the bush in the extreme summer's heat. Already the horses were showing signs of tiring, forcing them to rest a little earlier each day than they had wanted. At least they had a good supply of fresh water now. The men knew though that keeping the horses fit and healthy was critical to them arriving home safely, so if the horses looked tired they would rest them. Depending on the fullness of the moon, they could travel into the night a few hours, making up for any time lost during the day.

The trek from Kallara to Bourke was an easy one, nothing went wrong and the daily temperatures had settled back down to more like late spring. The earlier heat wave had passed, for the present at least.

They were happy to see Bourke again. Down on the wharves they asked after Captain Kirkwood and their friends from the Barrumba Queen, but no one had seen them since the chance encounter with them some months before.

They stayed in Bourke only long enough to see their friend Richard Fairclough; Writer of Bristol, England, safely on a Cobb and Co coach bound for Dubbo. From there, he could board a more comfortable train for the rest of his trip back to Sydney and the writing career that he believed awaited him. The Barlows were sad to see him off for he had been a real entertainer, amusing them with his wonderful stories and making some very memorable campfire moments.

They watched Richard's stagecoach head out on the southern road and immediately mounted their horses and rode out of Bourke in a nor-easterly direction towards the Culgoa River.

The Darling was still flowing gently with water from the late autumn northern rains, but the levels were noticeably dropping as they headed towards Queensland. The grasses in places had grown almost waist high and had since dried out, making the countryside ripe for summer bushfires. Also, because of the long grass, snakes were becoming a problem. On open ground, snakes can be seen at a distance and avoided, but in these conditions, a rider can be on top of a snake before he knew it. The men had to be aware that if a snake spooked the horses, they might stumble or rear up, throwing them out of their saddles. The ground and rocks would be very hard indeed if one fell from the height of a mounted horse, not to mention the fact that there would be an angry snake down there somewhere. They needed to stay vigilant.

Charles hadn't seen many wildflowers since they'd left the rocky plains. Now however, and following useful rains back in the winter months, in some places the ground was covered in nature's wonders of the outback.

The trees had resumed their majestic look, standing tall and reaching for the blue skies above, their leaves once again green and looking splendidly healthy. Small Australian native bees were hovering over every flowering wattle and native gum leaving one to wonder from where had they all suddenly appeared. Hardly a flower or bee for years during the droughts, but at the first sign of rain and then with the blossoming flowers, bees seemed to re-appear from nowhere. In places the ground was awash with red, yellow, orange, and white wild flowers. After many years of seeing the drought stricken Australian bush at its worst, in the spring of 1884 they were now seeing it at its very best. The one down side were the flies and they were everywhere.

Charles was again collecting seeds from the wildflowers to take home to his mother, and by now he had literally hundreds wrapped in a cloth that he kept safely in his saddlebag. His mother loved the colour red, so a great number of his seeds were from plants with red flowers, but he had plenty of yellow, orange and white also. The most precious of his collection was still the Sturt's Desert Pea from around Broken Hill.

One afternoon, about six days after leaving the Bourke district, they rode back onto Bungunnia Station and up to George Lamwith's homestead. John was pleased to hear that George had received his money some time back, and with it had come a bonus of good early spring rains. George told them that it certainly wasn't drought-breaking rain, but it was rain and to any man working the land, that was almost as good as money in the bank. Good rains provided fresh green grasses for the stock to graze and fatten on. As well, it filled the dams with much needed water. Rain provided for the future, more than anything else out there. Water was considered the true gold of the outback.

As they sat around the dinner table that night, John's thoughts were of Burton Downs and his family. He wondered if they'd received any rain up north, or would he be returning to a bleak barren landscape again, like the one they had left behind way back in the autumn. All of a sudden he felt a million miles from home. Perhaps it was Mabel and her wonderful home cooking, or just the female company. Whatever it was, John felt very homesick.

Funny thing homesickness, he thought to himself, it's such a lonely hopeless feeling. He was closer to home now than he had been for six months, yet at that moment he felt further away than at any time on their epic journey. He knew he couldn't take George up on his generous offer of resting at Bungunnia for a few days. His thoughts were all about home now.

He set his plan to head for home the next morning, much to the boy's disappointment for they had both been keen on resting a while. They were getting weary from the pace John had been pushing them to get home. His reasoning had been the oncoming summer heat, but they said nothing to him, not even when George made his offer to stay a while. He was after all their boss, as well as their father, and family loyalty and respect ran deep.

That evening they sat down to one of the best meals they'd had in a long time, a Mrs. Lamwith special. After the meal, while they were enjoying a glass of port together, George spoke on the subject of future business.

'I know a few cattlemen in this district who would be very keen to move some of their cattle to sale next autumn. If you and the boys are planning on taking another mob to Broken

Hill in the near future, then please keep us in mind,' he said with enthusiasm.

He paused for a moment to gauge any reaction from John. There was none forthcoming. John simply sipped at his port, enjoying the luxury of it all.

Matthew however had been taking in every word, 'If we planned another trek?' he asked.

'Yes, others in the district are aware of the results of our little arrangement, and are eager to cash in also, if another trip was to be planned that is.'

John still showed little interest. He was tired and weary, but Matthew wanted to discuss the matter in more detail.

'It appears Father isn't too interested. I think he just wants to get home, but I'd certainly be happy to discuss the prospect with you further', Matthew said keenly.

'I could set up a meeting with a number of them, if you were prepared to wait in St.George for about a week', George added.

Matthew looked to his father, 'Dad?'

'I'm sorry son. As you said, I only have thoughts for home. I haven't seen your mother or the children in a long time. The closer we get, the keener I am to get home.'

Charles, who had been quietly listening, joined the conversation; 'I'd be keen on another trip. I'd do it again, anytime.'

Again John added that he didn't want to wait around, but if both Matthew and Charles were that keen on the idea of another trip down south, he suggested that perhaps they could get in touch with George next autumn.

Matthew, a little unhappy at his father's lack of enthusiasm, fired back, 'I know it was hard work, but the rewards were good, we proved that. I think it's certainly worthwhile discussing further.'

There was silence for a moment or two and then Matthew spoke again, 'Dad, I think I'd like to discuss this further with these gentlemen in St.George. May I suggest that you head on home with Charles, and I'll stay behind to set up another cattle drive to Broken Hill next autumn? I can follow you home later. I think it's worth looking into.'

'Son, you're a man now, you don't have to prove that to anyone, but it's a long trail home alone.'

Matthew answered assertively, 'I'm an experienced bushman now. I'll follow the Maranoa to Mitchell. I'll be no more than a week behind you.'

After some debate, John knew, that at twenty-four years of age, Matthew was entitled to be treated as an adult, and this was a time when he had to let him make his own decision about the future.

'I always thought you'd take over Burton Downs, but I suppose there's plenty of time for that.'

He continued, 'If it's drovers you boys wish to be, then I guess I'll have to respect that and wish you luck.'

Matthew felt 10 feet tall. This was his moment, he was about to launch his own business and he couldn't have been happier. 'You can head off in the morning father, along with Charles. I'll take care of business and see you at home soon.'

Charles was a little annoyed. He wanted to stay with Matthew, but he also realised someone needed to look after their father. After such an epic journey, Charles had visions of all three of them riding home triumphantly together, but he realised that Matthew would be staying behind to set up their own business, and that was the way it had to be.

The boys slept well that night with the thought of what adventures lay ahead for them in the years to come. John also slept well. Perhaps the glasses of port helped.

CHAPTER TEN

The Storm
Thursday 21st March 4p.m 1994

In the eight days that Jock had been on the ground, he hadn't heard a single man-made noise. Not a plane, not a car or motorbike, nothing. It was a bit un-nerving. Over the years, Jock had spent a lot of time flying solo around the country, but he had never felt as alone as he was feeling right then. Thank God for his little visitor each morning. Without that little turtle around, he felt he could easily go nuts. If he knew there was to be a happy ending he could have enjoyed the solitude for a while, once the pain of his injuries subsided. However not knowing what lay ahead made it a worrying and lonely time. He tried hard to remain positive.

Time was slipping by, and he was getting a little unnerved by the whole dilemma. He had been out there for over a week and there had been not a single sign of human life. He could have been on the moon, or in the middle of the Pacific Ocean, it seemed that distant at times.

As the afternoon wore on, the sun disappeared behind a bank of very heavy clouds forming to the west. Definitely a storm brewing, he thought, and if it came his way it could be a great opportunity to replenish his water supplies. Not that his water supply was low, but the storm might provide enough rainwater to have a wash in. Perhaps even enough to clean his clothes and clean his wounds again. Fresh water, compliments of a Queensland storm, wouldn't go astray.

He set about pulling his bush water hole apart. He

needed the plastic sheets to keep himself dry when and if the rain did arrive. The nights were getting cold enough as it was, and the thought of being wet all night long was most unappealing.

He made a makeshift waterproof awning against the side of the plane with the plastic strips, using some branches and rocks as weights. Then he laid out any pieces of wreckage that he thought might catch and hold rainwater. He was going to be prepared if the storm passed through his region, as it looked like it might. He was glad for the activity. It helped to get his mind off his plight for a while at least. With his energy levels low and the pain still with his every move, he rested frequently.

The clouds grew darker as the afternoon wore on and the storm closed in. The air became very still and clammy, as it does just before a storm. Then it started to drizzle ever so lightly. A few leaves flew through the air and he knew the leading edge of the storm wasn't far away now. He got under his plastic covering and made some last minute adjustments, all the time keeping an eye on the western sky. It began to get very dark, and the feeling in the air worried him a little. The sky to the west had turned black. He spotted a patch of green in the clouds and the air suddenly turned very cold. He knew the signs.

'Hail, bloody hail,' he said out loud to himself. 'That's the last thing I need sitting out here on my own, to be blasted by a bloody hailstorm.'

He moved in under the fuselage as far as he could. More leaves were flying around now as the wind began to pick up. He could hear it whistling through the tops of the trees above him. The sky turned greener, a sure sign of hail.

Here she comes, he thought.

Suddenly the trees around him swirled over at over 45 degrees to the ground and a barrage of leaves washed across the sky. He wasn't surprised by the onset of the storm, but he was surprised where it came from. He had expected it to hit him from the west, but to his amazement it roared in over the rock wall behind him, from the south.

The trees twisted and buckled in the fierce wind, thrashing around as if in a washing machine. Leaves and debris were flying everywhere. He pulled himself as far beneath the fuselage as he possibly could.

Sheets of rain started pelting down. The odd small hailstones appeared flying in at a 45-degree angle, propelled by the fierce wind and making a deafening noise as they belted against the aluminium body of the plane. It continued its onslaught for a few minutes then the wind eased momentarily. Then, as if it were playing games with him it roared in again.

This time it was more like a tornado, slamming into the plane, ripping and tearing at anything in its path. From where he lay he could see part of the sky behind him. Pieces of debris from the wrecked plane were being tossed high into the air. Whole tree branches flew skyward, lifted by the sheer power of this thunderhead of destruction. He was glad it blew in from the south because the rock wall was protecting him from the flying debris. Even so, it was a terrifying time. The fuselage of the plane shook as the wind tried hard to lift it from the ground. He could feel the air pressure trying to drag him out from his haven. It roared on, not wanting to leave him alone. More debris, more hail, more wind. In a fierce storm, such as this one, time stands still. Your whole being is devoured by the moment. To say that being in a fierce Queensland storm and not feel fear would be a falsehood. They are terrifying acts of Nature. Jock felt that fear.

With the injury to his leg Jock couldn't move too far to escape the storms fury. Not that there was anywhere else to hide, he had about the safest place there was.

'Should the fuselage take off,' he thought, 'I'll crawl over against the rock wall. I might get wet, but at least I should be protected from the wind.'
None the less, he slid further under the plane as he could possibly squeeze.

More hailstones began flying in. They were larger now. Some were bouncing over the rock wall and tearing at the plastic sheets, slicing at them like a razor blade through paper.
Concerned that the hail would leave the plastic sheeting useless, he reached out and tried to pull it down, but in doing so the wind tore most of it from his grip.

Suddenly the fuselage of the plane shifted slightly as the wind pounded into in. Jock felt uneasy with the movement of the plane. He could get pinned under there if it moved again. He decided now was the time to find a safer place. Time to back up against the rock wall, wet he would have to be. At least there he could avoid the storm's fury and the flying hailstones, which by now were the size of golf balls. He crawled out from beneath the plane and slithered over to the rock wall. There he would huddle as close as he could to the rocky outcrop.

He reached the wall safely and decided that it was a good move. He was getting wet, but that was going to happen in such a savage deluge as this one anyway. There was a tiny overhang, almost enough to shelter from the wind and hail. He felt relatively safe, even though he now had a birds-eye view of the savagery of this beauty. He pushed his back into the rock face as hard as he could, watching as the hail shredded the trees of their foliage.

Suddenly, above him, and about 20 metres to his right, a tree appeared over the wall. It was a fair sized tree. He was preparing in his mind to watch it tumble over the edge to the ground below when a severe gust of wind lifted it into the air and projected it down into the valley. It flew through the air until finally, about 50 metres from where he was huddling, it smashed into an upright tree and literally exploded into hundreds of pieces. Mesmerized by the sudden explosion of bark and leaves, his attention was suddenly jolted back to the plane. He watched anxiously as the fuselage shook and lifted about a half a metre from the ground. The storm was trying to claim it, but it wasn't prepared to yield. Every time it rose, so too it would thud back down again. That went on for some minutes, the storm's fury versus the plane's weight. The plane won out. It stayed where it had crashed. The storm conceded.

The hail eased and then stopped altogether. One problem passed, but the storm hadn't danced its last dance. Sheets of rain followed, to the point where he could no longer see the trees in front of him. It was like a winter snow blizzard, a white out. It felt eerie as the valley in front of him disappeared from view. The rain was very cold. Jock was freezing cold. He remained where he was watching in awe as the storm continued its passage above him. The rain eased and the trees and valley slowly reappeared before him until finally the wind dropped to be nothing more than a gentle zephyr.

The violent storm had lasted only about ten or fifteen minutes, but it had left the area a total shambles. With the torrential rain that had poured down, Jock was now soaked to the bone, but he had avoided the dangerous wind and hail and for that he was thankful. He crawled back under the fuselage of the plane and covered himself with the remaining few shreds of plastic he had found.

The rain continued to fall lightly into the night. He took off his wet clothes and wrapped himself in one of the few decent sized pieces of plastic sheeting that hadn't blown away, and with another piece, he fashioned a cover over his head. At least he was relatively dry and now with the wet clothes off he was again quite pleasantly warm. The noise of the now gentle rain on the fuselage was almost soothing. He lay there watching the strobe lightning slowly fade until darkness again ruled his world. He slept.

The sun rose the following morning to be greeted by endlessly clear blue skies. Its welcoming amber light shone on over a scene of considerable devastation. There were branches from trees down everywhere and Jock could see sheets of aluminium glistening in the early morning sun, hundreds of metres away on the next hillside. They were obviously parts of his wrecked plane that had been blown there by the strong winds.

The storm had been a bad one, Jock thought, as he crawled back out to view the destruction, but it was a beautiful sight also; beads of moisture and left over raindrops were hanging from every leaf and sparkling in the morning sunlight. Christmas lights were never this good, he thought, as he looked in awe at Mother Nature's work. It was beautiful and tragic all in one. He felt a strong sense of wellbeing, like one feels after the passing of a storm, like setting out on a new life, a new beginning. It felt great to be alive. He just wished he wasn't alone. He was missing Mary and the kids badly. Nevertheless, with this feeling of a new life beginning, he set about collecting the water from his makeshift water catchers and clearing them of leaves and debris the storm had deposited in them.

Next he hung his wet clothes over the top of the plane to dry and then lit a fire to cook up some breakfast and warm his spirits with a hot drink, dressed only in a pair of jocks.

Once he'd eaten and delighted over his hot cup of tea, he worked out a plan to get things back into some sort of order. He was always one who liked things in their place. That was just his nature.

The first job that morning was to retrieve whatever pieces of plastic sheeting he could, to rebuild his bush water supply and for shelter should he need it again. Not that the plastic was much good this time, but then he could never have foreseen the strength of the storm and its winds. Again the fishing rod became useful. Rather than try and walk around the area he delighted and humoured himself by sitting down on a fallen tree and casting out the line, in the direction of some of the plastic sheets and eventually retrieved enough of them to fix his bush water trap. He laughed every time he missed his target, and gave out a joyful cheer whenever he succeeded. He retrieved enough for a small shelter if it looked like raining again. There were a few good-sized sheets just out of casting range, so he decided to walk out and retrieve them.

He supported himself on a broken tree branch, using it as a walking stick to shuffle along. It was the first time he'd tested out the injured leg. He knew it needed more time for it still gave him pain, but he was determined. The whole process had taken up quite a bit of effort and time.

By midday, Jock had his 'house' back in order and now that his clothes were dry, he was able to dress properly again. He smiled to himself at the thought of how strange it must look sitting out there in the bush, in only his jocks and fishing for lizards. He knew it would make for interesting stories to tell his children and perhaps even grandchildren in the years to come. All he had to do was to wait for the rescuers to find him or time enough for his body to heal enough to carry himself out.

The storm the night before was the second storm to have entered Jock's life in the past eight days. He'd survived them both, and although injured in the first, he'd come through the second with no more damage done. His 'house' had been rebuilt, so to speak, he'd replenished his water supply, and he still had some emergency food left and of course he had his fishing line. On top of all that, he had a clean set of clothes to wear, not quite the way he'd planned on washing them, but nevertheless they were relatively clean. The storm had just been a little interlude helping him pass time in what was becoming a lengthy ordeal.

He had to keep his hopes up though, as his old grandmother used to say, 'where there's life, there's hope' and he was determined to keep both. After all, aborigines had survived for nearly 40,000 years out there, and if they could do it for that long surely he could manage it for just a few weeks. He had water, he had some food, his health was still reasonable, and he had plenty of determination. After all said and done, the broken leg and ribs were just a small hindrance in the grand scheme of things. He was going to get out alive; he knew it and he hoped that Mary knew it also. Only the rescuers didn't. For now it was about staying as healthy as he could until the day came when he would be heading home. If only there was some way of letting Mary know he was alive and allay her fears, then he would be happy staying there for as long as it took.

By mid-afternoon, Jock was again preparing himself for what looked like another storm brewing to the west. He was wiser now, and he could prepare himself better in the event of another downpour. Keep it simple. Wrap himself in the plastic and either get under the fuselage or back up to the rock wall, depending on which way the storm blew in from.

With the approaching storm, every bird in the area squawked their loudest. Suddenly, for one brief moment, over the racket of the birds, he thought he heard a dog bark in the distance. He wished the birds would shut-up and he had a strong compulsion to yell out at them to do just that. He strained his ears searching for that distant bark again, but it didn't return.

He thought to himself, do dingoes bark? He didn't think they did. He turned to face one ear in the direction of the noise. Still he heard nothing unusual, just the squawking birds and the distant rumblings of another approaching storm. He turned his head the other way and listened with that ear. Still there was nothing. Maybe it wasn't a dog bark at all; perhaps it was his imagination playing tricks on him.

Maybe! Maybe! Maybe! For a brief moment he thought about the maybe's. Then he just as quickly stopped himself. Maybe can be a destructive word. There was no place for maybe's in his dilemma; he had to stay focused and positive.

A clap of thunder warned him that another storm was nearby. It was time to get ready again. He rolled up all but two of the remaining shredded plastic sheets, and packed them away securely under the fuselage. Of the two strips he kept out, he would wrap one around his body and put the other over his head when and if the rains came. This time he planned to stay dry and warm.

The Red Hill

Sunrise on Nundooka Station.
Wednesday and Thursday, the 20th and 21st of March.

After the big day out in Roma, and the excitement of the passing storm, Danny and his parents settled down for a good night's sleep back on Nundooka.

Next morning, Lucas and Danny got up with the rising sun and had an early breakfast. After breakfast, he said his good-byes to his mother and they left Nundooka and set off on the old motorbike, with Danny perched on the back with his arms wrapped around his father's waist. They were heading back out to join up with their mob of sheep and finally bring them back to the property.

They reached the mob about three quarters of an hour down the road, still in the paddock and still in the good care of Lucas's old mate Reg. The two men sat for a while enjoying a cuppa at Reg's campfire, chatting about the rains and the storm the afternoon before. After a few minutes Danny joined in telling old Reg about the school sport's day and how he'd run third in his main event, the 200metre final. Reg was impressed. Then Danny brought up the subject of the crashed plane, and they talked for a while about that as well, all offering their own opinions as to where it might be, and whether or not the pilot could still be alive.

Then the topic turned to hard times past and of their optimism for the region's future after the good rains of late. The talk of rain led Reg to offer his opinion that the weather patterns were right for another storm or two.

'More rain coming,' he said, 'maybe even today.'

Talk of storms and rain was always a popular topic to people on the land, so the two talked on a little while longer over another cup of tea and some toast over the open fire and then smothered in honey.

Danny in the meantime had tired of listening to the two farmers talking and had saddled up one of the horses.

'Is it ok dad if I go and look for the crashed plane? I bet no one has looked down this way!'

'That's fine Danny just don't go too far and head on back when you hear me start up the motor bike and toot the horn.'

'Can't figure that one out Lucas,' said Reg, as Danny headed out on a horse, 'Poor buggar's been missing for over a week now.'

'Poor buggar's been dead for over a week would be more like it,' replied Lucas.

'You're probably right there Lucas. I guess not too many people survive plane crashes at the best of times, but out here, you'd need to be a lucky man for sure.'

Around midday, Annie drove out with some lunch for 'her men' and was not at all surprised to see Lucas and Reg still sitting around the campfire talking and drinking their umpteenth cup of tea.

Country folk don't get together all that often, but whenever they did, every subject imaginable was tackled, and they're generally not inclined to rush things either. She thought it was good for Lucas to have some time catching up with an old friend. He'd been on the road for so long that she knew he would be enjoying the time to just sit and chat for a while.

Lucas liked people to think that he was a hard worker and Annie didn't want him feeling guilty about sitting around all morning talking, so she just casually joined in on the conversation.

The men appreciated the lunch, and continued talking after they'd eaten it. Meanwhile, Annie decided to mount up another horse and go and look for Danny. She was a little worried about Danny out riding on his own, or maybe she just wanted to show Lucas that she approved of him taking time with his old friend.

Having had to look after the property, as well as dealing with the tragic loss of their 'Poppy', she too hadn't had much relaxation time over the previous few months, and so was more than happy to get on horseback and ride out to look for her son.

She found Danny climbing a tree not too far away. He told her he was trying to get a better view of the countryside, to look for the plane. She persuaded him to climb back down and they rode over a few more hills together. Annie enjoyed the ride.

She felt good seeing different countryside for a change.

They returned to the campsite about an hour later and just in time to say good-bye to Reg. They'd chatted long enough and Lucas felt he should get the sheep moving again, to get some miles done'. He'd already lost a day and a half, although he felt satisfied that the time had not been wasted. He enjoyed the break, just to take time out for a while and not feel hurried. It was certainly a late start that day and around one o'clock they got the sheep moving again. Annie also left for Nundooka at the time her two 'men' broke camp.

They pushed on all afternoon without a break until they finally stopped to set up camp around sunset. As there were no storms or rain in sight, Lucas decided that the tent wouldn't be needed. They would sleep under the stars that night, besides he knew Danny loved open campfires.

They played a game that night, an old favourite, to try and pick which creatures made which sounds. It was a game they played often at Nundooka, before Lucas had gone away. They used to call it 'Spooks at night'. Lucas always felt to understand the night sounds would take away any fear Danny may have of the darkness. That night, between talking and playing 'Spooks', Danny had a terrific time, until finally tiredness overtook him and he settled down in his sleeping bag.

The following morning, Thursday March the 21st, was another one of those spectacular mornings that western Queensland knows how to produce. Cool, clean autumn air, the birds chirping with excitement at being alive, smoke from their fire hanging in the air creating streak-like patterns as the sun's rays tried to pierce through. Danny stoked up the campfire again until it was blazing, and then just sat in front of its warming glow and watched the amazing show a good fire can produce. Annie had brought them some eggs and bacon the day before and it didn't take long for Lucas to get the morning meal under way. The wonderful smell of food cooking on an open fire certainly helped to arouse their taste buds. Shortly after, along with a piping hot cup of tea, they enjoyed breakfast together, bush style.

With their stomachs suitably filled, the two packed up camp and got the sheep moving in a nor-easterly direction towards Nundooka. Within a few hours, the cool autumn air and slight cloud cover had been burnt away, and was now being replaced by a blazing hot sun.

They made good ground with the sheep and around the middle of the day, Annie drove up again, this time with freshly made egg and lettuce sandwiches and to wash it down, a couple of cans of cold lemonade from a small Esky. It was a pleasant break, albeit a short one, one they both felt they'd earned.

Lucas was pleased to see Annie, but at the same time, just a little annoyed that he felt she didn't think that he could take care of Danny. He kept his annoyance well under cover for he knew her intentions were good. Really though he had wanted a little time alone with Danny, some time spent together, just the boys, father and son.

She didn't stay long and within a half an hour they set out again. The sky began to cloud over and by mid-afternoon it looked very much like a storm might be heading their way. Lucas decided to stop earlier than usual and make camp just in case the storm turned out to be a bad one. For the third day in a row he hadn't driven the sheep very far, but he reminded himself, sometimes that's just how it goes out in the bush.

They put the old tent up. It was not looking like a night for sleeping under the stars, with the prospect of rain again. Danny set about making a campfire by firstly collecting as much wood as he could find and then stacking it up near where the fire was to be lit. That was his afternoon job now, and he liked it. 'Get another one of your fires going Danny', or 'put another log on your fire Danny'. They were 'his' fires now and that made him feel important. His father included him, along with the sheepdogs, the horses, and the old rusty motorbike, as being part of the team.

By 4 p.m. light rain was starting to fall and they both thought it best to shelter inside the tent, just going outside periodically to check on the sheep and to try and keep Danny's fire from going out completely. A little to the north of them Lucas could see a big storm was building. It looked mean, like it was going to be severe. The clouds were black with patches of green in them, usually a telltale sign of hail and severe winds. The rain they always needed. The wind and hail they could do without.

Lucas thought about Annie. Nundooka was to the north of them, and it looked like she would be right in line for the worst of it. The wind picked up and leaves began flying through the air. The trees were twisting and swirling overhead. He'd seen worse. Just a small blow, a bit of rain and it'll be gone in no time, he reassured Danny. But to the north it was looking decidedly ferocious. Someone, somewhere was going to get belted tonight, he thought.

The rain very rapidly became heavier and heavier. The campfire didn't take long to go out, but thankfully they didn't get any hail. They tucked themselves away inside the tent and hoped they'd tied it down securely enough to withstand the winds.

Within half an hour it had passed. When they reappeared from inside the tent they could see the tail end of the storm heading away to the east.

It's a wonderful time, after the passing of a big storm. There is a special stillness in the air. That calm, cleansing feeling that only the aftermath of a storm offers. Lucas thought to himself, that everyone should experience a Queensland storm at least once in there lives. He felt it was truly one of nature's wondrous offerings. The passing of this storm made him feel like he was part of a new beginning, a rebirth of sorts. It was a good sign he thought, almost like the bad times of the past few years were now behind him, and he could look ahead to a positive future again. He thought of Annie and hoped all was well on Nundooka.

They spent the rest of the night sheltering from the light rain inside the tent, although Lucas donned his Drizza-Bone a couple of times and went out to check on the sheep and horses. The rain continued lightly falling on and off throughout the night, but they stayed warm and cosy in the old tent. It wasn't long before Danny was dead to the world; it had been another big day for him on the road.

The next morning, Friday, the 22nd of March, saw Lucas and Danny waking early as usual. They first checked on the sheep, and then Danny lit one of his campfires and Lucas prepared breakfast. After a good feed in the belly, they were on the road again. There were signs everywhere that the storm the night before had been a fairly bad one, and the further they travelled north, the more debris they saw along the roadside and in the surrounding countryside. After about two hours of walking the sheep along the debris-scattered road, a Toyota Landcruiser made its way slowly through the mob of sheep and pulled up alongside of Lucas. A man and a woman got out, introduced themselves as Mary and Roger, and told him they were searching for Jock and the crashed plane.

The official search parties have been concentrating on an area around the main western highway. They had first started searching up around the Carnarvon Gorge and then moved down near Roma and now they're searching between Roma and Mitchell,' Mary explained.

Lucas questioned her, 'I heard about that! You're saying that you don't agree with them?'

'Well yes and no! Yes, it's very probable that he was following the highway and should have landed close to it. But then it was a very severe storm and he may have tried to fly south around it.'

'But wasn't the worst of that storm down our way?' Lucas asked.

'Yes it was. But it changed direction and built up suddenly surprising everyone, probably surprised Jock also. I'm just a little annoyed that they haven't spent more time searching down here, but they just won't listen to me.'

'You said landed. Everyone else is saying he crashed. Don't you believe he crashed?' Lucas inquired.

'They say he crashed, but I can't, so to me he landed somewhere, and I'm out here to find him.'

'I haven't seen anything unusual down here, and I don't wish to sound rude, but don't you think you're a bit too far south. We're over a hundred kilometres from Mitchell.'

'Well I would have agreed with you but for one thing,' Mary continued.

Lucas raised an eyebrow slightly, showing interest in her answer.

'Have you ever heard the story about the missing drovers?' Mary asked.

'What missing drovers is that then?' Lucas questioned.

'Well, late last century, two drovers went missing, a father and his son. They were on their way back from taking cattle to Broken Hill, when they disappeared somewhere in this district,' Mary explained.

'I've heard a few old timers talking about some drovers. My father mentioned it once or twice also, but no-one ever knew if it was a true story or just some ghost story made up in a bar one night.'

Roger, who was leaning against the front of their vehicle, asked, 'What do you mean by a ghost story?'

'Some say there's a ghost around the Maranoa. They've seen him riding a horse at night and heard him cracking a bullwhip. I never took too much notice of the story. Just some old drunk's imagination. If there's a ghost out here he's never bothered me.'

'What about a red hill then?' asked Roger.

'I think the red hill came with the ghost story, didn't it,' replied Lucas.

Mary was trying not to get annoyed with Lucas. She felt, like so many others, that he was treating the story lightly.

'I did some research on the missing drovers, and the story could well be true. I don't know about the ghost bit, but I believe in the red hill.'

She paused while looking for a reaction, and then continued, 'I'm running out of time. I have to believe in it, it's all I have left.'

Lucas realised that she was being serious and responded somewhat apologetically, 'I don't mean to make fun of the situation, but if a ghost story is all you've got left perhaps you should go home and leave the searching to the experts.'

Mary fired back an answer immediately, 'They all may be ready to quit, but I'm not. He's alive, I know it, and I'll go on searching until I find him.'

She continued, 'I found a poem that someone published about fifty years ago. It tells the story of two missing drovers and of a red hill that's said to be sixty miles north of where the two rivers meet. That's a hundred kilometres north of the junction of the Balonne and Maranoa rivers. That's right about here I'd say.'

'I'd agree with that, but tell me because I'm a little confused on something, what's the red hill to do with all this.'

'Didn't I mention that Roma Control Tower received a Mayday call from Jock the morning after he crashed and he mentioned a red hill. He said he was injured and he didn't know where he was, but he could see a red hill.'

Lucas nodded as if to say that he understood its place in the whole thing now.

'Look I'm sorry,' he said, 'but I don't think I can help you with much. I remember hearing something about the ghosts, and the red hill, but I never put the two together before. I was only a boy like Danny here. To me it was just a story. I didn't pay that much attention to it. My dad used to make up stories all the time. He was full of them.'

Lucas paused briefly as he shooed some pesky flies from around his eyes, and then he continued,

'I've never seen a red hill. It's just bloody scrub out here. The nearest thing to a red hill that I've seen is the occasional bunch of red wildflowers.'

He got Mary's full attention with the mention of red flowers and she questioned him on it, "What type of wildflowers?'

'Sturt Pea I think they're called. Sometimes after a good season of rain you'll see the odd clump around. They're very impressive, but I haven't seen any for a while, mind you, I've been down further south for the past year or so.'

'Can you remember where you saw them?' Mary asked in hope.

'I've seen the odd clumps around Nundooka. That's our property, about twenty kilometres north of here. You see them sometimes on the side of the road, but just a few flowers here and there. You've got to nearly fall over them to see them. Nowhere near enough to cover a hill,' Lucas stressed, 'but you also see yellow, purple, white, all different colours after rain.'

To Mary at least, that was confirmation of wild red flowers in the area. Also it was near the area where the drovers were supposed to have disappeared. She felt that Lucas thought she was a bit loopy, but the official search hadn't found any red hill, so who knows, maybe they were looking in the wrong area for the wrong thing. Jock saw a red hill that no one else could explain, so why not missing drovers, ghosts and flower covered hills. It was another explanation, and well worth pursuing at least. Jock was obviously injured when he made the call, and if all he could see was a hill with a reddish colour, then why not a large enough amount of flowers to catch his eye.

Soon after Lucas promised to keep an eye out for anything out of the ordinary, especially red flowers, Mary and Roger headed south in the Landcruiser. Not long after that Danny and Lucas saddled up, moved the sheep out from a fenceless paddock they had happily wandered into to graze, and in no time at all, were heading north along the roadside again.

As they rode slowly along, Danny told his father everything he'd heard or read about the crashed plane, and the little he knew about the search. Lucas was surprised that he hadn't heard more about it and was amazed that he hadn't seen any search planes, or rescue crews, looking down around where they were. He questioned out loud, as much to himself as to Danny, why if the rescue parties had searched up to one hundred and fifty kilometres north of the flight path, as Danny had told him, then why hadn't they searched one hundred and fifty kilometres south also. That didn't seem to make sense to him.

'Commonsense,' he told Danny. 'City people might all be

born with five senses, sight, smell, hearing, feel and taste, but they sure haven't got much when it comes to the sixth one. Maybe that lady we met earlier isn't as silly as I first thought. Perhaps she knows something all those experts don't. Crikey, some women have got another sense sometimes, that woman thing. Sometimes they just sense things that we blokes don't. She sounds like a very determined lady. If I were missing out in this country, I'd feel better knowing she was on my side.'

'Do you think he could still be alive?' Danny asked hopeful of a positive answer.

'I hope for her sake he is, but over a week out here, and probably injured, I don't fancy his chances. I sure as hell wouldn't want to be in his shoes right now. If he's still alive he'll be doing it tough out there alone.'

Lucas didn't dwell on it anymore and quickly put the plane and the missing pilot out of his mind. He had sheep to attend to and needed to keep them on the move before it got too hot.

The day had turned into another hot one, with the temperature climbing into the mid 30's. Around 1o'clock Lucas decided to stop for a while. They'd been pushing hard ever since Mary and Roger had stopped them four hours earlier.

Even though Lucas had put the crashed plane out of his mind, Danny hadn't. When they stopped he asked if his Dad if he could ride over to a line of hills about two kilometres away to the east, to see if he could see the lost plane.

Lucas reluctantly gave him the okay, providing he didn't get out of sight of the road or the sheep and providing he took one of the sheep dogs with him.

'Half an hour,' Lucas said. 'Make sure you're back in half an hour. We've still got quite a few good hours left in us yet.'

Danny agreed not to go any further than the first large hill and off he rode with one of the dogs following on behind. Lucas watched him for a while and then sat down in the shade of a gum tree to rest. It had been a hectic few days. In and out to Roma, the storm, all the visitors slowing them down, and now that Nundooka was almost in sight, it seemed like he couldn't get a good run at it.

About a half hour passed and Lucas was just about nodding off to sleep, when Danny came riding in at full pace.

He was very excited, 'I saw it,' he said gasping for air. 'I saw the crashed plane. I saw it! I saw it!'
Lucas got to his feet, 'You saw what?'

'I saw it reflecting in the sun. I saw it. I saw the plane.'

Lucas knew that Danny had been stirred up about the plane crash ever since the visit from Mary and Roger that morning, so he didn't take Danny any more seriously than a father would of his ten year old son who was just dying to solve the riddle.

He replied in a cool, but polite tone, 'I'm sure you saw something Danny, but it could have been anything reflecting in the sun.'

'No Dad, it must be the plane. What else would be out there, that far from the road?'

The comment made Lucas think for a while. What indeed would be out in that bush? Perhaps it was an old campsite. Roo shooters go bush after their prey at night, and then they usually sleep during the day. Maybe it was just the sun reflecting off their vehicle's windscreen in the distance. Or maybe something as simple as the sun shining on an old beer bottle left behind by one on an earlier trip. But Danny was insistent.

'Well, I suppose it wouldn't hurt to ride over there and

take a quick look', he replied. 'If it'll make you happy, I suppose there's little harm. Just a quick look though, I wanna get this mob home sometime before Christmas.'

'Thanks Dad.'

With his father away in the long paddock, and the recent death of his 'Poppy', Danny had been forced to growing up quicker than most, but still he had plenty of childish adventure left in him. In his mind, they rode out together, as if on a great adventure. Father and son, off to solve the great mystery of the missing plane and rescue the pilot.

They reached the top of the hill together and looked away to the east, in the direction that Danny had seen the reflection coming from, but there was nothing but trees, trees and more trees.

'Dad I saw it. I saw it shining in my face, right over there.' Danny pointed to the spot. 'Please dad, I'm not making it up, I saw it.'

Danny seemed so determined he'd seen something that Lucas thought about it a moment longer.

'I'm no bloody scientist, but the sun would have moved since you saw it about twenty minutes ago. So let's move our positions a bit and see if we can spot whatever it was you saw. If you move slowly that way and I go this way.'

Lucas had only moved about two metres when a bright reflection caught his eye. He called Danny over and they dismounted and both stood there together staring at a bright flash of light from the east. As they watched it began to lose its brightness and suddenly it was gone again.

Lucas took a small sideways step and there it was again, hitting him right in the face. It was a fair distance off, but from that distance it was definitely too bright to be a beer bottle. It had to be something bigger.

'Maybe it's a mining surveyor working the area,' he thought out loud, 'although there hasn't been any out this way for years, well not that I've heard of. Have you heard anything Danny?'

'No Dad, I haven't heard anything. I think it's the plane Dad, well it could be couldn't it?'
'Well I'm not sure what it could be.'

Usually if someone was out and about in an area, the 'bush telegraph' would let the locals know.

The bush telegraph is an Australian term for a local network of information and gossip passed on from one person to another by personal contact, CB radio, telephone or radio wireless. But the bush telegraph also had a mysterious quality about it. Sometimes information just moved from place to place by itself, with no apparent help from humans. It just happened.

'I think it's probably just a kangaroo shooter asleep under a shady tree down there, waiting for darkness to go out shooting again. I'd say it just the sun on the windscreen of his truck, but yeah I think it's worth a closer look.'

Lucas thought it best though to mark the location and direction from where they saw the light, so they could find it again later, if need be. They found some tree branches and fashioned a cross bound with some string Lucas carried in his saddlebags. He bashed it into the ground with the cross part pointing towards the area where they had seen the bright light. With that done then rode off in the direction of the light. Danny was understandably very excited. He really believed they were going to find the plane.

Lucas began to feel somewhat nervous the further they rode down the hill. What if it was the crashed plane, he thought, for sure the pilot would be dead and he didn't fancy coming across such a horrible scene as a fly blown, rotten, smelly corpse. If the crashed hadn't torn the body apart, wild animals probably would have by now. He didn't know whether to say anything to Danny, to prepare him for what they might find. He decided not to, after all it may not be anything like that, it was probably just a hunter and there was little point in worrying Danny unnecessarily.

With no idea how far the light beam had carried, they rode on slowly, scouting the surrounding area as they went. It could have been a kilometre or it could have been three kilometres, it was hard to tell out there.

After about twenty minutes slowly riding through the scrub, Lucas decided that they'd gone far enough and that they really should be turning back. Realistically, it was like looking for a needle in a haystack, he told Danny. But Danny was persistent, 'Just one more hill,' he begged, 'just one more, pleeeeeeease Dad?'

The terrain consisted of low rolling hills with the occasional rocky outcrop. Between the hills were flat areas of low, rather dense scrub. From a distance the hills didn't look very high, but as they rode into them, they were high enough to obscure their vision ahead. However the top of each hill provided some sort of view ahead. The scrub thick enough in places that Lucas realised they could ride straight past and whether it was a kangaroo shooter or the plane wreck, they might not see anything. They could be less than a hundred metres away and not see a thing.

Lucas looked around and picked out the highest hill and said to Danny, 'That's it mate, one more hill, that high one over there, but if we see nothing, we'll head back, I just can't spend all day out here looking for what might well be nothing at all.'

Danny knew that his father didn't like leaving the sheep

unattended so reluctantly he agreed. He knew that he had to, but he also realised himself just what his father already knew, that it was not going to be easy finding anything out there in that scrub.

'Maybe I can get some mates next weekend and we can ride out here and take a look around.'

'It's still a long way from home Danny,' he replied.

'Would be cool but.'

'We'll see, we'll see.'

They headed for the high hill that Lucas had pointed out and about ten minutes later atop the hill they dismounted and looked around. They could see in all directions for about three kilometres or so. Well they could see rolling hills surrounded by thick scrub.

It also showed Lucas how easily it could swallow up a man, never to be seen again. Surely though, if there was a plane down there, they would be able to see it, or at least some sign of it. He searched for a sign, a burnt tree, debris, a small unusual clearing, something! Anything at all!

Lucas realised he too was being drawn into the whole, larger than life mystery himself.

His thoughts were jolted away by Danny yelling out at the top of his voice from all of a metre away, 'Dad, Dad, there it is. There it is, the red hill, Dad... look it's the red hill.'

Lucas looked in the direction that Danny was pointing and sure enough, about three or four kilometres away to the south-east, on the side of a smallish hill, was a large patch of something red.

Lucas always carried a compass in his saddlebag. He took a bearing between his position and that of the red hill. It would be a long way through the bush and he knew he would need to be pinpoint accurate or they could miss the spot altogether. He looked back to the west and he could see the road snaking its way along in the distance. He took a bearing on that as well and then he wrote down his measurements.

He looked back at the red patch and shook his head in almost disbelief. There it was. Maybe that lady was right all along. Was this the mythical red hill, talked about over campfires and in pubs for over a hundred years? Was this the red hill that Jock, the pilot, had radioed in about? There was only one way to find out.

'Well Danny,' he said, 'we'd better take a closer look.'

Danny was more excited than ever, he was just about jumping out of his skin. This was the crashed plane, he just knew it, and he couldn't wait to get there.

'We've found it Dad! We've found the plane! We've actually found it, haven't we? Wait till Mum hears about this!'

Lucas was still just a little skeptical about it being the red hill that the lady on the road, and the pilot had spoken of, but at least now he had an open mind about it.

He spoke to Danny in a calm voice, 'We've found something unusual, that's for sure, but let's just wait till we get over there and see just what it is. It might be nothing to do with the crashed plane at all.'

They made their way down the hillside and into the scrub below. Once down in the gully they lost sight of the red hill, so Lucas used the compass to direct them towards their goal. They made their way about a kilometre through the scrub and eventually started making their way up the next hill. Again they could see clumps of bright red flowers on the western slope a few hills away. It looked like all together they probably covered an area about the size of an average city house block.

They pushed on through thick bush and finally half way up a hill they stopped. They both sat, leaning forward in their saddles and stared at the sight in front of them. It was quite beautiful. Out there in the middle of all that harsh scrub was this most beautiful hillside of wild red flowers with little jet-black centres.

After a minute or so, Danny interrupted the moment, 'I've never seen anything like them before. Can we pick some for mum, she'd like them?' Then he corrected himself, 'No, let's look for the plane first, then we'll pick some flowers for mum.'

Lucas quietly nodded and then mumbled, 'Sure looks like a red hill, doesn't it?'

Danny realised at that moment that his father just might be starting to believe that the plane might be here also. They rode around searching for the plane for another hour or so but found nothing. They found no sign of debris and no sign of human life anywhere. Lucas decided that it would take more than two people in that thick scrub to find any sign of the pilot or his wrecked craft. If he could convince the official search team that they were on to something positive, they could get searchers out there, perhaps even a helicopter.

It was now well after three o'clock in the afternoon and Lucas could see more storm clouds building up again in the west. He made the decision to head back to the road, find or make an opening into a nearby paddock, and bed the sheep down for the night. Then they could head in to Nundooka on the motorbike and report their findings by phone to the police constable back in Mitchell. Then hopefully, they'd have time to get back out to the sheep before the storm hit. He took more bearings on his compass and they headed back.

Sheep, unlike cattle, aren't likely to stampede if spooked by a storm, but Jock liked to be with them just in case something went wrong.

They rode back to the flowers, and picked a bunch for

Annie, then rode straight back to the road and the waiting sheep. Lucas looked for and found a gateway into a paddock just a little further down the road and moved the sheep into the paddock with the help of the dogs. Danny hooked the wire gate back up while Lucas fired up the motorbike and together they headed for Nundooka.

Annie was thrilled with the flowers and amazed to hear about the bright reflection and the red hill.

'Do you think it could be the plane, Lucas?'

'I don't know really, but it's certainly worth looking into tomorrow. The further we went, the more we looked around the more I started to believe it could be. We spoke to the pilot's wife this morning, she was out there looking for him and she reckons he's down this way somewhere,' Lucas told her.

'I thought he was supposed to have crashed further north somewhere, the other side of Mitchell?'

'Yeah so does everyone, but she's got other ideas, and you never know, she may just be right.'

Lucas quickly explained to Annie about the drover's tale and the red hill and that the pilot's wife Mary had done all this research into finding her husband. He confided to Annie that at first he thought her a bit crazy when she told the story. 'Maybe she's not so mad after all, maybe she got it right and they were searching in the wrong areas.'

Lucas rang the police in Mitchell and told the Constable everything that had happened that day, from the roadside meeting with Mary and Roger, all the way through to the red hill and the bright reflecting light.

Annie whipped up some scrambled eggs for an early tea for them and soon after Danny climbed onto the back of the motorbike and they headed back out to the sheep.

Lucas couldn't believe it, eighteen months on the road

where he'd hardly seen a soul the whole time. He'd seen nothing more exciting than the odd snake slither past, and now within days of finally getting home and all of this was happening around him. Big storms a plenty and now even red hills. Life had suddenly become very hectic. Soon there would be more people around than he would hope to see at a Saturday night dance at the bowls club. He thought about the solitude of the previous year and just briefly he missed it.

CHAPTER ELEVEN

The Final Effort
Friday the 22nd of March 7 p.m. 1994

Mary and Roger returned to Mitchell after a day of searching about a hundred kilometres to the south. This time instead on driving up and down roads though, they had driven across country wherever they could. It had been another hot, tiresome day, without finding any clues to help them find Jock. Still through it all, Mary remained in an up-beat mood and stayed very positive, 'Another day closer to finding him,' she told Roger as they climbed from the vehicle.

As they entered the foyer of the motel the local policeman greeted them. He presented them with the news that he'd received a phone call from a farmer at about 5 o'clock. The farmer had claimed to see a bright reflection on a hillside about a hundred kilometres south on the road to St.George. He, along with his son, had spent some time looking for the source of the reflection, but they couldn't find it. Instead they had come across a hillside covered in red flowers. He also mentioned that earlier in the day she'd spoken to them. He said to say he was the man with all the sheep.

Of course Mary remembered him. How could she ever forget a man and his son, along with hundreds of sheep, way out there in what to her was the middle of nowhere.

She hugged the policeman with joy, 'that is the best news I've heard in over a week, you darling man.'

They immediately rang search headquarters in Roma with the news, and after a number of short discussions with different officials there, Roma search headquarters finally began to take her seriously. They said they'd switch their ground search to that area and ring her back at the motel in an hour or so with the details. They arranged for three search and rescue vehicles to meet her at her motel at 7a.m. the next morning.

When the phone call finally came through at about 9pm, Mary was ecstatic.

'Finally,' she said to Roger, who had been sitting with her patiently consuming copious quantities of coffee, 'we're on the right track. I just know it.'

'It's a ray of sunshine indeed,' he replied.

'I truly believe we are on the right track, let's just hope we're not too late', Mary said in a quiet sad voice.

Roger was surprised at her statement, 'That's the first time all week I've heard you speak like that.'

'Like what?'

'In a negative tone, as if Jock may not be ok.'

'Sorry, it just slipped out. Of course deep down I've had doubts. I just didn't want them to know it.'

'Them, you mean the search crews?' Roger asked.

'If I'd shown any sort of doubt', Mary said, 'they might have stopped looking for a live person. I just don't think they would have tried as hard if they believed they were looking for a dead body.'

'It'll be fine, he's a survivor', Roger said in an uplifted tone.

'I hope you're right', Mary said.

'I am right, and you get those negative thoughts out of your head my girl. Tomorrow is the day. He's fine. Believe.'

She leaned over and put her head on Roger's shoulder, 'Beautiful man, beautiful friend, how could I have gotten through this week without you!'

'Hey, that's what friends are for.'

They stayed in an embrace for a long time until finally Roger pulled away, wiped a small tear from her eye, and told her it was time to try and get some sleep.'

Mary found it hard to sleep. She tossed and turned all night long, going over and over in her mind the clues that had led up to this moment. She was totally confident that they had the right area and she knew they were close now. She prayed many times that night. Her faith had never wavered since the day she received that horrible phone call telling her that Jock was down and missing.

Saturday March 22, 6.30 a.m.

Mary was up and ready early that morning. Perhaps up was the wrong word, for she never really went to sleep. She had lay there but had hardly slept at all. So during the night she had gone over her notes again. She had read the poem until the ink seemed to fade on the paper, and she had studied the maps. She went over and over everything in her mind. Finally this was it. This was the day they'd find Jock. She just knew it. It had to be. Everything pointed to it, well in Mary's mind it did. She prayed again as she waited for the rescuers to arrive. She prayed he had survived against all the odds and was waiting for her. She looked at her children who were sleeping so peacefully. She was happy to think that all of this drama hadn't seemed to affect them. In that area their grandmother had done a wonderful job keeping them occupied. She kissed them both on the forehead and hoped they would all be home in Toowoomba very soon. Was that too much to ask for, she wondered?

She looked out the front door impatiently as the sun slowly brought light to the day. Mary hoped that it would bring light back into her life as well. The pre-dawn sky was beautiful with baby pink and blue colours filtering through some far off clouds. She watched as the sky lost its baby hue and heralded the golden birth of a new day. As she watched the sun coming up she thought of her Jock and hoped that he was watching the very same sunrise. She knew deep in her soul that this was the day she would be released from the horrible shackles that phone call had bound her in nine days before. More importantly this was the day she prayed would bring an end to Jock's nightmare. She looked to the south, crossed her chest in a religious symbol, and waited for the rescue vehicles to arrive from Roma. This was the day, even if the results didn't come out the way she prayed for. She knew that if the searchers found nothing that it was almost definite that the search would be called off. Time had run out. She knew that, she understood that, she hated the thought.

About 15 minutes later a procession of 4WD vehicles appeared from the east. As they drove down the main street towards her motel, she noticed that each vehicle had a horse float in tow. She walked out towards the edge of the road and waved at the lead vehicle. These men were well prepared and looked very much like they were ready for business. Thank God, Mary thought to herself, someone has finally listened.

She loved every one of those men for their untiring efforts, but by the same token, she was frustrated by the way they had been so stuck in their old 'tried and true' methods of doing things. She felt they hadn't been prepared to open their minds up to a woman's intuition. 'She was too emotionally involved,' they told her on more than one occasion. Perhaps now, she thought, when they find Jock, they might be forced into thinking a bit more laterally in the future.

Knowing that a rescue team was on its way, the owners

of the motel had their dining room all set up and served them all hot breakfast before they left.

The air was full of positive vibes that morning. Something Mary hadn't seen in the rescue crews before. Everyone seemed to sense that finally they were on the right track. The chatter around the breakfast table was exciting to hear. She knew she had been right and now they all seemed to believe it also.

By the time they'd finished the breakfast feast, about ten more vehicles had pulled up out front, all prepared to join in the renewed search effort. The word had spread throughout the district on the 'bush telegraph' overnight and help was pouring in from everywhere. Even some of the original searchers had returned to help out in what they all seemed to believe was shaping up as the final act and they all wanted to be there.

At around 7.30, a convoy of about fifteen vehicles headed south towards Nundooka. It had been arranged to meet up with Lucas and Danny where they would guide them to the newly discovered 'red hill.' As they drove south that morning, it was hoped by all, that this was the red hill that Jock mentioned in his only radio message for help over a week before. By the time they reached Nundooka, the convoy numbered about twenty.

Danny was a little disappointed when he saw all those vehicles pull in through the front gate. He had thought that he and his father would be the ones to return and find Jock's plane by themselves, well that's what he'd hoped for at least. Lucas assured him that it was better for Jock to have as many as possible out searching for him, before it was too late. The young boy thought about it for a moment before realising that his father was right. As it turned out, when the rescuers arrived, they made a big fuss over him. He was made to feel like a real hero.

After about 10 minutes of discussions between Lucas and the leaders of the search crew, the rest were briefed on the plan. In wrapping the briefing up, it was announced that Danny would lead the search party all the way to the 'red hill' area. Danny was thrilled by the attention and ran inside to tell his mother.

'I'm proud as punch of you darling,' she told him. She kissed him on the cheek, and then slapped him gently on the bottom, 'Now go and find that pilot and bring him home to his family.'

'We will Mum, you watch, I know he's there and I know he'll be OK.'

With that Danny ran out the door, put on his bike helmet and climbed on the back of his father's motor bike, 'I'm ready Dad,' he called, 'Let's show them the way.'

They moved out through Nundooka's front gateway, turned left onto the St.George Road and headed south towards the red hill area. A convoy of vehicles with horse floats behind followed the motorbike down the road for about 20minutes, and when they reached the mob of sheep happily grazing in a paddock, they stopped by the side of the road. The horses were unloaded, saddled up, mounted and within minutes of arriving were following Danny and Lucas, now also on horseback, eastward into the scrub. Some 4WD's followed slowly through the scrubby bush as best they could. They headed east until they reached the handmade marker Lucas had constructed the previous afternoon.

After a brief discussion it was decided that four men on horseback, would head off in the direction towards the bright reflection to investigate further what it was that caught the sun's rays the day before and to report back on CB radio if they came across anything. The rest of the horsemen and the 4WD vehicles, who had by then caught up, would make their way over towards the red hill and start a search on foot radiating out from there.

From an elevated position on the next high hill they got their first glimpse of the red flowers a few kilometres away. Again the party set off, but this time they could see their target ahead. For nine days they'd been searching for something they couldn't see, searching in the bush for a mystery, but now solving the mystery seemed close at hand. A red hill, hopefully THE red hill was just a few hills away.

Sturt's Desert Pea was not native to this district, therefore most of the men had never seen them before, and when they arrived at the site, most stood and marveled at how truly beautiful the iconic Australian wildflower was. The flowers seemed such a contrast to the bland harsh Australian bush around them. Someone commented that they had a regal look, more at home on a banquet table than in the middle of the Queensland bush, with no one to enjoy such a beauty. The red flower, with its jet-black seedpod in its centre, was strikingly impressive indeed. The flowers had adapted well out there following the late summer rains. They had spread right up the side of the hill like a wild pumpkin vine. Some asked the inevitable question, why there? Why no-where else in the region? Just on the side of that one hill, in the middle of a thousand similar hills. To say it was a rare find would have been an understatement indeed.

Lucas also stood in wonder as he gazed up the hillside for the second time. He could sense something was going to happen there that day. He, like many others, believed that the flowers were a sign. The air was filled with an expectation, a sense that they were about to witness something special. Something they would remember forever.

Suddenly, one of the CB radios crackled into life. It was from the other search party, the men who had gone looking for the source of the reflection. Men gathered around sensing that this could be important. The other group reported that they'd found a sheet of aluminium hanging high in a gum tree. It was too high to identify for certain, but they were almost sure that it was part of a plane. It had to be from Jock's plane, what else would be hanging high up in a tree, dozens of kilometres from the nearest homestead.

A huge cheer went up as word spread about the find, and within minutes the whole 'red hill' team were heading out to join up with the other party, just a few hills away.

They didn't head back the way they had come, but instead headed across ground on the shortest probable route to the new sighting. Over the next hill their progress was slowed because of more than usual amounts of debris on the ground. There were trees and branches down everywhere, obviously from the storms over the previous nights and possibly from the earlier storm that had brought Jock's plane down. The area looked like a battlefield. They hadn't noticed much debris on the way to the red hill, but now they were up against a lot of storm damage. The main storm cell must have cut a narrow path through this part of the district. It appeared to be in a band only a few hundred metres wide.

It took them about 25 minutes to get through, until finally the two rescue teams stood together beneath a piece of shining aluminium, hanging rather precariously, high above them.

Another meeting was held between the groups, to decide on how they should go about the search for the plane and Jock.

They knew that the recent storm had been a savage one and that a light-weighted piece of aluminium could well have been tossed a number of kilometres by the strong violent winds, perhaps even more. But they knew they were on the right track. They now believed that Jock and his plane were around those hills somewhere. Now it was only a matter of where and how much longer it would take to find him. If he were alive it would be easier, they, and he, would have the use of sound and hearing. But if he was dead, his body could be lying anywhere in that scrub. For that matter a body could be in one of the millions of trees around. They had to find the crash site and if Jock were not with the wreckage, then they would have to reassess their options from there. First things first though, find the crash site. That would expose the plane, or what was left of it, and then hope and pray that Jock had survived.

The crash site

Just a short distance from the renewed search effort, Jock was sitting alongside his wrecked plane. He'd been killing time daydreaming about home, when from across the wide tree filled gully he thought he heard a noise. It sounded very much like the snorting sound horse's make when they blow air out through their nostrils and lips at the same time. He looked around in the direction from where the noise seemed to have come. He strained his eyes into the distances, but could see nothing. He sat in silence for a few minutes listening hard for that sound again, still nothing. Perhaps his mind was playing tricks on him after all he had been out there for nearly two weeks. He was injured and weak. Maybe the sound was only in his imagination, something like a mirage to a dying thirsty man in a desert.

He'd just about convinced himself that it was his subconscious playing tricks, when he thought he heard another noise. It was a long way off, and this time he thought it sounded like a motor engine revving. Also he thought this new noise was coming from a slightly different direction, a little more easterly. This second sound seemed to be more in the direction of the red hill.

He twisted his body around to look in that direction, and then propped him self up as if to get a better view, but there was still nothing, just trees and bushes, and that red hill. He listened intently, but again there was just the sound of the birds. If only they'd shut up for a minute, he thought, he might be able to better hear. He heard a thump, thump, thump sound behind him and quickly reeled around only to see a big old grey kangaroo bounding down the hillside.

Was he beginning to lose touch with reality? After all of his struggles, was he beginning to go crazy, was he hearing things that weren't there? He knew he couldn't handle that. He thought if it came to losing his sanity, going mad, then he'd rather be dead. What a terrible way to go, he thought.

Fear crept into his soul. He tried thinking of other things, but the thought of madness kept returning, over and over again. He wasn't prepared for that. He could handle the pain, the heat, the flies, even the incredible loneliness, but not insanity, he'd never thought of that as a possibility. For the first time since the crash Jock was beginning to panic at his own thoughts. The two sounds that he thought he'd heard were doing more damage to him than the crash itself. Injuries can heal, he thought, but if he lost his mind he could no longer help himself. The noises were real he told himself, they had to be real, he couldn't bear the consequences if they weren't.

Nervously he looked around in all directions, but again there was nothing but the solitude of his predicament. He flopped back down onto the ground and sat there with his head bowed in total silence. This was the first time he had felt vulnerable in the week or so since the crash.

There he sat, with his good knee bent up, his arms wrapped around it with his head buried in them. His other leg, still in the makeshift splint, stretched out in front of him. He felt no pain, just total despair. He was trying to force positive thoughts into his head, but the depression was taking over. He was now at his lowest point since his ordeal began.

'Cuppa tea' he thought, 'that'll pull me round.'

He searched for and found his last three teabags, then proceeded to prepare a small campfire. He had to stay positive he had to get actively involved in something, anything, to occupy his mind, even something as mundane as making a cuppa.

The main search party

While the rescue party was trying to work out who would look in what direction, Roger looked across towards Mary, just to see how she was coping with all that was happening. She had an odd look on her face, he thought. He walked over and stood beside her.

'I know he's here,' Mary said in a whisper. 'I can feel him nearby.'

She looked at the surrounding terrain for a few moments deep in concentration and then suddenly glanced up into the sky, into the gathering clouds.

An eerie quiet descended over the search party as one by one, everyone's attention was drawn to Mary. It was like she was in some sort of mild trance. She looked back towards a large hill just to the side of them. She stood quietly looking in that direction for a while. They all stood quietly watching her, wondering what was going on in her mind. Then out of the blue she turned back to Roger and said in a quiet positive tone, 'He's over that big hill there,' she said, 'I know it. I can feel it.'

Nobody moved and nobody said a thing. They just stared at the hill that Mary was referring to.

'I know you probably don't understand,' she said to Roger, 'but he's there. Don't ask me how I know, I just do.'

'Yeah I believe you,' he replied quietly.

'Do you? Do you really?' she questioned.

'I've followed you this far haven't I.' He paused for a moment, perhaps just to get her full attention. 'Take me the rest of the way. I'm with you. Let's go get Jock and take him home, one way or the other.'

'Where would I be without you, you beautiful man.'

They smiled at each other as only true friends can and then Mary turned and began walking in the direction of the large hill. Roger was caught a little unawares by her sudden movement, but took a couple of quick steps to catch up with her and they headed off together. He had no idea what Mary had in mind, but he felt he needed to be right there with her, just in case she was right and needed his support, either emotionally or physically. He knew that whatever they were to find over that hill, or the next one, there was a strong chance that it wouldn't end up the way Mary wanted it too. Jock may well be over the next hill, it seemed that he was around there somewhere, but was he alive, or was he dead. Chances were that he had not survived the crash or the ten days since.

Not a word was spoken by anyone they just fell into line a short distance behind Mary and Roger. She walked up a small rise and then stopped and looked around. After a short pause she headed off again as the others dutifully fell into line behind her.

They walked down through the low ground between the hills, still in silent procession, then up the side of the larger hill.

Lucas and Danny walked with their horses at the end of the line. Both quite puzzled by the almost bizarre trail of people hypnotically following Mary through the scrub. It was all a bit too quiet for one of Lucas' dogs who decided to break the silence by barking at a large goanna that had scurried out of the way of the procession and up a nearby gum tree.

The noise of the dog barking seemed to break the 'spell' and in no time most were chatting to each other as they followed along, some quietly voicing their opinions as to whether they should be following Mary or not. One felt they were going the wrong way. Others voiced that a woman's instinct was a powerful thing, and was worth pursuing. Most just couldn't work any of it out at all, they just followed, believing the whole thing was just a little bizarre.

The crash site

Not far away, Jock was busy collecting some small branches of wood to get his cuppa under way, when he thought he heard a dog bark. His head lurched up and spun around in the direction of the noise. Then came another bark, and another, and another.

A dog! Definitely a dog! Not a dingo, or any other animal, it was definitely a dog, and this dog's bark was closer than either of the sounds he thought he'd heard earlier. This was definitely closer. Was his long struggle about to reach its end, or was it just an illusion in his mind. His spirits lifted and then sagged again. First he thought he'd heard a horse, then a vehicle, and now a dog barking. Was he going mad or was help very close at hand. He tried to contain his inner excitement, just in case it was a mental mirage. He wanted to believe it so badly, but he resisted. Again his emotions soared and then deflated again, over and over.

Then he thought he heard the sound of muffled voices coming from the same direction of the dog bark. They were muffled sounds, certainly not clear, but they were human. 'They were definitely human voices, definitely, definitely, definitely,' he thought, 'humans with horses and vehicles and bloody barking dogs.' He wasn't imagining it this time. This was real. He heard real voices, real horses, and real dogs.

A massive wave of excitement ran through his body, and he tingled all over. His face burst into the biggest smile imaginable and he had no way of controlling it. It just took over his face, from one side to the other.

In the excitement of the moment, he tried to jump up from his crouched position, but it was not a good move. Reality surged back to him in the form of pain. He should never have jumped up on his leg unaided. He cringed back down to the ground as the pain raced up through his leg.

After a few moments of gritting his teeth and quietly swearing under his breath, the pain began to ease off. His mind began to clear again.

'What if they walk straight past me,' he thought. 'A hundred metres in this scrub is as much as a hundred kilometres anywhere else.'

'Make some noise,' he thought. 'Make a loud noise, get their attention before it's too late and they pass right by me.'

He grabbed a large piece of wood from his campfire stack and began banging it on the side of the plane's fuselage. 'They ought to be able to hear that back to Toowoomba,' he said to himself. Finally! People! Buggar me I've done it! I've bloody-well survived!'

The Last Hill

Mary reached the crest of the large hill first and stopped. By then the others were scattered up and down the hillside, most showing signs of their lack of fitness. The fitter ones were nearing the top and not far behind Mary. The not so fit ones, the rather overweight middle-aged men, were lagging a fair way behind. Those who were looking up would have noticed Mary stop and they probably thought she was puffed from the climb. Others still had their heads down, as you do when you're struggling up a hill, and wouldn't have even noticed her stop on the top.

However she had stopped dead in her tracks for a very good reason. There before her, in the small valley ahead, lay pieces of wreckage from a plane, Jock's plane. They were mainly small pieces scattered along the valley floor and in the scrub bushes covering the next hill. Also right in front of her was a rather long gouged out trail leading up to the tree line and a rock wall on the other side. To Mary and Roger it was obvious.

'He must have come down here and skidded across the ground.'

'Looks that way,' replied Roger.

There was debris everywhere when they studied the scene more closely. Mary couldn't believe she was actually seeing wreckage belonging to Jock's plane and that he must be down there somewhere, not more than a half a kilometre away.

She tried to stay positive about what lay in front of her, but her mind started to wonder into unknown territory.

'It looks bad, all that wreckage,' she said to Roger, 'how

could anyone survive that?'

Her eyes followed the gouged out trail across the valley floor and into the bushes and trees on the other side. Roger's eyes followed the same trail also.

'Does that look like the fuselage to you, in amongst those trees down there?' She pointed to the position. 'In front of that small rock wall.'

By now others had made their way to the hilltop. Someone beside her responded, 'Sure looks like it, doesn't it?'

She stood there looking for a while, trying hard to stay in control of her growing emotions.

Roger turned to those still clambering up the hill. 'It's the plane,' he yelled out. 'It's Jock's plane.'

His words suddenly hit home to Mary and an icy chill ran through her veins, 'What if he's dead?' she thought to herself. She had never allowed herself to think in such a negative way before. But now, as she looked down on all that wreckage, she felt scared.

'What if he's dead?' she whispered to Roger.

He didn't answer at first, he was pre-occupied getting the message to the others still clambering up the hill. For a moment she thought she couldn't walk down the hillside to the plane. What would she see down there, amongst all that twisted broken metal? Would she find her man, the love of her life, dead? She turned to Roger again, and again she whispered, although this time her voice was breaking with emotion.

'What if he's dead? I couldn't handle it Roger. I just couldn't.'

Roger put his hand on her shoulder, squeezed it firmly, and said in positive tone, 'Hey girl, don't give up now. He's this close.'

'But what if he is. After all this.'

'Well we don't know yet, so let's not cross that bridge just yet.

Anyway, what about that girl who was so determined he'd be all right, where has she gone all of a sudden?'

She smiled at him.

They both stood in silence until a voice from behind them interrupted the moment, 'Faith and courage my girl, faith and courage, that's what we must have right now and plenty of it.' She turned around to see the local priest who had joined the search during the morning.

'Thank you Father, I know, faith and courage.'

Mary could feel something powerful building up in side of her. The tears that were about to erupt in her eyes felt as if they were rising from a deep, deep well, way down deep inside her being. Her eyes began to tingle as they filled with emotion. Then suddenly, just at the point when she thought she was going to lose it, from over the other side of the small valley, came a banging sound. All eyes focused on the area just up beyond the tree line.

Roger looked down at Mary. She looked at him with disbelief all over her face and then, in a very positive reassuring voice Roger said,

'Hear that Mary? That's your man. He's alive my girl, he's alive.'

Mary couldn't believe it. Was it true? Had they finally found him, was he really alive. She stood there willing it to be true, listening for another banging noise.

Then, there it was again, a couple of bangs, a dull thumping noise that echoed slightly as it crossed the distance between the producer of the sound and them, the receivers. It sounded like wood hitting on tin. It had to be him; it couldn't be anyone else. Then when the sound stopped again, Mary had a chilling thought and she turned to Roger.

'Maybe someone found the plane before we did. What if it's not Jock at all, but just someone letting us know they've found the plane.'

'Mary,' he replied in a stern voice, 'I've followed your instincts for ten days now and you've brought me to this place. Now it's my turn. This time you'll have to trust my instincts. IT'S HIM, believe me, it's Jock and he's alive.'

Suddenly came another couple of noises from down in the small valley and this time it was followed by a muffled voice. It was hard for anyone to work out just what it was, but Mary recognised the voice.

'JOCKKKKKKK?' Roger yelled at the top of his lungs. He paused, waiting for a reply, but all that could be heard was a dozen or so birds flying out of trees, flapping and squawking as if a gun had been fired at them. Mary followed his lead and yelled just as loud as Roger had before. ' JOCKKKKKK !!!!!!!'

Her call was being pushed out by ten days of anguish, fear, frustration and raw emotion.

This time the scream was followed by total silence. This time, not a bird squawked, not a dog barked, not a horse neighed, just silence. Everyone stopped. They all listened, every one of them, to the last man, feeling Mary's emotion.

Then, without warning, after holding back for ten days, Mary's tears began to flow from her eyes, like a torrent streaming down her cheeks, uncontrollable and unchecked. Roger, who by now wasn't exactly dry-eyed himself, wrapped his arms round her and hugged her firmly.

'It'll be okay,' he said reassuringly. 'It'll be okay, I promise. We both heard the noise, didn't we? We both know it's him. I know he's all right. Let's go down there and get him and then you can take him home to Toowoomba.'

She looked at Roger for one last bit of reassurance. 'Take

him home to Toowoomba. Oh how good that sounds.'

He nodded back to her, nothing said, the nod was enough. They started walking down the hill together with Roger holding her hand.

Ten long days waiting

Jock heard another noise and tried to stand up but slipped and fell back down. He yelled out in pain. Then, still grimacing in pain, he heard a human voice away to the north of him. He couldn't work out what the voice was saying, for by the time the sound reached him it was distorted by a slight echo, but he knew it was a man's voice. It took him a moment to respond. His first thought was, 'am I dreaming? Am I imagining voices now?' It sounded like someone calling his name. He paused long enough to convince himself that he wasn't dreaming. This was real. Then he heard another voice. Again it sounded somewhat like his name being called out. This time it was a female voice. This voice he thought he recognised. It was Mary's voice.

He realised that a smile had made its way on to his face without any conscious help from him. It wasn't a funny, laughing smile; it was a smile of extreme relief. His struggle to stay alive and to keep on top of his situation had paid off. Their strong spirit and the love for each other had come through. It was almost over.

He stretched up towards where he'd heard the voices and yelled back as loud as he could,

'Down here, Mary! I'm down here!'

In the relative silence of the bush they all heard him. A loud cheer went up as Mary began to make her way down the hill towards the tree line in the direction the voice had come from. Every emotion was running through her body and her mind as she made her way past a mixture of plane wreckage and debris left behind by the crash and the storm.

Was he okay? - He sounded ok! - Was he badly injured? He had to have some injuries, she thought. The amount of wreckage in the valley bore witness to that. What would he look like if he were all right? - Bad cuts, broken bones! That handsome man she loved and married, would he look the same? Would he ever be the same man again after what he must have gone through? Surely the struggle of the past ten days would have some sort of impact on his mental state.

It is known that people who have been involved in disasters or some type of tragedy have great strains put on their personal relationships after such an event, some come out stronger for it, but emotionally some don't survive the trauma. Would this affect them, she wondered. Her mind was racing as she made her way across the flat towards the fuselage.

Tears were streaming down her face uncontrollably. Tears held back by more than a week of worry and grave concern, or tears of sadness for what she might find just ahead, but mainly tears of joy that her loved one was still alive. The tears rolled on freely.

Then, as she was heading across the flat ground following the deep gouge the fuselage had left as it skidded to it's final resting-place, and as if on cue in some outdoors theatrical play, she suddenly stopped.

Some of the rescuers had followed Mary, twenty or thirty paces behind as she headed down the slope. Some had remained at the top just watching as the final scene in this long journey played itself out before them. Some believed that this was Mary's moment and she should be the one to rescue Jock herself. After all it was her determination that had led to them being here.

At the moment that Mary stopped, they all stopped. All eyes fixed on the distant figure of a man, dressed in torn and dirty clothing, hobbling out from behind the fuselage ahead of them. He looked pale. He looked older. They stood in total silence as this man, with the aid of the stick, slowly limped his way out into the clearing towards Mary.

He looked up at her and smiled. Then his attention was drawn to the hill behind her. It was littered with not only trees and wreckage, but also people, dozens of them, like a line of ants winding their way towards him. He was taken aback for a moment at how many there were. Behind Mary he spotted his mate Roger.

'Good on you Roger, he yelled, 'I knew you wouldn't miss a good show.'
Before him was a sight he hadn't envisaged in his mind. Perhaps in the first few days of his ordeal he imagined the cavalry coming over the hill to rescue him, but as time dragged on he thought more and more that he would have to eventually walk out to safety by himself, no cavalry charging over the hills. But here they were, he could almost hear the bugler blowing the charge. What a sight before him.

'It's over,' he thought, 'I can finally go home.'

His focus was drawn back to Mary, standing almost dumbfounded, not thirty metres before him.

'Jock,' she called again, only this time it was not driven by the pent up pain and frustration, but more a loud sigh of relief. She began to walk quickly across the flat ground towards him, almost stumbling a few times over debris lying in her path, as he edged his way forward also.

It seemed like an eternity to the onlookers. In reality it

was probably only seconds, but it was one of those moments that perhaps only moviemakers truly capture by slowing the action speed down.

Finally they reached each other and embraced for a very long time. Then they could be seen speaking to one another. No one on the hillside knew what was said, although perhaps Roger had a fair idea, judging by the smile on his face. It would be left to every individual person there that day to put their own words to that very 'special' moment. Perhaps to some it didn't mean anything more than another search and rescue mission completed with a positive result. But it would be nice to think that some of them tried to take that magic moment with them and included it in their own lives, in their own relationships with their wives or girlfriends and with their children and friends. Perhaps they became better people for the joy of helping to find him alive and to return him to the ones that loved him most.

CHAPTER TWELVE

The last ride home to Burton Downs 1884

After a hearty home cooked meal at Bungunnia Station, Matthew hugged his younger brother, Charles, good-bye. Then he turned to his father and shook his hand and wished them both a safe journey.

It was hard for him to watch them riding away. After all, they'd been together every moment of every day for over six months, but he knew he wanted it done. The time had come for him to start the journey to his own future, to establish himself as his own identity. From then on the decisions would be of his making, his and his alone.

'Travel safely father and take good care of that young ragamuffin brother of mine.'

'Younger brother indeed - new partner more likely,' answered Charles with a smile on his face.

'I'll see you home in a few weeks then.'

John and Charles mounted their horses.

'Ride home safely, Matthew, your mother would never forgive me if you didn't.'

'Don't worry about me Father, I'll follow your path all the way.'

And with those final words the two Barlows rode away from the Bungunnia homestead heading north towards St. George.

Matthew knew he'd have to wait around while George Lamwith organised a meeting with other interested parties. He wasn't the type to just sit around, so instead he rode out to speak to a few local property owners himself. Then after a few days, and instead of waiting at Bungunnia Station, he rode ahead to

St.George and spent time talking to local businessmen, traders and farmers there. He was a young man with a new passion, his own business venture, and he wanted to learn all he could, so he talked, asked questions, and listened to everything they told him.

It was time well spent and he learnt a great deal about good crops and bad crops, good farm management practices and a little about irrigation. Everywhere he went people seemed to warm to this young man seeking knowledge and they opened their places and hearts to him without a second thought. It was a very valuable experience. He took his time.

By the start of his second week, George and Matthew had met with three different cattle breeders who were interested in the Barlow boy's droving some of their stock to Broken Hill or Dubbo, after the summer heat had passed.

By the end of the second week, Matthew had five cattle owners interested, with the promise of at least four hundred head of cattle to take down south next autumn.

He had not wasted a moment of his time. He spent time being shown how to irrigate fields from local water sources, including the newest asset to farmers, drilling into the Great Artesian Basin for extra water supplies.

He realised that if they were to continue breeding cattle on Burton Downs, as well as grow crops all year round, they could to well, where previously they had struggled. Water though was the key to it all, a steady supply was so important. He needed to find out more about this Artesian Basin. Was it available up in Queensland, if so how to achieve a successful drill. If not, then where was this underground reservoir located.

His new plan was to head home with this newfound knowledge and help to re-build the family property into a stronger, potentially more viable business for his father and mother. Then in a few years time, with his parents secure, he would feel free to look for a property of his own, along with Charles. He also thought that if he and Charles took one or two more combined herds of cattle to Broken Hill, or perhaps to another destination where the market prices were strong, they would have the finances necessary to buy their own land.

Finally, two and a half weeks after John and Charles had left St. George heading for Burton Downs; Matthew was also riding north on his final leg home. He headed out along the banks of the Maranoa, towards where the two rivers met with hopes of a bright future riding with him. There was very little water left in the river. By the time Matthew had passed the point where the Balonne ran into the Maranoa it had dried up completely, it was again a bone dry, dusty, creek bed, just like so many others in outback Australia.

In Queensland most of the rains fall in the summer months, with the winter generally being quite dry, unlike the southern parts of Australia where it is the opposite, wet winters, dry summers. That's not to say it doesn't rain in the winter up north, but rarely does it rain enough for the rivers to start flowing again. The rainfall that fell to the west of the Great Dividing Range the previous summer and early autumn, slowly made its way through Australia's dry barren heartland. It was once believed that all these rivers running inland would spill into a great inland sea. Adventurers and explorers proved that theory wrong in the early 1800's. A hundred streams, creeks and rivers eventually carry the rainwaters to the Darling and Murray River systems, through Queensland, New South Wales and Victoria and what's left eventually spills into the ocean in South Australia near the picturesque port township of Goolwa.

Up around Burton Downs, the creeks received water from summer storms, but the heat dried them out very quickly until they were again just dusty creek beds. Dams and deep waterholes were their main source of all year water supplies. That was limited, so the number of stock was also limited. They needed to find properties that had better water supplies as well as drill in the hope of tapping the underground reserves in the Artesian Basis, as it was now being known.

Matthew was a little concerned about the lack of available water on that last stretch home. He himself shouldn't have a problem, he was just one man with one horse, he could move quickly to the next known water hole or tank, but he was a little worried that his father and Charles would be slowed down by the number of packhorses they still had with them. It was getting hotter by the day and he knew a man could only last a few days out there in that heat without water.

He rode north and was somewhat relieved when he reached Mitchell, knowing that the trip from there to Burton would be safer. That dangerously dry, uninhabited section between St. George and Mitchell were behind him now.

He spent a day in Mitchell, just enjoying the hustle and bustle that the new railway tracks and bridge had brought to the township. When they passed through six months earlier they were still being built, but by now Mitchell was well used to the sound of steam engines puffing in and out of town, tooting their steam whistles as they passed, exciting the local children every time they did.

While in town he spoke to the bank manager about his plans for the future. He purchased some small gifts for his younger brothers and sisters from the new emporium the prospering town had attracted, and then headed north for Havelock Station. After renewing some old friendship and spending a night telling yarns by a large campfire, he turned east for the last two-day ride to Burton Downs. It seemed like he had been away for a lifetime, yet in other ways it only seemed like a few days.

The trip from St.George to Burton Downs had taken him only nine days, nine rather pleasant days where he found his own pace for a change. He enjoyed not being dictated to by the cattle, weather, ground conditions, bushwackers, or his father. He had found that he had time alone to think. The solitude was refreshing, something he hadn't had for many, many months, but now he was back in familiar territory and with it came a certain relief.

Burton Downs

Finally, on a hot sultry day, typical of mid-November, over six months after setting out, Matthew rode up the last hill of his journey. He stopped at the top. In front of him, a very welcoming sight. Something he had pictured in his mind so often while sleeping under the outback stars, the little Burton Downs homestead. He could see his younger brothers and sisters playing out the front. He spotted his mother hanging washing out to dry on their make shift clothesline to one side of the house. A small tuft of smoke rose from the kitchen chimney. 'Home,' he thought, 'it hadn't changed one bit. A beautiful little oasis in a dry hard landscape.' He smiled to himself. The type of quiet smile you get when you finally realise that you have achieved something special. It was a smile of quiet satisfaction. Although he was sitting on top of a small hill in Central Queensland he felt like he was on top of the world.

His moment was interrupted by a dog barking around the back of the house and then saw the old mutt run around the front and head up the hill towards him. One of his young sisters looked up at what the dog was barking at and spotted the rider on the hill. She took a moment to recognise him and then yell out, 'Look Mother, it's Matthew. They're home Mother. The men are home.'

Children ran out from everywhere, or so it seemed. They scampered up the hill towards him. More dogs barked, the children were yelling and Matthew sat there taking it all in. He was home at last and it felt good.

In all the excitement of the home coming welcome the children had forgotten for a moment about their father and brother, Charles. Matthew got down from his horse and walked down the hill with his young siblings to where his mother awaited him.

When he reached her she gave him a long loving hug. Then step back slightly and said, 'Look at you, my, my, my you look like a man. Left home a boy, came home a man.'

Then she looked towards the top of the hill and she immediately felt something was wrong. She had a confused look in her eyes as she looked back towards Matthew. Then one of the children realised what was missing from this reunion, and asked the question,

'Where is Father and Charles?'

His mother, Mary, cut in immediately, 'Yes, where is your father and Charles?

Matthew now looked confused.

'What do you mean, where are they? Aren't they home with you?' he inquired.

'No' said one of the children; 'you're the first one home.'

'The first one home! - You mean!'

He froze on those words, and then looked back to the top of the hill himself, as if expecting to see them ride over it at that very moment. It had never entered his head that he might return home before his father and brother; after all he had stayed on in

St.George for over two weeks after they'd left.

Mary took his hand and held it firmly. She had sensed immediately that something was wrong, and now it was being confirmed. She took a telegram from her apron pocket and showed it to Matthew. It said that John and Charles had left St.George and that Matthew would follow later. She knew they should have been home by now, weeks before Matthew.

With worrying tones to asked inquisitively, 'Just where are they then?', hoping that he had a viable reason for their delay.

There was silence, and then she asked nervously, 'Did something happen to them?'
Matthew still looked a little confused and replied slowly, 'I don't know Mother, they left St.George almost a month back. They should have been home weeks ago. They hadn't been seen in Mitchell, so I presumed, against my better judgement, that they had taken a shorter route home overland through the bush.'

'Oh Matthew,' she said as a tear appeared on the bottom of her eye which slowly broke its shackles and made its way down her cheek, 'something terrible has happened, hasn't it?'

'We'll find them Mother. We'll find them. I'm sure they're fine. They've just had a problem and been delayed somewhere. I'll go back out and find them. I leave tomorrow. They'll be held up somewhere waiting for me. I'm sure there is a perfectly logical explanation. Don't worry yourself unduly.'

Matthew's words were meant to comfort his mother, but he knew himself something had gone gravely wrong. He knew that they had not followed the trail that he had, so they could be anywhere out in the bush. He knew that a man could and would die quickly out there in that heat without water. He had to hope that they were laid up near a waterhole somewhere or for sure they would have already perished.

Within twenty-four hours of Matthew arriving back at Burton Downs, he was in the saddle and on the track again. He didn't head towards Havelock Station, time was an enemy now, so he made his way directly across country to Mitchell. Once there he alerted the local Police Constable of the missing men. Both immediately checked with the local business's to see whether anyone remembered seeing John or Charles in town in the past month, or whether someone might have seen them on the track. All their investigations drew a blank. No one had seen or heard anything of the two men.

Had they met with foul play? Perhaps they were simply sick or injured and lying somewhere out in the bush waiting for help to arrive. Or perhaps they had perished in the ever-increasing summer heat. Only two things were known for fact. The first was that they had definitely left St. George. Matthew had watched them ride north himself, and the second thing was that they hadn't passed through Mitchell. That meant only one thing, they were still out there, lost or dead somewhere between the two townships. Somewhere out in that almost uninhabited one hundred and fifty miles of rough scrub between St. George and Mitchell. Perhaps they had bypassed Mitchell altogether and gone straight from St. George to Burton. That thought did not bare considering. One thing to search around the known track, another think altogether if they'd gone overland

The Constable arranged for a search party to leave Mitchell the next day and search south along the Maranoa, the most likely route John and Charles should have taken. He also sent a telegram to the St.George Police alerting them of the missing men and requesting that they organise a search party to leave there and search north, also along the Maranoa.

The Mitchell party headed off following the dry

riverbed. Five days later, roughly half way between the two townships, the two search parties, each comprising of a police constable, an aboriginal 'black-tracker', as they were respectfully called, and a number of volunteers, linked up. The party from Mitchell, including Matthew, had found nothing unusual, no sign or trace of his father or brother at all. The search party from St. George informed the Mitchell party that they had found some old campsites along the river. However, they were unsure if it was the Barlow Boys who had camped there or someone else. The only other thing they noticed out of the 'ordinary', was the unusually large number of dingoes in the region. They were roaming in packs, which was somewhat unusual and a little worrying.

The two parties set up camp and settled down for the night under a clear starry sky on the banks of the dry riverbed. They went over what they already knew, and they went over what they thought might have happened. Everyone had a theory as to the fate of the two men from Burton, and it seemed that almost each theory was different in some way or other.

Some thought they had been attacked by one of the wild marauding packs of dingoes they had come across. Generally dingoes are very shy around humans, but if they were hungry enough, anything was possible. Others wondered if they had left the dry riverbed and taken a short cut overland towards Burton Downs. As the crow flies they could save days in travel time by taking a more direct route, but they would need to be sure of their water supply to take such a risky step. Matthew believed that was very out of character for his father, who had always chosen to take the safest option available in the past.

Some believed the two missing drovers might have run into trouble with an aboriginal tribe. Conflict between white settlers and aborigines was not uncommon in the past, but that idea seemed to be dispelled rather quickly by one of the black-trackers helping with the search. He reminded them that the local tribe had a history of living in harmony with the 'white fellas', but it was decided that it should not be overlooked as a possibility. To that end, the next morning, one of the black-trackers, set out to find the local tribe. He was to find out if they had any knowledge of the missing men. Later the next day, the black tracker re-appeared with the news that he'd found the tribe's camp. He was told they'd been out of the area for some months, on a walk-about looking for food. They had only just returned themselves and had seen nothing, but offered to watch out for any sign of the two in their wanderings.

Matthew couldn't believe it. They had been through so much over the months of droving. Now, so close to home, they had just simply vanished. For his mother's sake, he couldn't allow himself to think the worst. If only he had stayed with them, he thought? If only! But if-only's don't change facts and the facts were that they were missing without a trace and it was going to take an enormous amount of luck to find them.

The search parties decided there wasn't much more that could be achieved by staying out there. They had searched the most likely route along the Maranoa and found nothing. As well, the local aborigines couldn't shed any light on the mystery. So it was decided that the two parties return to their respective towns, via a slightly different route, up to about two or three miles inland either side of the Maranoa. To look for them any further inland would be an impossible task. They could be anywhere out there and it was simply too big an area to search. It could take years. They hoped that the men might have left the riverbed for food or safety and something had gone wrong stopping their return. It was still an unknown if they had made an ill-fated decision to short-cut overland to Burton. Next morning both parties bid each other farewell and headed out.

Matthew was not ready to give up hope. Although he fully understood why the others had to return, he stayed out there searching for another two weeks. He took the route further inland, believing now that his father may have made a short cut for home. He found it difficult to believe that his father would take such a risk, but then he couldn't believe they had found no trace of them either.

The problem was if they did go overland, at what point did they start that trek. Matthew studied the local maps. He found a creek that ran into the Maranoa about twenty five miles south of Mitchell. If they had followed it, they would cross the new train line east of Mitchell and from there nor-nor-east to the Hunterton Station, then on to Gunnewin, and then directly home to Burton Downs. The route would save about four days travel, but would have had his father and younger brother heading over very dry and unhospitable countryside. It was his last hope. He would head home along that route.

It was fast getting to the point where Matthew knew he was no longer looking for two living men, but rather he was searching for two bodies to take home, or at the very least, some answers to take back to his mother.

He took his time searching for clues, any clues. He rode on slowly. One afternoon, out of no-where, there appeared a thin ribbon of metal, stretching out as far as he could see in both directions. He crossed the new Brisbane-Mitchell railway line and made course for Hunterton Station, where they could shed no light on the whereabouts of the missing two men. They hadn't passed through there either, well not to the knowledge of the owners or stationhands. Matthew was running out of hope.

The summer heat was starting to beat down ferociously as the year of 1884 rolled into December. It was a long fruitless ride and finally Matthew brought himself to the conclusion that his father and brother were dead. He could search on in the hope of finding their bodies and some answers or he could head home before the death toll climbed to three. There was no choice. He headed for home.

At Burton Downs, Mary had been in touch with the local police on a number of occasions and by the time Matthew finally arrived home, she too had come to the realisation that her beloved husband and son were lost forever. Mary was relieved that her eldest boy had made it back safely and a hug and a quiet tear was all that was exchanged between the two after he rode in. No words spoken, none were needed for they both knew and felt the loss.

Time passed

The years rolled by without a trace of the two drovers. The story made its way into district folklore as the 'tale of the missing drovers' and was talked about often when locals got together over a cold beer or around a blazing campfire. Everyone had a theory, but no one knew for sure what had happened to John and Charles Barlow of Burton Downs.

Over the years stories surfaced about sightings of a strange red hill. It was said to be the blood of the missing men, spilling out from their resting-place and seeping down the hillside. And how often one too many beers could enhance the story. One farmer even went as far to say that over many years he had seen a fully saddled horse running free on more than one occasion, but he had never gotten close enough to catch it. He called it the 'Deadman's horse'. It was like a spirit horse searching for its rider. There were also stories from travellers and drovers, about seeing two ghosts walking along the

Maranoa at night. The stories changed somewhat from pub to pub, from campfire to campfire, but all were left wondering, just what did happen to the two missing drovers?

And so with time, and some very vivid imaginations, the 'tale' of the missing drovers became known as the 'legend' of the missing drovers.

Meanwhile Matthew had settled back down at Burton Downs and life moved on. He went ahead with some of the improvements he had planned with his father and Charles. He sunk a bore and got help to plough a number of paddocks. He introduced sheep to the property and in time built a small dynasty, helping to make the remaining Barlow family members comfortable. He helped his younger brothers Thomas and Will set up a property of their own, just as he had planned to do with Charles. He built a house for himself not far from the old family homestead on the Burton Downs property and eventually met and married a woman from the growing rural centre of Mitchell. It wasn't long before they had children of their own. The dream of becoming a drover passed with his duty of caring for the rest of the family.

Over the final years of the 1800's and into the new millennium, he made a number of trips down towards St.George, searching for some trace of his lost father and brother, but always to no avail. Every story and yarn ever told, that had made its way to Matthew's ears was in time checked out. His eldest son Henry also took an interest in the mystery and accompanied him on a number of his expeditions. Sadly too, they turned out to be the last trips he ever had with his son, for in 1916, the young Henry enlisted to fight in the Great War and was shipped overseas to the battlefields of Europe. He died in the horror of Belgium in 1917. His end came when an ugly cloud of yellow mustard gas descended over the trenches one night.

Whilst in France, the young soldier Henry had discovered a liking for the writing of poetry. Most of his poems were about his home and about Australia. He liked to write about happy times back 'on the farm' or about being out 'in the bush' and for that reason his poems were well liked. On leave, away from the harsh battlefields, he was known to entertain his fellow soldiers with recitals of his much admired poetry.

One of Henry S. Barlow's favorite poems was written about his grandfather. It was called 'The Tale of the Missing Drovers.' Many, many years later, that poem was to play a major part in another mystery. It was one of only two of Henry's poems ever to make it to print. The other made the local newspaper in 1932. It was submitted by his mother under the title:

Deadman's Road

The Great War beckoned, we did enroll
For Mother country, with heart and soul
An adventure awaited, and a great one at that
In uniforms new, and old slouch hat

To the fields of horror, we all were sent
Passing row after row of soldiers tent
Two by two down Menin Road we slogged
Through a land so badly battered and flogged

To the dreaded foe, so battle worn
We cursed and muttered words of scorn
These Flanders fields now mud and blood

The raining death, a torrid flood

Next the butcher's fields of Passchendaele
Nair question asked, the reason veiled
My boots were holed, my jacket torn
Oh for dry clean clothes to keep me warm

The maggots feed on passing life
No pride do they have and the stench is rife
Rats share my food and misery
At least they can choose to pack up and flee

My old buddy Jacko, bought it yesterday
Now in Flanders fields he'll forever stay
They found some bits, enough they said
To safely say "the poor bastards dead"

I'm scare 'THAT' fate is mine down the way
I hope it's quick, that I die where I lay
I'm scared of the pain I may have to face
I wish not to die in this horrible waste

Oh what I'd give to be home once more
To be greeted by mother at our front door
Still the battle rages just over the hill
It's a turkey shoot, it's a rabbit kill

Dare I dream of wheat fields round Narrabri
That sway and dance in freedom fly
The sun the warmth, those endless blue skies
The dust, the heat, those pesky flies

They seem so far, so far, so far
Oh how I'd love to see my old dar
Then a cry invades my moments thought
'Mustard gas' the call, and shelter is sought

It's cold, it's cold, so bloody cold
Our bread and cheese, tis covered in mould
The suffering, the fear, this bloody bog
Tis a strange world with yellow fog

Then it hit me like a thunderbolt
It knocked me down, a shocking jolt
Now the mud and blood is all over me
And worst of all, I can no longer see

An aid said 'boy, you'll be ok.'
But now it's dark, no longer day
Tis peaceful tho, no pain to bear
But I can hear the rats getting ready down there

The future and past, all melded to one
I remembered hearing a beating drum
Twas a funeral march, not only mine
And forever now my sun won't shine

The Generals, their armies, no reason came
The past now a memory, was it all in vain
So on foreign soil we lay in peace
The guns now silent, the battles ceased

Green grass is high, red poppies abound
Now the hum of silence, the only sound
But our graves still line the Deadmans Road
Tis our resting place, our new abode

And the fields round Ypres are quiet today
The battles gone, gone far away
Not quite the fields of Narrabri
Not quite the place I'd choose to die

But we did die here for a worthy cause
and on Remembrance Day take time and pause
To remember just why, we men were slain.
And remember us fallen, our suffering, our pain.

Generation after generation grew up and lived on Burton Downs until finally the property was sold to new owners. The new generation Barlows moved to Brisbane and the memories, the tales and legends were all but left behind, along with the gravestones on a small rise overlooking the little old homestead. On that hill were a number of generations buried between the 1880's and the 1950's. They're headstones are still there today, somewhat overgrown. Below them is an area of lush green grass and blooming wildflowers, watered by a bore that was sunk by Matthew just after he'd returned from his epic journey all those years before.

The names of Mary and Matthew Barlow are on the same headstone. Matthew had been buried with his mother, as he had wished, because, to his mother's great sadness, his father never was. Two of the gravestones are unmarked, and the ground beneath them untouched. That ground had waited all those years for the bodies of John and Charles, the two missing drovers. The hope was that one-day the mystery would be solved and the remains of the two could be laid at peace along with the rest of the family.

CHAPTER THIRTEEN

The Outcome

After the rejoicing and relief of finding Jock had settled down, questions began flying in all directions, all directed at Jock. As the rescuers looked over the wreckage, Jock was asked exactly what had happened. All believed it a miracle that he had survived the ordeal, not only the crash, but also the ten days alone with the injuries that he had sustained.

The search team's medical officer checked Jock's injuries as best he could, while Mary longed for the time when they could just be alone to talk quietly in private. For the moment however, he was the property of the world, and they all wanted a piece of him. Her turn would come soon enough. For the moment though she was over the moon with the knowledge that he was alive and in reasonable condition. There would be plenty of time for her and the kids when all the fuss had died down. She knew for now she would have to be patient a little longer.

The decision was made not to try and carry Jock out. It was felt it would be too rough with his leg as it was, so a radio call was made to Rescue Headquarters. They requested a helicopter be dispatched immediately, to airlift Jock back to the Roma Hospital.

Approval was given immediately and the chopper was in the air in less than half an hour with a full medical team on board. Mary also asked that her children, back at the motel, be informed that their father had been found and was alive and well. She knew the ordeal was beginning to distress them also, and that they would be relieved and excited to hear the good news.

The officer in charge made an announcement that a landing spot needed to be prepared for the expected helicopter to land safely. Everyone chipped in. They'd all come this far and wanted to see Jock safely in the helicopter and heading off to hospital before their mission was over.

Mary thought it an opportune time to speak to the group, before the ground clearing activity got under way. She asked Roger to get their attention.

'Excuse me fella's,' he bellowed out, 'Mary wants to say a few words.'

The area fell quiet, even the birds seemed to realise the special moment and stopped squawking. Everyone stopped what they were doing, and looked towards where Mary was standing by Jock

'Gentlemen, what can I say now that will ever be enough. How can I tell you now what I no-doubt will feel more and more as time goes on. To each and every one of you, for giving Jock and me your courage, and your precious time, we thank you so sincerely.'

She wiped a tear from her cheek and looked at Roger.

'To Roger, our dearest friend, who stood by my side, never once doubting me, never once letting me lose the way, we will love you always. You are the true meaning of friendship. Forever we will be indebted to you. Thank you!'

'To this beautiful young boy here,' she walked over to Danny's side, 'thank you for being so observant and persistent. You and your father found my Jock. You beautiful young man, if I could give you everything, I would. I hope that every day of your life is filled with as much joy and love as what I feel in my heart at this very moment.' She hugged him.

Then she looked across to Lucas and said, 'Thank you for finding the time to believe in your boy. He's a lovely boy and you should be very, very proud of him.'

She walked back over to where Jock was sitting, put her hand on his head and in one final gesture she added, 'Thank you all again. We will love you all, each and every one of you forever. You are our heroes.'

Someone in the group then called out, 'Three cheers for Danny,' and the response went up, 'Hip-hip, hooray! Hip-hip, hooray! Hip-hip hooray!'

This was a special day that would be remembered for years and generations to come, and they knew it. They may have searched in the wrong place originally, but they would learn from that. The final result was a good one, Jock was alive and safe now, and that was all that mattered. They must have felt so proud of themselves for persevering in his search. It was a personal challenge and huge milestone for all of them.

Search and Rescue groups have guidelines and protocol to follow and generally that all works well. But not every situation is copybook stuff, sometimes the unusual happens and it is from these situations that they all learn. The manuals get changed and improved upon and upgraded regularly. During this search they had made mistakes, but many a valuable lesson was learnt and the end result was a good one. Not one of them knew Jock or Mary before the crash, but each and every one of them gave their precious time for the rescue of a stranger, simply because he needed it. It is surely times like these that brave people, caring people, step up to be counted.

As work began on a clearing for the helicopter some took it in turns of getting souvenir photos of them with Jock and Mary, with the wrecked plane, Danny and his Dad, were happy to oblige, realising they simply wanted a souvenir to remember the moment, a record of their participation in the amazing adventure. The story no doubt would be talked about at parties and gatherings for years to come and those there that day wanted a record, as proof they had been a part of it. As sure as the sun rose and set in the sky, some people's versions of their part in the rescue would be exaggerated slightly or even more than slightly. There were probably thirty people there that day. In the years ahead there would probably be hundreds who would claim they were one of the rescuers who found Jock. At least some would have a photo to prove it.

Roger noticed Danny and his father off to one side with their horses, just quietly standing and watching, not quite knowing what to do or where to go. It all seemed a bit much for them. He wandered over and thanked them both for their efforts and asked them to come over and meet Jock.

Danny was quietly nervous and a little embarrassed as he walked across to where Jock was sitting up against a tree with Mary. There was also a medical officer in attendance securing a brace over Jock's broken leg.

'Jock,' he interrupted, 'this is Danny and his father, Lucas. They're the two who first saw the reflection of wreckage from your plane. They also were the first to find your little red hill, and called us in to help find you. Without them, we'd still be searching somewhere else.'

Jock hadn't been told much about how the rescuers had found him, so he listened with interest as Roger filled him in on the part that Danny and his father had played.

Jock reached up from his seated position and shook both their hands expressing his sincerest thanks, 'How can I ever thank you enough. Perhaps when I get out of hospital, you could come visit me in Toowoomba. We could get to know each other better. You can tell me your side of the story and I'll tell you mine. If you can't come to me perhaps I could come visit you from time to time,' he added with the deepest sincerity.

Danny got quite excited and looked at his dad for a response. Lucas nodded, 'Sounds great and if it's alright with you, I might bring Danny in to visit you in the hospital in a few days time.'
Mary welcomed the idea, 'I think that'd be lovely, I for one would like to get to know this young man a lot better,' she said rubbing her fingers through Danny's hair - 'You should be very proud of him, Lucas, he's a fine boy.'

The distant thumping of an approaching helicopter interrupted their chat. The noise got louder and louder, until suddenly, as if out of no-where it thundered over the tree tops and began to hover slowly downwards in a cloud of dust and dead leaves. The noise, being trapped by the small gullies and surrounding tree lines, became almost deafening, until finally when safely on the ground, the pilot cut the engine.

A medical crew of two climbed from the chopper and headed straight to Jock. Having already been treated by the para-medics with the rescuers, he was almost immediately lifted onto a stretcher and carried over to the chopper. The stretcher was secured to the floor as Mary also boarded and sat beside him in the observer's chair. The pilot fired the chopper's engines up again and the dust and leaf show resumed.

Jock looked back at his rescuers, now all gathered to watch the last act being played out, that being the helicopter leaving. He waved good-bye to them all and then noticed Danny standing to one side with his father. He gave him the thumbs up just as they were closing the door ready for take-off.

Jock reached over and spoke to Mary, who immediately stood up and leaned over and said something to the pilot. One of the medical crew slid the door open again and Mary climbed out. She ran quickly over to where Danny and Lucas were standing. Trying to get her voice above the noise of the helicopter's roaring engine, she yelled at Danny, 'Have you ever flown in a helicopter before?'

He shook his head to answer no.

'Would you like to fly to the hospital with Jock and me?' she asked.

'Wow, that'd be excellent!' Danny replied.

He remembered that he'd better get permission, so he looked around to his father and pleaded to him, 'Can I please Dad?

Lucas nodded his approval and then put his hand on his shoulder and pushed him gently towards the helicopter, 'Off you go then. I'll drive to Roma and pick you up in an hour or so.'

Mary interrupted, 'No need for that Lucas, the pilot gave the OK for both of you to fly with us.'

He looked at Mary as Danny took off for the chopper. 'Are you sure there's room for both of us?'

'The pilot said it was fine, so let's go.'

It would be Danny's first ever flight in a helicopter, so it was with nervous excitement that he climbed aboard followed by Mary and finally Lucas. Roger opened the pilot's cockpit door and told the pilot that he'd drive to Roma and pick Danny and Lucas up from the hospital just as soon as he could get there, but the pilot yelled back that he'd have none of it. He added that he'd be proud to fly Danny and Lucas back home to Nundooka, just as soon as he had seen Jock safely tucked away in a hospital bed.

As Roger closed the doors, Jock got Mary to ask the pilot for one more small favour. Would he mind flying low over the 'red hill', and he wanted to see just exactly what it was. The colourful hill had been the key to his rescue and he wouldn't mind getting a closer look at it.

The pilot accelerated the engine to maximum speed and slowly lifted off. The men on the ground grabbing at their hats and turned their heads from the windstorm as the helicopter headed north in a slow forward lifting motion and flew out low over the hills. When the pilot spotted the 'red hill', he also noticed a clearing just below the hillside, and instead of flying low over the area he made the decision to land the helicopter in the clearing. Mary leaned forward and inquired if there was a problem, to which he replied, 'No problem, I just thought you might like a real up-close look for yourselves. Bring me back a flower.'

When they'd landed in the clearing, Mary slid open the door and jumped out of the helicopter, along with Danny and Lucas, and the three ran over to the hill. Mary picked a few of the flowers and returned to the helicopter.

Sturt's Desert Pea is a blood red flower, the shape of a pixie's ear with a jet black eye in the middle. It grows in clumps of about four or five flowers on a smoky-greyish-green coloured vine-like stem. They thrive in the dry arid desert conditions of western New South Wales, most of inland South Australia and parts of the Northern Territory. They can also be found in the eastern deserts of Western Australia. However Queensland is generally considered too humid for them to survive in. They're a desert dweller, so it was a rare sight indeed to see them proliferating in this part of Australia.

'Sturt Peas, well I'll be,' Jock said with a hint of amazement in his voice. 'What on earth are they doing way up here? I didn't know they grew in Queensland.　thought they only grew down south,' he added.

Mary handed him a small clump of the blood red flowers. 'One things for sure, this pretty little flower, in the wrong place or not, certainly saved your life.'

The flight to Roma was an eye-opener for Danny and Lucas. The countryside took on a whole new appeal from a few thousand metres above it. After about 30 minutes in the air, they began their descent until finally came to rest on the grass covered football field right next to the hospital. From there on it was like royal treatment for Jock. He was whisked into an ambulance for the 100metre drive to the emergency entrance, then into a wheel chair and straight into a private room. Within an hour he was reunited with his children, who had been driven from Mitchell to Roma once the good news had reached them. They too had received special treatment, and had been driven from Mitchell to the Roma hospital in a police car with flashing lights all the way.

Nundooka Station

Later that afternoon, Annie Richards was in the kitchen at her Nundooka property, when she heard the sound of a helicopter getting closer.

A helicopter in that area was a rare thing. She'd heard a helicopter earlier in the afternoon, but it was a fair way off. This one was much closer she thought as she stood over the kitchen sink peeling potatoes for the evening meal. It got louder as it drew closer. She stopped what she was doing and walked outside to watch as it passed overhead, thinking that it was probably part of the search and rescue operation. She could see it immediately heading in from the east. As she watched she realised that it was getting lower and lower, as it approached the homestead. 'My goodness,' she thought, 'it's going to land here.'

And land it did, in a cloud of red dust, making it almost disappear from view. The engine was cut and the deafening noise began to abate as the overhead rotors slowed. The dust eventually began to settle and the helicopter reappeared from behind its cloak of ochre.

The passenger door swung open and to her surprise and amazement out climbed Danny. Then the side sliding door opened and out jumped Lucas. By the time the two had made their way over to the front of the house to greet Annie, the helicopter's engine was picking up power and in no time at all it was airborne again. They all turned and watched as the pilot hovered for a moment to wave good-bye and then he swung his craft sideways and in a thumping pulsating roar headed north-east towards Roma. The tiny craft quickly became smaller and quieter as it faded into the distant sky.

'How did you manage that then? A ride in a helicopter?' asked Annie.

Danny replied excitedly, 'He took us into the Roma Hospital and then he flew us all the way back out here. It was so amazing Mum!'

Annie sounded concerned, 'The Roma Hospital? What happened? Did someone get hurt?'

Lucas responded to her question first, 'No dear, well not exactly. We found the missing pilot.'

'What! Really! So he's alive?' Annie questioned.

'Yep, badly broken leg, a few cuts here and there, lucky buggar I'd say. He looked fine. Only needs a shave and a bath and he'll be new in no time,' Lucas said.

Annie was amazed, 'Well I never! Fancy that! Did he land the plane somewhere?'

'Hell no! The plane is in a million pieces all over a hillside not twenty kilometres from here. He's a lucky man all right. He's apparently been living on lizards since he came down,' Lucas added.

'Well what about the helicopter ride?' Mary wanted to know everything.

Danny answered, 'The man's wife was so happy that I helped find him that she asked if Dad and I wanted to help take him to the hospital in the helicopter and then they flew us home again. It was so cool Mum! I'm going to be a pilot when I grow up. Everyone looks like little ants from way up there, it's just so cool.'

Danny was so hyped up and full of excitement that he didn't stop talking for hours, and it was well past ten o'clock before he'd calmed down enough to get to sleep.

Meanwhile back in Roma, Jock was operated on the next day. He had to have his leg re-broken and set right this time. They put in a metal plate with four pins attached to the bone, to aid his recovery. The doctor told them that Jock had done the right thing by putting the splint on his leg to immobilise it. He had stopped the injured leg from sustaining any further damage. Even though his bones had begun to set wrong, the important thing was that no more damage had been done and no infections had set into the damaged bone during his ten-day ordeal. He was told he would probably need a further operation or two and it was very probable that he would walk with a limp at least until the leg was strong enough to have the plate and pins removed, but they were hopeful of a full recovery in time.

Three of his ribs had been broken but they were well on the way to mending themselves and the doctors concluded that he was indeed a very lucky man. They added that he quite obviously had a very strong will to live.

A few days later and still in the hospital, Jock had a surprise visitor. On his way through to Brisbane, his mate from the Jackson Oil Fields stopped off to see how he was. He too was fascinated to hear the whole story. Jock apologised to him for not getting the replacement parts to him when he needed them.

'No worries mate. When we'd heard you were down and unable to deliver them, we called in another charter pilot and got another set of parts out within 24 hours. You just get better and get yourself another plane. Sometimes we just have bad days. We'd be more than happy to give you another shot at doing it right.'

The two men laughed.

As it turned out, it didn't really matter anyway, the storms didn't bring enough rain to cause any real problems and the pumps weren't needed. It was all a bit of a false alarm.' Then he added, with a bit of a laugh, 'It was easier finding the new parts than it was finding you.'

He told Jock that the Oil Company had sent the company chopper to Roma for five days to help in the search and rescue mission. They had felt a responsibility, he said, to help, as Jock was on a mission for them. They would've liked to have helped longer but the chopper and it's pilot were needed back at Jackson on company business.

Jock was speechless. The quality of friendship shown by so many people was simply unbelievable. Not only by those who knew him but also by many, many more who did not!

A press conference was held in Roma with most of the people who'd been involved in attendance, along with dozens of reporters and photographers from the media. Danny was the one they all wanted to talk to. Jock was still in hospital and was unavailable for interviews. After it was all over Danny told his parents that it had been a little scary, with all the questions and the camera's flashing.

Danny caught the bus to school the following Monday morning and when he arrived he was greeted as a real hero. Over the previous two weeks he had imagined a day like this, never really believing that it would ever come true, but it had, and now all the other kids flocked around him all day long. Everyone wanted to talk to him, and every kid had a question to ask him. The media also turned up at school that day and followed him around interrupting normal school procedures. The school's principal was concerned about the disruptions, so, after a phone call to Danny's parents, decided to call another press conference. He told the gathered media to ask any questions they liked in a half-hour session, and then he asked that Danny and his family, as well as the school, be left alone to get on with their lives. The attention was disrupting the students and their studies, and it had to stop. He said that he appreciated the public's interest in the whole episode, but added strongly that the school had to be allowed to get on with teaching.

To the media's credit, they appreciated the situation and respected his wishes, restricting their contact to pre-arranged meetings and interviews.

Five days after his miraculous rescue, Jock returned to Toowoomba to recuperate with his family. He had to withstand the media knocking on his door, and phone calls twenty-four hours a day for the first week or so, all wanting an exclusive inside story. The story had become the talk of Australia. Everyone wanted to know the story from start to finish.

Finally after being hounded for days with all types of offers, Jock called a news conference himself. He told the gathered faithful that Mary had decided to write a book on the story, and that they had signed a contract with one of the television companies for the rights to their story. He added that it hadn't been his wish to 'sell' his story, but that he had been encouraged to do so as to stop the constant hounding from the journalists and photographers. He realised they were only doing their jobs, but it was having a profound impact on his family's life and his recovery and he didn't want that to continue. They'd been through enough already, he said.

Mary was stunned by his announcement.

'What's this about a book?' she asked as soon as the newshounds had left.

'A spur of the moment decision dear, I thought it would get them off our backs! Anyway it's not such a bad idea when you think about it.'

'What me write a book?'

'Why not? I've got the story and you've got a way with words. We always said you should write a book. Well here's the perfect story to work on, and if the books any good the television thing should follow. Hell, if nothing else, it should get me some money for another plane.'

Meanwhile in the days that followed the rescue, the police cordoned off the area around the crash site and had set up a camp nearby, until Air Safety Control Inspectors had completed their investigation of the plane and the surrounding area for their reports. The Inspectors removed the engines from the site and shipped them back to Brisbane for closer inspection. From such an isolated location, it would be too difficult and too expensive to shift all of the pieces out, so, once they had completed their investigation most of the wreckage was simply left where it laid.

In no time at all, onlookers and tourists came from near and far to see the site of one of Australia's most remarkable real life dramas. An area had to be set aside, on a nearby hill, about fifty metres from the plane wreckage, for onlookers to view the scene. Once the Air Safety people had left the area it was pretty much open season. The barriers came down and almost like crows on a carcass, the souvenir hunters started to clear the area of the debris.

Sadly the red hill sustained a great deal of damage also before the Wilderness Society stepped in and roped that area off. They were forced to erect signs around the hill asking for help in protect the plants and the native bush for the future. The red flowers had long since gone, awaiting the next good downpour on their little corner of the world to make their re-appearance.

After two months recovery back in Toowoomba, and with the all clear and blessing from his doctors, Jock was ready to go back flying again.

The Insurance Company paid out his insurance policy within twelve weeks. Along with some money received from the sale of his story to a television show, Jock and Mary went to Melbourne about 3 months later and took delivery of a second hand Beech-Craft Twin Engine 10-seat passenger commuter. The almost new plane was not unlike the one he flew out to Jackson that fateful day.

After a few instructional flights over the following few days, they flew out of Melbourne and headed north to Toowoomba. They stopped briefly there to pick up a couple of passengers, Jock's mother-in-law and of course the kids then headed for Roma and Mitchell on a person to person thank you mission. A few hours later they landed in Roma and promptly hired a car to take them on the rest of their crusade.

They started with the local services and from there got names and addresses of those who had given so much time in finding him. Some were no longer available, but those who were still around Roma and Mitchell were thanked personally. It took four days to eventually get around to thanking each and every one of them.

They stayed four nights in Roma and then drove on to Mitchell where they stayed a further two nights. There they stayed at the Mitchell Motel and this time insisted on paying the bill. Following an invitation from Danny and his family, they also stayed a day and a night out at Nundooka.

On the seventh day Jock told Mary he had some business to attend to, something he needed to do alone. He drove back to Roma, fuelled up his plane and flew out to the Jackson Oil Fields. On board with him he had the original package of parts he'd left Brisbane with two months earlier. The package had been recovered at the crash site and returned to Jock along with his fishing line, his thermos flask, and some other personal items. He'd made himself a promise after the crash, that if he ever got out of there alive he'd deliver the package to Jackson, finally completing his long journey. The next day, after doing just that, he flew back to Roma, got into the hire car and headed back to Mitchell. It was a Sunday and a reception had been arranged for them all at the new Mitchell Civic Centre.

The Mayor of Mitchell was the first to speak. He praised everyone for their wonderful efforts in finding Jock and in bringing him back safely. The Search and Rescue chief was next, and he was followed by the president of the local branch of the C.W.A (the Country Women's Assoc.)

Finally it was time for Jock to say something. He stood up proudly and thanked everyone again. He kept it short and in closing he announced that Mary had a few words to say as well.

Mary stepped up to the podium and spoke in more detail. She too thanked everyone, paying special attention to young Danny for being so vigilant. She also spoke about Jock's recovery back in Toowoomba and dwelt on what the future held for them and their family. She promised the people gathered there that day, that she would write her book about the whole event and when completed, she would like to return to Mitchell to launch it there in the new Civic Centre. She spoke about Jock's struggle near the red hill and also about what she had discovered about the old tale of the Missing Drovers.

She went on to say that if it weren't for 'that' poem, she would never have gone as far south as she had. She may never have bumped into Danny and his father, and that being the case Danny probably wouldn't have noticed the reflection from a piece of the wreckage in the treetops. It had certainly been an amazing set of coincidences that led to his discovery, she added.

She said she was still intrigued by that poem, but added that the riddle of those missing drovers would never be truly explained without T.Wilson, the person who had submitted the poem to the Show Society, way back in 1953. In closing, she read the poem to the gathering. She then thanked them all once again and left the podium to a warm round of applause.

With all the speeches out of the way, everyone settled down to enjoy the customary afternoon tea and informal chat that is such a part of country gatherings. It was a good opportunity for Jock and Mary to mix and mingle again with the people and to enjoy their company on that sunny Sunday afternoon.

A little bit later, a small middle-aged lady came up to Mary and quietly interrupted.

'Excuse me,' she said politely, 'if I may introduce myself, my name is Teresa Green. I live in Roma.' She continued, 'before I was married my name was Teresa Wilson and I grew up with my family on a small farm just outside Mitchell here. I'm the one who submitted that poem to the Show Society. It was a long, long time ago, when I was still a young lassie. I

think it was my grandfather who wrote it, before I was born.'
Mary looked at her with a huge smile on her face then put out her hand to shake Teresa's.

'Well lovely to meet you Teresa Green! If you have some time, I have a million questions to ask you.'

The two ladies excused themselves from the group and found their way to a quiet corner of the Civic Centre to talk some more about the poem.

'I believe I am a direct relative of the missing drovers,' Teresa said while sipping a cup of sweetened black tea.

'One was in fact my great-great grandfather, John Barlow, and the other was his second oldest son, Charles.'

'It's such a fascinating story,' replied Mary. 'Please do go on'.

'The story was always a bit vague,' Teresa said. 'Much of it was never known, and some has been lost through the generations. About all we do know for fact, is that they were never found, and their bones still lay out there somewhere between here and St.George.'

'There was a third drover you know,' she said, 'he was the elder son, Matthew.'
She paused to take another sip of her tea and then slowly wiped the corner of her mouth with a petite white lace handkerchief. 'Apparently he stayed behind in St. George for some time, letting the other two go on alone, and when he finally arrived back to his home, he must have realised something had gone terribly wrong. They all lived on a property up Injune way, known as Burton Downs.'
Mary was totally absorbed in the story Teresa was telling her.

'Matthew, the one that survived, apparently went back on a number of occasions searching for his father and brother but he never found any trace of them. They had just simply disappeared.'

Teresa continued by saying that many years later, one of Matthew's sons, Henry, heard a rumor about where the missing drovers were supposed to be buried and where a hill of wild red flowers could be found.

After a top-up of her cuppa, she went on, 'It was said that the hill of wildflowers was somewhere between Mitchell and St. George. I'm really sorry but when your husband went missing I never thought about that old tale. He may have been found much sooner if I had only paid more attention.'

'Water under the bridge now,' replied Mary, 'besides it all ended up fine in the end. Do go on with the story though.'

'Well as I remember it, it was all such a long time ago, but Matthew and his son searched in vain for the graves and the flowers but nothing was ever found, not a single trace. The earth just seemed to swallow them up.'

Mary was enthralled, 'Do go on, it's such an amazing story.'

'Henry was my grandfather,' Teresa said, 'he died in France during World War One in 1917. Henry had a daughter in 1914 before he went overseas, that was my mother, Mary Ann. She told me some of the story before she died, but she had been very sick and by then she couldn't remember most of it. It was a pity but I wasn't really that interested earlier, when she still had her full memory. You know we lose so much when our old people die,' she said with sadness in her voice. 'Some years later, when I was clearing out some of my mother's old things, I came across the poem and a short story that someone in the family had written. Unfortunately I lost the story in the floods of 1965, but the poem, thanks to the Show Society's publication, has survived. I think that my grandfather wrote both the story and the poem, but there's no way of knowing for sure now.

Mary couldn't get enough of the story, so the two decided there to look into the story as far as possible and if they could solve the mystery they would write their findings down for everyone.

Teresa believed that there could never be an end to the story without knowing where and how the men had died. She suggested, now that the red hill had been located, they should get together along with some of her relatives and find the time to go out to the area and have a closer look around. At least now they knew where the red hill was and after all, if the legend was right, the two men's bones or some trace of them might still lay out there somewhere. True the hill of wild flowers had been found by accident, but that was more than anyone had managed to do in over a hundred years.

Mary was elated at the prospect of bringing the story to its eventual conclusion. The story had fascinated her right from the start and she was more than keen to see it to its end. They agreed that it would be best to go out there as soon as possible, before the tourists and sightseers did any more damage to what might well be an historic gravesite.

Later, back in the motel's dining room, the two talked on into the night and by then Jock was just as excited by the intriguing story as they both were. He also knew, that once Mary got her hands into a project, there was no turning back or stopping her. She was on a mission again.

Mary rang Lucas at Nundooka, and asked him if he would like to act as their guide and take them back out to the crash site and the 'red hill'. It didn't take much talking before he too was keenly interested in the whole idea of searching for the missing men. He said he'd thought about going out there many times himself to have a look around, but he'd been too busy on his own property. He added that he could use a couple of day's break and he'd be happy to act as their guide, so long as they didn't mind Danny tagging along also.

Next morning Mary, Jock, Teresa, and one of her cousins, Malcolm, were again heading down the road to St. George. They stopped at Nundooka to pick up Lucas, Annie and Danny and continued on to the crash site.

Jock told them he felt a strange feeling pass through him when he saw the site again. It wasn't fear, but it was a feeling touched with considerable sadness, he said. It was more like the feeling you'd get when you wake up from a bad dream, you know it can't hurt you, but just the same you're glad it's over.

They set out on foot for the red hill and the first thing that struck them all was that the red hill was red no more. The beautiful flowers had long gone and that special hill looked just like any other hill, nothing special about it now.

They searched the surrounding area for most of the day and then late in the afternoon returned to Nundooka. Arrangements were made with Lucas to take them out again bright and early the following morning. They stayed at Nundooka long enough for a refreshing cuppa and then drove back to Mitchell, arriving just on dusk.

That night in their motel room, they received five telephone calls from different people who'd heard about their new search for the missing drovers. They were interested to hear if they'd found anything out there. Mary was pleased with the interest being shown. Ever since Jock had been found, and after Mary had told everyone at the reception about the poem on the missing drovers, there had been renewed interest in the tale.

It was indeed an intriguing story, a little bit of history, and a piece of their heritage that didn't have a final chapter. Mary also received a phone call from the local newspaper. They had heard on the wind about the renewed search and were looking for a story. The journalist arranged to meet them next morning and join the search.

At six o'clock, the radio alarm in the motel room suddenly burst into life. The voice, a very distinctly proper voice announced, 'It's six o'clock...time for the news,' after a short piece of dramatic music, 'Good morning, David Taylor, with ABC News.'

Following a few reports on Australian and world events an item came to their attention as the newsreader ploughed on. 'The small town of Mitchell, in western Queensland, is again the centre of attention this morning with another dramatic search about to get under way.'

'Seems like we've made the news headlines again dear,' Jock said as he put the kettle on for their morning starter. 'Half of Queensland will be plodding through those hills soon, all trying to solve the riddle, and that might not be such a good thing. They might find something useful and then again they might be more trouble than they're worth. I think a small group of twenty or so would be useful.'

Mary by then was in the bathroom, 'How did they hear about it so soon?'

'Bush telegraph's been working overtime again I suppose,' he replied.

About a half an hour later, they headed out of Mitchell again, only this time there was another three car loads of helpers following behind. The word was getting around fast and they had the feeling that with each day that passed they would probably see more and more people joining in and they still weren't too sure if that was a good thing or a bad thing.

When they reached Nundooka, they were surprised to see six more people waiting with Lucas and Danny. The ABC News, beaming its information out over the vastness of outback

Australia had, for better or for worse, helped spread the word. It seemed many people wanted to be a part of this new mystery in Mitchell.

By the time they reached the sight that morning there was no fewer than twenty-six willing searchers.

'Well, I guess the more searchers there are, the better the chance of finding something,' Jock said as they got out of their hired four-wheel drive vehicle.

'It would have been nicer if we had been left alone though,' said Teresa, who sounded a little disappointed with all the attention.

'I think I agree with you, Teresa,' replied Jock, 'but realistically we could be out here for months looking. They've got to be an asset.'

'It just doesn't seem right though. We're searching for my relatives bodies or gravesite, and these people are just out here for an adventure.'

'Don't take it personally Teresa,' said Mary, 'the more eyes out looking, the better chance of finding something useful. Perhaps then you can lay them to rest properly, with a priest and prayers and all.'

'I know you're right Mary, but it still seems wrong somehow.'

'Most of them are good souls Teresa. They have good hearts and good intentions. Most of these people helped me find my Jock remember.'

The group fanned out and searched in all directions for about four hours, until around midday, as had been previously arranged, they all met back at the base of the red hill for a lunch break, and to collate any information they may have gathered.

One of the last searchers to return for lunch was Teresa's

cousin Malcolm, and in his hand he had an old metal buckle that he'd found in deep grass just two hills over. It was passed around while they ate sandwiches that Annie had made up earlier. Generally it was agreed that it could have been a buckle from one of the original packhorses. It looked old and it was very rusty and certainly very different to anything anyone had seen out there before.

After lunch the main search was moved to the area where the buckle had been found, and over the next few hours a number of other items were retrieved. They found a number of small plants that were identified. None were in flower, but it was agreed that they were Sturt's Desert Peas. The group was overjoyed and it was widely agreed that it was an omen. They general consensus was that they were close to where the men may have come to grief.

Around four the search parties met back at the base camp for another gathering to discuss whether there had been any more findings and to plan the next day's search.

Jock was sitting on the ground near the fire that had been started to boil a billy. He was sitting there in somewhat of a daze; deep in thought, watching Danny put more wood on the fire. Danny picked up a small piece of wood and as he threw it on the fire Jock noticed an unusual marking on it. He jumped up and grabbed a water container that was nearby and threw the water on the fire. The flames went out instantly as they hissed a spurt of steam into the air. Jock reached in and quickly grabbed the piece of wood from the shouldering pile and flicked it to the ground. His sudden action surprised everyone. When he was sure the piece of wood had cooled enough, he picked it up again. He held it up to look at the marking he thought he had seen. Sure enough, on the face of the flat piece of wood was six carved letters, 'J.B. 1884'.

There was a hum of voices as they all tried to take in exactly what it was they were looking at. Breaking the silence, one of the searchers said in a loud voice, 'J. B. one, eight, eight, four. That could be John Barlow, 1884.' Another agreed with him and, as if on queue, the rest of the group spontaneously cheered.

For the second time in two months, those normally quiet hills erupted to the sound of people cheering. Both times it had been for the discovery of missing humans. The first time it was the finding of a man in trouble, and the second time it was for one apparently long since dead, but in a sense, both had been saved.

Jock thought about it for a while and then called out, 'Does anyone know where this piece of wood came from?'
He paused awaiting an answer, but none was forthcoming immediately.

'Who collected the firewood?' he asked in a slightly more questioning tone.
A timid, nervous voice broke the silence; 'I collected all that wood yesterday. A whole big pile of it,' and then almost apologetically added, 'Dad asked me to.'

'It's alright Danny,' Jock replied, 'I didn't mean to yell at you, or frighten you, but you know you've probably done it again. You may just have found the biggest clue yet.'
Jock walked over to Danny and said quietly, 'You've done well, Danny,' and then putting his hand on his shoulder for reassurance and added. 'Do you remember where you got the wood from?'
Danny didn't have to think long at all. 'Sure,' he said as he pointed straight to a clump of large bushes not far from the campfire. 'I got most of it over there. Some was just on the ground and some of it was under those bushes.'

A few searchers began walking over in the direction that Danny had pointed, when another called out to them that perhaps Teresa should be the one to go over and have a look first. After all, he said, if there was anything over there, it would be fitting for her to find it.

Teresa looked a little overawed by the whole situation until Mary joined her and took her by the hand and with a little encouragement they walked towards the bushes together. They both looked around for a short while without finding anything, while the rest of the group watched on. Then Teresa disappeared under some of the low hanging foliage of one of the bushes. A minute or so later she reappeared. She was seen speaking to Mary and shortly after both disappeared beneath the bushes together. A buzz of excited conversation erupted from the rest of the searchers, who had been standing quietly around the campfire. A few minutes passed until Mary reappeared from under the bushes. Silence greeted her as she looked towards the anxiously waiting group.

'I guess we've just solved the riddle,' she called, 'I think we've just found the missing drovers.'

She then walked back up to the campfire, leaving Teresa under the bushes. She told them that it looked like their gravesite. They had found what they thought were parts of a skeleton. Just small pieces of bone, she said, but they were pretty sure they were human remains. She said that Teresa was a bit emotional when they found the bones, and that perhaps she should be given a moment or two alone.

It was getting late, but no one had plans of going anywhere. This was too good a story to walk away from now. The men sat around talking to each other and sipping on hot brewed tea for about five minutes, until Teresa reappeared. Total silence greeted her as she slowly walked back up to the campfire.

'After all those years, I'm sure we've just found my great-great grandfather and his son.'

The expectation that she was about to cry was strong, both in her, as well as from the assembled group, but she resisted her natural instinct and kept composed. 'It's just amazing down there,' she said with the hint of a small shake of her head.

'All those years they've just lay under those trees and no-one could see them.'

She raised her hand to expose an old tin. 'This was down there, half-buried in the dirt, but I couldn't open it.' She passed a small pocket-knife, along with the tin to Jock.

'You found them when you crashed here. Would you like to open it and see what's in it.'

Jock took the tin and gently tried to screw the lid open. It was rusted on, so he used the knife and tried to wedge it under the lid. After a bit of levering and some muscle, he lifted the lid off. Inside was a piece of old material. He carefully took it out and unfolded it in the palm of his hand. Once unfolded, the material revealed an old-fashioned gold pocket watch and chain. He also noticed that scribbled on the inside of the material was a note.

'Interesting,' he said, 'there's something written on the material.'

He handed the watch and chain to Teresa, and then began to read the note out aloud.

Father injured in fall ,
dingoes scared horses
all food lost - waited two weeks for Matthew
Father is poorly no food - no water left
don't know what to do,
fear father will not make it

He paused for a moment as he perused the next line. He looked at Teresa and then over to Mary with a saddened look, then he continued solemnly,

Father died – I think 7 or 8 Nov 1884.
Praying for Matthew to come.
3 weeks now - can't last much longer - very weak
Lord save our soles - so sorry mother
Love you all. Love you all

THE END

Where the Wattle Blooms
Four Aussie stories

The Ghost of Dugong Island
A ghost mysteriously returns to his old haunt searching for something or someone he left behind.
Set in historical Moreton Bay, Queensland.

Eighteen Thirty Five
The adventures of a young teenage convict, and his struggle to survive after the ship he is being transported on is wrecked along the S-E Tasmanian coast in 1835.

Let the Canefields Burn
Sometimes there are things you have to do in life to satisfy the heart. This is the story of a man who returns to the place of his childhood.

One Hell of a Storm
The story of a young man caught in the middle of Cyclone Tracy during the Christmas of 1974.

For copies of **'Where the Wattle Blooms'** please contact the publisher, InHouse Print, as mentioned at the start of this book, or the author at www.rufusjohnpuppets.com

Aussie Fact and Fun, a book of Aussie trivia and Aussie history is well under way.

The Journey, the story of my grandfather from 1910 to 1919, should be ready by 2016. The story starts in Reading England when my grandfather, as a young teenager, was sent to an orphanage. Soon after he was shipped to Australia to train as a farm labourer. After being sexual abused at his first assigned job at the age of 14, he ran away and survived by his wits. In 1916 he shipped out for the battlefields of Belgium and France. In 1919 he returned briefly to Reading to find his sisters and the father who had put him in the orphanage.

www.ingramcontent.com/pod-product-compliance
Lightning Source LLC
Chambersburg PA
CBHW060937030726
47503CB00003B/631